T0006164

THE DISAPPEARANCE OF TRUDY SOLOMON

THE DISAPPEARANCE OF TRUDY SOLOMON

· A FORD FAMILY MYSTERY ·

MARCY McCREARY

CamCat Publishing, LLC
Brentwood, Tennessee 37027
camcatpublishing.com

Hardcover ISBN 9780744303308
Paperback ISBN 9780744304022
Large-Print Paperback ISBN 9780744304053
eBook ISBN 9780744304152
Audiobook ISBN 9780744304176

Library of Congress Control Number: 2021937773

Book and cover design by Maryann Appel

5 3 1 2 4

For Dad—
The best tummler in the Catskills.

CHAPTER ONE

Monday, October 22, 2018

MY PALMS were sweatier than usual. I glanced around before reaching into my desk drawer to rub Secret on them. Yes, that Secret. The anti-perspirant. There was going to be lots of handshaking today and I wasn't sure I could avoid it. They finally solved the case. Missing August 6, 1978. Found October 22, 2018. Forty years, two months, and sixteen days. And the answer . . . right under their noses the entire time. Dad didn't know yet. My plan was to stop by Horizon Meadows Residences after my shift to break the news.

Sally McIver strode across the precinct floor and planted herself on the edge of my desk. "Hey Susan, can you believe it? Wait until your dad hears the story."

The story. The one that consumed my life forty years ago. A case my mother derisively referred to as a “Big *F*-ing Deal.” Emphasis on the *F*. For years, the disappearance of Trudy Solomon confounded my father—the lead detective on the case—until it faded away, yet not completely. Like a chalkboard where you can see remnants of math equations long erased. The cold case of Trudy Solomon. No strong suspect. No obvious motive. No forensics to test. No computer databases to mine. Just gumshoe detective work that yielded few leads and no resolution. Until now—until this fluky stroke of luck.

Someone leaked the story to the press. That didn’t take long. Trudy was found only a few hours ago. An unruly group of reporters swarmed the police station. I held no animus against reporters—like locusts, they were harmless when just a handful were flitting around the halls, but they had a way of causing damage when they got all riled up around a potentially juicy story. I had been dodging them all morning. I wasn’t sure how much more I could offer up than what Ray Gorman, the detective (and the guy who shares my bed), had told them. *He’s* the one who connected the dots and found her. I could only assume I was the *human interest* side of the story. They’d want to know how Dad reacts to the news. They’d want to know if I knew about this case back when I was thirteen and if so, how it impacted me and how I felt now. But that was my story. Not theirs.

FOUR WEEKS ago, Monticello Police Chief Cliff Eldridge called me into his office. A day like any other day. A day stuck at my desk while Internal Affairs reviewed my case. A day with my gun locked away. A day feeling spasms of pain in my right thigh, a throbbing reminder of the bullet lodged in fatty tissue. I had returned to the station exactly one week earlier, on September 17, cleared for desk duty and not much else. Shuffling papers. Watching surveillance tapes. Answering phones. Monitoring police vehicles. They called it restricted duty. Felt more like purgatory—*am I in or am I out?* My future as a detective resting in the hands of others.

"We just got a call from a senior investigator with the New York State Police." Eldridge glanced at a piece of paper on his desk. "John Minot. Ever hear of him?"

"No, sir."

"His unit found skeletal remains along Route 9W in Ulster County. He ran up against a wall trying to identify the body, so he started going through regional missing person reports." Eldridge paused and peered over his cheaters. "Do you know where I am going with this?"

"Are you saying this could be Trudy Solomon? Are the bones forty years old?"

"They've been there for some time, but they haven't determined how long yet. Detective Minot claims they roughly match the description of Trudy Solomon. Female. Caucasian. Late twenties, early thirties."

"Holy shit. And cause of death? Is that known?"

"Gunshot to the head. Close range."

"Jeez."

"Minot is looking for a relative of Trudy's so he can run a DNA test to confirm or rule out that it's her. He thought we might have something in the files, people we can contact. But this case has been dormant for so long, we'll have to do a little digging on the relative front." Eldridge shifted slightly in his chair, then cleared his throat.

Two short grunts. "I know you, Susan. You're gonna want this case. I can see the gears turning in your head right now. But you know the situation. You're on desk duty until you are cleared by Internal Affairs, the department shrink, and your doctor. If it were up to me, I'd hand this to you to follow up. But it's not up to me."

"Who are you assigning this to?"

"Ray and Marty. I told them to keep you apprised, and if they need help, the kind you can do from a desk, they'll let you know. Okay? That's the best I can do right now."

"And my dad? Can I let him know?"

"That's up to you, Susan. But I would keep it to myself until we know more. No need to get his hopes up—then dashed. Probably best not to replay 1978 again. You were too young to remember, but I'm not."

Oh, I remembered. When the world is crashing down around you during your preteen years, you remember everything. F-U Mother. With an emphasis on the F. I decided not to tell Dad until there was a definitive answer. Eldridge was right. No need to dredge this up prematurely.

In the weeks that followed, Ray and Marty sifted through local and national databases to find a living relative of Trudy Solomon. Not a soul emerged. But Ray did hit upon something odd. When he did a search on Trudy Solomon's social security number he found it was still in use, associated with a medical bill for a patient in Massachusetts. That patient was a woman named Gertrude Resnick who had the same birth date, February 16, 1951, as Gertrude (aka Trudy) Solomon. Eldridge gave them the go-ahead to travel 250 miles east to a hospital in Lowell, Massachusetts, to question her.

In the early-morning hours of October 22, Ray awoke early to make the trip. "Wish you could come with us," he whispered in my ear. Then he leaned over and kissed my forehead before I had a chance to draw the blankets over my face. "Y'know, you're kinda cute when you're mad."

"Then I must be cute all the time."

BY MIDAFTERNOON I was getting antsy waiting to hear from Ray as to whether the Trudy in Lowell was in fact *our* Trudy. From the moment the body was found until now—what felt like the longest four weeks of my life—I had been in a constant state of agitation. Between keeping this discovery from my dad and awaiting clearance from IA, I couldn't remember a time in my adult life that sucked more. Well, except for being shot . . . and almost dying.

I was in the police-station bathroom, trousers at my ankles, when Ray finally called me.

"Hey. Did you talk to her yet?" My voice echoed around me in the little stall.

"Gertrude Resnick? Not yet. We're about to go in. Did you get your gun and badge back?"

"Yeah. A half hour ago."

"Super. We'll celebrate tonight."

I stared at the inked heart on the stall door. The initials SM and EP scribbled in its center. Sally still refused to use this stall after Elaine Pellman broke up with her nearly two years ago. I suggested she paint over it, but Sally insisted it should live on, like her pain.

"Susan. You there?"

"Yeah. Sure."

"You okay?"

"Yeah. It's just been a long morning. Lots of paperwork and shit."

I was definitely not in a celebratory mood. Sure, IA exonerated me, but many folks in this town certainly hadn't. In the end, it came down to my word, an officer in good standing, against a criminal's word. The fact I was shot probably helped my case. Thing is, I shot and killed the person who *wasn't* holding the gun. And Calvin Barnes's family still wanted answers.

I splashed cold water on my face. I tried not to look in the mirror, dreading what I would see staring back at me. But I glanced up anyway. I'd seen better days. A recent botched dye job turned my curls from chocolate brown to bluish black. Which would have been cool thirty years ago when I was going through my punk-rock phase. The concealer I applied this morning was doing little to mask the charcoal-tinged bags under my eyes. Even my blue eyes seemed dingier. No longer bright as cornflower, they were murky like an oil-slicked ocean.

I grabbed a couple of paper towels and patted my face dry. Then I scrounged around my bag and removed some essentials—concealer, lipstick, eyeshadow, blush. Ah, the wonders of makeup. A dab here and there, and voilà, I didn't look half bad for a been-through-the-wringer, fifty-three-year-old detective.

A NEW sign greeted me at the entrance to Dad's digs: Welcome to Horizon Meadows Residences. What I wanted to know is who came up with the name Horizon Meadows. Did they just pick two random words and throw them together? The place was *literally* in the woods. You could barely imagine a horizon. And anything that might once have been a meadow had been subdivided and built on. So why not call it Forest Haven or Sylvan Acres? Maybe because, for the residents of places like this, the horizon was a metaphor for what awaits them all.

After his second heart attack, Dad relented, but not without complaint. Claimed he would die within six months of moving, as he put it, to an old-age home. He was convinced he would be reduced to a drooling, blithering, incapable clod.

That was two years ago.

Then a few old guys from the police force moved in. At seventy-seven, Dad was the reigning Horizon Meadows bridge and shuffleboard champion. He and most of his buddies were in Level One. Independent living. A decently appointed one-bedroom apartment with an emergency call button in the bathroom. Bud was in Level Three, a floor in the building that featured a nurse on duty at all times. And poor Andy. Level Four. Dementia got the best of him, but he joined them in the dining hall on his better days. A few months ago, he asked my father to put a pillow over his head when he reached Level Six. I doubt Dad would oblige. But, then again, I wouldn't bet on it.

As I made my way through the lobby to the computer room, I wondered if Dad had gotten wind of the Trudy Solomon story. If he had, I was pretty sure I would have heard from him. I spotted Dad on the far side of the computer room helping Agnes navigate her granddaughter's Facebook page. "Hey, Dad. Hi, Agnes."

Agnes leaned toward Dad like a lion protecting her cub. "Hi, Susan," Agnes purred. "Will told me about your brush with death. I prayed for you every night. And well, here you are, looking wonderful. Prayers answered. God is looking out for you."

"*He* must have heard you." I glanced at Dad—eyebrows raised, admonishing my sarcasm. "Thank you, Agnes . . . I'll take all the help I can get."

"Well, well, well. The prodigal daughter has returned. How's the bullet wound?"

"Dad, I'm fine. I've got some news for you." I glanced sideways at Agnes. "Can we find a quiet place to talk?"

Agnes patted Dad's arm. "We can do this later. I'll be right here when you return."

It was unseasonably warm for late October, the temperature hovering around seventy degrees, so we headed out to the benches behind the main building.

"There's been a break in the Trudy Solomon case." I paused to study his reaction. Skepticism. "She's alive. Ray found her."

His mouth twitched and one eyebrow lifted ever so slightly, signaling a shift from incredulous to unconvinced. "Are you sure it's her?"

"One hundred percent sure."

"What happened to her? Where's she been all these years?"

"That's still not clear. She has Alzheimer's. Has had it for a while now."

"Then how do you know it's her?"

I told him how they found skeletal remains that jogged the case open, then traced the social security number to Gertrude Resnick. I told him that she'd identified herself from a Cuttman Hotel work ID photo, proclaiming "me," and then verbally identifying her husband, Ben Solomon, when shown a picture of him.

"Holy shit. Holy . . ." He paused and shook his head. "Where is she?"

"In an Alzheimer's care facility in Lowell, Massachusetts."

"Well, I'll be damned. A social-security-number trace. Seems so simple."

"Dad, things were different back then. You couldn't just plug a social security number into a computer. Don't second-guess yourself."

Dad shifted his attention to his shoes and poked at the dirt with the tip of his worn loafers. "And the remains that were found? Has she been identified?"

"Nope."

"So now what? Is Ray going to find out what happened to Trudy? I mean, maybe she was kidnapped? There could still be a criminal element to this."

"I think you know the answer to that. Eldridge is not going to put any more resources on this."

"Did he say that?"

"Well, no. But where's the crime? She's been found."

"Don't you want to know what happened to her?"

"Sure, I'm curious. But—"

"Ask Eldridge to reopen the case. Or take a leave of absence. Help me figure this out. We had the beginning. We now have the ending. Let's figure out the middle."

"Are you kidding? For what reason?"

"Do I sound like I'm kidding? This has haunted me for decades. I deserve to know what happened. We finally have a break we can work with."

WHAT WAS with this *we* shit? Nineteen seventy-eight was one of the worst years in my life. Grandpa died. Mom and Dad separated. My best friend dumped me for a new best friend. Mother hit the bottle hard. And a woman who went missing pulled Dad out of my orbit. The funny thing was, I'd been obsessed with this case too. But looking back, it was hard to discern if it was the mysterious nature of the case itself that intrigued me, or my desire to bond with my father over something, anything. I pestered him incessantly about leads, suspects, witnesses. He was so sure she was kidnapped or murdered. But there was also a theory floating around that she simply wanted to walk away from her life. And I just wanted to know how that was even possible. How did she do it? Why did she do it? Where did she go? Did anyone help her? Trudy captured my imagination. I imprinted on her at a time when I wanted to disappear, reinvent myself. But I was thirteen—what did I know about how to do such a thing?

"I'LL THINK about it." My palms started sweating profusely again. *Palmar hyperhidrosis*—the clinical term for excessive, uncontrollable sweating of the hands or palms. The bane of my existence.

TRUDY

"QUITE A day," the nurse said, pulling the comforter over Trudy's chest and tucking the edge under her chin. "Quite the day, indeed."

"They found me," Trudy whispered, then thought, Was I lost? They wanted to know my secrets, but I locked my lips so the words wouldn't come out. The words stayed in my mouth. They have no business being said.

The nurse settled onto the La-Z-Boy in the corner of the room. She pulled two knitting needles, a half-knitted sweater, and a ball of yarn out of the bag beside her. "That picture. That was something. Jogged your memory, huh?"

Trudy lowered the comforter just enough to free her arms. "That was me!" Trudy squeezed her eyes shut to concentrate, to remember how she dolled herself up for that ID picture for the Cuttman Hotel. Ben didn't like the photo. "He said I looked crazed."

The nurse quieted the knitting needles. "Who said that?"

Trudy didn't answer. She thought about all the questions those two nice policemen had asked her. Lots of questions.

"Who said you were crazy, Trudy?"

"The man in the picture."

For a split second, Trudy remembered what happened that summer. There and gone in a flash. Just squiggly lines and misshapen circles. There and gone in a flash.

CHAPTER TWO

Tuesday, October 23, 2018

RAY AND I were two months shy of our sixth anniversary as a couple (two of those cohabiting). Before Ray there was Simon. Before Simon there was Evan. Before Evan there was Phil. A pause between each one. Phil was my high-school sweetheart. Nine months after graduation our daughter, Natalie, was born. A year later we got married.

Four years later we called it quits. My one and only marriage. If you're not good at something, why keep doing it? Being a mother, though, *that* I was good at. I would just think about what my mother would do in any parenting situation and do the opposite. Reverse role modeling.

"Are you going to do it?" Natalie asked, juggling a twin on each hip. Both redheads, like their mother, inherited from Phil. The ringlets and long eyelashes were my genetic contribution.

"Here. Give me one of those." I lifted one of the boys above my head and slowly lowered him until our foreheads lightly touched. A squeal escaped and I inhaled his warm, somewhat sour breath. "I've got Henry, right?"

"Yes, Mom. I've got Charlie. So . . . what have you decided?"

"I haven't. I'm afraid Dad will obsess over this again, and at his age, well, I don't think he can handle the stress." *On the other hand, this might actually be a good thing for Dad, give him something to keep his mind active.*

But I kept that thought to myself.

"And what about you? Can you handle the stress with everything else that's going on?"

"Natalie, I'm not one of your cuckoo patients. I got shot. I shot someone. I'm dealing with it." I secured Henry in the swing that hung in the doorway between the kitchen and the dining room. "Besides, I told my father I would seriously think about it."

"Mom, you almost died. And you killed someone. Maybe wait a few months. Get your sea legs back." Natalie placed Charlie in the bouncy chair across from Henry. "So, if you were to look into the case, where would you start?" She too was not immune to the pull of this case.

"Your grandfather wants to work backwards from Lowell. Backtrack using her social security number. I would prefer to work forward from the day she failed to show up for her doctor's appointment at Monticello Hospital. Handle it like any cold case that gets resurrected. Interview people who knew her, reexamine evidence, review police reports, find inconsistencies in witness statements. We now know she wasn't murdered. Dad had been convinced she was. That probably led him down a few wrong paths."

"And to what end? What does it matter now?"

There was no way to explain to Natalie why this mattered. This case brought back so many memories, and not all of them good. It was just an itch I needed to scratch. Like a mosquito bite—small but irritating. The nagging feeling that knowing what happened to her would right all the wrongs from that year. But I wasn't in the mood to get into all that.

"Your grandfather is convinced that something nefarious went down. He believes if Trudy had just run off, he would have found her. He wants to make sure justice is served." Yeah, something like that. He also had that itch. And I was pretty sure it was bigger than mine. Jock itch, maybe.

"The Cuttman no longer exists. Monticello Hospital no longer exists. Come to think of it, very little from back then still exists." Natalie crouched in front of Henry's swing and planted a kiss on the top of his head, then looked back at me. "So, exactly where are you going to start looking?"

YOU CAN'T tell now, but Sullivan County was once a thriving, vibrant area. Especially in the summers. To understand this area's ascent you have to go back to the turn of the twentieth century. Think *Fiddler on the Roof: The Sequel.* At the end of the show (or movie, if that's your thing), Tevya, the dairy farmer, leaves his little village of Anatevka for America. If there was a part two, he would find himself on the teeming Lower East Side of Manhattan. He would look around, shrug, and say to himself (in Yiddish), *"On the one hand, I have found myself a job in a factory so I can support my family, but on the other hand*"—inflection rising—"*this is no place for a dairy farmer. Where can I go to earn a living and breathe fresh air?*" He learns he can borrow a *bisl* of money from the Jewish Agricultural Society and buy himself a farm in Sullivan County, New York—ninety miles north of the city.

Eli and Fanny Cuttman were real-life immigrants from Russia who purchased hundreds of acres of land for farming. They bought the Round Valley Farm sometime around 1910 and took in boarders, charging them seven dollars apiece (chamber pot included). When they passed away in the 1940s, their son, Sam, and daughter-in-law, Sylvia, inherited the property. I don't know if you would call them visionary, but they (and other boardinghouse owners) saw an opportunity. Boardinghouses were torn down, and in their place, sprawling hotels were built to attract the growing population of Jews looking for respite from the sweltering summers in the city.

In the first half of the twentieth century, Jews had limited vacation options. They were barred from hotels and country clubs up and down the east coast. A gentleman's agreement, this was called, an innocuous-sounding term that was anything but.

In the second half of the century, as anti-Semitic restrictions waned, it was family tradition and nostalgia that kept them coming to this region. The hotels had a lot to offer: idyllic settings boasting indoor pools, outdoor pools, golf courses, ski hills, nightclub shows, athletic fields, dancing lessons, exercise classes, bingo, shuffleboard tournaments, bridge and mah-jongg, tennis courts, camps for kids and teens.

But the biggest draw was the food. Three meals a day. All you can eat. Just a two-hour drive from steamy New York City. "The Jewish Alps," Dad would say. Others called it the Borscht Belt.

Sam and Sylvia Cuttman had two daughters, Rachel and Deborah. The older daughter, Deborah, eloped with a bellhop and moved to New Jersey. Rachel went to Barnard College but never graduated. She returned to the hotel when she was nineteen years old to help run it when Sam became ill. She too married a bellhop, Stanley Roth. Rumor was that she had no choice. Scott was born less than nine months after their wedding. Then, in a span of eight years, Rachel gave birth to three more children: Meryl, Lori, and Joshua. When Sam and Sylvia retired in the early seventies, Stanley and Rachel seized the reins. To ensure a loyal staff, Stanley installed his own family—his brother and sister-in-law, David and Diane, several cousins, and an uncle—in various management positions.

Lori Roth and I were inseparable from kindergarten through seventh grade. At the time of Trudy Solomon's disappearance, we were still best friends, so I spent a good chunk of my preteen years at the Cuttman. The outdoor pool was the grandest among all the hotel pools: Olympic size, with three diving boards of varying degrees of difficulty. If Lori and I just wanted to hang out, we would head over to the game room and spend every quarter we had on pinball, air hockey, and the jukebox. At night we danced at the teen disco or sat at the nightclub bar drinking Shirley Temples. As the owners' daughter, Lori was practically royalty there, and she and her siblings were treated with special deference by the staff. None of the Roth kids demanded such treatment; it was just the natural order of things. For many members of the staff, it was a way to get in good with Stanley and Rachel—especially Stanley, who was deemed by many to be a demanding, if not demeaning, boss.

By the end of eighth grade, Lori and I were no longer speaking to each other. So my days hanging out at the Cuttman dwindled with our fading friendship. You could say we drifted apart. But that would be kind. There is this moment when your family's socioeconomic status starts to matter. Around thirteen years old—when the desire to be popular short-circuits girls' brains—is usually that moment. Lori was the daughter of a hotel owner. I was the daughter of a cop. Her mother went to Manhattan to shop. My mother went to the local liquor store. She wore Jordache jeans. I wore Lee's. Our bond couldn't survive class-consciousness.

After our friendship soured, I would sneak onto the hotel grounds. Take a swim. Hit the game room. Dance at the disco. Sometimes Lori would spot me. But she kept her distance. One night I got stopped by a security guard who told me Rachel would call the cops the next time I stepped foot on their property. Claimed she didn't want the "townies" using the facilities. I was reduced from best friend to pariah in a matter of months.

One by one, the siblings peeled off to college—none of them were interested in coming back to the area to run the hotel. In 1995, Stanley and Rachel sold the Cuttman to an Indian guru who transformed it into an ashram. According to Dad, the Roths left the area with a nice windfall to pursue other interests.

And so the demise of the Catskills area began. The *Dirty Dancing* days were long over. Other hotel owners were devising their own exit strategies. Vacationers were no longer flocking to the area. The now grown-up kids, the ones who had come with their parents to these hotels, were not enchanted with the run-down rooms, dated lobbies, dilapidated athletic facilities, and kosher menus. The nail was hammered into the coffin when the gambling referendums failed to pass in the early aughts. Potential buyers fled. Abandoned hotels crumbled. Weeds proliferated. Graffiti adorned building walls. Sort of like the ruins of the ancient fortress of Masada in southern Israel—without the UNESCO World Heritage Site status.

Natalie was right. The last twenty-five years had not been kind to this region. Anyone associated with the Cuttman was long gone. Trudy's old friends were God knows where . . . or dead. I had worked cold cases before, but this one was akin to trying to locate the delicate seeds of a white dandelion after you blew them off to make a wish.

I STOPPED by Horizon Meadows on my way to the police station to give Dad the bad news. I had a litany of excuses. Suspects and witnesses left long ago. The hospital, where she was last seen, was closed. The Cuttman nonexistent. Our victim, or whatever she was, couldn't piece together two sentences. Ray thought it was a bad idea. I had a bum leg. And, my near-death experience was messing with my head.

Dad wasn't taking no for an answer. He pulled out the "I'll be dead soon" card. And even though I was expecting that, it still stung. But then he offered up something unexpected.

"What if I told you I know how to get in touch with Ben Solomon? The husband."

"You know where he is?" I asked, realizing my mistake the minute the words came tumbling out of my mouth. He'd set an ambush, and I strolled right in.

"You can say we're like pen pals. Although these days it's more like email pals. You know I always suspected he had something to do with her disappearance. But he insisted he was as much in the dark as anyone. He over-insisted, if you know what I mean. What's that line from Shakespeare?"

"The lady doth protest too much?"

"Yeah, that. He made it a point to get in touch with me every so often, trying to prove his innocence. I figured it couldn't hurt to write him back, stay close to him if he did or said something stupid. My Spidey sense always tingled when I was around him."

Dad was the White Rabbit and I was following him down the rabbit hole. "What makes you think he'll have a different story now that she's been found?" I asked.

"People get spooked when a missing person reappears all of a sudden or a witness pops up out of the blue. Maybe he's afraid she said something to someone, so he tries to cover his ass and reveals something new, something self-incriminating."

"Talking to this one guy isn't going to break this case open—you know that. We would need to get in touch with people who knew her from the hotel and her hometown to piece this thing together. And Lord only knows where all those folks ended up."

"I know."

"You know what?"

"I know where they are. They don't call me the Computer King of Horizon Meadows for nothing. There's a Facebook group called Summers at the Cuttman. And guess who runs it? One of the Roth kids. And get this: hundreds of staff and guests from the 1970s have joined. There's also a Growing Up in Mill Basin, Brooklyn, 50's and 60's group. That's where and when Trudy grew up. We put out a few feelers, see what we can reel in. Like throwing chum to the sharks. See who bites."

You know that proverbial fork in the road? I was standing right in front of it. And both paths seemed shitty.

Left, I tell Dad to let it go. She's been found. End of story. He gets pissed. Right, I ask Eldridge for permission to look into the case, opening that little door to crazy Wonderland.

I get sucked into the vortex of the worst days of my childhood. But, damn, I'd be lying if I didn't admit I was somewhat curious.

CHAPTER THREE

Wednesday, October 24, 2018

HAVING NEARLY drained my glass of Bud, I signaled the bartender for a refill. If I hadn't become a detective, I would have seriously considered bartending. Some people laughed when I confessed this offbeat occupational fantasy. And maybe it was silly. But it was the truth. I thought there was something alluring about standing behind a bar, owning a space that no one can intrude on, concocting cocktails or simply tapping a beer line, getting to know the regular clientele or hearing a story from a stranger passing through town. I would prefer a hotel-lobby bar over a local saloon. A place filled with out-of-towners, mainly business folks, married or single, male or female, who were susceptible to one-night stands.

Men ordering single malt scotch, neat. Women ordering dirty martinis, dry. *What's a nice girl like you doing in a place like this?* and bearing witness to other corny pickup lines. Then you go home at night without the weight of the world on your shoulders. (Well, unless a patron slipped someone a roofie or a customer who had one too many got into a car accident. Then some amount of guilt would fall on your shoulders, proving no job was fully without consequences and burden.)

Sally came up behind me, reached over the bar and pilfered a slice of lime from the fruit tray. She inserted it in her mouth, creating an illusion of big green lips, and sucked the juice out.

"Hey there, stranger." She winced and shuddered, a delayed reflex from ingesting the tart lime. "Have you decided yet?"

"I caved. I told Dad I would ask Eldridge about reopening the case."

"Well, I guessed wrong. Definitely thought you would take a pass."

"I'm doing this for my father. He's convinced there's a criminal element to this, and with no statute of limitations for kidnapping, he could go to his grave knowing he got his man."

"And you? What do you think?"

"I'm not sold on that theory. I'm more inclined to think she wanted to start a new life and figured out a way to erase herself. Which I find intriguing. I think it would be kinda cool to figure out what happened to her between the time she disappeared from here and reappeared in Lowell. Give her a life story. Without it, it's like she never existed. Alzheimer's has robbed her of her story. Maybe we can tell it for her."

"And if Eldridge says no, will you take a leave of absence and do it on your own?"

"I would prefer to do it officially, but I'd consider it."

"And Ray, is he okay with this?"

"Ray is ambivalent. He tossed out that I was free to do whatever I wanted, although he thinks it's a waste of time. Natalie thinks it's a bad idea. But that's the psychologist in her. She wants me to reduce the level of stress in my life, not pile it on. It would have been nice to have their full support, but I get it." I reached for the bowl of bar nuts and scooped out a few. "If Ray told me he was going to take a leave of absence to work on a case his father couldn't solve, I would've probably told him he was . . ." I gazed at the assortment of nuts in my palm. "Nuts."

Sally waved to the bartender and yelled, "Guinness!" She pounded her fist on the bar. "I think you should do it. You're the best detective in this precinct. Hell, probably in all of Sullivan County. If anyone can crack this case, you can."

"Before this whole Calvin Barnes thing I might have agreed with you. But there are still some people in this community who think I should be fired, that I got off with a slap on the—"

"Fuck what the community thinks. You should be exalted as a hero, but instead they're accusing you of racial discrimination. For God's sake, you were shot."

"Yeah, but the guy I shot in return wasn't the one holding a gun. It was Wayne Railman who pulled the trigger—so the white guy shoots me, and what do I do? I shoot the Black guy because I could have sworn *he* had the gun. Perhaps, in a snap judgment, I fired at the man I *assumed* was threatening my life. Y'know, implicit bias."

"Don't you dare blame this on some split-second thought process." Sally crinkled her face. "Man, I would just like to see all these armchair cops walk in our shoes one day. If they knew you like I do, they would know this is so bullshit."

"So I should tell them I voted for Obama, twice, and attend Black Lives Matter meetings?"

"If it helps change minds, hell yeah." Sally took a swig from her fresh pint of Guinness and a little foam mustache formed on her upper lip. "Get Rhonda to vouch for you. Having the lead organizer of the local BLM chapter on your side has to count for something."

"I'm not so sure Rhonda *is* on my side. I haven't heard from her since this thing happened." I pressed my slightly sweaty fingers against the icy beer mug. "Can we change the subject?"

"Sure . . . has the Jane Doe skeleton been ID'd yet?"

"Nope. Not sure how involved our department will be with that . . . the remains were found in Ulster County. Not our jurisdiction."

"So, when are you going to talk to Eldridge about Trudy Solomon?"

"Tomorrow morning."

"Let's make a toast." Sally raised her pint. "To Trudy Solomon. Here's hoping she's had a good life."

CHAPTER FOUR

Thursday, October 25, 2018

MY SIT-DOWN with Eldridge went better than I thought it would. I got the feeling he too was curious about what happened to Trudy Solomon. Eldridge's mother worked at the Cuttman as a waitress in the main dining room back then, and although she had not been friends with Trudy, I'm sure her disappearance was a topic of conversation and speculation in the Eldridge household. When Eldridge joined the force in 1981, the Trudy Solomon case had been active but back-burnered. My father was still assigned to the case and he was given some leeway to investigate new leads as long as he kept closing his other cases. Eldridge dabbled in it, as did all the rookies who thought they had the chops to break the case. It never hurts to get a fresh pair of eyes on a case like this, but eventually resources dwindled, new cases took priority, and Trudy's husband wasn't applying much pressure. By 1982, Ben Solomon had remarried. The Trudy Solomon case officially closed in 1983.

Eldridge said he would let me know his answer after he had a chance to discuss my request with his superiors. He would prefer to keep it official, as opposed to me playing private detective with Dad.

"Well? How'd it go?" Sally asked as I passed her desk on the way to mine.

"Hard to say. He'll let me know in a few days."

When Sally walked into the precinct ten years ago, I was the only female officer in the place. Today there were four of us. Four women, twenty-one guys. A handful of them testosterone-infused, dick-measuring jerks. So we put a lot of thought into determining who wins our Biggest Jackass of the Precinct contest every year. Jerry Houseman was the reigning champ, holding the title for three years. Last year was a close call, but wearing a Red Sox cap pushed him over the finish line.

Those guys may have given me a hard time when I started (and I was the daughter of a well-respected detective), but Sally had two tours in Iraq under her belt when she walked through that door, which meant respect from the ranks on day one. She enlisted in the army the week after 9/11. Her dad, Dennis McIver, was a bit of a local legend himself. Cop turned bar owner. Every Boxing Day he invited law enforcement from surrounding counties to enjoy a free meal at McIver's Pub. The tradition started in 2002, when Dennis returned home from Ireland with his new bride, Fiona McDougal from Doolin. Best beef stew this side of the Atlantic Ocean. Getting on Sally's bad side got you banned from McIver's Pub. Nobody crossed Sally.

My thigh started to throb. The tightening sensation usually gripped me during moments of anxiety. The meeting with Eldridge wasn't especially stressful, so I was pretty sure that was not the cause. I had a feeling it was related to what I was planning to do later this morning. I hobbled over to my desk. Sally followed me.

"You okay?"

"Yeah. It's nothing. The bullet is acting up and my hands feel like Niagara Falls on a rainy day." I sat down at my desk and rubbed my hands on my pants. Sally pulled open the drawer and pointed to the Secret. I shook my head. Too many people around. I glanced at the mounted clock behind Sally's head. Nine on the dot. Two whole hours until my visit with Mom. Two hours of a throbbing thigh and uncontrollable sweating. Fuck it. I uncapped the Secret and applied it to my palms.

MY MOM'S house, the house of my teenage years, was frozen in the seventies. I walked through the front door and stepped back in time. Orange shag carpeting in the living room, mustard-colored appliances atop faux-brick linoleum in the kitchen, and throughout the first floor of the house, aging wallpaper blooming with orange and pink flowers. The once-vibrant colors were yellowed from decades of cigarette smoke settling on the petals. I stood in the doorway outside the kitchen, peering in. Usually there would be a stack of dirty dishes in the sink, but this morning the plates were nested neatly in the plastic drying rack. The counters were wiped clean and only a coffee mug and spoon sat in the sink. Probably the cup of decaf Mom drank before bed in an attempt to palliate the likely morning hangover.

I poked my head into the living room, half expecting to see Mother lying on the couch with an empty vodka bottle at arm's length. Instead, I saw a tidy room with the throw blanket neatly folded on the back of the sofa and the pillows arranged symmetrically in the corners. Felix the Cat (a name my mother bestowed upon her feline companion during one of her lighter moods) was curled up on a tartan swivel chair. She lashed her tail when she spied me but didn't move from her perch.

An episode of *The Twilight Zone* flashed through my mind. An alien from Planet Clean had taken over my mother's body. Either that or she'd hired a maid, which fell more into the fantasy genre. I doubled back to the foyer and noticed other oddities. You wouldn't call them oddities in most households—vacuumed rugs, dusted banister, a lavender-scented air freshener plugged into a wall socket—but in my mother's house this was more than a little weird.

The cop in me kicked in and I tiptoed upstairs. The timbre of what sounded like rap music was emanating from my old bedroom. I stood still outside the door trying to make sense of what my eyes and ears picked up. *What was going on behind that door?* I crept down the hall to my mother's bedroom. I put my ear against the door. Light snoring. I turned the doorknob, opening the door just enough to stick my head in. The rancid smell of stale cigarettes escaped, causing me to involuntarily shudder and tighten my nostrils. The room was pitch-black, but light from the hallway streamed across the carpet and onto the bed, illuminating the curved outline of my mother's body under the covers. She stirred for a few seconds but remained asleep. I twisted the knob and carefully closed the door. *Okay, now what?* Door number one or door number two? I knew what awaited me behind door number two if I disturbed my mother. So I headed back over to door number one.

I knocked gently.

"Come in." A male voice. Wasn't expecting that.

I opened the door with a fair amount of trepidation, and was a bit thrown by what I saw. A twenty-something Black guy sat at my desk. The glow from the laptop computer bounced off the lenses of his wire-framed glasses, giving him an otherworldly vibe.

If there was an alien sitting there I would have been less surprised.

"Hello," he said. "Are you here to see Vera Ford?"

"Yeah. I'm her daughter. And you are?"

"I'm Thomas. Thomas Dillon. Vera—your mother—told me she told you about me . . . that I'm living here and helping out."

I kept my expression neutral and raised my eyebrows. He lowered the music, then stood up to shake my hand. I instinctively wiped my hand on my shirt before offering it to him.

"Susan, right? I'm an orderly at Horizon Meadows, and I got to talking to your dad one day and told him I didn't have a place to live. He asked me if I was any good at cleaning and straightening up messes and I told him that my ma was the finest hotel housekeeper in the Catskills and taught me a whole lot. He said I could stay here if I kept it tidy."

"And my mother went along with this?"

"Well, at first, no. But your dad spoke to her a few times. He convinced her to try this out temporarily, see how it goes. We hardly see each other anyway. If I'm not at Horizon Meadows, I'm at Sullivan County Community College over in Loch Sheldrake or in here studying."

I didn't know what shocked me more—these living arrangements or that Dad was having conversations with my mother. I glanced over at his computer.

"She doesn't mind the music?"

"I play it real low or wear my Beats. She hasn't complained about that."

"You okay with her . . ." I searched for the right word. "Lifestyle?"

"It's a small price to pay for a roof over my head. It's what your dad calls a symbiotic relationship."

"Uh-huh. So, what are you studying?"

"Criminal justice. Got one more semester to go after this one. Hoping to get a job at Woodbourne Correctional, maybe become a cop. For one of my classes I had to interview a police officer or detective and I'm thinking, when am I going to find the time to interview a police officer? I'm telling this to your dad, and he's smiling the whole time. Then he tells me he was a cop, then a detective." He paused to see if he still had my attention (he did), took a breath, and continued. "I was bouncing around, sleeping on friends' couches, my car, the park if it was warm out, sometimes the staff overnight room at Horizon. I don't mind cleaning and straightening up in exchange for this room, and your ma, she ain't no real bother, really. I have an auntie like her. I know what it's like. Your dad told me—"

"See, Susan, I ain't no bother." Our heads turned on cue, like a pair of synchronized swimmers. My bathrobed mother swayed in the doorway. "I mind my business. Thomas here minds his. He has a word for it. What's that word?"

"Symbiotic, Ms. Ford. But it actually means—"

"So, Susan, what brings you around for a visit?"

I locked eyes with Thomas, and for two people who didn't know each other, we shared a moment of understanding. I led my mother out of my—now his—room and pulled the door shut. The faint sound of hip-hop resumed.

MY STOMACH growled. The last thing I had eaten was a granola bar four hours earlier at seven o'clock that morning. Mother was in the shower and, from past experience, I calculated she wouldn't be down for another twenty minutes or so. When I opened the refrigerator, I was confronted by an assortment of condiments and leaky Chinese food containers. I leaned over to examine a container of cottage cheese, but I wasn't keen on opening it and seeing whatever science experiment was germinating inside. Yesterday's vestige of coffee was in the carafe, so I washed it out and started a fresh pot. From the pantry I unearthed a box of Ring Dings a few months past their sell-by date. I had bought into the urban legend about Twinkies, and figured if they can survive for decades, so too can its sister Hostess snack cake.

Mom liked to say I inherited the *skinny gene* from Dad's family, that I could eat anything and not gain a pound. But in the last few years I noticed my belly and thighs taking on a life of their own. The skinny gene was no match for menopause. I put the Ring Dings back where I found them.

The coffee machine beeped—I poured myself a fresh cup of coffee and assessed the kitchen. Hats off to Thomas and his cleaning prowess. Floors were not sticky. The microwave had only a few flecks of food clinging to its innards. The old appliances (the dishwasher was strictly for show) could pass as a deliberate decorating decision by a seventies-inspired interior decorator.

Even the oak table had a bit of shine to it. I splayed my fingers on the Formica counter. The cool surface instantly chilled my warm, moist palms.

"Good, you made coffee," Mom said, limping over to the coffeepot. Recent knee-replacement surgery hadn't improved her gait. "To what do I owe this visit?"

"I'm here because Dad said you wanted to talk to me."

She dumped three spoonfuls of sugar in her coffee and sat down at the kitchen table. I joined her. She fiddled with the pack of Marlboros on the table. The bright bulb above us accentuated her telltale signs of being an unrepentant smoker: vertical wrinkles above her upper lip, deep crow's-feet along the outsides of her eyes, sagging upper arms and breasts, and a yellowish stain on the insides of her middle and pointer fingers. A missed hairdresser's appointment left her with about an inch of gray hair at the roots. *Miss Sullivan County 1961*. If the light was right and you squinted, you could still see why she won the crown. The announcement in the local paper (the framed clipping still hung on the living-room wall) showcased her winning attributes: chestnut brown hair, blue eyes, 5'5", 115 pounds, 33-22-34. But now, at seventy-five, she looked older than Dad at seventy-seven.

"Oh right." She pulled out a cigarette and lit it. She inhaled deeply and exhaled slowly, relishing the rush of nicotine to her system. "He told me about Trudy Solomon. I think it's a bad idea for you to drag your father into this. He's not well."

I stood and retreated to a corner of the kitchen to avoid the smoke. A shitload of questions had hit me all at once. Why was Dad talking to her about this? What concern was it of hers if we did a little snooping? Why, all of a sudden, did she care about my father's well-being? What angle was she playing?

"Is this any of your business?" I waved my hand in an attempt to dissipate the smoke, but it was already penetrating my hair and clothes like a blood stain on carpet. "This is what you want to talk to me about? And here I was thinking it might be something important, like maybe apologizing to your granddaughter for almost killing the twins."

"Don't go on exaggerating, Susan. I merely left the oven on for a few hours. It got a bit hot; nobody was in danger of dying."

"You don't know that. Natalie and Frank can't even rely on you for a few hours to watch the kids. How difficult is it to stay sober while babysitting?"

"I wasn't drunk, but whatever. I'll apologize," she mumbled. "Now, as to why I wanted to talk to you . . ."

I leaned against the counter as my mother rambled on about how selfish I was by playing into Dad's fantasies. That I was riling him up. I got the feeling Dad made it sound like this was my idea, not his. Or maybe she was confused.

"Why do you even care what Dad is up to?"

"I just think this is a bad idea, especially with the trouble you're in and Will's heart issues."

My Dad's heart issues. The reason I came back home. I had tried my own little disappearing act after graduating college. Well, not so much a disappearing act—more of an attempt to leave the past behind. I had married Phil Morley at the start of freshman year at SUNY Albany. He took a job as a second-shift security guard, so he could watch Natalie during the day while I took classes. It was difficult, but we managed. That is, until the end of senior year, when I caught him with the stay-at-home mom in the neighboring apartment. Truth be told, I wasn't insanely angry. Quite the opposite, really. I'm pretty sure we wouldn't have gotten married in the first place if it wasn't for Natalie.

A new life was calling. Away from Phil. Away from Albany. Away from the Catskills. That's when Trudy Solomon popped back into my consciousness. I so wanted to believe she ran away, reinvented herself, became a stronger person. A different person. *Could I do that?*

With Natalie in tow, I headed south to the city, hopeful my art history degree would land me a decent job. Mom thought I was crazy. ("Good luck raising a kid in New York City on an entry-level salary and no husband," she slurred during a typical unpleasant phone call.) Dad, as usual, was absorbed in a case. ("I'll try and get down to see you and Natalie next week," he said, week after week.) I shed my married name and reverted back to Ford. Managed to get a job pretty quickly—unit production assistant for a movie company. Between child support and my small paycheck, I was able to afford a cramped two-bedroom in Brooklyn's Boerum Hill neighborhood. Second floor of a three-story brownstone. No elevator. One of the bedrooms the size of a walk-in closet.

Then came Evan Smith. An on-again, off-again relationship, heavily reliant on sex. Too much sex, if that's even possible. Didn't matter if we were in a state of bliss or a time of war—the physicality of this relationship kept us in each other's orbit. That was until he was caught embezzling funds from his company. I should have done the dumping, but he dumped me when the trial was over.

Twice burned, I threw myself into my work. I quit the production assistant job when a friend offered me a job as a location scout for a production company—which offered better pay and more independence. I ran around the five boroughs, New Jersey, and Connecticut cajoling homeowners, businesses, parks and recreation departments for use of their properties. My colleagues were in awe of my public-record sleuthing. I was dubbed Queen of ACRIS—the Automated City Register Information System—which listed owners of lots, blocks, and individual buildings. I once managed to convince a gas station owner to give our crew half a day to shoot a commercial near the pumps for a cologne called Antifreeze. I became a masterful liar, telling home owners we would leave their homes as pristine as we found them. In reality, their homes looked like crime scenes after we packed up and left. I guess the appeal of having one's home in a movie overrides their obligation to read the fine print of the contract. But I also became masterful at smoothing things over.

Then in 1999, I got the call. *"Susan, come home. Dad had a heart attack."* Good-bye Brooklyn. Hello Catskills.

"Susan, you listening?" Mom grumbled, breaking into my flashback.

I wasn't. Didn't matter—I knew what she wanted. "I'll give your two cents some thought," I said, keeping my sarcasm in check. But I knew that I would, once again, do the complete opposite of what she wanted.

I KNOCKED on my bedroom door. I wondered if Thomas knew about the Calvin Barnes fiasco. Who around here didn't?

"Come in," Thomas shouted over the music.

I handed him my card. "If things go south here, or you want to chat about a school project, feel free to call me."

He took my card and jammed it into his back pocket. "Appreciate that."

I closed the door but remained planted in front of it. *Should I go back in and get a read on the situation or let it go? Understand where he stands on the matter. Understand where his sympathies lie: With Calvin, unarmed teenager, shot by a cop? With me, injured in the line of duty, trying to get drugs off the street?* The decision was made for me when I heard glass shatter downstairs, followed by a flurry of curse words. Clearly, this was a sign. I turned and headed toward the kitchen to deal with another one of Mom's mishaps.

TRUDY

TRUDY SAT in the cafeteria waiting for her Coke. "Maxine?" she yelled to the young woman sitting a couple of tables away. "Maxine?" she repeated. "It's me."

The woman smiled politely and nodded her head.

Trudy stood and approached the woman. "Hi Maxine!"

To Trudy, Maxine was a real friend.

Her only real friend.

Someone she could tell her secrets to. Someone who wouldn't blab all over town. Maxine had her own fair share of trauma and bad luck. That's how you bond with a person—shared experiences that others dismiss as trivial . . . or tell you to just get over.

"Hi . . ." The woman glanced at Trudy's hospital bracelet. "Ummm . . . Ms. Resnick?"

Trudy blinked, then laughed. "So formal. La tee da."

"I'm afraid you have me confused with someone else. Maxine, you say?"

"Don't be silly." Trudy crouched down and whispered, "The plan is in place."

"The plan?"

"Right. We shouldn't talk about it here." Trudy glanced around, then sat down. She leaned in close to the young woman. "I'm a bit nervous."

"No need to be nervous," the young woman said, patting Trudy's hand. "I'm sure whatever it is will turn out just fine."

"I can always count on you, dear friend, to make me feel better."

CHAPTER FIVE

Tuesday, October 30, 2018

ELDRIDGE GAVE me the go-ahead this morning. He framed it to his superiors as an under-the-radar assignment, keeping me out of public view while the Barnes controversy settled down. Said the higher-ups had great respect for my good old dad, William Ford, and approved his role as consultant.

We were given two months and a small travel budget to figure this out. That gave us until New Year's Eve—a ridiculously tight deadline for a cold case with a tepid lead. Dad was certainly up for the challenge.

Me, I was still a bit uneasy about digging around in the past when my present was kind of a mess right now.

"What's your plan of attack?" Ray asked, tossing three hamburgers and buns on the grill. Two for him, one for me.

"I thought you weren't interested."

"I wasn't. But now that you're actually doing this, I am."

I leaned against the deck railing, weighing the pros and cons of involving Ray.

"Y'know, Eldridge doesn't want me dragging you and your pals into this. He doesn't want his detectives distracted by this investigation."

"Well then pretend I'm just your boyfriend and you're bouncing ideas off of me. Besides, I broke this case. It would be pretty cruel shoes to leave me in the dark."

Cruel shoes. Ray started using this expression a few years ago after reading *Cruel Shoes*, a collection of short stories by Steve Martin. ("It's the greatest work of literature I've ever read," he insisted.) I told him I'd think about it, that I'd make my decision after dinner. I went back into the house and headed to the fridge to get salad fixings. My rear pocket vibrated. I glanced at my phone and let it go to voice mail. But it would have been cruel shoes to ignore the message, so I immediately texted Dad to let him know I was eating dinner and would call back later. Now that we had gotten the green light, he was champing at the bit to get started. Me, I preferred a day or two to process this. I needed to steel myself, psyche myself up. To make sure I was ready to embark on this wild-goose chase, which could bring relief or misery, or both.

Besides, I planned to see Rhonda tomorrow. She called me out of the blue, although I had a feeling Natalie instigated it. Before the twins were born, Natalie attended Black Lives Matter weekend meetings at the Episcopal church and worked with the group to organize marches and raise money for Black candidates running for office. The death of Natalie's best friend spurred her to activism, she claimed.

Her friend, Autumn Sanders, drove to Georgia two years ago for a job interview. Two weeks later she was dead. The cops said she was weaving through traffic and changed lanes without signaling. When they asked her to get out of the car, they claimed she was uncooperative and had to use minimal force to get her to comply. She was tossed into a jail cell. That *minimal* force resulted in a few broken ribs, causing internal bleeding. No one checked on her throughout the night. By morning she was dead in her cell. But the dash cam told a different story. Autumn changed lanes to presumably let the cop car go by. She wasn't weaving in and out of traffic. In fact, there wasn't another car in sight. When she moved over, the patrol car moved over behind her and turned on the lights and siren. There was no sound on the recording, but you see Autumn get out of the car after some back-and-forth conversation with the officer.

When she stepped out, the cop grabbed her hair and slammed her to the ground with zero provocation. Zero. His partner exited the squad car, and in full view of the lens, spit on her. Then he kicked her repeatedly in the gut, and once in the back for good measure. Did these guys not realize their vest cams were activated? Or did they not care, because they'd done it before and were never called to task? What they didn't know was that Autumn's father worked in the New York State Attorney General's office as one of the lead prosecutors. When you know the *right* people . . . justice tips back in your favor. One cop was now rotting in jail. The other got off with a reprimand—but later lost his job when a hacker exposed his Facebook page full of racist, misogynistic, anti-Semitic, and homophobic tirades. Seems he was an equal-opportunity hater.

I opened the slider to let Ray back in with the platter of burgers. "Dad just called. I have a feeling he's going to be calling me a lot. I'm going to have to put up some guardrails."

"Knowing Will, he'll be bugging the hell out of you. You sure you want to do this?"

"I've already said I would. I'm not going back on my word."

"Roger that."

"And, I'm not starting until Thursday. So, don't ask me what I plan to do until then. I need a couple of days to gather up the old files. And besides, I'm having lunch with Rhonda tomorrow. I'm hoping she can help me with my prob . . . the shooting incident. Maybe tamp down some of the animosity." I laced my fingers together and cracked my knuckles. "But I haven't spoken to her since this happened. I'm not even sure Rhonda is on my side."

"But she's agreed to see you. Do you think she's meeting with you to ream you out? I doubt that. She knows you would never purposely shoot someone based on their race. You were on those police reform committees. You attended BLM meetings, for God's sake."

"It's not that simple."

"I don't know, seems pretty simple to me. You saw the flash of a gun, and in that split moment you had good reason to believe it was Barnes who shot you. The whole thing stinks."

CHAPTER SIX

Wednesday, October 31, 2018

RHONDA WAVED at me from a booth near the back of the diner. I was just five minutes late, but her near-empty glass of iced tea told me she'd been sitting there for some time. She shut her computer lid as I settled into the seat across from her. We engaged in small talk about the twins, my dad, her son. I ordered an egg-salad sandwich; she got the turkey club. As luck would have it, we ran out of small talk just as the waitress arrived with our plates.

"Half the group is willing to give you the benefit of the doubt." Rhonda stabbed one of the sweet potato fries with her fork and sighed. "They think it's important to show that the Black Lives Matter movement can recognize the difference between unjustified and justified police action, that not every incident is racially motivated, and we are a reasonably minded movement. They believe that if Calvin was white, the outcome would have been the same. However, the other half are spitting mad. It's happened yet again, and this time in their own backyard. They just don't believe what the cops are saying, how things went down. I've heard the word *cover-up* a few times."

"Which half do you stand with?"

She took two bites of her sandwich before answering. "It doesn't matter where I stand, Susan. Even if I was on your side, I can't go to bat for you, at least not publicly." She stabbed another fry and took a sip of iced tea. "But I think there are some in the group who would go public to defend you, if that's what you're hoping. Your daughter intimated as much. Folks really respect Natalie—her free counseling for kids at risk has been a godsend, and I think many see this as a way to pay it forward."

"I don't want to pit the members of the group against each other. I was hoping that you, as the head of this chapter, would be willing—"

Rhonda held up her left hand, palm facing out, fingers spread. "I have to stop you right there. The last thing I need is a splintered group, with me as the axe. Why do you think I suggested we have lunch here in Middletown, where no one will see us together? But if it makes you feel any better, I'm pretty sure if you fired your weapon, you had good reason to."

"I appreciate that. I wish I could convince others I had no choice."

"I didn't know Calvin Barnes, but I know people who knew him. They said he was a good kid under the influence of his not-so-good brother."

"I know he's being portrayed as this straight-A student who was in the wrong place at the wrong time. It's bullshit," I snapped. The waitress glanced over at us, her facial expression a mixture of curiosity and alarm at my rising voice. I inhaled sharply and slowly exhaled. "He *was* a good student up until a year ago. That's when he decided dealing drugs was more important than homework. He wasn't some innocent kid caught in the crossfire. He was there setting up a buy. I saw it with my own eyes."

"You've seen his parents on TV? They claim he was tagging along with his older brother Melvin and had no idea he was going to pick up a few bags of weed. His brother said you shot him when he was just standing there with his hands up."

"Yet, that's not what happened. Calvin was clearly in charge. His brother Melvin and the guy who shot me, Wayne Railman, were there for his protection." As I spoke Rhonda gazed down at my clenched fists, then back at me. I relaxed them slightly, forming misshapen donut holes. "And it wasn't just a *few* bags of weed. There was easily four ounces on that table. Not to mention quite a few sandwich bags full of Oxy. Intent to sell is a Class D felony."

"The problem people have is the cops say one thing and the victim's relatives say another, and—"

"Whoa Rhonda, victim? Really?" I squeezed my fists tight again, my fingernails dug into my moist palms. "Victim connotes that he is innocent in all this. He's not." I unclenched and stared at the little half-moon indentations.

"I'm just telling you what other people think. What you're up against. Too bad the department didn't get the funding yet for the body cams. I think that would have helped your case. But without it, it's hard for these folks to just take your word for what went down."

I knew Rhonda had limited options here.

A difficult balancing act. She couldn't go all in for me but she wasn't about to leave me stranded by the roadside. I relaxed my shoulders, which had inched up toward my ears. "That's why I was hoping for your support on this. You've known me for, what, three years now? Have I ever given you any reason to believe I would shoot someone out of some kind of animus, consciously or subconsciously?"

"It's not that—"

I leaned forward and whispered, "I've gotten a couple threatening notes tucked under my windshield wipers. A few heavy-breather calls to my home phone in the middle of the night."

Rhonda bowed her head and clasped her hands, as if she was praying. She shook her head, then asked, "Threatening in what way?"

"Watch your back kind of thing."

"Jeez. Tell you what, let me think about it. Okay?"

We sat silently for a few minutes. The waitress must have sensed we had run out of things to talk about and appeared at our table. "Anything else, ladies?"

"Just the check," I said. "My treat. I really appreciate you making the time to talk to me."

"I appreciate the generous offer, but I think we should split the bill."

I got Rhonda's drift. She didn't want this to look like a bribe. Even if it was just eighteen dollars.

"Look, I know you want my support. Let me think about my next move. I'll get back to you by the end of next week. It's the best I can do," Rhonda said, clearly intent on putting an end to this discussion. "So I hear that you're resurrecting the Trudy Solomon case."

"You know about that?"

"Uh-oh. Am I getting Natalie in trouble here? She mentioned it to me yesterday."

"No worries. I'm sure it'll be all over town soon enough. Yeah, I'm looking into it. With her turning up alive we might have a better chance of finding out what happened to her. Plus we have a lot more technology at our disposal for sleuthing."

"Did you know my mother was assigned to the doctor Trudy was supposed to see the day she went missing?" Rhonda said.

I looked up from signing my half of the bill. "Interesting. I had no idea your mom worked at Monticello Hospital."

"Yeah. My mother was a student nurse there around the time Trudy disappeared. She even has a scrapbook with newspaper clippings about it."

"Did the police interview her back then?"

"I don't know. I would imagine so. Maybe your dad would remember. My mom's name is Clara Cole. She works at Horizon Meadows now, caring for Alzheimer's patients. Isn't your dad a resident there?"

"He is. Level one, independent living." I tapped the side of my forehead. "Still has all his marbles."

I made a mental note to add Clara Cole to the list of potential witnesses we needed to interview, currently a list of one: Ben Solomon. It was quite possible that everyone else associated with this case was dead, living elsewhere, or memory-impaired. What in the world had I gotten myself into?

CHAPTER SEVEN

Thursday, November 1, 2018

DAD'S PICKUP truck had been rear-ended earlier in the week, leaving him stranded and making me his glorified chauffeur. When I pulled up to the entrance of Horizon Meadows, I spotted him—head tipped and sitting slightly slouched on a concrete bench. A human question mark. At his feet were two bankers boxes full of forest-green file folders. The first time I saw those folders was in 1978. The last time was in 1999, about two months after graduating from the police academy, when I couldn't help but take a sneak peek at them. I raised the rear hatch of my Prius and hoisted the boxes into the cargo area. I hadn't seen the contents of these boxes in nineteen years, but I remembered Dad's organizational system.

Each file folder was labeled with a color-coded sticker. Blue for witnesses. Green for suspects. Purple for friends. Yellow for theories. Orange for leads. Within each file were manila folders containing witness interview notes, suspect statements and alibis, potential motives, and biographical info extracted from Trudy's friends and acquaintances.

No one could ever accuse Dad of not being organized. It was clearly one of the many reasons he parted ways with my disorganized, messy mother. If cleanliness was next to godliness, he was in the orchestra section, front row, and she was up in the balcony, last row. He lived a clutter-free and tidy life even before he got wind of Marie Kondo. But when his buddies bought him *The Life-Changing Magic of Tidying Up* (as a gag gift for his seventy-seventh birthday), he ratcheted up his obsession to the next level. The nurses told me he was going apartment to apartment trying to convince his neighbors to embrace the KonMari movement. Maybe this explained his desire to get Mom's life in order.

"Are these all the case files?" I asked as we simultaneously buckled in.

"That's everything. Eldridge brought them by yesterday."

"You hungry? Want to stop somewhere first?"

"I've been waiting four decades to dig back into this case and you think I want to stop and get something to eat? Susan, I'm an old man. I ain't got time to spare. Let's just get to it."

I headed west on Route 17B toward Bethel. Fifteen minutes later, we arrived at my house. The gravel crackling under my tires aroused Moxie from her favorite resting spot on the porch. Moxie's mother was a black Labrador Retriever. Her father, unknown. That mysterious breed produced tufts of light-brown patches on her sides and belly. But her boxy build and curious face were clearly in the Lab camp. She lazily lifted her head as if to decide whether it was worth getting up. It was; she stood when I stepped out of the car. She could only go so far on her twenty-foot tie-out and arthritic hind legs, but she managed to limp down the three steps with her tail in full swing.

"How old is the old mutt now?"

"Thirteen. I read on some dog website that that makes her eighty-two in human years. You're just a few years younger than her."

I squatted to release her from the tie-out and she followed us inside. To avoid a conversation about my housekeeping skills (or lack thereof), I had tidied the place the day before. Even so, Dad couldn't help but surreptitiously poke around and assess my ability (or inability) to keep only those things that "sparked joy." I was more like my father than my mother when it came to being a pack rat. Not particularly sentimental, I tended to discard things without contemplating their future personal value.

Ten years ago, I bought this house from a woman who was moving to Asheville, North Carolina. I figured it was a good investment if the gambling referendum passed. If not, well, I had a nice lakeside cottage just ten minutes from Yasgur's farm, the Woodstock Festival site. The previous owner had left her furniture, a mishmash of eclectic pieces that either elicited compliments for my aesthetic eye toward shabby chic or raised eyebrows for my inability to create a coherent style. I converted a barely used three-season porch into a cozy home office. The narrow five-by-ten room provided just enough space for a desk, chair, and one filing cabinet. Too small for Dad and me to spread out the contents of the boxes, let alone be in the room at the same time without getting in each other's way or on each other's nerves (since we both tended to pace).

Ray said we could commandeer the dining room. We rarely used it anyway—we preferred eating breakfast at the kitchen island and dinner on the living room couch, usually watching foreign detective shows on Netflix (cozy mysteries where British hamlets with silly names were awash with murder and mayhem, or gritty crime procedurals with psychologically damaged cops, usually of the female persuasion).

Earlier in the week, I had purchased a portable whiteboard on which to hang pictures of our suspects (should we determine foul play) and map out a visual time line of Trudy's movements after her disappearance. Dad sipped coffee while I rummaged through the boxes. I found a faded Polaroid of Trudy and stuck it in the upper left corner of the white board. Then I taped a picture of Trudy's husband, Ben Solomon, on the board under a column marked "Suspects." Suspected of what, well, we were not really sure. Yet.

"So Dad, why is Mom under the impression that reopening the case was my idea. And what's with the guy you've rented—"

"Oh yeah, that. Meant to tell you. It slipped my mind because of all this," Dad said, sweeping his arm across the table. "Nice kid. Needed a place to stay, and your mother needs some help. Housekeeping was never her strong suit, so I matched them up. It's not like you use your bedroom."

"Okay, but—"

"As for why she thinks it's your idea to investigate this thing, I kinda positioned it that way. I wasn't in the mood to get into a dustup with her, so I laid this at your feet. She'll get over it. Sorry about that."

"Why is she so adamant that we shouldn't do this?"

"Not sure, except she wasn't thrilled with this case forty years ago either. She thought I was obsessed. Perhaps she's afraid you'll get obsessed. It does take a lot out of you to grind on one case for years."

"Well, I'm game for an obsession right now, so, how do I put this kindly . . . F-U Mom."

"That's the spirit! So, here's what I'm thinking. First, let's see what other hits we can get on Trudy's social security number. See where it leads us. Second, let's put out feelers on those Facebook groups I told you about. And third, let's determine whom we can interview from these old files. Figure out who's still alive and worth having a conversation with."

"Okay. I'll run the social. You do the Facebook stuff."

I never really embraced Facebook the way many of my friends and colleagues did. I rarely posted anything. I logged on once or twice a week to see what my "friends" were up to. I guess I was more of a Facebook voyeur. Natalie, however, was a prolific poster. Mostly pictures of the twins, but also dishes she cooked, political articles from liberal-leaning news outlets, vacation pictures, and dogs-doing-cute-things videos. If she wasn't on Facebook, I probably would have never signed up.

"Before I dive into Facebook, I'm going to email Ben Solomon," Dad said. "He's living in Ellenville these days. Maybe he'll meet us for coffee. He seemed genuinely shocked when I phoned him and told him Trudy was alive. He asked me if that makes him a bigamist. That was his first concern. Himself. Didn't even ask if she was okay or what had become of her."

"And you still think he had something to do with her disappearance?"

"I just don't think he's as innocent as he claims to be. A friendly face-to-face over a cup of joe might yield some tidbits of information we couldn't get out of him forty years ago."

Nodding, I powered up my laptop and plugged Trudy's social security number into the database. It was linked to two medical records. One was associated with the Lowell memory care facility where Ray had found her. Prior to that, her social security number was linked to a 2008 stay at a mental hospital in Belmont, Massachusetts. Nothing before that date, which meant she never filed for taxes, nor was she employed (unless she took money under the table).

Was this purposeful? Did she just want to live her life under the radar? Had she been hiding from someone? Or, as Dad suspected, had she been held against her will until she became a burden or of no further use to her captor?

When Dad finished typing his email to Ben, he clicked over to Facebook. "The Mill Basin Brooklyn page is public, but in order to post on the Summers at the Cuttman page, I have to seek permission from the site's administrator."

"And that would be?"

"Meryl Roth." Dad tilted his head forward and peered over the rim of his reading glasses. "Being that you were friends with her, maybe you should ask to join."

Meryl was older than her sister Lori by two years. Although I had been best friends with Lori, I never really hung out with Meryl. She rotated in a different orbit. I wasn't exactly jealous of her, but I sure did envy her. She was the definition of seventies cool. Big hair, perfectly coifed à la Farrah Fawcett. The trendy wardrobe: Frye boots. Tube tops. Tight-fitting designer jeans. Daisy Dukes. Candie's platforms. The stretchy wrap skirts made famous in *Saturday Night Fever.* She was the first girl to buy a mood ring. Everyone followed suit. "I wasn't exactly friends with her. But I get your point—it probably makes more sense if I join this group."

When we were done requesting entrée into our respective Facebook groups, Dad made his way, once again, to the bathroom. He didn't want to talk about it. And that was fine with me—did I really want to hear about his prostate? He claimed it was under control, nothing to worry about. ("Old man problems," he groused.)

I removed the folders from the boxes and laid them out on the table. Our plan was to read every scrap of paper in these files, get ourselves reacquainted with the case and make note of who was still alive and could be interviewed.

"Dad, do you know Clara Cole?" I asked when he reentered the dining room. "She's a nurse at Horizon Meadows."

"Sounds familiar, but I'm not conjuring up a face."

"She's Rhonda's mother—"

"Rhonda?"

"Local BLM organizer."

"Right. Go on."

"Well, it just so happens she was a student nurse working for Trudy's doctor at the time of her disappearance." I pulled Clara's witness statement from the pile and handed it over to Dad. "It looks like your partner Sam interviewed her."

"Well, son of gun. Small world."

My computer dinged, alerting me to a private message in Messenger.

OMG! Suzie Ford!! How the heck are you? I stalked over to your FB page and see you still live in the borscht belt (ha ha)!!! And that you followed in your dad's footsteps. Should I address you as Detective Ford? LOL! What brings you to the Summers at the Cuttman group? Looking to reconnect with old friends? I also moderate our high school FB page. Check that out! Lots of fun memories there!! Best, Meryl

Suzie. A name I thought I would never hear again. When I turned thirteen, Suzie just didn't feel right. It felt babyish. And Dad sometimes called me Suzie-Q, which embarrassed me in front of my friends. The name on my birth certificate was Suzanne. At the time, I felt that was too stuffy. (Still do.) I wanted to change my name to Natalie (I had just seen *West Side Story*), but no one would abide by my wishes. So, we settled on Susan. Dad got the hang of it almost immediately. But it took my mother nearly a year to remember to call me Susan. Maybe it was the vodka. Maybe she didn't give a shit.

As for the rest of the message, OMG! was right. So many exclamation points! What was protocol here? *Should I reciprocate with the same level of enthusiasm?* I didn't want to come across as a cop badgering her Facebook group. Just needed to give enough information to intrigue her, but not too much to scare her away and lose access to the group. I remembered Dad saying that Stanley Roth was livid about the amount of police presence on his property and blamed the investigation for canceled reservations that year. His anger was enough to draw Dad's suspicions, but there was no circumstantial or hard evidence to implicate the family. There was also pressure from the upper echelon of the police department to leave the Roth family alone. The Roths and other hotel owners were powerful people with political friends who gave generously to police charitable funds. Dad pushed the envelope as far as he could.

Hi Meryl! Yup, still here in the Catskills. The area is starting to turn around with gambling on the horizon! I'm actually working a cold case and was hoping to find Cuttman people who might be able to help me—staff and guests who were there in the mid 70s. A little stroll down memory lane might help me solve the case!! Also, would love to get in touch with

Lori. It would be great to say hi to her after all these years. How are your folks? Your brothers? Hope all is well!! Best regards, Susan

Six exclamation points felt about right. As for the sentiment about Lori, perhaps over the top. "Love" seemed a bit much. I changed "love" to "like" and hit send. When I reloaded the "Summers at the Cuttman" page a few minutes later, I was a member of the group.

"Hey Dad. I'm in." He shot me a thumbs-up. "I'll let you know if Meryl says it's okay to post about the case."

"Well, I'm not asking for permission. I'm diving right in." Dad peeked over his laptop. "What's with these piles?"

"I sorted the old interview files, separated the living from the dead. The doctor Trudy had the appointment with is dead. Max Whittier, the guy from the parking lot who saw Ben drop off Trudy, is dead. Trudy's best friend at the time, Maxine Cohen, is dead." I scanned Maxine's file. "According to her statement, she was shopping in Middletown when Trudy disappeared and claimed to have no idea as to what might have happened to her."

"Maxine Cohen. Kinda remember her. A down-on-her-luck type."

"But her neighbor, Eleanor Campbell, is alive and, get this, she still lives in Monticello. All the Roths are alive. I saw a post on the Cuttman page about the parents living in Florida. They must be, what, in their late seventies?"

"Yeah. I went to high school with Rachel Roth. She was a year ahead of me, so that makes her seventy-eight. She was quite the looker back then. By any chance, did you find interview notes with a guy named Lenny? He was the hotel coffee-shop manager at the time. Another piece of work."

"Yup, he's in my alive pile. What's his story?"

"Trudy complained to Rachel that Lenny constantly groped and harassed her, so Rachel fired him. He was escorted off the property. Rachel said he was spitting mad at Trudy. Yelling shit like 'you'll be sorry' and 'you better watch your back.' But he had an alibi for around the time she was dropped off at the hospital. Even so, I think he's worth looking at again."

I flipped through the Leonard "Lenny" Berman file. "Well, what have we here? A police record. Seems harassing Trudy wasn't his first rodeo. Got picked up for solicitation." I loosened the staple that secured his mug shot to the arrest sheet, separated the two documents, and tacked the photo to the whiteboard under "Persons of Interest."

"I'm going to call that mental hospital in Belmont," Dad said. "See what I can find out about why she was there. Do you have the number?"

I jotted down the phone number of McNair Hospital and handed him the piece of paper. "Before you call, I want you to eat something. I made a sandwich for you . . . it's on the counter."

I needed him to slow down, take care of himself; I feared he would fulfill my mother's prophecy of being killed by this case. I could've used a bite myself, but a ding from my computer pulled me back into the dining room.

Hi Susan!

I remember when you changed your name from Suzie to Susan. Sorry about that! Old habits die hard!! So, you're trying to solve a cold case. Sounds intriguing. This Facebook group could use a little excitement. It would be cool if you crack the case with info from one of our group members! You should friend Lori (her married name is McDonald. Which didn't go over well with the parents). She lives in Venice (California, not Italy!). I'll give her a heads up that you'll be getting in touch. Josh is still in the hospitality business. Runs a bed and breakfast in Vermont with his husband (that also didn't go over too well with my parents—although they did attend his wedding). Scott lives in Florida. Pretty successful guy—owns a bunch of car dealerships. He's recently divorced from Wife Number Two (that's what we call her; the earlier one is, you guessed it, Wife Number One). He recently got engaged to future Wife Number Three. My parents live in Jupiter, Florida. Mom is in pretty good health (knock on wood). Dad has had some health issues, but my mother is caring for him. I'm living in New Jersey these days. Earlier this year I retired from my life as a literary agent (I've taken up genealogical research—trying to piece together our family tree!) Hope all is well with you! Best, Meryl

My palms felt like a bed of moss covered with a thin membrane of morning dew. Just hearing about the exploits of the Roth family threw my palmar hyperhidrosis into overdrive. I unsealed a mason jar full of fireflies. Just try recapturing those motherfuckers. Meryl will tell Lori (if she hadn't already) that I reached out to her. *Will she expect to hear from me?* Lori and I did not part ways amicably. It was more like a slow burn of cruel gestures and remarks as we grew out of our childhood "best friends forever" promise.

I typed "Lori Roth McDonald" into the Facebook search box. There she was. Her page was private, so all I could see were a few photos. In one, she was holding a baby with the caption "Yikes! I'm a grandma!!" This family loved their exclamation points. I hovered over the Message icon. *Here goes nothing.*

Hi Lori,

Hope this message finds you well. Meryl and I connected through Facebook and she might have mentioned to you that I would be getting in touch. First things first . . . I'd like to get the "elephant in the room" out of the way . . . I know our friendship crumbled in high school, but I do look back fondly on the good times we had in elementary and beginning of high school. Whenever I pass the hotel grounds, I think of all the mischievous things we did! I heard you went to Boston University, and currently live in CA. I paved a different path. Went to SUNY Albany after high school (after a gap year), worked as a location scout for a production company in NYC for 10 years, but when my dad had a heart attack I came back home and enrolled in the police academy. Followed in my dad's footsteps, so to speak. Would love to hear what you're up to, but I'd understand if you would prefer to keep the past in the past.

Friendship crumbled? Was there a better word or phrase to use there? Disintegrated. Dissolved. Terminated. Ceased to exist. Ended in a barrage of mean and vicious backstabbing. I stuck with *crumbled* and hit send. Back at the Summers at the Cuttman page, I composed a message about the Trudy Solomon case.

Cold case investigation needs your help! Looking for friends, co-workers, acquaintances who knew Trudy Solomon (nee Gertrude Feldman). She worked at the Cuttman Hotel from 1974-1978. She went missing on August 6, 1978. There's been a recent break in the case. Link to news article below. Monticello Police Dept. trying to piece together her life or determine if any criminal activity was involved in her disappearance. Please PM if you have any recollection of her that you could share. Any little detail will be helpful! Thank you, Detective Susan Ford

There, done. No turning back. I headed into the kitchen for a cup of coffee. Dad was on the phone with the mental hospital in Belmont doing what he did best: convincing the person on the other end to, as he put it, cough up the goods. I was only half listening, but it sounded like they kept putting him on hold as they shuffled him from one department to another. I took my coffee back into the dining room and surveyed the files in front of me wondering how I ended up getting sucked into this. I banished that thought and resumed the task of separating the living from the dead.

"Pack your bags, Susan. We hit the road on Sunday," Dad proclaimed, bursting into the dining room like he was raiding the place. "The doctor who treated Trudy still works at McNair, the hospital in Belmont, and is willing to chat with us, but only in person. Dr. Jacqueline Blanchard is her name. She said she's available Monday morning, so I figure we drive out there on Sunday and stay overnight at a nearby hotel. And get this, Trudy was admitted as Gertrude Resnick. Same last name as in Lowell. Dr. Blanchard can't discuss any medical issues because Trudy is still alive—doctor-patient confidentiality and all that—but she told me she always thought how strange her situation was, and how they couldn't get in touch with the woman who brought her there. And here's the kicker . . . the doctor said that back then the police were sniffing around as well, as Trudy was thought to be a possible witness to a murder. So we might want to head over to the local police station while we're there to see if they can shed some light on that."

"Holy shit. How long was she in that hospital?"

"Five years: 2008 to 2012. She was moved to the Lowell nursing home when McNair shut down their Alzheimer's unit."

"In 2008 she would have been fifty-seven. That's awfully young to have Alzheimer's."

"Early-onset. We've got a couple of them at Horizon. One woman is in her early fifties."

Dad's computer dinged.

"Well, lookie here. If it ain't my good friend Ben. Says he's willing to meet with us tomorrow morning at Mo's Diner in Ellenville. Wish we had this Internet thing back in my policing days. Makes tracking down people *too* easy."

I hadn't seen Dad this excited in a very long time. Mom, as usual, was wrong. Even if there was an innocent explanation to Trudy's disappearance, at least Dad felt useful again. He seemed invigorated, to the point where he actually looked a few years younger. There was a spring in his step. An unmistakable energy in his voice. *He found the thing that sparked joy*. Me, I was still waiting for the fuse to light.

TRUDY

TRUDY PEERED out her window at the parking lot below, looking for the car that was supposed to pick her up. She scanned the lot. Is that Max, the guy from the post office? I mustn't let him see me. She slid the curtain along the rod. She waited a few seconds then parted the curtains. He was gone.

"Good morning, Trudy," the nurse said as she entered the room.

Trudy suddenly stepped away from the curtains.

"Sorry, did I give you a fright?"

"I have to go downstairs," Trudy said. "A man is going to pick me up."

"A man? What man?"

Trudy brought her finger up to her lips. "I can't tell you. It's a secret." Trudy peered out the window again. "There. There. The green car. He's here."

The nurse walked over to the window and glanced down at Dr. Meadows' green Buick.

"That's Dr. Meadows, Trudy. He's coming to work."

Trudy closed her eyes. I got in a green car. A different green car. I was taken away.

She remembered for a moment. There and gone in a flash.

CHAPTER EIGHT

Saturday, November 3, 2018

"HOW DID the meeting with Ben go, babe?" Ray asked. "Did he sing like a canary?"

Sing like a canary.

Another expression Ray often used.

Sometimes it felt like I was in a hardboiled detective novel when talking to him about a case.

He was as dead as a car on a subzero morning, sweetheart. He went through a Mickey Spillane phase, read at least five Mike Hammer books a few years back.

Next up was Robert Parker, then James Ellroy. He got me into Sue Grafton. I'm up to *G is for Gumshoe*. At the rate I read, I was pretty sure I'd be close to retirement by the time I'd make my way through the series.

"If you're asking if he confessed, no, he didn't sing like a canary. He pretty much stuck to the story he told Dad back in seventy-eight. He dropped her off in the hospital parking lot and drove off. Came back an hour later, and when she didn't materialize, he went in to find her. The receptionist told him that she never checked in. He left, spent the day looking for her around the hotel and asking her friends if they'd seen her. That night, when she didn't come home, he called her in missing. Cops told him to come by in the morning and file a missing persons report."

"Ah, the old twenty-four-hour rule."

"We did manage to get a bit more information about her state of mind. He said their marriage was on the rocks but he didn't bring it up at the time because he thought it would make him look suspicious. He also said she'd been very agitated for about a month before her disappearance. Claims he found her crying several times and that she had become mopey and withdrawn. Jumpy too. Like if he walked in a room, he noticed that she startled. At one point she told him she was looking for work at a different hotel, that she didn't like working at the Cuttman anymore. But it was midsummer and no one was hiring."

"So, perhaps something or someone put a scare in her," Ray said. "Maybe she was in some kind of danger."

"In the old police report, Ben described a thin-faced, lanky guy with a bushy mustache. He supposedly spotted him chatting up Trudy several times in the months before she disappeared. Dad thought Ben made the guy up, trying to mislead him. He asked around, and no one else corroborated this sighting. But when he pushed Ben on this yesterday, Ben said he definitely remembers this guy. Claimed he could still pick him out of a lineup, if we found him . . . Wait a sec." I walked over to the dining-room table and sifted through the papers. "Look at this drawing."

"Holy shit. I was wondering who that—" Ray caught himself. "Sorry, I peeked at the files."

I rolled my eyes, letting it slide. "I think this is the guy Ben described. This police sketch was loose at the bottom of the box, so I thought it might have been from a different case and mistakenly ended up in there. Dad didn't mention a sketch. But he might have forgotten about it."

I taped the mustached man to the whiteboard under the Person of Interest heading and scribbled "hotel worker/vendor/guest?" above his portrait. His eyes were narrow, eyelashes long, almost feminine. His cheeks were sunken, with long dimples extending from the bottom of his cheekbones to just below his lower lip. His jaw descended to a point, creating the illusion of a diamond. Handwritten in a neat cursive below the pencil-drawn face was a description:

White Male, mid-to-late 30s
Brown hair (curly) / Blue eyes
6'1" / 175 lbs

I snapped a picture of him with my iPhone.

"When Dad asked Ben about Mustache Man, he said we should talk to Stanley or Rachel. Ben thinks he was associated with the hotel, perhaps as a contract worker or vendor, so the Roths might know."

"Why didn't your father follow up on this back then?"

"Like I said, he thought Ben was blowing smoke. No one else claimed to have seen this guy. And Stanley wasn't exactly cooperative. He wanted the police off his property, not snooping around even more."

My phone dinged, alerting me to an incoming text message.

Dad: *Another lead from the Brooklyn website page. A friend of Trudy's got in touch with me and would like to talk to us. I'm hoping she knows how to FaceTime. Or else we add Brooklyn to our travel itinerary.*
Me: *What's wrong with using the phone?*
Dad: *You know the phone sucks when it comes to interviewing. We need to read facial expressions. Makes for a better interrogation.*
Me: *She's a witness. Not a suspect.*
Dad: *Doesn't matter. Maybe we head to Brooklyn after Belmont. Add a day to the trip.*
Me: *Whatever you think is best.*
Dad: *Any messages from anyone on Cuttman page?*
Me: *Nope.*
Dad: *Lori?*
Me: *Nope.*

After telling Ray about the woman in Brooklyn, I headed upstairs to pack. I was pretty sure Dad was just looking for an excuse to spend a few days away from Horizon Meadows and turn this into an adventure. Relive the good old days. I threw in extra underwear and socks—just in case.

CHAPTER NINE

Sunday, November 4, 2018

ALONG WITH my suitcase, I stowed the two boxes of files in the trunk of my car. I figured it would be good to have them with us in case we needed to refer to an old fact or theory. Our plan was to meet with Dr. Jacqueline Blanchard in the morning right after breakfast. Then, hit the road no later than two o'clock so that we would arrive in Brooklyn in the evening. Dad had arranged to meet Trudy's high-school friend on Tuesday morning.

I glanced over at Dad in the passenger seat. His expression was that of an eager kid headed to the candy store. Grinning ear to fucking ear. A case that stymied him for decades now had a chance of being solved. And I could only imagine how satisfying that must have felt. Definitely a whole lot more rewarding than beating your old buddies at shuffleboard.

“So, who are we seeing in Brooklyn?” I asked. I’d been so busy sorting through the boxes and piecing together the time line of events that it occurred to me late last night I’d never asked him her name.

“Sandra Leer.”

“Chandelier?”

“First name Sandra. Last name Leer. As in dirty look.”

“Are you serious? What were her parents thinking?”

“Right? I went to school with a guy named Peter Peterson. And I thought that was weird. Poor guy had a stutter. His parents eventually transferred him out of public school to St. Peter’s Catholic School in Liberty. I wonder if he’s still alive. I’ll have to look into that.”

“You’re making that up.”

“It’s the damn truth. God’s honor.”

We had one stop to make before we headed east. Google Maps instructed me to turn right onto Mullover Street, a narrow stretch of road littered with mobile homes.

“There it is,” Dad said. “Just as Ray described it. White with rust-color trim and a green awning. The residence of Mr. Coffee Shop Manager, Leonard Berman.”

Dad banged on the door. A guy with shoulder-length greasy hair opened the door a crack. His cheeks were pockmarked with red splotches, his nose broken and self-healed several times. Yet, if you looked closely, mentally erased the top layer, you could see that Lenny had been a handsome man in his youth.

“Whoa, old man. Take it easy or you’ll bust my door down. Don’t wanna be suing you for property damage, now.”

"Lenny Berman?" I asked.

"Yeah. Who wants to know?"

"I'm Detective Susan Ford with the Monticello police and this is ex-Detective William Ford. We'd like a quick word with you about an old case. Hoping you can help us."

"Ex-detective. Huh? You two related? Or is the last name a coincidence?"

I ignored his question. "You worked at the Cuttman in the seventies. Do you remember Trudy Solomon?"

"No. Should I?"

"She's the coffee-shop waitress who went missing in seventy-eight. A few days before that, you were fired for harassing her. Does that jog your memory?"

"Oh yeah. Her. What about it? I had nothin' to do with that. I told the cops back then."

"Do you recognize this guy?" I held up my phone and showed him the police sketch of mustache man.

Lenny removed his glasses and squinted. "Um, no. He don't look familiar."

"So you never saw this guy hanging around the hotel. Or bothering Trudy?"

"Like I said, I never seen him. Why you askin'?"

"We found Trudy." His expression didn't change. "Alive, living in Massachusetts."

"Yeah, so why you buggin' me?"

"Just trying to figure out what happened, that's all. She's not well, and we just want to know what happened to her after she went missing."

"Well I don't know that dude in the picture. And I don't know nothin' about Trudy. Now leave me alone." He pulled the door shut.

I opened the car door for Dad. "Do you believe him?" I asked.

"Not a single word."

AT THE midway point between Monticello and our destination, Dad took the wheel. Said he wanted to drive for an hour or so. I leaned my head against the passenger window and closed my eyes. Not to sleep, but to think. Why was I doing this? On one level, I was simply indulging Dad's fantasy of finding out what happened to Trudy. Giving him one last hurrah. I was just along for the ride. A diversion while the Barnes shit show sorted itself out. But on another level, I was actually excited about the prospect of breaking this case *with* him. It was what I had wanted when I was thirteen—I was always thrilled when he would run ideas past me, treat me like one of his buddies. Would I have been so gung ho about taking on this case if he wasn't my sidekick? Or I, his? Who was I, Sherlock or Watson? Or were we more like superheroes—Batman and Robin—exposing a villain and seeking justice?

I opened my eyes and twisted in my seat when the car slowed down.

"Just a bit of traffic ahead," Dad said, pointing to the red line snaking across the GPS screen.

I nodded wearily, thinking back to the year Trudy disappeared, 1978. That year, a dividing line in my life. *Before and after*.

Before April 1978 my family was whole. I had a best friend. My grandfather took me fishing and camping. Every Sunday night, Dad and I would watch *Quincy, M.E.* or *Columbo* or *McMillan and Wife* and try to solve the case before Jack Klugman or Peter Falk or Rock Hudson did. My mother had no more than a glass of wine (or two) at dinner. On second thought, I might be wrong about that particular memory, as it was my father who woke up early in the morning to make me breakfast, get me off to school. He made excuses for her. *She has a headache. She has a tummy ache. She wants to sleep in a bit.* Sleep it off was probably more like it. But when I came home from school, she always had an afternoon snack ready and was chatty about her day and genuinely eager to hear about mine.

After April 1978, everything went to shit. Lori started hanging out with other girls. My grandfather succumbed to a heart attack in his sleep. My father moved out. On a Sunday night, no less. And Mom began declaring, "It's five o'clock somewhere!" as she poured herself a drink, usually around noontime.

This was not to say that Dad wasn't there for me in those *after* years. He came around the house quite often. Often enough to make me think he was looking to reconcile with Mom. Typically, it was under the guise of having to fix something: the doorbell, the garage door, the dishwasher. Once in a while, he would bring me a book. ("You gotta read this, Suzie-Q, oops, Susan," he would say, handing me a dog-eared paperback by Agatha Christie, Dick Francis, or P. D. James.)

I wasn't exactly sure when Dad became obsessed with the Trudy Solomon case. But he did. If memory served me correctly, his frustration set in around November that year—when I saw less and less of him. The Cuttman was a summers-only resort, opening shortly before Passover in the spring and closing soon after the Jewish high holidays in the fall. By Thanksgiving, any remaining staff were long gone. Following up on leads and interviewing witnesses became increasingly difficult. But Dad was determined to find new avenues of inquiry. He would read and reread the case file, trying to tilt his theories sideways and backwards, hoping to dislodge a new piece of evidence he could pursue. This was also around the time my mother forbade him to talk to me about the case. She told him it was giving me nightmares (it was not). She told him the other detectives were starting to worry about him (they were not). She told him he should just move on, that this case just wasn't worth the stress (which made him more determined to prove her wrong). If I had to surmise a reason for her insistence, I would venture it was because she had it in the back of her head that life would just go back to normal if Dad let go of the case and came home.

"Ready to take over?" Dad asked, exiting the highway. "I need to stretch and pee."

BY THE time we checked into the hotel, we were too tired to even nurse one drink at the bar, so we headed straight to our rooms. As I nodded off to sleep I heard the familiar ding. I tried to ignore it, but curiosity won out. The bright light of the phone blinded me for a moment, but when my eyes adjusted, I saw a message notification.

> *Hi Suzie! How nice to hear from you. High school sure was not a good time for us, but hey, we're adults now. If you want to know the truth, high school was awful for me. I did things I'm not proud of. But I'm not that person anymore. I saw your post about Trudy Solomon. I'm racking my brain trying to remember it. Something about a missing counselor? Meryl tells me that she told you I live in Venice, Ca. So beautiful out here. My husband and I adopted a child and she just had a baby of her own. Life's been pretty good, typical ups*

and downs. Would love to hear what you're up to (especially with the case!). If you're up for a real chat my number is 310-555-2618. Cheers, Lori.

I blinked at the screen. My eyes were moist, but my palms were remarkably dry. Maybe, in times of scarcity, the body made triage decisions about where to deploy its moisture.

CHAPTER TEN

Monday, November 5, 2018

BEFORE MEETING Dad at the hotel's breakfast buffet, I wrote to Lori letting her know I would call her in a few days. I figured I'd be pretty distracted these next two days, but I was also looking for an excuse to delay this reunion.

At nine forty-five we pulled into a visitors spot at McNair Hospital.

At ten o'clock the receptionist directed us to sit in the patient waiting area.

At five after ten we were ushered into Dr. Blanchard's office, where two leather wingback chairs awaited us. Dr. Jacqueline Blanchard was seated behind an antique mahogany desk, spine straight, fingers folded together. One-inch-long, fire-engine-red fingernails popped in contrast to her crisp white lab coat. Her Adam's apple was quite pronounced. The doctor who sat across from us hadn't always been a woman. I glanced at Dad, but saw no indication that he was cognizant of this fact.

After quick introductions, Dr. Blanchard reiterated what she told Dad on the phone. "As I mentioned, I'm happy to provide some information about Trudy Resnick, but I need to steer clear of her medical history." Her voice was breathy and light, and much higher than I had imagined given her likely past.

Dad nodded. "We understand."

"She was admitted on July 23, 2008, for extreme distress. I can't go into more detail—doctor-patient confidentiality—but I can tell you it's a good thing she sought help. She was accompanied by a woman who, as you can see here, signed her name on the admission paperwork." Dr. Blanchard flipped around the open file and slid it toward Dad. "Martha Stuart."

"Martha Stewart? Like the cook on TV?" Dad asked, taking out his reading glasses.

"Only she spelled it s-t-u-a-r-t."

He glanced down at the signature. "And what did this Martha Stuart look like?"

"If memory serves me correctly, she was very attractive. And you can tell she had money. Expensive jewelry. Designer clothes. Carefully manicured nails." Dr. Blanchard glanced quickly at her own carefully manicured nails and lowered them under the table. "Guessing late fifties, perhaps early sixties. But I'm not very good at discerning a woman's age. Especially back then when I was a . . . younger."

"Do you know who she was? A relative? A friend?" Dad asked.

"She seemed more like a relative than a friend, if you know what I mean. More like a caretaker than a buddy."

"Did she ever visit Trudy?"

"No. In fact, soon after Trudy was admitted, we tried to contact this woman to get more information about Trudy, but the number she gave us was out of service. And the address she provided was nonexistent. The police tried to track her down as well, but they too were unsuccessful in figuring out who she was."

"When we spoke by phone last week, you mentioned something about a murder. Do you have reason to believe this woman or Trudy was involved?" I asked.

"Trudy was in my care for four years, and not once did I think she was involved in anything nefarious. I mean she was in a bad way, but more like shock. And fear. Not guilt. Many witnesses placed her at a grocery store at the time of the murder. The police interviewed her a few times, but she was quite confused. We didn't realize it at the time she was admitted, but she was in the very early stages of Alzheimer's. Early-onset Alzheimer's; Trudy was only fifty-seven at the time. As far as Martha Stuart, I have no idea if she had anything to do with the murder. We only spoke briefly during admission intake."

"Can you tell us about this murder?" Dad asked.

"That I can. It was a pretty big story around here. Trudy's husband was stabbed to death."

"Trudy's husband?" I turned sideways and rested my hand on Dad's arm to prevent him from reacting with an onslaught of exuberant profanity. I felt him grip the armrest of his chair and he casually nodded, signaling he got my message loud and clear.

"Yes. Ed Resnick. Trudy found him dead on the floor in their kitchen when she returned from grocery shopping. Stabbed in the neck with a knife."

It was clear from his faraway stare that Dad was processing this information. And my mind was going into overdrive. We thought Trudy (or the person who kidnapped her) changed her name to Resnick to avoid being found. But it sounded like she had remarried. Without first divorcing Ben. Or maybe she just took his name to give the appearance of marriage. Perhaps this was a case of Stockholm syndrome—maybe Ed Resnick kidnapped her and she developed an affection for him as a way to survive. Or maybe she was kidnapped by someone else, got away, and met Ed. But then why wouldn't she have gone to the police? So many theories were competing in my head.

"I have a newspaper clipping of the story in her file." Dr. Blanchard shuffled through a few papers and pulled out a *Boston Globe* article dated Monday, July 21, 2008—the day after the murder. A picture of Ed Resnick appeared below the headline "Waltham Man Murdered in His Apartment."

I pulled out my phone, hit the Photos icon, and held it up to the newspaper. "Well, I'll be damned." I angled the photo toward Dad.

"Holy . . ." Dad bit his lower lip. "Cannoli. I guess Mustache Man does exist."

"Did exist, Dad. Did exist."

DETECTIVE JOHN Flannery led us to an interrogation room through a maze of desks, haphazardly arranged on the second floor of the two-story Waltham Police Department building. Just an hour earlier, Dad had called the station to inquire about the Ed Resnick murder. He was patched through to Detective Flannery, who introduced himself as the head of the homicide unit's Unsolved Case Squad.

"The building is undergoing some renovation and we're short on private office space at the moment," Detective Flannery explained as we entered the small, windowless room.

"No need to apologize," I assured him. "We know what that's like."

Dad recounted the story of Trudy Solomon and how we were looking to piece together how she'd spent her missing years. "We want to determine if she was the victim of criminal acts or has knowledge of criminal acts committed by others."

Flannery listened with his head bobbing slightly to the right, as though an invisible string was tugging his ear toward his shoulder. For a man in his fifties, his skin was quite smooth and rather pink, like Silly Putty. The changes in his expressions were hardly discernible, a slight eyebrow lift, a quick purse of the lips, an upward twitch of his nose that made his nostrils look cavernous—each understated movement linked to a revelation in Dad's story.

Then it was Detective Flannery's turn to talk. "First things first, Trudy was not Ed Resnick's wife. The lead detective on the case—Reginald Masters—found no marriage certificate to back that assertion. It appears Trudy simply took Ed's last name. The Waltham lease listed a reference—a landlord who owned a couple of buildings in Allston. Detective Masters tracked down the landlord and, as you can see from a copy of that earlier lease, they also signed as Ed Resnick and Trudy Resnick. Some landlords back then were funny about renting to unmarried couples—which might explain why they did that. Anyhow, they moved into the Allston apartment on February 1, 1990 and then moved to the Waltham apartment in 1995. He found nothing predating this Allston lease."

In a burst of excitement, Dad slapped his hands against his thighs. "Jesus . . . sorry, continue," he said.

"According to Detective Master's report, Resnick was killed sometime between one and two-thirty in the afternoon, while Trudy was out shopping at a nearby supermarket. She also stopped at a drugstore to pick up a prescription. An asthma inhaler. His. Not hers. When she entered the apartment she screamed, alarming her next-door neighbor, who called the police. Based on the trajectory of the stab wound, Resnick was stabbed in the neck by someone who was three-to-four inches shorter than he was, so . . . five seven or five eight." He slid a piece of paper across the desk. "It's in that coroner's report. According to Trudy's statement, a knife was missing from the kitchen. She said she was certain of this because it was housed in one of those wood multi-knife holders. But it was never recovered, leading Detective Masters to believe this was a spur-of-the-moment attack, not premeditation. But he couldn't say for sure. There's also the possibility of—"

"A robbery gone wrong? Was anything taken?" Dad asked.

Detective Flannery tilted his head forward and peered over his glasses. A subtle scolding gesture. Clearly, he was not accustomed to being interrupted.

"The place was sparsely furnished, and the few items of value—his watch, a camera, his wallet—were all in the apartment. He was a plumber and general fix-it guy . . . had an expensive set of tools sitting in the front hallway. And there was some evidence to suggest he was not just some random victim. When Detective Masters pulled Resnick's bank records, he discovered monthly cash deposits of two thousand dollars, each dating back to 1995, a good thirteen years before his murder. So, I'm thinking some kind of extortion scheme. Or skimming. When he questioned Trudy about it, she claimed not to know anything about it."

"Can we speak to Detective Masters?" I asked.

"Unfortunately, he died a couple of years ago." Detective Flannery opened another file that lay on his desk. "There's one more thing that may, or may not, be related. The police were called to Resnick's apartment a year earlier, in 2007, by a neighbor who heard arguing and reported it as a domestic dispute." He looked down at the file. "The neighbor's name was Cynthia Lambert. But the officer responding to the call found two men in a heated argument. One was Resnick, the other—" He glanced down at his file again searching for the name. "Seems this other guy had a solid alibi for the murder, though. Masters tracked him down and questioned him. Says here he was on an airplane headed to Las Vegas for an automobile dealers conference. His name . . . oh here it is . . . Scott Roth."

CYNTHIA LAMBERT was easy to track down. The police report noted she was a student at Brandeis University at the time of the domestic-dispute call. A quick check on LinkedIn, searching both Cynthia Lambert and Brandeis University yielded Cynthia Lambert-Alcott working at an ad agency in Boston. Social-media sites, digital fingerprints, forensic DNA, CCTV cameras . . . tools Dad could only dream of when he was working cases back in his day.

She agreed to speak to us, but we didn't have enough time to meet in person and get on the road by two o'clock, so we decided to FaceTime with her from the confines of my car. Cynthia was backlit by the late-afternoon sunlight pouring through her office window—her haloed head filled the screen of Dad's iPhone. As I merged onto the Mass Turnpike, Dad summarized the Trudy Solomon and Ed

Resnick cases to her and our reason for wanting to get in touch with her.

"Wow! I'm not sure how much help I can be," she said, her voice chipper and eager, clearly excited to assist in a police investigation.

"Sometimes witnesses don't know what is, or isn't, helpful. Even a small detail can help our investigation. For instance, did you hear what they were arguing about?"

"No. It was muffled, but loud. I thought it was Trudy and Ed."

"Did Trudy and Ed fight often?"

"Not often, but Ed had a short temper and he could rip into her. Sometimes she came over to my place while he cooled down. She would say it was nothing. That he was all bark and no bite. Just needed to let off steam."

"So if fighting was not that unusual, why did you call the cops?"

"Well, it sounded worse than usual. But I guess that's because it was actually *two* guys and Trudy yelling at each other. Which surprised me because they never had anyone over."

"See, that's an important detail. It tells me they were reclusive. Kept to themselves. Kept a low profile," Dad told her.

"Interesting. Yes, I would say that was true about them. If I can make another observation . . . I got the sense he was protecting her, not controlling her."

"By any chance, did you see the other guy?" Dad asked, likely wanting to confirm that the person who claimed to be Scott Roth actually *was* Scott Roth.

"Well, I lingered outside my apartment. I was curious. But I also wanted to make sure that Trudy was okay. I got a look at him when he left the apartment, which was about five minutes after the cops left."

"Can you describe him?" Dad asked impatiently.

"Um. I think so. The guy looked to be in his midforties. But it was hard to tell because he had a severe receding hairline. Curly hair, but because he had lost so much of it on top, he had that Bozo the Clown thing going on. He was tall, but not towering. Kinda good-looking. Even with the bad hair. He was dark. Not Black, mind you. Just dark hair, dark eyes, tan complexion."

"Hold on one sec. Gonna text you a picture," Dad said.

After a few minutes of silence she replied, "Yup, that's the guy."

Dad fist-pumped the air. "Is there anything else you could think of that might be helpful. Anything you heard or saw?"

"Like I said, after the police left, they were all more civil to each other. When they parted ways, the guy said, 'You should report him,' and Ed said something like, 'Not going to happen. I need the money.' When I asked Trudy about that later, she said I must have misheard. I never gave it another thought. Well, not until you sent me that message on LinkedIn."

"How come you didn't report this to the police?"

"Why would I? This conversation happened after the police left. Besides, it never occurred to me that it was important. Just two guys having a disagreement over money. Wait. Do you think this balding guy had something to do with Ed's murder?"

TRUDY

"GOOD AFTERNOON, Trudy," Dr. Meadows said.

Trudy looked around the office. This reminded her of something. Ah, yes. That lovely doctor Jack. Jack Blanchard! "I remembered something," Trudy said to Dr. Meadows, tipping her head to one side.

"Wonderful."

"He had lovely hands." She thought about those hands: long and lean. He waved them around like a magician.

"Martha left me with Jack." She smiled because she remembered to call her Martha, just like she told her to do. "Martha said I can keep the money if I keep a secret."

"What secret?" Dr. Meadows asked gently.

"About Ed. He's dead." She sucked in her lips and pressed them tight against each other. Think. Think. The past felt fuzzy again. Names, dates, places disappearing slowly, like an aging Polaroid—the once vibrant colors now muted and hazy. "Ed wanted the money. He kept asking for the money. Now he's dead."

"Ed who, Trudy?"

Trudy shook her head. "Ed?"

CHAPTER ELEVEN

Tuesday, November 6, 2018

DAD AND I met in the breakfast lounge of the Day's Inn in Marine Park, which, according to Google Maps, was a ten-minute drive to Sandra Leer's house in Mill Basin.

"Good morning, Dad." We thought about sharing a room to save some money, but decided that having alone time during this road trip was worth the extra ninety-six dollars.

"Oh, I forgot to ask you . . ." Dad began as he poured milk over his Cheerios. "Dr. Blanchard. A man, right?"

"Well, actually a woman. Although, yes, I think she once *was* a man."

"Like *Tootsie*?"

Well, at least he hadn't lost his observational skills. "No, Dad. Not like *Tootsie*."

He knitted his brow. "Oh! I get it. Like Bruce Jenner?"

"Ding. Ding. Ding," I said as I tapped my nose three times. "Hey, some good news on the witnesses front. Last night I heard from three people who responded to my message on the Summers at the Cuttman Facebook page. They claim to have information we might find helpful. I'll set up calls with them when we get back home."

"Man, this is really coming together, Susan." Dad picked up his bowl of Cheerios and downed the last drop of milk. "Let's go!"

"MY PARENTS bought this house in the midsixties for fifteen thousand dollars," Sandra Leer told us. "I'm putting it on the market next week. Guess how much?" Before we could venture a guess, she answered her question. "Seven hundred thousand. Can you believe that? This little house with a postage-stamp backyard going for three quarters of a million dollars. I told them to sell this house years ago. Glad they didn't listen to me."

I looked around at what seven hundred thousand got you in this part of Brooklyn. A seventeen-hundred-square-foot semi-attached house on a twenty-one-hundred-square-foot lot. Three small bedrooms, one and a half baths, a living room, eat-in kitchen (no dining room), and finished basement. Probably not mentioned in the listing: a shared driveway with your neighbor. That was bound to lead to some interesting turf disputes.

"It's the neighborhood that's driving up the price. If you drive a few blocks further in, you'll see the ornate McMansions. The real-estate agent calls the area *very desirable*," Sandra said, rolling her eyes.

"My partner and I interviewed Trudy's neighbors that summer," Dad said. "But I don't have you or your parents on the list of people we spoke to."

"Trudy lived a few blocks over, so we weren't exactly neighbors. I don't think her neighbors would even know me. We usually hung out here, at my house. She was embarrassed to have friends over. Her mom was something of a pack rat. Y'know, a hoarder." She air-quoted *hoarder*.

"So what can you tell us about Trudy?" I asked, steering the conversation back to the matter at hand.

"Oh yes. Of course. Trudy and I were friends in high school. James Madison High. Fun fact—we were two years behind Chuck Schumer."

"The senator?" Dad asked.

"Yes. We weren't friends with him, but I remember Trudy had a crush on him. Wouldn't that have been something if she'd dated a future U.S. senator? But neither of us were dating material back then. A couple of plain Janes. We pretty much kept to ourselves. I wouldn't say we were loners, but we were lonely. She tended to keep to herself, so she wasn't invited to any parties, nor did she join any clubs or activities. I broke out of my shell in college, but she didn't want to go. She struggled in school. If you read her letters, you'll see why."

"Are these the letters?" I asked, pointing to a short stack of papers in the middle of the table.

"Yes. My unprofessional diagnosis is dyslexia. Although back then, before anyone had any real understanding of learning disabilities, she just figured she was dumb." Sandra cast her eyes down to the table covered with memorabilia. "Anyway, my mother passed away two months ago, leaving this house to my brother and me.

Neither of us wanted to move back here or manage it as a rental property, hence the For Sale sign. We've been taking turns going through old stuff, tossing what we don't want to keep, donating the rest. In some way it's been an interesting trip down memory lane. My mother kept photo albums, diaries, letters, art projects, school records."

As I scanned the table I wondered if my mother kept any stuff from my youth.

"In a box labeled 'Sandra,' I found letters Trudy wrote to me the summer you claim she disappeared. Only, at the time, I didn't realize she disappeared . . . I just thought she stopped writing to me."

"Why did you think she just stopped writing to you?"

"I graduated law school in the spring of 1978 and was studying for the bar exam. I told her that I needed to concentrate on the exam and she wouldn't hear from me for a while. She took it as a slight, as you'll see in the last letter she wrote to me. She was definitely going through a rough patch, and well, I pretty much told her I didn't have the time to help. When you read the letters, you'll see she was upset about something. She doesn't spell it out, but it sounds like she was being harassed by someone at the hotel. After taking the exam, I wrote to her to apologize, but never heard back." Sandra sighed. "I assumed she didn't want to forgive me. I certainly didn't think something bad had happened to her. I was so wrapped up in my own shit, I just figured she'd moved on with her life, and I was no longer a part of it."

"So you never heard from her again?" Dad asked.

"No. I moved away soon after the exam. I was pretty burnt out and spent nearly two months gallivanting around Europe before returning to look for a job. When I landed a junior position at a law firm in the city, I was working sixty to seventy hours a week."

"Do you mind if we take these letters? We'll send them back to you after we've had a chance to read through them."

"If you think it will help, sure."

"One last question and we'll be on our way," I said. "Have you ever heard Trudy mention an Ed Resnick?"

"Ed Resnick? No. But there is a mention of a guy that she refers to as S. R. in the letters. All she said is that she's scared of him but doesn't want to reveal who he is, hence the initials, I guess. Now I feel somewhat responsible for what may have happened to her. I could have done something about it, if I just—"

"Don't blame yourself," Dad said. "Would've, could've, should've is not going to change a thing." Pretty sure he said this not only to assuage Sandra's misgivings but his as well.

⁂

"S R—SCOTT fucking Roth?" Dad snarled, lingering in front of the car door.

"Or Stanley Roth. Or any hotel worker or guest with the first initial S and the second initial R."

"C'mon, Susan. We find out that Scott paid a visit to Ed, had some mysterious argument with him, and you think he is not the person Trudy is referring to in the letters?"

"Scott was eighteen at the time of Trudy's disappearance. Do you think he was harassing a twenty-seven year old woman?"

"Ever see *The Graduate*? And she wasn't even as old as Mrs. Robinson. Maybe they had an affair and she broke it off, and he, being young and in love, couldn't take no for an answer."

"*The Graduate*? Really, that's the basis for your theory? And from Sandra's description of Trudy, I wouldn't exactly call her a seductress. Besides, why would Scott get into a beef with Ed years after Trudy left?"

"Okay. Point taken. Let's just run down what we have established."

As I turned the key in the ignition, Dad fished around the glove compartment for a pad and pencil. He licked the end of the pencil with his tongue and flipped back the cardboard cover of the spiral-bound notebook. My phone rang as I pulled away from the curb. I pressed my thumb on the speaker icon embedded in the steering wheel.

"Hello?"

"Where are you?" Chief Eldridge's voice crackled through the audio system.

"Still in Brooklyn. I'm heading home now."

"Good. Good. I need you to come in first thing tomorrow morning. This Calvin Barnes thing just became a bit of a shit show. Did you get a chance to speak to Rhonda? We could really use someone on your side right now."

"What happened?" I released my right hand from the steering wheel. The moisture left behind quickly dissipated.

"The family's lawyer just filed a civil suit."

My heart rate ticked up a few notches. I glanced over at Dad and he flashed a reassuring smile. "I spoke to Rhonda. I'm pretty sure she isn't going to come out publicly to support me. But she said there are members willing to go on the record and give a positive character assessment based on my work with the group."

"Okay. Try and make that happen soon. Is Will with you?"

"I'm here, Cliff."

"Okay. Any new developments in the Trudy Solomon case?"

"As a matter of fact, there are," Dad said. "We'll fill you in tomorrow."

"Sounds good. And Susan?"

"Yeah."

"Hang in there."

No words passed between us as we listened to a Foreigner song on a classic rock station. When a Led Zeppelin tune came on, Dad lowered the volume knob.

"How about we theorize a little and figure out our next move." Dad patted my right arm. "At the very least, it will keep your mind off the Barnes case."

I squinted at the gas indicator and calculated how far into Connecticut I could get before having to refuel. Norwalk, maybe Fairfield.

"Susan. You listening?"

"Sure, Dad." I took a deep breath. "Okay, we know that Trudy and Ed were together from at least 1990. Let's assume for a moment that Ed is the mustached guy Ben saw hanging around Trudy at the hotel. Did she run away with him, did he kidnap her, or did they run into each other years later and start dating?"

"I'd like to go back and see Lenny. I sensed he knew something when we showed him the police sketch of Ed. And he didn't flinch when we told him Trudy was found . . . alive. Now that we have a name, let's lean on him a bit harder. Make him think we know more than we know."

I drummed my fingers on the steering wheel. "We also need to interview the woman who lived next door to Trudy back in 1978 . . . uh, what's her name?"

"Eleanor Campbell."

"Yeah, her. She might have seen Ed lurking about. If she and Trudy were close, maybe Trudy confided in her about an extra-marital relationship or a stalker."

“And we need to get in touch with Scott Roth,” Dad said. “Somehow, he figures in this. He knew Trudy was alive in 2007, yet kept that fact to himself.”

“According to what Cynthia just told us, it doesn’t sound like Scott was putting the squeeze on Ed for money. It sounded like he wanted Ed to snitch on someone. So, it’s entirely possible Scott knew what Ed was up to.”

“So if not Scott, who was Ed’s mark? That’s the person with motive.”

“Yup. But we also can’t dismiss that Trudy might have killed Ed . . . perhaps before she went to the grocery store. Cynthia said they dusted it up every so often.”

“The autopsy report indicated a person three to four inches shorter than Ed. That would map out to Trudy. But y’know who is also three to four inches shorter than Ed? Ben. He was the one who had mentioned the Mustache Man. Maybe he tracked him down. Revenge for absconding with his wife.”

“Interesting theory, Dad. But, you said yourself he seemed genuinely surprised when you told him about Trudy. We should keep in mind that it could’ve just been a random murder . . . a robbery gone sideways.”

There was traffic ahead. I pumped the brake gently. Dad’s head was down as he scribbled in the tiny notepad. He looked up momentarily when the car came to a full stop, frowned, then went back to writing.

“Just some construction ahead,” I said. We sat silently for a few minutes. I sorted through the suspects and motives in my head. I sensed Dad was doing the same.

Dad tapped the eraser end of the pencil against the dashboard, sounding like the opening bass line of Jefferson Airplane’s “White

Rabbit." "Cynthia Lambert said that Trudy was involved in the argument. So, contrary to her statement to Detective Masters, she did know about this money." Dad paused, stared down at his notebook and scribbled something. "What about the people who contacted you through Facebook?"

"We're talking to a lifeguard tomorrow—Brian something. A guest and a cocktail waitress said they can chat with us on Wednesday. I'll confirm the times with them and let you know."

"And then there's the woman who escorted Trudy to McNair Hospital, Martha Stuart. Not sure how we'll track her down, but let's not lose sight of the fact that she gave false contact information." Dad wagged the pencil at me. "That makes her suspicious in my book."

Dad pulled out the letters Sandra Leer gave us and leafed through them. My thoughts drifted to the Facebook messages. The lifeguard claimed to have information I would find *enlightening*. Wanted to *get something off his chest*. The cocktail waitress wrote that she could *shed some light on Trudy's marriage*.

The guest was friends with Scott and wanted to talk to me about a conversation they had about Trudy soon after she disappeared. I wasn't keen on rolling this case around in my head for the next two hours.

"Dad, do you mind if I switch on a podcast?"

"Depends. What podcast?"

"*My Favorite Murder*. I think you'll get a kick out of it. It's these two women chatting about true crime stories."

For the next hour we listened to the podcast's hosts banter about the kidnapping and murder of Polly Klaas in Petaluma, California.

"Can we listen to another?" Dad asked.

"Sure."

He took my phone and scrolled through the list. “Episode 46, ‘Skippers Unite,’ sounds interesting. It’s about the two serial killers Leslie Allen Williams and Israel Keyes.”

“Let it rip.”

By the time I dropped Dad off at Horizon Meadows, we had listened to three episodes of *My Favorite Murder*. I drove home in silence, needing to clear my head of murders and kidnapping. However short-lived that would be. Ray would be eager to hear what we discovered on this little road trip. But I had one more thing to do before laying out the case to Ray. I killed the ignition and called Lori Roth McDonald.

RAY LEFT the porch light on, but I stumbled up the stairs anyway. *Gotta remember to fix the loose board on the second step.* I could see the glow of the television from the entryway. Ray’s head was tipped slightly forward. I gently placed the keys in the glass dish and tiptoed into the living room. When I turned off the television, Ray twitched.

“Hey babe,” he mumbled.

“Sorry. Didn’t mean to wake you.”

“No worries. I was just resting my eyes.” He stretched his arms to the ceiling and stood quickly as if to prove he wasn’t asleep. “So, how’d it go?”

For the next thirty minutes, I laid out the plot for him and he occasionally interrupted with a *wow* or a *holy shit*. Then I told him about my conversation with Lori.

All in all, my chat with Lori went much better than I thought it would. We had different versions of our “breakup.” In her version, we simply got interested in different things and became different people when we hit our teens. She recounted a story about how I once tried to get her to smoke weed and although she acted all cool, it scared her. ("You were so badass, so rebellious," she said. "I just felt like a goody-two-shoes who wanted to get good grades and not get into trouble.") That sincerely surprised me. I didn't see myself as some rebellious hooligan. I pretty much toed the line. I skipped class once in a while, or snuck into the movie theater, or blew curfew (by no more than an hour) if there was a party down by the field. But I never got in *real* trouble. Didn't really want to.

"So I smoked pot once in a while or snuck out at night a couple of times," I said to Ray. "I wasn't Sandra Dee. But I certainly wasn't John Bender. Or the female version of John Bender."

"Who the hell is John Bender?"

"Really? Judd Nelson . . . played this rebel character named John Bender in *The Breakfast Club*." He shook his head as I rattled off the cast: "Molly Ringwald? Ally Sheedy? Anthony Michael Hall?"

"Never heard of 'em."

I scrunched my face and shook my head. *Was he asleep during the eighties?* "Anyway, she got the sense that *I* didn't want to be friends with *her* anymore. I have to say, it's pretty damn interesting how we saw things so differently. She even claimed she had no knowledge of her mother banning me from the hotel grounds. Not sure I believe that."

After Lori and I aired our perceived slights, the mood shifted. I could have been wrong (and perhaps it was wishful thinking), but I felt we settled into the familiar banter of old friends. Then we got around to Trudy Solomon. When I told her about the resurrection of the case, she claimed she barely remembered it. I reminded her that we sleuthed around the hotel interrogating guests and staff if they had seen her, but Lori insisted she had no recollection of ever doing that. She didn't even recall her father reaming us out when he caught us questioning the bellhops. To me, that case was everything. It was a way to get closer to my dad. It was mysterious and fascinating. But to her, it was probably just a game, nothing particularly meaningful or memorable. I asked her if she was still close to her siblings, and she said she spoke frequently with Meryl, occasionally with Joshua, but rarely heard from Scott. I didn't mention Scott's possible involvement. I figured I could bring it up when I better understood how he fit into all this.

I trudged up the stairs feeling the weight of the past two days. Exhausted was putting it mildly. But I wasn't taking any chances. I shut the bathroom door, opened the cabinet door under the sink, and reached behind the rolls of toilet paper. There it was . . . the bottle of Percocet prescribed to me after a bullet ripped through my thigh. The last two pills. "Hello you."

CHAPTER TWELVE

Wednesday, November 7, 2018

ELDRIDGE'S OFFICE was enclosed in glass. He usually kept the blinds rolled up to signal that his door was always open. But this morning the blinds were drawn, the door shut. Fluorescent bulbs buzzed like mosquitos above my head.

"I'm not going to sugarcoat it, Susan. I read the civil complaint last night. They feel confident in their version of the story, and all we have is your word against theirs." Eldridge came around from behind his desk and sat on the edge. "You really should've waited for backup. But I'm not here to lecture you about that again."

"In hindsight, I get it. But they would have been gone by the time backup showed up."

Eldridge shook his head. "Look, I know you're a fair-minded cop. You've got an outstanding record. But there are two witnesses, and yes, I know they're criminals, saying that Calvin Barnes's hands were in the air when you shot him. I'm just asking you to think very carefully about the statement you gave claiming you saw something in Calvin's hand. Are you one hundred percent sure?" I threw up my hands. "Do you think I'm making this up?" I said, perhaps a bit too defensively. "Chief, when one of your officers sees a gun pointed in her direction, are you suggesting she should say, 'Hey, time out everyone, did you just pull a gun on me?' Yes, I'm damn sure I saw a gun."

Eldridge slid his fingers back and forth along his throat. "Whoa there, Susan." He hopped off the edge of the desk and towered over me. "It all happened very quickly, and the mind can play tricks in a situation like that. Tell me again what happened." He sat back down at his desk and clasped his hands like a prim schoolmarm. "From the beginning."

I closed my eyes. I played the scene out in my mind as I had done dozens, probably close to a hundred, times before. I opened my eyes and recounted, once again, how that night unfolded. "I had just gotten off duty and was driving past the abandoned warehouses when I spotted two parked vehicles. That's when I saw flashlight beams bouncing off the windows from the inside. At first I thought, no biggie, probably a bunch of underage kids drinking. But when I peeked inside the window I saw Calvin and Melvin Barnes, Wayne Railman, and two other guys standing around a table with an assortment of drugs laid out, like they were perusing merchandise at a flea market. At that point, I didn't know who was selling or who was buying. I went back to my car, called for backup, and then positioned myself by the window. Watching them conduct business, I was able to discern that Calvin, Melvin, and Wayne were the sellers. Then they started packing up, and well, I decided to go in . . . with my gun drawn. I yelled for everyone to get on the floor. Melvin Barnes heeded my command, and laid down on the ground, but the two buyers took off toward the side exit. I could see Wayne Railman off to the side, to my right, on his knees. Calvin Barnes was about ten feet in front of me, pointing what I thought was a gun and yelling, 'Kill the bitch,' and that's when I felt the bullet hit my thigh. I didn't realize it was Wayne who had shot me. I thought Calvin had shot me, and I thought he was going to go for the kill, so I took aim at him and fired. Wayne ran over to Calvin. He said, 'Hang in there Calvin. That bitch will pay for what she done.' Then Wayne stood up, aimed his gun on me, and that's when backup arrived. Wayne dropped his gun and got down on his knees with his hands on his head, yelling, 'Bitch, you killed Calvin.'"

I took a breath and wiped away an escaped tear. "I was just so sure Calvin Barnes also had a gun in his hand."

Eldridge plucked a tissue from the silver box on his desk and offered it to me. "Were you able to get any character references?"

"I'll remind Rhonda. She said she would get back to me this week."

Eldridge stood up from the edge of the desk, signaling the end of the reprimand.

"Is there anything else, sir?"

"Not at the moment. Go find out what happened to Trudy."

WITH THE Eldridge meeting in the rearview mirror, I spent the next hour setting up phone meetings with the lifeguard, the hotel guest, and the cocktail waitress. With limited time and funds, Dad agreed that Skyping would have to suffice. The lifeguard wrote to tell me he could hop on a call later that day. The hotel guest and the cocktail waitress were both available the next day.

It was noon and I had some time to kill, so I drove to the warehouse. I hadn't been back there since the reconstruction exercise back in early September. I parked my car in the exact spot I parked it that night. August 25—it was unusually hot and muggy for late summer, and a cluster of gnats encircled me when I got out of the car that night to chase away what I thought were teenage boys drinking in the warehouse. The place was a frequent rendezvous point for underage drinking. I should have let it go. Ignored it.

Now the cold was biting. It was just shy of twenty degrees, but the relentless wind from the north made it feel a hell of a lot icier. Although the warehouse where the shooting had taken place was abandoned, the small one across from it was owned by a local Hasidic guy, Mordecai Little. He operated an antique store a couple hundred yards up the road and kept excess or in-need-of-repair inventory in this warehouse.

I walked around the perimeter of the abandoned building. The police tape had been taken down a few weeks ago. When I got to the front door I hesitated, then took a deep breath before turning the handle. The air was slightly warmer inside, so I slid off my gloves and shoved them into my pocket. I stood in the spot I stood in that night and conjured up the figures of Calvin, Melvin, Wayne, and the two buyers. *What did I see in Calvin's hand?* I'd been so sure it was a gun. Was it possible I saw Wayne's gun and assumed Calvin had one too? Maybe Eldridge was right. The mind playing tricks in a stressful situation. Or maybe it was unconscious bias. Did I harbor unacknowledged prejudice against minorities? I'd like to think not, but I was not that naive to believe I was immune from such thinking.

A wave of nausea sent me fleeing outside to the corner of Mordecai Little's warehouse where I upended my breakfast. I remained doubled over until the last remnant of my breakfast sandwich landed on the grassy area between my feet.

My back ached and I stretched skyward with both my arms to relieve the tension.

That was when I saw it.

A white, baseball-sized CCTV camera lodged under the eave facing out to where my car was parked. My mind started to race. Was this camera operational? How long had it been there? Could there be footage from the night of the shooting? Did it even matter, since this camera was outside, not where the incident occurred?

I snapped a picture of the CCTV camera with my phone and texted Eldridge asking him if anyone was aware of this. I immediately saw the three dots indicating he was texting me back.

> ***Cliff:*** *Let me check. But you are not to get involved. I'll have Marty run this down*
> ***Me:*** *Today?*
> ***Cliff:*** *Yes today*
> ***Me:*** *Ok*

I checked my watch. Dad and I were supposed to Skype with the lifeguard at two. It was nearly one o'clock and I had told Dad I would meet him at his apartment at one-thirty. My mouth was sour; I scrounged around the inside of my car for gum or mints. All I could find was an empty Altoids tin. I was not sure how long that water bottle had been sitting in the cupholder. Perhaps a week. No more than two. I rinsed out my mouth with the two inches of tepid water and spat it out before slamming the car door shut.

I FOUND Dad in the game room playing pool with one of his buddies. He was holding a pool cue in his left hand and a little square box of blue chalk in his right palm. He placed the chalk on the edge of the billiards table and lined up the shot. Two women were perched on barstools nearby. They applauded when Dad sank a ball into a pocket. His cheerleaders.

"Two more shots, Susan," he said, rubbing the chalk onto the end of the tapered cue. "The two ball, then the eight ball."

Dad leaned over the table and hit the white cue ball, applying a little English. The cue ball, now besmirched with a powdery blue dot on its smooth surface, spun into the blue ball, which in turn swiveled into a side pocket. Without saying a word, he strode over to the other side of the table. With the tip of the pool cue, he tapped the far corner pocket to indicate his intention. He rested the cue between his thumb and forefinger, bent forward at the waist and tapped the cue ball with just enough finesse that it ricocheted off the far bumper and careened into the eight ball, knocking it into the corner pocket. The two women clapped and gushed. Dad bowed slightly at the waist while making flourishing circles with his right hand as though he were honoring a king . . . or in this case, two queens.

"You owe me a beer, Mitch." He inserted the cue in the wall cabinet, then reset the fifteen balls in the plastic triangle. "Be with you in one second, Susan." He sauntered off to the corner of the room and yakked it up with a couple of guys playing cards.

Dad the hustler. Dad the show-off. Dad the eligible bachelor. Dad the socializer. When he looked over at me, I overdramatized looking at my watch. He slapped one of the guys on the back and finally headed my way.

As we exited the game room, I told him about my little discovery at the warehouse.

"Sometimes it's luck that turns things around. Like the social security number in the Solomon case," he said. "This could be your lucky break."

"I'm not counting my chickens just yet. It's a long shot that there even is a recording, let alone something worthwhile on it. But as you like to say . . . never leave a stone unturned."

"HELLO, BRIAN."

Dad and I huddled on his couch so that we both fit in the frame of my laptop computer. Brian appeared to be sitting on a barstool at a kitchen island. I could make out a high-end stovetop behind him. A Jenn-Air or a Wolf. The one with the red knobs. I took the lead and laid out the case from the moment the state troopers found the bones along the highway (the body still unidentified).

"You mentioned that you can offer something enlightening, something only you would know that might help us understand what happened to Trudy," I said.

"What I'm about to tell you I haven't told anyone . . . except my wife. When I saw your inquiry on Facebook, well, I just felt it was time to come clean. Actually, my wife prodded me. Maybe this is information I should have shared with the cops forty years ago, but I couldn't. And I'm not sure it would have made a difference—"

"Just tell us what you know," Dad interjected, a trace of impatience in his voice.

"Well, here goes . . . I had an affair with Rachel Roth." Brian paused, perhaps expecting Dad or me to say something. But we were stunned into silence. "I was twenty-two, she was thirty-eight. She was the most beautiful woman I had ever seen."

Well, Dad was right about one thing.

The Graduate.

He'd just pegged the wrong couple.

"Rachel was looking for attention and affection. Stanley was a philanderer, getting it on with the women who stayed at the hotel for weeks while their husbands worked in the city."

"And Rachel knew about this?"

"Rachel said they had an understanding, an arrangement. They were essentially a married couple living separate lives. And she was fine with that. 'Together for the kids,' she said. But seeing that they are still together, they must have decided to make it work as empty nesters. I'm sure it has to do with all the money they got after they sold the hotel. I don't know the details, but I remember she told me that her father made Stanley the beneficiary of the hotel. So he probably ended up controlling the purse strings. Which meant she was stuck with him if she wanted to live high on the hog."

"What does this have to do with Trudy Solomon?" Dad asked.

"Just getting to that. The reason I contacted you was because of a conversation I had with Rachel about a week or so after Trudy went missing. She was very concerned about Scott. He was a moody kid, didn't get along with Stanley at all. Didn't get along with anyone, really. A bit of a loner. Rachel suspected Scott was somehow involved with Trudy because she saw them together a few times, usually whispering and trying not to be seen."

"And you didn't mention any of this to the police, because . . .?" I asked.

"I just couldn't say anything. She begged me to keep our affair a secret, and I was afraid if I was pressed on what I heard from her, there would be questions as to how I knew all this. And Rachel didn't want Scott questioned by the police. She arranged to have him stay with her sister in New Jersey for the rest of that summer—then he went off to college."

"Do you think Scott was involved in Trudy's disappearance?"

"I honestly didn't think so at the time. I spoke to Scott before he left and he told me I got it all wrong. That Trudy was just a friend and I should mind my own business and go to . . . well, he alluded to the fact that he knew about me and his mom. But I always got the feeling he was hiding something. Something which may, or may not, have anything to do with Trudy's disappearance. It just seemed like he was in a bad place that summer . . . even before Trudy went missing."

Like a huge pane of skyscraper glass crashing down onto the pavement, my notion of Rachel Roth shattered into a million pieces. She'd been June Cleaver to my mom's Joan Crawford. The perfect mom who tended to her four children, kept her home immaculate, knew all the repeat guests and staff by name, didn't smoke, sipped the occasional cocktail, attended Sabbath services every Friday evening, and stood lovingly by her husband's side every Sunday greeting new guests. Was it *all* a facade?

"Did you continue to see Rachel after the summer?" I asked.

"No. She broke it off. I was just her summer boy toy. Thinking back on it, I would say she was pretty manipulative. Got what she wanted by hook or crook. I'm pretty sure I was not her first dalliance. Nor her last."

I glanced at Dad, who looked shell-shocked by the conversation. I turned back to the screen. "Anything else you want to get off your chest?"

"Nope. That's all I got. I have to say I felt relieved when you posted that Trudy was still alive. I've been carrying around some amount of guilt because I never told anyone about this. I mean, like I said, Scott didn't seem like the kind of person to harm someone, but in hindsight that was for the police to figure out. I was just a dumb kid thinking with my dick, not my brain."

"One last question. Did you know an Ed Resnick? Skinny guy with blues eyes and a bushy mustache." I positioned the sketch in front of the laptop camera.

Brian squinted, then shook his head. "Not ringing any bells."

Within seconds of ending the Skype session, Dad finally said something. "Fuckety fuck fuck."

Yeah. Sounded about right.

TRUDY

TRUDY AND her nurse sat hip to hip at the edge of the exercise pool.

"You know what would be lovely, Maxine?" Trudy said to the nurse.

"No. What?" the nurse replied.

"I should take swimming lessons. Problem is, I don't think Ben is going to let me. He said he didn't want some guy touching me." Trudy tittered.

"You can do whatever you want, Trudy. You don't have to listen to Ben."

Trudy leaned in closer to the nurse. "You have to admit, the lifeguard is super cute."

"You got a crush on him?" the nurse asked.

"I do NOT." Trudy held up her thumb and pointer, spread a few inches apart. "Okay, this much."

The nurse laughed.

Trudy thought about the lifeguard. And the rumors. Him and Mrs. R. "Brian only likes older women."

"Really now."

"Oh yeah. But I don't blame Mrs. R." Trudy leaned in closer and whispered, "Her husband . . . um . . . he . . . well, he wasn't . . . nice to her." She sat quietly, splashing the water with her feet. Then suddenly stopped and said softly, "He wasn't nice to anybody."

The nurse patted Trudy's thigh. "You wanna swim, Trudy?"

"I never took swimming lessons. Ben wouldn't let me."

The nurse reached out her hand. "C'mon, I'll show you."

CHAPTER THIRTEEN

Thursday, November 8, 2018

SNOW WAS accumulating on the roads, so I drove a bit slower than usual as we made our way to Lenny's trailer home.

"Man, that story sure was something." Dad and I were still reeling from yesterday's conversation with "Brian the Lifeguard," the name we'd bestowed upon him. His real last name being somewhat of a tongue twister—Przeciszewska. "I would have been happy to oblige Rachel's need for attention and affection. Man o' mighty. You know, that was the year your mom and I separated. I was unofficially a bachelor. If I only knew. I was still in my prime then. Maybe not twenty-two, but a virile thirty-seven year old."

"Jeez Dad. TMI. I really don't want to hear about your crush on Rachel Roth. And you weren't exactly a bachelor either. You came around often enough to make me think you still wanted to reconcile with Mom."

"I came around to see *you*. I remember that summer like it was yesterday. You changed your name from Suzie to Susan. Remember that? Man, that drove your mother crazy."

I turned onto Mullover Street and spotted Lenny's Honda Civic parked under a makeshift carport erected next to his trailer home. As we got out of the car, Lenny stepped out the door. He lit up a cigarette and leaned against the railing, eyeing us as we walked along the broken stone path to his doorway.

"You're going to catch a cold standing out here like this in that flimsy coat," Dad said, blowing into his cupped hands. "What do you say we go inside?"

"I'm fine just here. Don't like it? Leave." With the cigarette dangling from his lip, Lenny zipped up his windbreaker jacket.

"Fine. Have it your way. Just trying to save you some medical expenses."

"Yeah. Well, I have insurance. Whaddah you want? I already told you everything I know."

"We don't think you did," I said. "People who knew Ed Resnick tell us he knew you," I lied.

"Who?" Lenny said without missing a beat.

"You know who. We showed you his picture last time we were here," Dad said, taking the police sketch out of his pocket and unfolding it. "Tell you what. You tell us about Ed and Trudy and we'll not pursue a search warrant for these premises."

Lenny took a long, slow drag. He tilted his head sideways to blow out the smoke. He was obviously stalling, weighing his options.

"Here. Let me see that."

Dad handed him the sketch. "Yeah, that could be Ed. I kinda remember him. We hung out once in a while. Heard he got killed years ago."

"You know about that?"

"Word got back to me. Can't remember who told me. I was a junkie back then. Memories shot to hell. Clean now." Then he held his fingers like a gun to his head and pretended to shoot himself. "But still fucked up in the head."

"So tell me, when you hung out with Ed, did he mention his plans to leave the area with Trudy?"

"I guess since he's dead it don't matter that I'm tellin' you this. But yeah. He talked about it with me. Told me to keep it on the DL. Said he needed to protect Trudy. Someone gave him five thousand dollars to, as he said, start a new life. I think he went to Rochester. His mother lived there."

I felt the vibration of my phone in my coat pocket. "Hold on. Gotta take this." I walked just far enough away from Dad and Lenny for some privacy, then swiped to answer. "Hi Rhonda."

"Hey Susan. Wanted to let you know that I spoke to some of the members and we got a few takers willing to give character statements on your behalf."

"I really appreciate that. So I guess this means you're sitting on the sidelines?"

"I'm afraid I have no choice. This is the best I can do. And Susan, I do believe you did what you had to do. But my hands are tied."

"Sure, sure. I understand. Just to have a few people willing to do this is great. Really, I appreciate you doing this for me."

"Should they call the chief and make arrangements to give a statement?"

"Let me check with Eldridge and I'll get back to you."

As I headed back over to Lenny and Dad, I could hear them talking about football. Dad was always good at building rapport with just about anyone.

Slick lawyers, slime-ball criminals, little-old-lady witnesses, cagey suspects, attractive women. I wished I'd inherited this skill, but in this department I was more like Mom—small talk just wasn't my thing. I liked to get straight to the point.

Sidestep the chitchat.

"Sorry about that. Urgent matter. You were talking about Ed get-ting five thousand dollars to start a new life? You know from whom?"

"I dunno. But he did drop the word 'she' into the conversation when he told me about the cash. He also told me to keep my mouth shut about it. He was holdin' something over me, so I kept my end of the bargain. But seein' that he's dead and Trudy has been found, I guess it don't make no difference now."

"What was he holding over you?" Dad asked.

"I was skimmin' some money from the coffee shop. Gonna arrest me? Pretty sure no one gives a shit anymore."

"Do you know if Ed was shaking down someone?"

"If he was, I don't know nothin' about that. Haven't spoken to the dude since he left here."

"Do you know if his mother is still alive?" I asked.

"Haven't a clue."

"Okay. Do you happen to know his mother's name?"

Lenny pulled off his glasses and pinched the top of his nose with his thumb and middle finger. "Something with an M. Marjorie. Margaret. Mildred? I can't recall."

"And his father?"

"Never brought him up. Got the feelin' he didn't have a father. Are we done with this interrogation? I'm gettin' cold."

"We can go inside if you like," Dad said. Lenny shook his head.

"Just one last question," I said. "What line of work did he do around here?"

"Ed was a heating and air-conditioning maintenance guy. Did work for a few of the hotels in the area. There, I answered all your questions."

As Lenny turned to go back into his trailer, Dad said, "Thing is, Lenny, I think there are some things you're still not telling us."

"My brain might be a little fried, ex-Detective William Ford, but I just told you everything I know about Trudy Solomon and Ed Resnick." Lenny spun around and flicked the butt of his cigarette over the railing. "Now leave me the fuck alone."

"YOUR THOUGHTS?" Dad asked when I started the engine. Cold air blasted from the vents.

"I think you're right about what you said back there. I think he's still holding something back. But he did give us some info we can follow up on. Looks like Trudy and Ed headed to Ed's mom in Rochester. I can do a search for an M. Resnick in that area. See what I can find out about her. Might have to add Rochester to our travel itinerary."

"After your mom's father died, I never thought I would set foot in Rochester again. He used to drag me there on business trips. Back then, him and his brothers would get together and party 'til dawn. Your grandfather was the only one of the four brothers that left the area. Your mom was eleven at the time."

"Funny, I don't recall Grandpa being much of a party animal." I clearly remembered him scolding my mother about drinking too much.

"About the time you were a toddler, he got himself cleaned up. His younger brother died in a drunk driving accident. The oldest brother died from liver disease." Dad sighed. "That will take the wind out of your sails."

An uncomfortable silence settled over us, brought on by this detoured conversation about my mother's uncles. After a few minutes of solemnity, I intruded on the quiet. "I don't think we are looking at a kidnapping case, Dad. It sounds like Trudy and Ed planned to leave, and someone helped finance it—Ed's mother, a relative, a girlfriend of Trudy's, perhaps. Someone who can easily part with five grand."

"So what's our next move?"

"I would love to have a chat with Scott. Find out why he was visiting Trudy and Ed in oh-seven. Problem is, I don't think Eldridge is going to fund a little side trip to Florida."

"I've got some money socked away," Dad said. "And I can't think of a better way to spend it."

"When the twins turn eighteen and need tuition for college, I'll remind them that their great-granddad tapped into their college fund because hunting down the Roths in Florida was more important than their educational future."

Dad laughed. "Those boys are going to Harvard on a full scholarship. They won't be needing any of my hard-earned dough."

WE HAD a couple of hours to kill, so I headed to the police station.

Dad wanted to bring Eldridge up to speed on the case and I wanted to see if Marty was able to get in touch with Mordecai Little about the surveillance camera. We had scheduled calls with the ex-cocktail waitress and the hotel guest for later in the afternoon. Both preferred audio over visual, so no faces for Dad to read. And in the evening, Dad was primed to chat with Clara Cole about Trudy's missed doctor's appointment. We also planned to hit up Trudy's old neighbor, Eleanor Campbell, tomorrow—unless the predicted snowstorm held us hostage in our homes. Luckily, she still lived in Monticello so we didn't have to go far. And the Facebook list grew by one person overnight—an ex-bartender named Carlos Rodriguez. Claimed he overheard an argument between Stanley Roth and Trudy a few weeks before she went missing. He thought it might have relevance to the case.

"Dad, why don't you head in? I've got a few calls to make. I'll catch up with you in a few."

I actually didn't have any calls to make but my leg was aching and I didn't want him worrying when he saw me limp toward the front door. I sat in the car, the heat blasting and Bruce Springsteen blaring. Five minutes. Ten minutes. Fifteen minutes. I wiped my sweaty hands on my coat, adjusted my hat, pulled on my gloves, and stepped out of the car. There were about three inches of snow on the ground.

Dad was in Eldridge's office, filling him in on our conversation with Brian the Lifeguard and our second chat with Lenny Berman. I planted myself at my desk and fired up my computer. An email from Carlos Rodriguez was sandwiched between a *New York Times* news story about climate change and a CVS ExtraCare coupon for household cleaning products. Said he could FaceTime on Monday morning at ten o'clock.

A PS at the end of the email: *I remember you and Lori Roth ordering Shirley Temples with extra cherries.* I remembered drinking those sweet concoctions at the bar. But I had no recollection of a bartender named Carlos. I googled him. He was a renowned "urban artist," living in SoHo, who painted murals for city beautification projects. His commissioned work was on display in all five boroughs, as well as in cities across the United States and Europe.

I clicked over to his website, BlightToBeauty.com. A cool animation erupted on the screen—a shadowy figure spray-painting a funky, graffiti-style Blight to Beauty logo onto the side of a building. Rodriguez's bio revealed that he lived with his husband, George, and two tabby cats, April and Leslie.

Marty tapped me on the shoulder and asked me to follow him to Eldridge's office. He closed the door behind me and motioned for me to sit in one of the two chairs in front of Eldridge's desk. Dad stood to leave, but I let him know that he was welcome to stay. He sat back down.

"I got in touch with Mordecai Little," Marty said. He paused, perhaps waiting for some kind of signal to keep talking, but Eldridge didn't move.

"Yeah? And?" I said impatiently.

"The camera was installed a year ago, so it was there and I missed it during the investigation. Granted, the thing is the size and color of a cue ball and camouflaged under the white eave, but—"

Eldridge cut him off. "There's enough blame to go around, let's just continue."

"He said sometimes it's on and sometimes it's off. All depends on whether or not he remembers to activate it. He also said he rarely checks it, only if he suspects something has been stolen from his warehouse. The good news—it's a wireless webcam and whatever is recorded he saves on his computer."

"So he might have footage from that night," Eldridge said to me.

"Except he won't give us the log-in info," Marty added. "He wants to be present when we look at the footage. And he wasn't planning on coming back to the area until spring."

"Can I talk to him? Explain the situation . . . the urgency," I said.

"We explained the situation to him," Eldridge said. "He said he'll call us tomorrow. See what he can do about coming up sooner. But with the storm coming, we might be looking at next week."

"Not sure what you're hoping to find, Susan. It's just footage from outside the warehouse," Marty said. "What we really need is footage from *inside*."

"It's something," I seethed. "Which is better than the whole lot of nothin' I have now."

THE PHONE lay flat on my kitchen counter as I tapped out the number. The ex-cocktail waitress, Rita Mayer, answered with a sing-song hello.

"Hello Rita. We got you on speaker phone. I'm here with retired Detective William Ford."

After some chitchat about the inclement weather, now forecast to be an ice storm, I asked her about Trudy.

"I really hope I'm not wasting your time, but your Facebook post got me reminiscing about those days, and well, I have a story to share that might shed some light on what was going on with Trudy and Ben at that time."

"Rest assured you are not wasting our time," Dad said. "We've spoken to several people who thought the same thing. And they really helped us."

"Okay, well, can I give you some history first? Put my story in context?"

"Sure," I said.

"When I first started working summers at the hotel, I was a cocktail waitress. That was 1974. I was eighteen, on my own for the first time. I was starting college that fall and thought this would be a fun way to make money. Trudy and I roomed together that summer in the staff quarters. She was five years older than me. I thought of her like a big sister. I remember singing silly songs with her. She could be quite funny."

"Did she confide in you about what was going on in her life?" I asked as I retrieved a pitcher of iced tea from the refrigerator.

"Yeah. I could tell her stuff and she could tell stuff to me. She didn't have many friends, pretty much stayed in most evenings. It wasn't that she was shy, she just wasn't super social, if you know what I mean. Introverted."

"So she wasn't seeing anyone at the time?" I asked, then turned to Dad. "*Want some?*" I mouthed, holding up the pitcher.

He nodded.

I grabbed two glasses from the cabinet.

"Actually, she was. That's when I first met Ben. She was dating him—they had met the year before. He was a local guy, supervised the housekeepers and porters. When I came back the following summer, they were married. Which surprised me. He wasn't a very nice guy. I'd say rough around the edges. Not too attractive neither. He looked like that troll in the *Three Billy Goats Gruff* book."

"I've looked over all my old notes and for some reason neither my partner nor I interviewed you in 1978," Dad said, then took a sip of iced tea. "*Oooh, that's good,*" he mouthed to me.

"I worked summers there until 1977, the year before Trudy disappeared. I had no clue about it until I saw your Facebook post."

"So you didn't keep in touch with her?" Dad asked.

"By 1977, we weren't close anymore. She'd stopped confiding in me. Ben was a control freak and a bit of a goon. It was like she was prohibited from socializing with the girls from the hotel. I never heard him threaten her, but he had a threatening presence, if that makes any sense. It wouldn't surprise me one bit if she ran away and tried to hide from him."

"We think Trudy ran off with another man," I said. "Earlier today I emailed you a sketch and a newspaper clipping of a guy named Ed Resnick. Does he look familiar to you? Did Trudy ever mention him?"

"I have it open on my screen now. Sorry. He doesn't look familiar. And I'm pretty sure I never heard the name Ed Resnick."

"Do you think if Ben found out who Trudy ran away with that he would harm that person?" Dad asked.

"I think he had the temper for it. That last summer I was there, I snuck into the housekeeper's hut to get extra towels one time and I saw him shove his sister to the floor. She was holding a baby in her arms. Ben yelled at her to get off the property, and said something like 'I told you never to bring that kid up here. Get out before you're seen.' He was a bully. I confronted him and thought he was going to hit me, but he just stomped away. Then I asked his sister if she was okay. She said yes and left in a hurry. But I could tell she was frightened of him."

"His sister? You sure?" Dad asked.

"Yeah. I didn't know it at the time, but when I told Trudy about it, she said it was Ben's sister. I think her name was Joy . . . no, Joyce. She was about ten years older than Ben. Single mom. Lived in Middletown. Trudy told me the baby was adopted and Ben helped out with expenses. Trudy was miffed at that, because money was tight for them all the time."

When we ran out of questions, I thanked Rita and disengaged the speaker.

"Man, o' fucking mighty," Dad said, shaking his head. "So Ben has a sister. That was news to me."

"Yeah. News to me too. I'm surprised that a single woman could adopt a baby back then. Especially a woman that didn't have the means to support one. Did that strike you as odd?"

"I guess." Dad let out a slow, long breath. "Time to have another chat with Ben."

"Do you think it's worth chatting with his sister too . . . if she's still alive?"

"Hell ya. I'll chase that down. Who's up next?"

"Michael Coleman, a hotel guest who was friends with Scott. We got about twenty minutes."

"You got beer?" Dad asked. "That iced tea was nice, but I'm in the mood for a brewsky."

"Help yourself. If you don't like what's in the fridge, there are some craft beers in the cooler downstairs. Ray's doing some beer-of-the-month-club thing and it's pretty hit or miss."

Dad stared at his choices in the refrigerator, then retreated to the basement. He came back with an IPA from a Vermont brewery and sat down at the dining-room table. "Let's get through this next call and then run down all the shit we still need to do." Dad took a sip of beer, then examined the label. "Pretty good."

Michael said he would call us. I was hoping the guy could shed some sunshine on what Scott was up to that summer. I whiled away the time by updating the Trudy time line and rearranging the white board. I moved Ed Resnick from the Suspect column to the Victim column. We were fairly confident Ed did not coerce Trudy—she seemed a willing participant in the plan to leave the area. If she was scared and he was protecting her, who was he protecting her from? And why?

And did that have something to do with *his* murder thirty years later?

It was already ten past three. Ten minutes past the time Michael was supposed to call. Dad stood up, paced the room a couple of times. He walked out to the living room. A few minutes later he was back in the dining room. He pulled out a chair. I thought he was going to sit down, but he pushed it back in and walked into the kitchen. A few minutes later he came back into the dining room with a can of peanuts.

"Want some?" Dad placed the peanut tin on the dining room table.

"If Michael doesn't call within the next fifteen minutes, I'll email him, reschedule, okay?" I grabbed a handful of peanuts.

"I need to be back at five o'clock. That's when I'm meeting with the nurse . . . Clara Cole. And I got that poker game with the guys at—" My phone rang. "Finally."

I swiped to answer. Before I had a chance to say hello, I got bombarded with a slew of breathless apologies.

"No worries, totally understand," I replied. "Hold on while I put you on speaker phone."

"Michael, hey, this is retired Detective William Ford. Thanks for speaking with us today."

"Sorry for being late. A meeting ran long, then my wife called. Crazy day."

"Well, we'll try to keep it short," I said. "You mentioned a conversation you had with Scott Roth that you think may have a bearing on this case?"

"Yeah. I actually saw that newspaper article about finding Trudy Solomon before I saw your post on Facebook. It reminded me of something Scott told me about a week after her disappearance. Scott and I, and a few other guys, went to a local bar and he got pretty drunk, well, we both got drunk. Anyway, we were all coming up with theories about Trudy's disappearance. Scott was pretty quiet at first, but then he turned to us, and very seriously said, 'She was probably murdered. And I'm pretty sure my father has something to do with it.'"

"Did you believe him?" Dad asked, his eyes wide, his mouth hung open.

"Stanley was a mean SOB, but this sounded like the ramblings of a drunk teenager pissed at his dad."

"Did Scott say anything after that?" I asked.

"He laughed and said something to the effect that he was just messing with us. But later that night, as we stumbled home, he said he wasn't kidding, that he had reason to believe his father was involved in her disappearance. So it was hard to know what to believe. I told him he should say something to the police. He said he would. And that I should just stay out of it."

"Well, he never gave a statement," Dad told him. "In fact, he was shipped off to his aunt's house, maybe with a stern warning to keep his mouth shut."

"Man, he swore to me he would. Otherwise, I might have . . . well, I might have said something. I bet Scott was relieved to learn Trudy was alive this whole time. That his father didn't murder her, like he thought."

"Well, he knew a while ago," Dad said. "We recently discovered that Scott knew she was alive back in 2007. So the question is, why did Scott *think* his father killed Trudy in 1978?"

"That I can't help you with. I left the hotel a couple of weeks after Scott departed. That was my last summer there before college, and I never went back."

"How well did you know Scott?" I asked.

"Pretty well. My parents started going to the Cuttman when I was thirteen years old, and that's when I first met Scott. We would stay there for four weeks, usually all of August. Scott and I would hang out together. He said he preferred hanging out with the guests, not the staff. It was clear he hated the whole hotel scene."

"Did you keep in touch with Scott after that summer?" I asked.

"No. He was what I would call a summer friend. But I ran into him in November of 2001. I remember because it was soon after 9/11 and we chatted about it. He knew someone. I knew someone. Anyway, we bumped into each other on a beach in Florida. Told me his parents sold the hotel in 'ninety-five and were swimming in dough. I asked him if he got a piece of the action and he said he wanted nothing to do with his father or the hotel. But he was pretty successful by then—owned a few car dealerships along the Florida coast—so it wasn't like he was hard up for money. I do keep in touch with his sister, Meryl, through Facebook. She's told me about his failed marriages and his kids. But he's not on Facebook, and the few times I've emailed him, I've gotten no replies. If he's shunning the past, he's doing a bang-up job of it."

No sooner than we hung up on Michael, my phone rang. *Eldridge* flashed on the screen. I let it go to voice mail. I was in no mood to chat about Calvin Barnes. When the voice-mail message registered, I hit play. "*Hey Susan. I just heard from John Minot. He just ID'd the bones. Call me ASAP.*"

THE SNOW was falling at a pretty good clip. Six inches on the ground. Supposedly four more to go until this changed over to sleet and ice. Eldridge offered to discuss the Jane Doe case over the phone, but I told him we could stop at the precinct en route to Horizon Meadows. We still had enough time to meet with Eldridge before Dad's chat with Clara Cole.

"A local, Renee Carter, thirty-one years old," Eldridge said, handing me the manila folder with the forensics report. "Minot got a match from a local dentist whose father filled some of Renee's cavities. We lucked out—he kept all of his father's patient files."

Dad grabbed the folder from my hands. "Shit. She's the woman whose landlord reported her missing in the spring of 1977. We just thought she skipped town to avoid paying rent." Dad turned to me. "She was a prostitute, Susan. And I'm ashamed to say that we jumped to that conclusion. And just so you know, she had a history of doing that."

"So you assume something bad happened to Trudy, because she worked at the hotel, but Renee, being a prostitute, simply ran off. Jeez, Dad. I mean, did anyone even bother to investigate . . . even a little?"

"There's more to this story, and it's a doozy," Eldridge said.

"Before you go there, I just want to say that we did investigate. We interviewed the landlord, who was somewhat of a recluse, an agoraphobe, I think is the term. Never left her apartment—so she wasn't able to provide much information. She said the only interaction she had with Renee was when Renee slipped the rent check under the door. We searched Renee's apartment and there was hardly anything there. It appeared she had packed up her things and left."

"Did it occur to you that someone wanted you to think that?" I asked, halfway between miffed and surprised that Dad would dismiss this case so easily. "So ironic. Trudy *did* run away and Renee was murdered."

"We did treat this as a missing persons case . . . even collected the few remaining items from her apartment . . . but there was nothing to lead us to believe something nefarious happened to her. So we thought she ran."

"Will, no one is accusing you of not doing your job. Now we have a chance to investigate further. Right that past wrong. Okay? So, here's the crazy part . . . Minot retrieved the evidence box you assembled . . . which contained a pacifier."

Dad jumped up and started pacing. "That's right! The landlord said Renee had a newborn son—heard it crying at night. She told us she wrote a note to Renee to let her know that having a child in the apartment was not allowed, so she assumed Renee found another place. But she wanted us to find Renee and get the last month's rent. We just didn't have the resources for that back then."

"Okay, Dad. We get it. You had good reason to believe she left the area."

Eldridge cleared his throat. "Do you want to know what else we learned?"

Dad and I nodded like admonished children.

"Minot was able to pull DNA off the pacifier. Hoping to maybe get a match to the dad and hoping he might be in the system. Turns out dad's not in the system and mom isn't either, because—get this—Renee was not the baby's biological mother. However, the boy *was* in the database. Had a bar brawl a few years back and got arrested. His name . . . you're ready . . . Jake Solomon."

"What the—?" Dad exclaimed.

"And get this, a woman claiming to be his mother, a Joyce Solomon, posted his bail. And she is none other than Ben Solomon's sister. So, answer me this, how the fuck did Renee's supposed son end up with Ben's sister?"

"Holy shit. Is it possible the two cases are related?" I asked. "I mean, is it just a coincidence that Ben is connected to both Trudy and Renee, two women who mysteriously disappeared from the area?"

Dad stopped pacing. "Un-fucking-believable."

"God, I hope Joyce Solomon is alive," I said.

Dad clenched his right fist and hammered it into his left palm. "Man, I can't wait to hear Ben's explanation. It should be a doozy."

THE TEMPERATURE was rising according to the gauge on my dashboard. Still below freezing, but in a few hours the temperature was supposed to hit thirty-two degrees and these snowflakes would change to ice pellets. After dropping Dad at the entrance, I slowly drove away from Horizon Meadows, mindful of the fact that the Prius was not an ideal car for slippery roads and whiteout conditions. I cranked up the windshield wipers and gripped the steering wheel tighter.

When I turned into my driveway, a pair of headlights swung in behind me. Ray's Jeep. *Had he been behind me this whole time?* As I unlatched my seat belt, he tapped his knuckle on my window and waved.

Then he ran inside.

"Hey babe," he said when I opened the front door and stepped in. "I saw you leaving the station. I was nervous about you driving home in that environmentally friendly death trap you call a car, so I followed you. Wanted to make sure you made it home in one piece."

I peeled off my coat and stood directly in front of him. The top of my head level with the bottom of his chin. He reached his arms straight out, pulled me in, and squeezed tight.

"How's the Solomon thing coming along?" he asked when he released me.

"It's crazy. We simply wanted to find out what happened to Trudy and in the process we've stumbled upon two murders, one possible baby abduction, and an apparent extortion scheme. We've uncovered a lot of crazy shit related to this case—and the thing is—we still don't know what really happened to Trudy Solomon."

"Wait. *Two* murders? A baby abduction?"

"Oh yeah. The plot has thickened, my friend."

TRUDY

"TRUDY, THIS is Rita. Rita, this is Trudy," the nurse said. "Rita is moving into the room next to yours."

Trudy giggled, then sang, "RITA RITA bo-bi-ta. Bo-na-na fan-na fo-fi-ta. Fee Fi mo-mee-ta. Rita. Your turn."

Rita glanced at the nurse and then back at Trudy. "I'm sorry. I don't know that song."

"Of course you do. We sing it all the time."

"Trudy, this is Rita Messinger. Do you know a different Rita?"

Trudy scrunched her face. This wasn't the right Rita.

My Rita had bouncy blonde hair, doe eyes, and legs like a Rockette.

"Where's my Rita?" Trudy asked. "Rita was my friend. She told me Ben pushed his sister. His sister bowls, y'know. Ben said I can't bowl. He says I'm . . . I'm . . . spastic."

"Well that's not nice," said Rita. "Who's Ben?"

"We think Ben was her husband," the nurse answered.

"Not a good husband, it seems," said the wrong Rita.

Trudy scowled. "I'm no spring chicken. Gotta get married. Tick tock. No one else knocking at my door. That's what my ma said." A smile spread across Trudy's face. "Wanna learn the song?"

CHAPTER FOURTEEN

Friday, November 9, 2018

“HOW DID your conversation go with Clara Cole last night?” I switched the audio to speaker and laid the phone on the dresser.

“She’s a pretty interesting lady. Kept all the newspaper clippings from the case in a scrapbook. Said it fascinated her because she was scheduled to assist the doctor who was supposed to see Trudy on the day she disappeared. She also told me what the appointment was all about. Which, back then, the doctor wouldn’t disclose. Trudy was being treated for depression. Only back then it was referred to as—and I’m quoting Clara here—‘problems with living.’ She said that this particular doctor prescribed benzodiazepines to many of his patients.”

"Benzowhat?"

"A class of minor tranquilizers, like Valium."

"Ah yes, Mother's Little Helper. I guess her life wasn't all sunbeams and rainbows after all."

"Why do you sound so far away?"

I parted the curtains. "Just looking outside," I yelled.

I shut my left eye to minimize the intensity of the sunlight bouncing off the white carpet of snow and ice. My property had been transformed into a picture postcard, the limbs of the elms and maples encased in ice—glassy cocoons glistening in the low morning sun. The green needle tips of the spruce trees poked out from under several inches of snow. The lake was motionless, hardened by a thick layer of grayish ice. Stunning, really, until I spotted my car and reality set in. *Shit.* A four-foot snowdrift, sealed in place by a thick layer of ice, sloped against the driver's-side door.

I peered down at the snowfall measuring stick planted in the yard. It was half hidden, which meant about twenty inches had accumulated since the snow started falling yesterday morning. But from this angle it was hard to see how much was snow and how much was ice.

"Mighty beautiful out there. But treacherous," Dad said. "I don't think you'll be making your way here any time soon, so we'll have to postpone our meeting with Trudy's neighbor, Eleanor."

I picked up the phone and switched off speaker. "Yeah. I'll be spending the better part of the day digging out my car. Did you email Ben?"

"Last night. No response yet. Will let you know the minute I hear from him. Just told him I wanted to follow up with a few questions. Didn't mention Jake or Joyce. Didn't want to get the door slammed in our faces."

"Okay. Keep me posted. I'm going to do some online sleuthing later and try to find Ed Resnick's mother."

RAY HANDED me a mug of coffee. "I brewed more than usual. We're going to need some extra caffeine to shovel this shit."

Moxie stood at the door, whimpering to get out. This was her kind of weather. I opened the door, grabbed the tie-out, and hooked it onto her collar. *Okay*. Her favorite command, giving her permission to do the thing she was itching to do. She bounded across the porch and leaped into the snow like a puppy. She wasn't expecting a layer of ice, which impeded her ability to frolic. She stepped gingerly across the yard, the weight of her body disturbing the icy surface, startling her every time she sunk into the snow. I pulled out my phone and shot a few seconds of video to send to Natalie.

I figured now was as good a time as any to tell Ray about my trip to Florida. "Dad and I need to talk to the Roths. He booked us a flight to Fort Lauderdale out of Stewart. We leave on Thursday."

"Do they know you're coming?"

"Nope. Dad is pretty sure they'll refuse to see us if we ask. So—"

"They might refuse to talk to you even if you manage to get in front of them. That's a lot of time and money wasted."

"Perhaps, but it's warm and sunny there. Dad could use a little vacation." *So could I*, but I kept that thought to myself. Ray mumbled. "What was that?" I asked him.

"Nothing. I'm trying to think up reasons why this is crazy, but y'know, if I were in your shoes, I would be on the next plane down to Florida myself. So, I get it."

"Ready?" I said, pulling on my snow pants.

Ray gulped down the rest of his coffee. "Let's do this."

"I'M TOO old for this shit," Ray said, stomping the snow off his boots. "That is heart-attack snow."

I had given up twenty minutes earlier. After thirty minutes of chipping away at the ice that hermetically sealed the driver's-side door, I got in and started the car, hoping the blast of heat would melt the buildup of ice on the windows. The heater barely helped and the winter sun was too weak to do much melting. And really, there was no point in digging out my car . . . Ray's Jeep was parked behind my Prius. Neither of us was going anywhere today. The good news was that the temperature was supposed to hit the midforties around noon and stay mild and sunny for the next few days. Mother Nature would finish the job.

Ray planted himself on the living-room couch and fired up *Game of Thrones*. When I had finally made the decision to watch it, Ray told me six seasons of the series had already aired. It seemed too big of a commitment to start bingeing now. ("Maybe the next time you get shot," he teased.) As a sword fight ensued, I flipped open my laptop and began my search for Ed Resnick's mother, whose first name might, or might not, start with the letter M. If she gave birth to Ed at an early age, say twenty, she would be eighty-nine now. The chance that she was still alive was pretty slim, so I started with a search of the obituary listings in the local Rochester newspaper, the *Democrat and Chronicle*. The paper's obituary section was powered by third-party software called legacy.com—yet another technology that would have been helpful to Dad back in the day.

I typed *M* in the box for first name and *Resnick* in the box for last name and adjusted the time frame from *last 3 days* to *any time.* Three hits. Maude. Millicent. Marilyn. I read through each of their obituaries and there was no mention of a son named Ed. I clicked back to the search page and left the first-name box blank and typed "Resnick" in the last-name box. I got a few more hits, but one name caught my eye. Tammy. Two *M*s in the middle of the name—a plausible memory snafu of an ex-drug addict. I clicked on Tammy Resnick's obituary, who died in 1993 of cancer, and there it was in the second-to-last paragraph: *Tammy Resnick is survived by her children, Ed Resnick of Waltham, MA, and Naomi Silverton and her husband John of Hull, MA, and Alfred Resnick and his wife Suzanne (Metz) Resnick of Weymouth, MA; grandchildren Michael and Sandy Silverton; and several nieces and nephews.* Interestingly, no mention of Trudy as Ed's wife or significant other. I searched the legacy.com database for Ed's siblings, Naomi Silverton and Alfred Resnick. No obituaries. Didn't mean they weren't dead. Was it worth hunting them down? Would they even know the answer to our questions: Did Ed's mother give him five thousand dollars? Did they know why Trudy and Ed left this area without telling anyone? Was Trudy a willing participant in her so-called disappearance? Would they know if Ed was extorting money from someone?

I was beginning to feel achy from chipping and shoveling and stood to stretch. I peeked into the living room. The television was off. Moxie was in her dog bed, out cold. Ray was splayed out on the couch with a paperback tented on his chest—the book moving up and down as Ray breathed in and out. I headed upstairs, closed the bedroom door, and called Dad.

CHAPTER FIFTEEN

Saturday, November 10, 2018

THE ADVIL I took the night before had worn off. Snow shoveling did me in. My biceps, pecs, lats, and lower back were punishing me for not exercising on a regular basis. When I turned my head to the left (the only body part I could move), I saw a blank space where Ray should have been. The digital clock on Ray's bedside table illuminated the time: 8:34 am. I let out a strange animal noise and sluggishly lifted my torso.

"Ray?" I yelled toward the bathroom. "You in there?" I reached for my robe, which hung on the edge of the footboard. "Ray?" No answer. I walked over to the window. His Jeep was gone, the driveway was shoveled, and my car had been freed from its icy encasement.

The icicles that formed under the gutters dripped furiously onto the wooden deck, making a plinking sound. I leaned my forehead sideways against the pane to read the outdoor thermometer. Forty-one degrees. Thank you, Ray. Thank you, Mother Nature. One less thing to deal with today. I peeled off my robe and stepped into a very hot shower.

A hand-scrawled note was propped up against the coffeemaker. *Didn't want to disturb you. Headed out early to catch up on work.* I crumpled up the paper and deftly basketball-tossed it in the garbage. *Score!* I texted Ray to ask if he'd fed Moxie. He had, but forgot to give her incontinence medication. I signed off with a heart emoji and thanked him for freeing my car.

I texted Dad to let him know I was no longer imprisoned at home and would pick him up at eleven o'clock. He had called Trudy's neighbor, Eleanor Campbell yesterday and she'd agreed to see us today. Said she was pretty much homebound (unclear if that was because of the weather or a medical condition), so to stop by anytime.

Then I made the mistake of checking Facebook. A private message from Meryl awaited me in Messenger.

> *Hi Susan, I got a call from my mother yesterday and she was quite distraught over the investigation you have re-opened. She said dad is in a pretty fragile state these days, and she believes this rehash of the case, which nearly ruined the hotel, will only make things worse for him. I told her that this has nothing to do with her or dad, but she did ask me to reach out to you and explain the situation. She's hoping you would find it in your heart to let this go, especially since Trudy has been found alive and well. Best, Meryl*

No exclamation marks this time. And no mention of Scott. What were they afraid we would find? We were pretty sure Scott was involved. Stanley wasn't looking all that innocent. And, we had an inkling that Rachel knew something. I wrote a response to Meryl.

Hi Meryl, The last thing we want is to do is upset your parents. We're pretty much wrapping up the case. We heard from some Cuttman staff and guests after I posted that message on the Facebook group. Turns out Trudy left of her own volition. She was going through a personal crisis and took off with a friend. We have a few lingering questions about why she left and some trouble she ran into years later, but we're sure this has nothing to do with your parents. Best, Susan

I called Dad and recited the messages to him. "What do you think?"

"Well, you're not exactly lying. But you're pretty close to the line."

"I'm rethinking our visit to Florida to talk to Rachel and Stanley. I say we leave them alone . . . for now. Focus on Scott."

"Are you saying we keep our reservations but pay Scott a visit instead?"

"Yeah. Meryl didn't mention Scott. It's quite possible he has no idea the case has been resurrected. He's somewhat estranged from the family and he doesn't have a presence on social media. If he's in the dark, that could work to our advantage."

"Fine. But if we find out they are involved in some way—"

"Right. Then we'll deal with it."

I hit send, hoping my message would appease Meryl and her parents. In a way, I was kind of glad this happened. I thought questioning them at this stage was a bit premature. If they were involved in either Trudy's disappearance or Ed's murder, it was unlikely they were going to feel remorse and confess all of a sudden. We needed to know more before confronting them. Besides, Scott was the person who kept popping up, like a jack-in-the-box. Shove him down, crank the handle, and back up he sprung, over and over again. He thought his father killed Trudy. Why? He was seen furtively chatting with Trudy. Why? He was sent away that summer. Why? His initials appear in a letter Trudy wrote to her friend Sandra. Why? He argued with Ed and Trudy in 2007. Why? He was estranged from his parents. Again, why? Maybe, just maybe, an unannounced visit would rattle Scott enough to cough up some answers to these questions.

When I stepped outside I spotted a folded piece of paper tucked under my windshield wiper. Ray leaving me another note, I assumed. I plucked it out and unfolded it.

You won't get away with murder

I whipped my head around. Had this been here earlier in the morning? I racked my brain trying to visualize if I saw the note when I peered out the window. No way. I would have seen it. Whoever stuck it there did it in the past hour. And managed to do it in day-light with me—alone—in the house. I refolded the paper and tossed it in the glove compartment.

"WOULD YOU like some coffee?" Eleanor Campbell led us to her living room. "I just put on a fresh pot," she added, to make sure we didn't think it was an imposition to accept her offer.

"I can always go for a cup of Joe," Dad said. "Susan takes hers black. I like a little milk."

A birdcage in the corner of the room jailed two parakeets. The blue one perched on a swing, the yellow one paced sideways on a bar. Both squawking incessantly since we'd walked into the room. Eleanor motioned us toward a dark green velvet-upholstered Queen Anne couch, the armrest near the window faded to mint. Dad and I miscalculated the firmness of the cushions and quickly sank deep into the innards of the sofa.

"Don't worry, they'll quiet down. My budgies get excited when visitors come around, which, unfortunately, is not very often," Eleanor said. "Now, if you'll excuse me for a moment, I will get the coffee."

"Susan, I think I'm gonna need your help getting out of this sofa," Dad whispered. "And those birds are driving me fucking crazy."

His face transformed from a scowl to a smile when Eleanor reentered the room.

She deftly balanced three mugs on a silver tray and set it on the coffee table in front of us. She handed one of the mugs to Dad, perhaps aware of his sunken predicament.

Dad took a careful sip. "Coffee is very good. And your birds are quite lovely."

"Aren't they? A birthday present from my sister a few years ago. *Melopsittacus undulatus*, or more commonly known as budgerigars. The blue one is Shirley and the yellow one is Laverne. Shirley knows a few words, but Laverne just sings. *Right*, Shirley?"

"Right!" Shirley shrieked.

"You're such a *pretty girl*," Eleanor said.

"Pretty girl. Pretty girl," Shirley mimicked.

Dad's eyebrows arched upward and his mouth formed a little *o*. "Well, I'll be a son of gun. That's something. That's something, all right. So, Ms. Campbell—"

"Please, call me Eleanor." She touched her collarbone and batted her lashes.

"Eleanor. Do you remember when we met, forty years ago? I was the lead detective on the Trudy Solomon case. I was here with my partner Sam."

"I do. I remember quite well. Haven't lost my faculties yet. I'm eighty years old and manage just fine, *thank you* very much."

"Thank you!" Shirley chirped.

Eleanor lowered her voice to a whisper and leaned in toward us. "I have to be careful what I say around Shirley. She repeats about fifteen words and not all of them are—how should I put this—rated G." She batted her lashes again. Was this a tic or an attempt to flirt with Dad?

Dad snorted, then cleared his throat. "Eleanor, I have a copy of your original statement if you'd like to read it," he said, offering her the document. She took the paper and placed it in her lap. "You mention a woman who you said visited Trudy's house twice, a few weeks before she disappeared."

"Yes, I remember that. Trudy asked me not to tell anyone about her, but I felt obligated to tell the police . . . in case she was tied to Trudy's disappearance."

I pulled a sheet of paper from my bag—a printout of Tammy Resnick's obituary. "Is this her?"

"No. Definitely not her."

"How about this woman?" Dad handed Eleanor a photograph of a young Rachel he'd clipped from an old magazine article about the hotel during its heyday.

Eleanor lifted her dangling pink-framed reading glasses, adjusted them on the end of her nose, and examined the photograph. "No, that's not her."

"You sure? Take a second look."

Without looking at the photo, Eleanor said, "I am one hundred percent sure this is not the woman who visited Trudy. I would certainly remember a woman who looks this beautiful. Not that the other woman wasn't attractive—she was, but not like this. The woman I remember seeing had lighter skin and straight blackish hair . . . like your color," Eleanor said to me. "This woman has dark brown hair with bouncy waves," she said, pointing to the picture.

"Anything else you can recall about this woman?" Dad asked.

"She was thin, but had an ample bosom. Oh, and she smoked. But who didn't back then? On one of the visits she wore a blue-and-white-striped kerchief."

"How about her?" I asked, holding up a faded picture of Maxine. "Do you recall seeing her around?"

"That's Trudy's friend, Maxine. As you can see, she is plump with stringy blonde hair. Not too attractive either. Obviously, not the mystery woman."

"And this guy. Have you ever seen him?" I handed her the sketch of Ed Resnick.

Eleanor studied the sketch. "I've seen him, but not visiting Trudy. My brother George, God rest his soul, worked at Monticello Hospital, head of maintenance. This guy worked for him occasionally. I was at my brother's house one day, and this guy came by to pick up a paycheck. I think his name was Ted . . . no, Ed."

"You've got some memory there, Eleanor," Dad said.

"That, my health, and these birds are what keep me in this house. My nephew wants me to move to Horizon Meadows or

Lochmore Manor, sell the house. No siree. I plan to die here with my budgies. Not in some nursing home. And if my Laverne and Shirley go before I do, I'll just get two more."

I knew Dad wanted to say something positive about Horizon Meadows, tell her she would be less lonely there, that it was not what she imagined, but he kept his mouth shut. He had a good rapport going with this woman and might need her assistance in the future to identify the woman who visited Trudy.

"Would it be possible to speak with your brother about Ed?" I asked.

"Afraid not. George died ten years ago. Heart attack. Left me his car though, that green Pontiac out there. Still runs."

"Saw that. A Pontiac Grand Am. They don't make 'em like they used to," Dad said. He leaned forward. "Did you gift or loan Trudy five thousand dollars?"

Eleanor reached for her collarbone again and chuckled. "Oh my, no. I was lucky if I had a few hundred dollars in my bank account back then."

"Okay, well, we've taken up enough of your time," Dad said, rocking slightly back and forth in an attempt to launch out of the couch. "You've been very helpful. Very."

"Are you sure you don't want to stay for lunch? I've got cold cuts and fresh bread in the fridge." Again, her eyelashes fluttered. "I could make a few sandwiches."

Dad managed to get to his feet with a slight assist from me. "That's very generous of you, Eleanor, but I've got to get back to Horizon Meadows. Promised my buddies I would join them for lunch today. And then I've got a billiards tournament this afternoon."

Maybe he was planting a seed in her mind, nudging her toward a less lonely life if she sold the house.

But knowing Dad, he just couldn't leave without defending his lifestyle.

I SAT in my car and read the text messages Eldridge had sent while I was driving Dad back to Horizon Meadows. Mordecai Little would be driving up on Tuesday to give us access to the recorded files. He also spoke to three BLM members who were willing to provide character references and go on record about my work with the local BLM chapter and the community outreach programs I had organized.

Every part of me was sweating, not just my hands. My heart was revved up. Not panic-attack level, but pretty cranked up. I rolled down the driver's-side window a few inches in an attempt to clear the steamy windshield and windows.

My phone rang. "Unknown Number" flashed on the screen. "Hello, this is Susan," I said hesitantly, expecting it to be one of those robocalls.

"Hi Detective Ford. It's Thomas."

Thomas? Did I know a Thomas? Did we interview someone named Thomas?

Before I could ask 'Thomas Who?' he said, "Thomas Dillon. The guy living in your old bedroom."

"Oh, yes. Hi Thomas. What's up?"

"Your mom asked me to clean out your bedroom closet. Seems she's been using it to store old stuff. But it started to overflow, so she wanted me to get rid of anything that was broken or of no future use. Perhaps sell some things on Craigslist. Anyway, once I got everything out of there, I found something of yours."

I tried to recall if I had left anything behind when I moved out in 1985. "Okay, what is it?"

"It's a diary. And I swear I didn't read it. It's locked, and there's no key. It was lying flat on the corner of the shelf above the hanger rod. I didn't want to toss it without your consent."

"Is it yellow with a fuzzy flower on the front?"

"That's the one."

I wanted to say, burn it. "I'll be over later today to pick it up. And Thomas—"

"Yes ma'am?"

"Please don't let my mother see it."

THOMAS HANDED me a pair of scissors and I cut the piece of cloth strap securing the lock.

"Like a little time capsule," he said.

"A time capsule from hell," I told him.

"Seems you turned out okay, maybe a little burnt around the edges."

"Actually, I'm more like lava cake. Burning on the inside, soft and spongy on the outside."

Thomas nodded and smiled. "If you say so. Your mother should be back shortly if you want to stick around."

Should I stick around?

Here was my chance to ask Thomas his thoughts on the Barnes case.

"Unfortunately, I can't wait around for her. Lots to do today. Oh, and no need to mention I was here." I waved the diary like a tambourine. "Or that you gave me this." I jogged toward my car, hastily putting distance between me and the conversation I should have had with Thomas.

THE SLICED-OPEN, six by nine-inch, pale yellow, cloth-textured journal with a felt appliqué daisy affixed to its cover sat on the dining-room table, patiently waiting for me to remove my coat, hat, and gloves. I was less patient, and hurried to undress. I had been tempted to start reading it when I got into the car back at my mother's house but thought better of it. Didn't want Thomas to come out to the curb and ask what I was still doing there. Or worse, have Mom return from her errands and see me crying (or screaming) in her driveway. Not that I thought reading the diary would evoke either of these emotions, but better be safe than sorry.

I probably wouldn't even have started a diary if Dad hadn't given me this one. He'd bought the diary soon after he moved out, April 2, 1978. That date was permanently etched on my brain like intricate carvings on a sperm whale's tooth. When he presented the diary to me as a gift, he told me a police shrink had said it would be "a helpful way for me to work out my feelings about their separation." I threw the diary in my desk drawer.

About one month later, while searching for some stickers, I came across it. Lori had shared her diary with me the week before. Mostly musings about boys she liked, the disgruntled teachers who clearly had no business being in their chosen profession, and basement parties where kissing games were taking precedence over dancing and gossiping. If Lori kept a diary, I figured, then so should I. Once I had written a few entries, I could read my diary to her. It's what best friends did. Although Dad bought me the journal as a cathartic exercise to calm my angst about their split, none of the entries between May 3, 1978, when I started writing, and June 1, 1978 made mention of either one of them. The first entry was a single paragraph about going to the movies with Lori to see *Return from Witch Mountain* and spotting Bonnie and Joe making out in the movie theater. All my entries in May were simply one or two paragraphs describing what other kids were doing. How I felt about these incidents was conspicuously absent—as if what I thought or felt didn't matter.

The first entry that had anything to do with my family appeared in early June.

6/3/78

Good Morning Diary,

Sorry I didn't write last night. I was super tired. Yesterday I found out from Sharon that two Broadway shows are coming out as movies this year. They are Grease *and* The Wiz. *Me and Lori already put it in our calendars to go on June 16th the day* Grease *opens. Mrs. Gold took the class to see* Grease *on Broadway last year and I have the album. I know every word to every song. Although Sharon told me that new songs were added to the movie. They better be good! Today is a half day at school. So I'm thinking it is going to be a good day.*

This day ended up sucking. My family is royally fucked up. They keep hinting at getting back together but I think Mom might be dating someone. She must have forgotten I had early release today. Sixth graders came to the school for a tour. Lori volunteered to be a tour guide but I didn't want to be in the school when I didn't have to be. So mom must have forgotten this. Like she forgets everything!!! So what happened is that I'm walking up the driveway and I see mom hugging this man on the front porch. They didn't kiss or anything like that. From a distance he looked handsome but I didn't get to see him up close because I hid in the bushes when he drove by. I waited fifteen minutes so my mom wouldn't suspect I saw anything. Should I tell dad? I'll decide tomorrow.

Sharon. That must be Sharon Katz. Star of the school plays. Always with her nose in a book. I seemed to recall she went to Harvard. Or was it Yale? And, contrary to what I wrote about going to the movies with Lori, I was pretty sure it was Dad who took me to see *Grease*. I flipped to June sixteenth and there, in all caps, I wrote: "SAW *GREASE* WITH DAD. IT WAS GREAT! I LOVE THE NEW SONGS!" It was the only entry for the day. No reference to Lori or why our original plans fell through. I turned back to the June 3 entry. The first paragraph (like all the entries before it) was written in a neat cursive handwriting with carefully drawn letters tilting slightly to the right. In the second paragraph, the letters were bigger, rounder, and angrier. A mix of cursive and block script. Tilted left and right. A little hole pierced the page where a period should have been.

What disturbed me most about this passage was that I had no recollection of the man on the porch. It seemed pretty traumatic at the time. Didn't traumatic events stay with you? Or were these the types of unwelcome memories buried in the core of your brain, like crabs that burrowed into the sand to make themselves harder to capture?

I flipped through the diary, scanning the entries for another reference to the man who hugged my mother. After leafing through movies I'd seen, parties I attended, friends I gossiped about, and a few arguments with my mother, I found another entry about this man.

8/1/78

Dear Diary,

Everything about this day sucked. I saw that guy again. The one mom hugged a few weeks ago. I never told dad about him because I got the feeling things were going better between mom and dad and I didn't want to ruin things. I came home early from swimming at Lisa's pool and they were talking in the kitchen. They didn't see me and I didn't go in but I could hear them whispering and laughing. And then mom told him to not worry, because he'll never find out. What the hell!!!! And that isn't even the worst of it. Me and Lori got into a huge fight today. She's been hanging out with that bitch Marilyn. Marilyn's dad is some big shot lawyer and her mom is a doctor so they have a ton of money.

The two of them were going on and on about all the new clothes they were going to buy for eighth grade and they totally ignored me. Lori then told me she left me out of the conversation because she said my family doesn't have enough money to buy the clothes they were planning on buying so what's the use of me going with them to the mall. She said it would be like torture.

Although I had no recollection of the time I saw Mom hug that man back in July, this day, August 1, 1978, I suddenly and fully remembered. One of those deeply buried crabs clawed its way to the sand's surface and I nabbed it. The fight with Lori at her pool. The overheard conversation in the kitchen. With this day firmly in my mind, I tried to picture the man. But he was seated at the table with his back toward me. And I, trying not to be seen, was crouched midway up the stairs out of their view. The conversation rising and falling, so I was only able to catch a few words here and there. And although I could not recall what Mom and that man discussed, the argument with Lori sharply crystalized in my mind. There we were, best friends, standing together at the starting line. On your mark, get set, go. What ensued was a drawn-out marathon, a series of slights and insults that would unfurl over a full year before we both reached the finish line. The end of our friendship (although I was pretty sure she reached the end before I reluctantly did). And this was the day it began—the day the starter's pistol sounded—with the not-so-subtle jab at my lower socioeconomic status. Her remark, a kick to the gut. I grabbed my towel and hastily pulled my T-shirt over my bathing suit. As I stormed off, she yelled, "What, Suzie, what did I say? I was only trying to make it easier for you." When I turned back, I saw Marilyn smirking. Her new friend Marilyn, and probably that girl Sharon, encroaching on our friendship like the moon slowly overtaking the sun during a total solar eclipse, until all I felt was darkness and stillness and a sense of foreboding. Did she really believe she was making life easier for me? Or was she deliberately sowing the seeds of our breakup, seeing an opportunity to climb the social ladder? And she climbed it, all right. By the time Lori was a junior, she was the third-most popular girl in high school, behind Marilyn Jones and Tracy Edgar. By senior year, Lori eclipsed

"Not something I really want to chat with her about. Besides, even though this was forty years ago, I'm not so sure she would come clean about sneaking around with another man. It's even quite possible she doesn't remember. Vodka can have that effect."

"Well, I have no memory of her dating anyone that year. If you really want to know, you're going to have to ask her."

"Do you remember taking me to the movie *Grease*?"

"Now, that, I remember! You told me that Lori was sick . . . or grounded . . . something like that . . . and you really wanted to go. So I was your stand-in. I even remember going to Lefty's before the movie for your favorite dinner—French onion soup and a cheeseburger." Dad paused and then deftly changed the subject. "So, Susan, the Resnicks. Should we give them a call?"

"Sure. Why don't you call them, and if they are willing to talk with us, we'll just squeeze them in between Carlos, Ben, Joyce, Jake, and Scott."

"Carlos?"

"The Cuttman bartender."

TRUDY

"WOULD YOU like to watch some television?" the nurse asked, fiddling with the remote.

Trudy nodded. "Is Laverne and Shirley *on?"*

"Laverne and Shirley?"

"Isn't that your favorite show?" Trudy asked.

"I remember that show," the nurse said. "Two girlfriends who worked in a beer plant sharing an apartment. Well, I don't think that show is on anymore."

"We just watched it the other day. Remember, I came over after that fight with Ben."

"Um, well, let me check the TV listings, okay?"

"Eleanor, you should not have told Ben that I had a visitor. He insists on knowing who my friends are and what I'm doing at any given moment. He just likes being in charge."

"Well, here's a show we can watch. The Kids Are Alright*."*

Trudy slapped at her head. "Eleanor, you can't tell Ben about this woman!"

"What woman?" the nurse asked.

"You know. The woman who came to visit. The one with the blue-and-white scarf." Trudy glanced over at the television. "In fact, don't tell anyone."

"Okay, Trudy. Our little secret."

Trudy frowned. More secrets.

CHAPTER SIXTEEN

Sunday, November 11, 2018

JOYCE SOLOMON was alive and easy to find. She lived in Liberty, a couple of towns over from Monticello. We decided to ambush her in the morning before talking to Ben in the afternoon.

We didn't want Ben sounding the alarm with his sister before we had a chance to speak with her. In a ploy to determine if she was at home, Dad dialed her landline. When she picked up, he asked for George. I heard her reply, "Sorry, you must have the wrong number."

On the fifteen-minute ride to her house, Dad fumed nonstop about how pissed he was, being deceived by Ben. I didn't blame him one iota, so I let him vent.

"Yes?" Joyce asked, slightly cracking open the glass storm door. She was short and redheaded, like Ben. But that was where the similarities ended. Joyce's facial features were soft and gentle—muted gray eyes, lightly freckled cheekbones, ivory complexion, heart-shaped lips à la Betty Boop. Delicate burgundy curls fell generously onto the shoulder pads of her winter coat.

"Good morning, Ms. Solomon. I'm Detective Susan Ford, and this is my father, retired Detective William Ford. May we come in?"

"I was just about to head out to pick up some groceries. What's this about?"

"Just need to ask you a few questions about a cold case we are working on. We also have a few questions about Ben."

Joyce pushed open the storm door to let us in. Dad and I stepped over the threshold and we all stood huddled together in a dark entryway.

"I haven't seen or heard from Ben in months, not sure how much help I can be."

"We really just need a few minutes of your time. Is there a place we can sit and talk?"

Joyce led us out of the entryway and into a cramped living room, where a sofa, recliner, television console, and coffee table took up most of the space. Along one wall was a narrow book case filled with trophies. Bowling trophies, to be precise. About one hundred of them, in varying shapes and sizes. Bowling plaques dating back to 1957 were mounted on the walls.

"Yours?" I pointed to the bookcase.

"Every last one of them. Got a big tournament coming up next week, so I'm hoping to add another one to my collection. I play in a senior league now. Ain't too many of us left." Joyce turned toward Dad. "You look familiar. Do I know you from somewhere?"

"Well, I don't bowl, so we didn't cross paths at the local lanes. I'd say we're about the same age. Perhaps we mingled at some of the same high-school parties."

"Perhaps. It'll come to me. You said this was about some cold case and Ben. Not sure what I can possibly help you with."

"A couple of months ago, state police discovered skeletal remains along 9W in Ulster County. A woman shot point-blank forty-one years ago, in 1977. She was a Jane Doe until a few days ago. A dental X-ray gave us her name—Renee Carter," I said. Joyce attentively nodded her head, but did not react to the name.

"I don't know a Renee Carter." She shifted in her chair slightly, stiffened her back, sat up straighter. "As I said, I really do have to get going."

"That may very well be." I paused, perhaps for effect, but more so to make sure what I was about to say was clearly understood. "She had a baby that somehow ended up with you after she was murdered."

Joyce's eyes widened, then squinted. She leaned toward us, and for a moment I thought she was going to pitch forward out of the recliner. "That can't be. I adopted Jake." She swallowed hard. "I wonder if she was the mo—"

"What adoption agency did you use, Ms. Solomon?" I asked.

"I . . . I . . . can't remember. I'll have to go through old files." Joyce yanked up the collar on her coat. "Look, I really have to go."

"I'm afraid we need to straighten out a few things first," Dad said.

"I remember you now. You're the detective who was looking for Trudy. I saw you interviewed on a TV news program. They found her, right?"

"Yes ma'am, I was the detective assigned to Trudy's case. And yes, she's recently been found alive. The case was reopened when

Renee Carter's skeletal remains were found—we initially thought it was Trudy. In the course of our investigation, we've uncovered new evidence in both cases and we're chasing down leads. Now this can be pure coincidence, but your brother is connected to both of these women."

"Ben told me—" She stopped.

"Ben told you what?"

Her gaze darted around the room. Her demeanor changed from proud bowling champ to petrified child.

"Ben told you what?" I repeated.

"Are you sure this murdered woman was Jake's mother?" she stammered.

"Well, here's the thing, Ms. Solomon," Dad began. "Renee was *not* Jake's biological mother, but he was in her care. We do not know who his biological parents are. It was DNA on a pacifier found in the apartment that led us to Jake, who was in our system. We're still trying to sort out why Renee had him. And how he ended up with you."

Joyce sat erect and still. She lowered her head slightly and her gaze settled on the coffee table. We waited a few minutes for her to reply, but she maintained her perfectly still pose.

"You were about to say something that Ben told y—"

Her head shot up. "I don't know. Really. I don't know why I said that. I don't really talk to Ben. We're not very close."

"Ms. Solomon, I didn't even know about you until last week. Ben never told us he had a sister. We learned of your existence when we interviewed an ex-employee of the Cuttman who was friends with Trudy. Why did Ben keep you a secret?"

"How would I know? You'll have to ask him about all this. I . . . I really have to get going," Joyce said, rising from the recliner.

"Here's what we think happened," Dad said. "Ben took that child for you. Or the two of you cooked up this scheme together. So, if you know something, trust me, it is in your best interest to tell us."

Joyce slowly slumped back down on the recliner. She momentarily cradled her head in her hands. "My husband and I tried to have a baby, to no avail. He died when I was thirty-five, and I never remarried." She leaned toward Dad and touched her bottom lip, as if she was letting him in on a secret. "At one point, I was sleeping around, trying to get pregnant. That's how desperately I wanted a baby. I tried to adopt, but back then, no adoption agency would let a single woman on welfare adopt a child."

"And how does Jake factor into this?" Dad asked curtly, his patience worn a bit thin.

"One day, Ben turns up with Jake. He told me the runaway mom had no relatives and the baby would be put in the foster care system. I just assumed it was one of his employees at the hotel." She glanced around the room; her gaze landed on a display of family photographs wedged between bowling trophies. "I convinced myself it was fate. That I was meant to have this baby."

"You do realize this was illegal?" I said.

She inhaled sharply, then let out a slow breath. "When you are desperate to have a baby, you do desperate things. But we certainly wouldn't have hurt anyone."

Dad lowered his head and peered over his glasses. "So you're saying Ben just turned up on your doorstep with a baby?"

"That's exactly what happened." She cocked her head to the side. "You can't possibly think Ben killed this woman. I mean, I find that hard to believe. He would never do that."

"We have a witness who saw Ben shove you. That sounds like violent tendencies to me," he said.

"I don't recall that incident, but he could pitch a fit if he was upset. I was living in Middletown at the time, and he told me to never bring the baby up this way. I once did and boy, did he get mad. Maybe that's what this witness was referring to. He had every right to be upset . . . he didn't want anyone asking questions. But Ben isn't a bad person. He actually helped out with some expenses at the beginning. When Jake turned five, I went back to college and got a good-paying job as a bookkeeper and office manager, and since then we managed just fine."

"What have you told Jake?" I asked.

"About wha—?" She looked up seemingly confused, as if she'd started believing that Jake's origin was perfectly normal. But within a second her face crumbled. "I've never told Jake. He doesn't know. I thought about telling him when he became a father—his daughter is ten now—but I just couldn't. I've held this secret for such a long time . . . the truth is what feels like a lie now." Joyce pulled a tissue out of her coat pocket and dabbed her eyes. "What . . . what do you plan to do? Will I go to jail?"

"That's for the courts to decide. By law, Jake should have been placed in state custody and the Department of Child Services would have been responsible for his well-being." I shifted my attention to Dad, and then back to Joyce. "Also, if the police knew a child was left behind, their investigation into Renee Carter's disappearance would have gone in a different direction. Your cooperation in this matter will have some bearing on what happens to you."

Dad cleared his throat. "This investigation is just getting under way, Ms. Solomon. For all we know, you had a bigger hand in this than you are letting on."

"A bigger hand? What, now you think *I* killed that woman?"

"We have no evidence to suggest that . . . right now. Although wanting a child is certainly motive," Dad said. "We will be speaking with Ben this afternoon. If he was just the recipient of this child, as you purport, then he just might know something that could shed some light on who murdered Renee."

"You are not to contact Ben. It's important for us to interview him without the taint of a heads-up," I said, trying to strike a balance in tone between threatening (to make sure she complied) and compassionate (to gain her trust). "As for Jake, I suggest you come clean. He'll want to hear this from you, not us or some nosey reporter."

"Will you give us your word that you will not get in touch with Ben before we've had a chance to speak to him?" Dad asked.

Joyce let out a long sigh. "You have my word."

DAD AND I arrived at the diner early. We grabbed a booth near the front so Ben could easily spot us when he walked in. If he walked in. If Joyce was innocent as she professed, we felt pretty confident she would keep her word and maintain radio silence. However, if she was in cahoots with Ben and tipped him off, well, he was probably halfway to Timbuktu by now. Neither of us had eaten lunch, so Dad called over a waitress and we ordered two cheeseburgers, two Diet Cokes, and fries to split. At ten past two, the bell over the front door tinkled and Ben walked in.

I thought about how Trudy's roommate described him—troll-like. Spot on. His untamed carrot-orange hair grew vertically from his squarish head. His eyebrows, like two warring caterpillars, twitched inward above beady eyes. His shoulders were bowed, making him appear shorter than he actually was, which was short to begin with. Maybe five seven.

He spotted us immediately.

But before he could sit down, Dad slid out and excused himself to go to the bathroom. I knew the ploy. He wanted to trap Ben in the booth. Ben sat across from me, and we engaged in small talk (the weather, my dog, his phlebitis) until Dad reappeared and slid in next to Ben on the red vinyl bench seat.

"I see you got the fries," Ben said. "Best in Ulster County."

"Feel free," Dad offered.

Ben reached over and plucked two fries from the plate and stuffed them into his mouth. "So, what is so important that we must meet again in person? Did you figure out what happened to Trudy?"

"We're still working on that," Dad said. "But there's something else you might be able to help us with."

Ben eyed the door. It just dawned on him that he was trapped.

Without implicating Joyce, Dad laid out what we knew about Renee Carter and Jake Solomon. The agitation started almost immediately and then it built. His cheeks turned a deep shade of crimson. A vein bulged from his thick neck. He slammed his fists on the table, then he hip-checked Dad in an attempt to dislodge him. Dad managed to keep his butt firmly planted.

His old police instincts took over and he grabbed Ben by the shirt collar and pushed him up against the seat. Sally and her partner, Ron Wallace, who were waiting outside for my text signal, ran in.

"Ben Solomon. You're under arrest for the murder of Renee Carter and the kidnapping of an infant. You have the right to remain silent. Anything you say . . ."

"I did not—NOT—kill Renee Carter!"

". . . can and will be used against you in a court of law. You have the right to an attorney. If you cannot afford an attorney, one will be provided for you."

"This is bullshit! I didn't kill anyone!"

The diners, who had been mostly quiet but riveted to the action in our booth, took out their cell phones to record the arrest. I kept my head down. The last thing I needed was to be the star of some viral video making the rounds on Twitter.

"We'll chat about it at the police station," I said as Sally handcuffed him and led him out of the diner and into the waiting police car.

RAY LEANED forward in his chair and asked Ben if he would like something to drink, ignoring the public defender seated next to him. Ben bobbed his head yes, and Sally walked in with a can of Coke. Marty leaned against the mirrored wall, playing the role of casual observer. Dad and I were cloistered behind the two-way mirror. Ben had asked for a lawyer immediately upon entering the interrogation room, so now, one hour later, we were finally getting down to business. Ray tried to talk to Ben before the PD showed up, but he just sat there, his arms crossed over his chest, in stony silence.

"I hope you've got a good lawyer here, Ben, cuz you're in a heap of trouble," Ray began. "So, I'll just lay my cards on the table, and when I'm done it will be your turn. Your confession here today will have bearing not only on your future, but your sister's as well. Capisce?"

Ben nodded.

"Please state for the record that you understand what I just said."

"I understand."

"Good. Now we have an understanding that the truth will work to your advantage over any bullshit you try to shovel. And my partner over there . . . he is the king of bullshit detection. Now, let me roll this back for you a bit."

Starting with the discovery of the skeletal remains, Ray summarized both the Trudy Solomon and Renee Carter cases, emphasizing Ben's connection to both of them. "I showed you mine, now you show me yours."

Ben glanced sideways at his court-appointed PD, who nodded. "I didn't kill Renee Carter. And I certainly didn't kill Ed Resnick. I didn't even know who the hell Ed was until you just told me." Ben looked over at Marty. "And that is not bullshit. He's the guy I described to Will Ford forty years ago, and Will's the one who didn't believe me at the time that the guy existed. If he took off with Trudy, I have no fucking idea why."

"Tell us how you came into the possession of the baby, Ben," Marty asked, taking a seat across from Ben.

Again, Ben glanced over at his court-appointed PD and the PD nodded. "My sister had nothing to do with this. And I did what I did to save that kid from a life of foster care and God knows what. I get a call out of the blue from this guy I hardly knew who tells me that some prostitute ran away and left her baby in her apartment. He remembered me mentioning how my sister really wanted a kid. Claimed I went on and on about it at a poker game one night. So he rang me up and asked if I wanted this one. That's it. End of story. I picked up the boy and delivered him to my sister. Every day after that I checked the newspaper to see if someone was looking for the mother and son, and nothing. Maybe I would've returned the kid if I saw that someone was looking for him. But nothing."

"And this guy who called you out of the blue? Does he have a name?"

"Yeah. Lenny. Lenny Berman. A scumbag if ever there was one."

I CHECKED the rearview mirror. Sally and Ron were two car lengths behind us. Ray and Marty behind them. It took less than an hour to get a search warrant.

"Three times a charm," Dad said on our third trip to Lenny's trailer home.

"Do you think Lenny killed Renee?" I asked. "Or for that matter, Ed? Maybe he lied about the last time he saw him."

"I honestly don't know what to think."

The three cars pulled up in front of Lenny's carport. The Honda nowhere in sight. One by one the headlights cut out. Sally and Ron unholstered their weapons and held them barrel down as they approached the front door.

"Leonard Berman," Ron yelled, pounding on the door. "Police. Come out slowly with your hands on your head."

Silence.

Ron pounded the door again. "Leonard. You've got nowhere to run. Come on out!" Ron waited ten more seconds before kicking in the door with a single blow. He raised his weapon and crossed the threshold. Sally stepped in behind him. Twenty seconds later we heard Ron yell "clear."

Sally appeared in the doorway, holstering her gun. "Place has been cleaned out."

Ray and Marty entered the trailer home. Dad and I leaned against my Prius. Eldridge had warned us not to interfere with the search. Not our case.

"Nice night," Dad said. "Dark enough to see the Milky Way."

"Speaking of the Milky Way, you hungry?" The last time we ate anything was two o'clock at the diner and it was now approaching eight o'clock.

"I'm good. I grabbed some granola bars at the station." Dad reached into his coat pocket and offered me one.

"Thanks. Y'know, it would have been funny if you had Milky Way bars stashed in your pockets."

Ray stepped out, shaking his head, and waved us over. "Nothing left behind. Clothes gone. Food gone. Even the wastebasket was emptied. Must've known we were onto him."

"So now what?" Dad asked.

"We'll track him down. When did you last speak with him?"

"Three days ago . . . Thursday. Gives him a bit of a jump on us."

CHAPTER SEVENTEEN

Monday, November 12, 2018

I LIFTED my sleep mask and gradually opened one eye. The sunlight streamed in through the gaps in the blind slats, forcing me to squeeze my eyes shut after detecting the presence of a hangover. It was low grade. Not as bad as I thought it would be. On a scale of one to ten, a four. Sally had invited me out for a drink after our raid on Lenny's place. Two pints of Guinness and a couple of shots of tequila didn't quite do me in. But I had to call Ray last night to drive me (and Sally) home. "I'd rather be mad than sad," he says whenever I rouse him out of bed in the middle of the night to get me home safely. Which was no more than four or five times a year.

"Hey babe," he whispered. "You okay?"

I groaned and turned into a fetal position.

"Wanna have sex? Heard it's a great cure for what ails you."

I thought about his proposition. "Sure. Just give me a sec to empty my bladder."

When I reentered the bedroom, Ray was sitting up against the headboard reading my old diary.

"Enjoying it?" Truth be told, I had no qualms about him reading my diary. For the most part, it was just the ramblings of an insecure kid. Perhaps he would gain some insight into my deep-rooted self-doubt brought about by feeling rejected by family and friends. Or maybe he would just get a kick out of it.

"As a matter of fact, I am. It's like a little peek into your preteen mind. And the stuff about your mom . . . that's some crazy shit."

"I don't think she was as mean as I made her out to be. I think a lot of that is the perception of an angry thirteen-year-old." I leaned over and grabbed the diary out of his hands. "If you want to have sex, we'll have to stop talking about my mother."

I straddled Ray, bent over, and kissed him gently on his lips. He moved his hands down my back, cupped my bottom and in one deft move maneuvered me facedown on the bed. Then he straddled me, massaged my neck and back, steadily moving south until he reached my coccyx bone, where he lingered for a few minutes longer. As promised, he spent the next fifteen minutes curing my hangover.

"Mind if I shower before you do?" Ray asked, rising from the bed. "Go back to sleep if you like. I'll walk Moxie."

I mulled over getting more shut-eye, but instead reached for my diary. I flipped through to the latter part of that year looking for another reference to the mystery man. Nothing. At the start of eighth grade, in September of 1978, my fury was directed at my mother—her binge drinking, her lackadaisical attitude in trying to reconcile with Dad, her constant harping about my father's obsession with the Trudy Solomon case, her snide remarks about my frizzy hair ("I hear Dippity-do works wonders"), my skinny frame ("Are you anorexic or something?"), my smattering of pimples ("There's a product called soap for that mess on your face"). Midway through eighth grade, around February 1979, my attention pivoted away from my mother to my waning friendship with Lori. There were a few good days, which were easy to spot, because my handwriting was fluid and orderly.

"I thought you'd be fast asleep by now," Ray said, stepping out of the bathroom with a towel wrapped around his midsection. His hair damp and wild from towel drying. A speck of shaving cream along his jawbone. "Your headache is going to come back if you keep reading that thing. Seems to me you should let the past stay in the past."

"Says the guy with the happy childhood."

Ray's childhood was the complete opposite of mine. Ray was three years younger than me, born in 1968, one year before his parents, Celia and Daniel, married. His parents spent the first year of his life living on a commune with other unwed couples with young children. They eventually tied the knot at the Woodstock Festival, both just twenty-one. The ceremony, as legend had it, performed by a traveling minister. After the festival, they hitchhiked across America, little Ray in tow. When they came back to the east coast, they decided to settle in Hurleyville, a couple of towns over from where I grew up in Woodbourne—just in time for Ray to start kindergarten. Ray and I attended the same elementary school (grades one through six) and high school (grades seven through twelve), but our paths never crossed because of our age difference. Ray described his parents as free spirits. ("Hippies—the real deal," he would proudly say.) His mom taught art at the elementary school. He once told me she would kiss all the plants before leaving the house every morning and greet each of them when she came home in the afternoon. Every so often, when we passed a street musician or heard a particular song on the radio, he would tell me the story of how one day he came home from school and found his mother hunched over on the couch plucking a guitar. She'd passed a pawn shop while out shopping and seen it in the window. "It called to me," she told him. Armed with beginner guitar books, she taught herself to play. At night, she would practice and he would fall asleep listening to her sing songs made famous by Cat Stevens, Joan Baez, Carole King, and James Taylor. His dad was a lineman with New York Telephone and Telegraph. No matter how tired his dad was, he never said no to a game of catch or a math problem to solve. If he was angry, he didn't curse—instead, he would use euphemisms like *fiddlesticks* and *schnitzels.* They marked anniversaries and birthdays and holidays by buying gifts for people less fortunate than themselves.

With savings and pensions, they were able to retire at fifty-nine. And they knew exactly what they wanted to do. "Get on the road, like the old days," they said. That was eleven years ago. One morning, they set out in their Subaru to shop for a recreational vehicle at an RV dealership in Vermont. They put a down payment on a thirty-nine-foot Fleetwood Discovery, and according to a credit-card receipt found in his dad's jacket, celebrated at a nearby restaurant. They left the restaurant at eight o'clock, and at ten o'clock a drunk teenager plowed into the Subaru. Head-on. The nineteen-year-old driver died instantly. As did Ray's parents. The sole survivor, the drunk man's girlfriend, was in a coma for weeks. Ray was still married at the time. To a woman named Angie. His daughter,

Samantha, was nine. He withdrew from his marriage and plunged himself into his work. ("The grief felt insurmountable," Ray said.) It wasn't long before Angie found herself in the arms of another man. He'll tell you he didn't know how he did it, but Ray managed to attend all of Samantha's dance recitals, school plays, and parent-teacher conferences. ("If I didn't, I knew my parents would scold me when I got to heaven," he said to Samantha years later.)

Ray's savior was the drunk guy's girlfriend, Marisa. Two years after the accident, she came to see him. To apologize. Marisa knocked on the door, probably expecting to be yelled at or shooed away. But he invited her in. She explained to Ray it took two years of therapy to finally work up the courage to face him and ask for forgiveness. She was consumed with guilt, felt she hadn't done enough to dissuade her boyfriend from getting behind the wheel.

She said to Ray, "I knew he was drunk. I was tipsy myself. I knew he shouldn't be driving. My parents always said I should call them if I was ever in this situation and they would pick me up. That they would rather be mad than sad. That they wouldn't judge me or punish me. But I didn't call them. I didn't—"

But before she could finish, Ray wrapped his arms around her and they sobbed as if the accident had occurred the day before, raw and vivid in their minds.

They started a program called "Better Mad Than Sad," which became part of the local drivers ed curriculum. Parents joined their kids for a fifty-minute session in which parents pledged to pick up their kids or their kid's friends, no questions asked, no judgment passed. Years later, a study proved this program prevented scores of teenagers from getting behind the wheel drunk. It also saved Ray's life, metaphorically speaking. A few years ago, he created a foundation in his parents' name—a one-thousand dollar scholarship awarded annually to two high-school seniors who had taken part in the program.

I sometimes thought I was drawn to Ray because he had such an idyllic childhood. When we first got together, I pressed him constantly on his family life, and tried to imagine his mother as my mother. *Would a loving, caring mother have made a difference? Would I be less cynical, more affable, less stoic, more trusting?* My therapist would say, "Don't blame your mother for your perceived shortcomings. You can either play the victim or take responsibility for the way your life turns out. You make your own choices." Did we?

I swung my legs over the edge of the bed and steadied myself. Turns out sex was not the cure for what ailed me. I needed two Advil and a hot shower.

OUR FACETIME meeting with Carlos the Bartender-slash-Building Muralist had been postponed a few hours. Someone defaced one of his murals in Brooklyn and he needed to do a bit of repainting. An emergency, he said, because a production company planned to shoot a music video in front of it that very night.

I stared at the two whiteboards in my dining room. I had bought a second one when the single case morphed into two—the disappearance of Trudy and the murder of Ed. But now there was a third case. Eldridge had put Ray and Marty on the Renee Carter case, but the connection, however tenuous, was enough to warrant my inclusion. Ray promised to keep me apprised of any new developments.

I called Dad to let him know Carlos couldn't speak to us until later in the evening. The minute I hung up, my phone rang, and thinking it was Dad calling me back, I answered without looking at caller ID.

"Hi Dad, forget something?"

"Um, hello?" A woman's voice. "Is this Detective Susan Ford?"

"Yes, sorry, thought you were someone else." I pulled the phone away from my ear to look at the number. It was local.

"It's Joyce. Joyce Solomon. I have a favor to ask of you."

JOYCE AND Jake were seated in the front section of the coffee shop, along the windows that offered a view of Broadway, the main thoroughfare that ran through the town of Monticello. It was eleven thirty, too late for breakfast and too early for lunch, so we pretty much had the place to ourselves. Two men sat at the counter reading newspapers. Three mothers and three baby strollers were tucked into a back corner of the cafe.

Joyce and Jake sat across from each other, so I sat down next to Joyce. There was something familiar about Jake, but I was pretty sure I'd never met him. He rose slightly to shake my hand. If he stood up straight, he would tower over me. I was thinking six-two, six-three. Dark, looping curls framed his boyish face, making him appear younger than his forty-one years. He was handsome, with almond-shaped eyes, hazel with flecks of green. His cleft chin was deep and long, rendering the illusion of an upside-down heart. His hawkish nose gave him an aristocratic air. He definitely came from a gene pool of good looking people.

When Joyce called this morning, she said Jake wished to speak with me. The night before, she had told him everything. He had questions. Questions she couldn't answer, and she hoped that I might be able to fill in the blanks. I told her we still knew very little. But she insisted.

"What is it you want to know?" I asked.

"I would like to know more about this woman, Renee Carter, why I was in her possess—" he cleared his throat, "why was I with her, if she was not my birth mother, and I want to hear about the circumstances surrounding her death."

"At this time we don't have information regarding your birth parents or how you came to be in Renee's apartment. There is an investigation underway. As for her death, well, she was shot and buried along the highway in Ulster County. There was a small cross made of sticks and string near the remains. That usually indicates remorse and some kind of relationship or connection between the killer and the victim. In this case, between Renee and whoever caused her demise."

"Interesting," Jake said. "Go on."

"Either the murderer or an accomplice contacted your uncle and offered up the baby—you, that is—knowing that Joyce desperately wanted a child. We are chasing down a lead now." I turned to Joyce. "Do you know a Lenny Berman?"

She shook her head.

"Did she have any relatives or friends?" Jake asked. "Someone you can speak to? Maybe someone who knew my birth parents?"

"Detective Ray Gorman is looking into all that. I'm sorry to say that the police did not do a thorough job of investigating her disappearance. They assumed she simply left the area. Have you thought about doing a DNA search? That's how we found you. Your arrest for a bar brawl a few years back put you in our system."

"Oh yeah, that. I was just breaking up a fight, although no one believed me at the time. I always thought I was in the wrong place at the wrong time. But now I'm beginning to think I was in the right place at the right time." He turned to Joyce and then back to me. "If it wasn't for my DNA on file, I would have never found out the truth." Joyce lifted her hand to place over Jake's curled fist, but he inched his hand away. "How do I go about doing a DNA search?"

"I've never done it, but I have friends who have. They ordered a DNA test kit from a company called Ancestry. You simply spit in a tube, mail it back, and they analyze the results. If you have relatives who've done it, you can find them through the site if they've opted to make their results public. My friend found a number of distant cousins."

Jake gulped down the last of his coffee. "Well, it's something to think about."

BY THE time we got on FaceTime with Carlos, it was close to eight o'clock. Once again, Dad and I were seated side by side on his couch trying to get both our faces into the frame. Carlos sat patiently still as we maneuvered the laptop.

He was an exceedingly handsome man. Tan, with deep wrinkles. Two rows of perfectly straight teeth, each gleaming like a freshly-painted picket fence. Eyebrows arched like little tents above moon-shaped eyes. A long goatee, speckled gray, tapered down to just above his heart.

"You're still as cute as a button," Carlos said. His voice, a deep baritone, magnified his attractiveness.

Was I cute? I was pretty sure at thirteen I wasn't cute. Frizzy hair, pimply face, bushy eyebrows weren't exactly features I would call cute.

"I remember you and Lori Roth ordering Shirley Temples with extra cherries and twirling on the barstools, pretending to be adults drinking at the bar."

"You have a great memory," I said wryly, trying to conjure up spinning and role-playing but drawing a blank. Why were some memories like flashing neon lights, bright and easy to visualize, while others—like this one—dim and elusive? "So, Trudy?"

"Ah yes, sweet woman, but . . . how should I put this?" He paused, then said, "Jittery. Always seemed anxious, on edge."

"Yes, we've gotten that impression from others. You mentioned you overheard an argument with Stanley Roth and Trudy Solomon that you think has relevance to the case?"

"Yes. The reason for this call! We were short-staffed in the nightclub one night, so Trudy offered to help out after her shift in the coffee shop."

"And this was when?" Dad asked.

"I'd say late June. Definitely before July Fourth weekend. I remember because we usually didn't get busy until that weekend, but there was some kind of convention or large group at the hotel, and we weren't fully staffed for the summer yet."

"Got it. Just trying to establish a time line."

"Sure, I understand. It was the end of the night and Trudy was in the back area cleaning up and I was at the bar closing out the cash register. Mr. Roth walks in, plops down on a barstool and says, 'Hey PR, give me a Johnny Walker Black and soda.'"

"PR?" I asked.

"Yeah, that's what he called me. PR for Puerto Rican. And, trust me, it wasn't a term of endearment. He knew how to put people in their place. PR get me this. PR get me that. And never a tip. Cheap bastard. Anyway, he hears Trudy yell out to me that she's almost finished. He then asks me if that's Trudy Solomon back there and I tell him it is. He slams his drink down and stomps back there. At first I don't hear much, but then I hear voices raised. I peek in to make sure she's all right. Mr. Roth has his finger right up to her chin and calls her a . . . the 'c' word. He then tells her to keep her f-ing mouth shut. Then he storms out. Trudy was shaking like a leaf. I asked her what that was all about, and she just said it was nothing and that she had it under control. Well, it didn't look like nothing to me. But she told me to let it go."

"Did you ever see an incident like this again—between the two of them?"

"No. But I quit at the end of July. Mr. Roth was just too much of an a-hole to put up with. I was just starting to paint seriously then. Decided to move to the city and take some classes and check out the gallery scene."

After thanking him for sharing this story, Dad asked him questions about a few of his murals. He had researched some of Carlos's work and was curious about how he got started. I thought it would appear rude to get up, so I remained planted on the couch.

"I was hawking my paintings in Washington Square Park until a friend of a friend asked me to paint a mural on the side of a library building in Harlem to promote literacy. A news crew came out when it was done, and then things started to click. Commissions were slow at first, but steady enough to afford the crazy downtown rents. My big break came in 1984, when I was commissioned to paint a mural in Washington, D.C., honoring the two hundred and thirty-seven marines killed in Beirut. After that, well, let's just say, I'm not in danger of starving anytime soon. Once a PR bartender at the Cuttman Hotel working for a bigoted SOB, now a well-known muralist. Go figure. And what is Mr. Roth doing? Last I heard, drooling and losing his marbles. Y'know what that is right there? That's karma."

WHEN I arrived home, I found Ray perched at the edge of the recliner absorbed in *Game of Thrones*—a battle scene in which zombie-like skeletons were attacking a ragtag army fleeing by boat. I lingered at the threshold between the entranceway and living room, letting the scene play out. I tiptoed in and sat on the couch. He reached for the remote and hit the pause button.

"So, did you learn anything?" he asked.

"I think we now know why Trudy would have been looking for another job. She was scared of Stanley. He threatened her to be quiet about something. Maybe Stanley was trying to protect Scott. But that still doesn't explain why she just up and left without telling anyone."

"Perhaps you should see Stanley when you're in Florida. You're still going, right?"

"Yeah, we're still heading down to get some answers out of Scott. But Stanley's got health issues, and I told Meryl I wouldn't badger him. I'm going to stick to that promise." For now at least.

CHAPTER EIGHTEEN

Tuesday, November 13, 2018

SALLY ESCORTED Mordecai Little to a small, windowless room in the precinct, where Eldridge, Ray, Marty, and I were already assembled. Six chairs were pushed up against one wall, but I think we were all too antsy to sit. At least I know I was. Four computers—two PCs and two Macs—sat on a long table pushed up against the wall across from the door. A 65-inch television monitor hung on the wall perpendicular to the bank of computers. Ryan Beamer, our forensic tech guy, was seated in front of one of the PCs.

Mordecai shook hands with Eldridge and nodded in my direction, momentarily making eye contact. He took a seat at the computer table, pulled a laptop from his briefcase, placed it in-between two of the desktop units, then fired it up. We watched quietly as Ryan configured Mordecai's laptop to play, via Bluetooth, on the television monitor. When the two screens mirrored each other, Mordecai retook the reins and logged into his webcam feed—he refused to divulge his password to anyone, so he was in the driver's seat. He scrolled through dates until the cursor landed on August 25, 2018.

"Ready?" Mordecai asked, glancing around—his curled *payot* moving to and fro as his head swiveled.

Everyone nodded and mumbled some form of yes—*yeah, yup, uh-huh*. He clicked on the link. He slid the time marker to eleven o'clock, around the time the boys said they showed up at the warehouse, and hit play. One car was already there, a Toyota Camry. In it, you could make out the silhouettes of Calvin Barnes, Melvin Barnes, and Wayne Railman. My hands were warm and moist, so I wrapped them around the chilled Diet Coke can in front of me. At eight minutes past eleven, they got out of the car and huddled by the trunk. They talked for about three minutes. Then Calvin stretched his arms above his head like he was warming up to exercise.

"Go back," I shouted.

Mordecai slid the time marker slightly to the left.

"There. Right there. Stop it there."

"Holy Toledo," Eldridge said.

Tucked into Calvin's jeans was what appeared to be a Glock 45-caliber pistol.

"We did not recover a Glock 45," Marty said.

"Then where the fuck is it?" I asked.

"Mr. Little, our apologies. Please continue," Eldridge said, shooting me a one-more-outburst-like-that-and-you're-out-of-here look.

Wayne opened the trunk and Calvin removed a cardboard box about the size of a microwave oven, presumably filled with the drugs. Melvin lifted out a scale. Wayne pulled out the Sig Sauer P938 he shot me with and shut the trunk. Wayne whispered something in Calvin's ear and Calvin nodded. Then they headed toward the entrance of the abandoned warehouse. Thirteen minutes later, Wayne emerged from the warehouse. He turned his back to the camera and assumed a peeing position, the bulge of the Sig Sauer visible in his waistband.

When headlights illuminated the darkness, he zipped up and sauntered back into the warehouse. Melvin then came out and leaned against the trunk of his car as a Jeep Cherokee rolled up behind it. The two buyers emerged and were led into the warehouse. The time marker read 11:33. At eleven-forty, the headlights from my Prius can be seen bouncing off the two cars as I approached. I parked my car perpendicular to the Jeep. I got out of my car but left the door wide open. I walked over to a side window and peered in. I hurried back to my car to fish my phone out of the console and called for backup.

I headed back to the window to monitor the situation inside. I stood by the window for nearly five minutes. Then I crept over to the warehouse entrance.

I remembered exactly what I was thinking: *They're packing up, getting ready to leave, and backup is almost here. I can get everyone down on their bellies and keep them mollified until backup arrives.* What the hell was I thinking? Me against five guys doing a drug deal. What I should have done was quietly move my car out of sight and wait. If backup failed to show before they left, I could have opened an investigation and set up a sting.

Do it the right way.

Instead, now I was sitting in this stuffy room with an aching leg, sweaty palms, and a blazing headache, watching a grainy black-and-white video. A video I hoped would save my ass.

"SO NOW what?" I asked Eldridge.

"We searched that place high and low, Susan. No one found a Glock," Marty replied.

"Well, it didn't just disappear into thin air. And this time around, how about we search the place higher and lower," I spat out in a tangle of desperation and anger.

"Susan, you're not doing any searching. I'll get the guys on that as soon as possible," Eldridge said. "Meanwhile, Marty, you head down to Woodbourne Correctional and interrogate the hell out of Melvin and Wayne. And folks, I don't want to be reading about this new piece of evidence in the newspaper. I will inform the sheriff, but it doesn't go beyond that. We don't need this leaking until we know what happened to that gun. I don't want the void filled with conjecture."

"What about telling Rhonda? She's been helping drum up support for me among the BLM activists. I think it's important she knows. She'll keep it quiet, I know she will. If we're going to gain her trust, I'm pretty sure holding evidence back from her is not a way to earn it. Let's treat her like she's on our side—because she actually is."

"Let me think about it. But for now, mum's the word."

"You're mighty quiet about this," I said to Ray when we were alone in the room.

"Just taking it all in."

"What do you think happened to the gun?"

"I've got a theory kicking around in my head." Ray squinted and scratched at his cheek, thinking through whatever crazy idea was floating around in his noggin. "Maybe Wayne or Calvin kicked it under a stack of pallets. There were a ton of them in the warehouse at the time. Some stacked eight feet high. Maybe there wasn't a thorough-enough search under those things. You said that Wayne ran to Calvin after you shot him. You were down on the ground at that point with your own injury. You might have missed what happened."

I closed my eyes and tried to visualize the scene. "There was a stack of pallets about three feet to the right of Calvin."

"There you go. And then, when Wayne and Melvin learn no Glock was found, they're thinking you'll get blamed for killing an unarmed teenager. Melvin's revenge for you killing his brother."

"Interesting theory, but the warehouse has been cleared out. If there was a gun under those pallets, someone would've seen it."

"Or taken it."

CHAPTER NINETEEN

Thursday, November 15, 2018

THE PLANE was delayed a couple of hours due to inclement weather, pushing our arrival time at Palm Beach International Airport to two o'clock. The soupy combination of heat and humidity greeted us as we stepped out of the terminal to wait for the shuttle that would take us to the rental-car outpost.

Before takeoff, Eldridge had called to assure me that Marty would spend the next couple of days hunting down the Glock. Ray thought that even if they didn't find the gun, the video just might be enough to fully exonerate me. Eldridge wanted as much proof as possible, which meant finding the gun and pressuring Melvin and Wayne to recant their concocted story. But when Marty went to interview Melvin Barnes yesterday, he didn't budge from his original testimony. "*Calvin didn't have no gun.*" When Marty showed him the video, Melvin shrugged and accused him of video manipulation. "*That shit looks photoshopped to me. You cops know every trick in the book.*" That prompted Eldridge to send the video feed to a digital forensics lab for authentication to ward off any further accusations of evidence tampering.

By the time I got to the rental counter my well-behaved curls were having a temper tantrum. I extracted an elastic hairband from my baggage and pulled my frizzy mane back in a high ponytail, where it would probably stay for the next few days.

"Cute do," Dad said when I met him outside the men's bathroom. "We all set?"

On our way to the Holiday Inn in Boca Raton, we rehashed our plan. Namely, how we would convince Scott to divulge what he knew. He was the keeper of two puzzle pieces—and in my estimation, the most critical pieces of information to solving this thing. First, why did he think his father killed Trudy Solomon? Second, why did he go to see Ed and Trudy in Waltham?

After checking in, we decided to get a bite to eat before heading over to Scott's house, which was situated along the intracoastal in Deerfield Beach. We figured we had a better chance of catching him at home later in the evening, after work. Besides, after a month of ice and snow, a leisurely dinner on an outdoor patio was hard to resist. Perhaps it was the consequence of a long travel day or the heat we were not used to, but neither of us talked much during dinner. We limited ourselves to one drink, a local IPA, one of those overly hoppy brews that were all the rage.

I glanced around at my fellow diners. The patrons were chic and well coifed. My old jeans and faded T-shirt made me think of that classic Sesame Street lyric, "One of these things is not like the others."

When it was time to go, Dad grabbed the check. "This little expedition is on me. Remember?"

SCOTT'S HOUSE was lit up to the point where we thought he might be having a party. But there were no cars in his driveway or on the street in front of his house. Even the path lights, flanking a stone walkway across his lawn, were illuminated.

"Well, here goes nothing," Dad said as he opened the car door.

I've done the "we need to ask you a few questions" stroll up to doorsteps hundreds of times, but this time felt different. Really different. Nerve-wracking. Stomach-lurching. Throat-tightening. My entire body was as sweaty as my palms. I swallowed hard a few times.

It was all I could do to keep my shit together before coming face-to-face with someone from the Roth family. I could have just walked back to the car and let Dad do the interview. He could certainly handle this without me.

About halfway up the walkway, Dad stopped (perhaps sensing my desire to make a dash for the car). He stepped in front of me, grabbed my upper arms, and bore his eyes into mine. "Susan, you can do this. These aren't the Roths from your youth. They hold no power or superiority over us anymore." I nodded perfunctorily. He released my arms and we continued up the walkway to the door.

Dad reached for the doorbell. The one light that wasn't on, the porch light, flickered to life. A young woman, about thirty years old, opened the wood door. She did not open the glass storm door. The resemblance was uncanny. Lori Roth. Same hair, wavy and auburn. Same eyes, round and hazel. Same eyelashes, long and thick. Same chin, pointy with a clef.

"May I help you?" she said loudly, her voice penetrating the glass door.

"Is Scott home? I'm an old friend from Upstate New York," I yelled. "I'm—we're—working on an old missing-persons case that we think Scott can help us with."

She unlocked the glass door, wedging it open about six inches. "Okay. He's working in his office upstairs right now. What are your names? I'll let him know you're here."

"I'm Susan Ford, and this is my dad, Will Ford. I am . . . *was* friends with his sister, Lori."

She closed the wood door. But not all the way. Three minutes later she swung open the wood door and stepped outside.

"He can't see you right now. He's on a call. He asked me to take your phone number and he'll give you a call."

"We're only in town for a couple of days," Dad said. "We are happy to wait out here until he finishes his phone call."

"Please go. He made it pretty clear he doesn't want to talk to you tonight."

"Are you his daughter?" I asked.

"Yes. Amanda—Mandy."

"Nice to meet you, Mandy. You look just like your aunt—Lori," I said.

"So I've been told." She smiled coyly and the resemblance became even more pronounced. "I haven't seen her in years. But we keep in touch through Facebook and Instagram."

"Can you let your dad know we just want to ask him a few questions? He's not in any trouble. We just need him to fill in some blanks about an old case we are working on," I said, scribbling my phone number on a page in my note pad.

Mandy took the paper and tucked it into her jeans pocket. "I'll be sure to give this to him."

When we got halfway down the walkway, I turned around. Except for one lamp-lit room on the second floor and the flickering of a television on the first floor, the house was now completely dark.

"I don't know, Dad. This might have been a wasted trip. If I was a betting girl, I would put long odds on getting a phone call from him."

"Maybe we pay a visit to the dealership."

"He owns four dealerships. Two are within fifteen miles of here, but the other two are several hours away." A melodious *beep-beep* rang out as I unlocked the car doors. "Are you suggesting we drive to each one?"

CHAPTER TWENTY

Friday, November 16, 2018

IT WAS six in the morning. The sun had lifted off from the horizon about fifteen minutes earlier. Deep crimson and bright purple clouds dotted the eastern sky. I yawned. One of those big, vocal ones that last a good five seconds.

I peeled back the tab on my plastic coffee lid and took a sip. Dad fiddled with the radio tuner, landing on a local sports station. A chocolate croissant smiled at me atop the dashboard. Dad bit into his blueberry muffin and an avalanche of crumbs cascaded down his shirt and into his lap.

"This really brings me back," Dad said. "Stakefast, we used to call it." He brushed the muffin crumbs onto the floor.

We were parked three houses down from Scott's driveway. Our hope was that he would turn right out of his driveway toward his Delray Beach dealership, so we wouldn't have to bank a U-y. If he decided to go to his dealership in Pompano, he'd probably be heading our way, and we'd have to duck out of sight before we started tailing him. That meant we risked losing him if his destination was one of the other two dealerships, the one in Vero Beach or the one in Miami. I still couldn't believe Dad had talked me into this insane ploy.

As each hour ticked by, the temperature climbed a few degrees. The TV weatherman assured us it would be less humid today. I reached around to the cooler perched on the backseat and grabbed a bottled water. I eyed the sandwiches, potato chips, and the six-pack of Diet Pepsi we had bought at Publix last night, just in case we got stuck here through lunch (I did manage to convince Dad that six o'clock in the evening was quitting time). I was already hungry and it was only nine-thirty.

At ten o'clock, a car appeared at the edge of Scott's driveway. It inched out and the distinctive Mercedes grill came into view. He turned right. I counted to five and then pulled away from the curb. Ten minutes later we arrived at Roth Mercedes Motors. I snagged a spot across the street from the entrance. Scott turned into the dealership lot and parked in front of a metal signpost marked "Reserved." When he emerged from his car, I raised my binoculars and adjusted the dial to zoom in on his face. It had been quite a while—forty years to be exact—since I had last laid eyes on him. He had not aged well. Maybe it was the paunch. Maybe the lack of hair—he was nearly bald, except for a few strands of hair that stood straight up like baby grass sprouting from newly seeded soil.

"Ready to do some car shopping?" Dad asked.

"A Mercedes? I wish."

My anxiety from the day before had been replaced with Zen-like calm. Perhaps it was because now that I'd seen him, he didn't remind me of the Scott I knew in my youth. Or perhaps it was because the element of surprise was gone. This didn't feel like much of an ambush.

He had to know we were coming. He could have hidden out in his house or ditched us, but he didn't. He drove to his nearest dealership, almost making it too easy. If this was a game of cat and mouse, he made for a lousy rodent.

We stepped into the brightly lit showroom. A thirtysomething woman broke from a group of suited-up men. Her four-inch stiletto heels click-clacked on the white tile as she hurried toward us like a heat-seeking missile. To her, we probably looked like two dupes looking to buy a fancy car. Her cream-colored blouse did little to hide the outline of her lace bra. Definitely intentional. Her ample backside was squeezed into a black pencil skirt. Hair like Morticia Addams—long, shiny, straight, licorice black. Skillfully applied makeup accentuated her wide eyes, high cheekbones, and full lips. She was both intimidating and accessible. Presumably, a perfect combination of assertiveness and cool poise to be a successful luxury-car salesperson.

"Welcome to Roth Mercedes. Have a car in mind, or browsing?" she asked, with a practiced vocal fry. She held out her hand. "I'm Christie Lamont."

Dad grinned like a besotted school boy and shook her hand. "It's a pleasure to meet you."

I cleared my throat. "Actually, we are here to see Scott Roth," I said. "I have a feeling he's expecting us."

"Um, okay. Follow me."

I smacked Dad's arm when I caught him ogling her rear end. *STOP IT!* I mouthed.

We ascended a spiral staircase, the centerpiece of the showroom, to a floor of glass-enclosed offices. Probably for the guys in finance who are called in at the last minute of a deal to sell you the unnecessary extras—floor mats, rust protection, extended warranty, mud flaps. At the end of the hallway was a door to a private office. The affixed plaque read SCOTT ROTH. Christie knocked on the door to the beat of "Shave and a Haircut . . . Two Bits."

"Come in."

She opened the door and poked her head in. The unmistakable scent of Lemon Pledge escaped. "A couple of folks here to see you, Scott."

"Yes, I've been expecting them."

Christie ushered us into Scott's expansive office, then stepped back out and closed the door. The room felt more like a movie set than a place where actual work got done. On one side of the rectangular space, a toffee-hued leather couch with two matching leather chairs formed a semicircle around a mahogany coffee table. *Modern Dealership*, *Dealer Magazine*, and *Auto Dealer Today* were meticulously layered in three piles, tiered with the most recent issue of each magazine on top, only the titles of the older issues peeking out from underneath. On the other side of the office, Scott was seated in a leather swivel chair behind a massive mahogany desk. The stapler was positioned perfectly parallel to, and in-between, a Scotch Tape dispenser and a Post-it Notes dispenser—all branded with the Roth Motors logo. Twenty or so cobalt-blue ballpoints, also sporting the Roth Motors logo, poked out of the pen holder. No errant clear plastic Bic or No. 2 pencil to break up the uniformity. The only item on the leather-lined desk blotter was a closed spiral notebook, about the size of my old diary. A pen stand with two fancy pens was positioned dead center above the blotter. On the mahogany credenza behind Scott was a Dell computer, the screen black. Next to the computer sat a tiered folder holder, each slot containing one manila folder. Each folder's purpose designated by a type-written label on its tab. The intense order of everything made me uncomfortable.

For Dad, this must have been nirvana. Scott motioned us to sit in the plush upholstered chairs across from him.

"I take it you're here regarding Trudy Solomon," Scott said. His voice flat and monotone. No pleasantries to start the conversation. No *Hi Suzie, great to see you after all these years*. He continued, "I heard from Meryl that you found her. Case closed, right? So, what's your purpose in stalking me?"

"We've got a few unanswered questions," Dad said. "Questions we thought you might want to avoid answering. For instance, you knew back in 2007 she was alive and well, yet you never reported this to the Monticello police. Why?"

"You know about that, huh? Well, to what end? She was alive. And the case was long closed. I figured, let her live her life the way she wanted to. It was obvious to me she wanted to remain missing. She had no relatives, and she told me she didn't want Ben to know where she was."

"Was she afraid of Ben?" I asked.

"How would I know? I just know she wanted a new life. Is that it? Are we done here?"

"Not quite." I paused, holding his emotionless gaze for a few seconds. "We interviewed a few hotel workers and guests from that summer, and they were all under the impression that you thought your dad killed her. Now, why would that be?"

His head remained forward, but his eyes fixed on the ceiling. He shook his head slowly, then puckered his lips so that they disappeared into his mouth. He rested his pointer finger under his nose and his thumb under his chin. "Not ringing any bells for me. They must be mistaken."

"All of them? Mistaken?" Dad asked.

"Memories fade. Or get warped. This was forty years ago and I was eighteen years old. You expect me to recall what I said or thought in 1978?"

"Okay. So how about 2007? That's just eleven years ago. Why did you go see Ed and Trudy?" I asked.

"I ran into them on the street in Boston and they invited me over."

I wondered how long it took him to come up with that line. He had eleven years to settle on the reason he was in their apartment, should anyone ask him, and this was what he was going with?

"I think we are done here. I'm sorry I couldn't have been of more help." He stood up.

"We know about the extortion. We know you went there to discuss it with Ed. We also suspect the blackmail scheme is tied to his murder." Dad recited it exactly the way he had practiced. Assertive but not overly threatening.

Scott's stoic expression dissolved. In its place, a fusion of surprise and anger. A whisper of flush surfaced on his cheeks and spread upward to his forehead. "Get out of my office now," he barked in staccato, as if each word were its own sentence.

"Looks like we hit a nerve there, Susan," Dad said without taking his eyes off Scott. "This is a murder investigation, Scott. There is no statute of limitations on murder. So, I suggest you do yourself a favor and tell us what the hell you were doing at Trudy's in 2007."

Scott clearly understood we were out of our jurisdiction, with flimsy evidence, and no authority to actually arrest him. He had no intention of cooperating or shedding any light on the case and seemed to take great pleasure in showing us out of his showroom with nothing to show for it.

Turned out Dad had a Plan B.

TRUDY

TRUDY HEARD two men arguing outside her room. She held her palms over her ears.

Dr. Meadows poked his head in. "You okay?"

"Is that you, Ed?"

"No, Trudy. It's Dr. Meadows."

"Why are Scott and Ed fighting? Is this about the money?"

"No one is fighting. Just a little commotion in the hallway."

She could have sworn she just heard Ed shouting that they deserved every penny. Only he said goddamn penny.

"They were fighting about the money," Trudy insisted.

"Well, everything is fine now," Dr. Meadows replied.

Trudy knew everything was not fine. Why was Dr. Meadows lying? "Ed is really mad. Scott wants us to stop. Said twelve years is enough. But Ed said no."

"What needs to stop?"

"The money. That's what they're fighting about," Trudy replied, confused that Dr. Meadows wouldn't know this. Didn't he just hear them fighting? "Every month. Like clockwork. Tick. Tock. Can't stop."

"No need to worry about that anymore, Trudy." Dr. Meadows smiled and closed the door.

The two men started arguing again. Then she heard a loud knock on the door. Ed told her to be quiet. That the police were outside. That he would do all the talking.

CHAPTER TWENTY-ONE

Saturday, November 17, 2018

DAD CALLED the airline last night, canceled our flight back to New York, and rebooked us on an early-morning flight to Logan Airport in Boston.

He had gotten in touch with Ed Resnick's siblings the day before after our fiasco of a meeting with Scott and they'd agreed to meet with us. ("And hey, since we are going to be in Massachusetts, why not visit Trudy Solomon?" Dad said.)

Sure, why not? As long as we got back in time for Thanksgiving. Natalie would never speak to us again if we failed to show up for the one holiday she seemed to cherish above all others. ("What's better than a whole day of cooking, eating, and washing dishes with family?" she reminded me every year. "Root canal?" I always replied.)

The flight was uneventful—on-time takeoff, landing fifteen minutes earlier than scheduled. Naomi Resnick lived south of Boston, in a coastal town called Hull. That's where Dad arranged to meet both Naomi and her brother, Alfred. The Alzheimer's facility Trudy lived in was north of Boston. Our plan was to see her the next day.

Dad fiddled with Google Maps as I drove us out of the rental car parking lot towards 93 South. Estimated driving time, forty-five minutes. I hated driving around cities I didn't know. Especially ones like Boston, notorious for confusing road signs and impatient drivers. And rotaries.

A couple of miles after crossing the Hull town line, we passed through a two-block commercial district—grocery store, bank, real-estate office, hardware store, nail salon, bakery, diner, pharmacy, liquor store, sub shop, post office. As the saying goes, "Blink and you'd miss it." Then came streets designated from A through Z (although the last street sign we passed was XYZ Street, so perhaps they ran out of streets along this stretch). We continued on a narrow two-lane road that separated the ocean from the bay, driving past a lifesaving museum, a yacht club, a cemetery, and what appeared to be an overdeveloped cluster of condominiums built on a tiny island connected to the peninsula by a bridge. As we approached a bend in the road, Google Maps directed us to take a right and a couple of lefts. "*Your destination is on the right.*" We pulled up in front of a brown foursquare in need of a paint job.

Naomi must have seen us pull up. She opened the door and stepped out onto the porch cradling a fluffy white dog.

She waved.

As we climbed the three steps, she said, "I wanted Popeye to meet you out here. He's very excitable and pees in the house when strangers walk in."

"Cute . . . dog," Dad said. Dad didn't consider these little dogs, dogs. He considered them glorified cats. ("Dogs have owners. Cats have staff," he would joke, quoting a T-shirt that walked past him one day.) He was not a fan of cats . . . or little dogs.

"Popeye, now you be a good boy. No pee-pee." She looked up. "Would you mind letting him sniff you? It would really help," she said, reverting back to an adult voice.

Dad and I held our hands under the dog's nose. I glanced down at the welcome mat: AHOY MATEY, WELCOME ABOARD. After this ten-second meet and greet, Naomi held open the door and directed us to a navy-blue sofa. Blue-and-white-striped pillows embroidered with anchors were lined up along the cushions. The lamps were replicas of lighthouses. A ship's wheel hung on the wall facing the sofa, flanked by a pair of long oars. The coffee table was a flat-top lobster trap (not a replica, the real deal) with a thick pane of glass on top and several reddish plastic lobsters inside. A collection of shells and sea glass laid in piles on the window sills.

Naomi headed to the kitchen and quickly reappeared with a pitcher of lemonade and a plate of chocolate chip cookies. She handed us coasters constructed of nautical rope and placed the pitcher on a fish-shaped tray. When I lifted a cookie from the plate, an octopus's eye stared up at me.

A toilet flushed upstairs. A few moments later, a gray-haired man descended the stairs, gripping the banister and taking one step at a time.

"Hello everyone," he said when he reached the floor. He took a few steps and held out his hand to Dad. "Alfred Resnick. Naomi told me you were stopping by to discuss Trudy and Ed. That you might have a new lead in Ed's murder."

He shook my hand and sat down on the leather recliner—the one piece of furniture that felt out of place in this over-the-top, under-the-sea decor motif.

"Well, we appreciate you seeing us on such short notice," I said. "We won't take up too much of your time."

"Let's start at the beginning," Dad said. "What can you tell us about Trudy and Ed when they arrived in Rochester?"

Alfred gave a go-ahead nod to Naomi. "They wanted us to be quiet about their whereabouts. To pretend they were married. Trudy claimed she was in fear of her life. So we played along."

"Who was she afraid of?" I asked.

"She didn't say."

"Her husband?"

"Perhaps. But like I said, they told us very little, and we respected their privacy," she said. Naomi glanced at Alfred again. He nodded. "There's something else you should know. Well, maybe you know already." She cleared her throat. "Trudy was pregnant."

I puckered my lips to suppress the outburst of *what the fuck* exploding in my head.

Dad didn't even flinch. "Go on," he said flatly. He once told me that a successful interrogation is like a poker game—never give away what's in your hand and you stand a better chance of winning. He thinks people tend to blab if they think they are telling you something you already know.

"She wasn't showing when they got to Rochester, but it didn't take long until it was noticeable. The thing was . . . Trudy was not handling the situation well . . . in her mental state."

"Her mental state?" I asked.

"Ed said she suffered from anxiety, bouts of depression. Made worse by . . . " Naomi scooped her hands around her belly. "We weren't sure she could handle caring for a baby, let alone two."

"Two?" I asked, poker face intact. At least I thought so.

"Twins."

I wanted to stand up, release the tension building inside me. But I didn't want to interrupt this flow of information. I also didn't want to appear rattled. But what the hell was going on? Ben's babies? Ed's babies? Lenny's babies? Stanley's babies? Scott's babies? Someone else's babies?

Whose fucking babies were these?

As though reading my mind, Dad asked, "Was Ed the father?"

"He didn't say. We didn't ask," Alfred said.

"If you had to guess?"

"Honestly, I don't know. *We* don't know," Naomi said, eyeballing her brother. "Al and I weren't close to Ed, and we got the feeling their predicament was none of our business. At one point, he had to have Trudy hospitalized. She was on the verge of a nervous breakdown—practically catatonic in the last few months of her pregnancy, waiting for it all to be over. Like I said, she was in no condition to handle the stress of motherhood. And we got the feeling Ed wasn't keen on being a dad."

"What happened to the babies?" Dad asked.

"They were put up for adoption. There was an adoption agency in New York City that specialized in placing twins. So Ed managed all that."

"We did a search on Trudy's social security number. We did not find a mental hospital or any hospital stay in 1978 or '79."

"All I know is that the adoption agency covered all the expenses. That might explain why," Naomi said.

"Abortion was legal in 1978. Why didn't she just have an abortion?" I asked, getting myself back into this conversation with a question Dad would probably never ask. Which was made crystal clear when he shot me a look that said, *I can't believe you just went there.*

"We weren't privy to why they made that decision, but I think the adoption agency applied a lot of pressure."

"Okey dokey," Dad said, his verbal cue for pivoting to a new line of questioning. "We were told that a woman gave them five thousand dollars to start a new life. Was that you or your mother?"

Alfred snorted. "Besides the fact that she didn't have two nickels to rub together, our mother was as cheap as the day is long. There is no way she would give anyone that kind of money."

"You sure of that?" Dad asked.

"I can't be one hundred percent sure, but I would bet Popeye's life on it."

"Oh Al. Stop it. That's disgusting."

"You know what I mean," he said to Naomi. "You think Mom would give five thousand bucks to Ed?"

"No." She turned to me and Dad. "Al's right. Mom didn't have that kind of money. And if she did, she certainly wouldn't part with it. Our dad left her very little. She lived on a small fixed income. And no, I didn't give them the money. If he asked, I might have. But he didn't."

"Was Ed the youngest of the three of you?" I asked.

"Yes. He was a bit of a surprise baby. I'm ten years older than him. And Al is two years older than me. Our parents' marriage was on the rocks—maybe they thought a baby would bring them together."

"And did it?"

"Not really. They bickered all the time," Naomi said. "My teenage years weren't the happiest time of my life."

I nodded in solidarity, but caught myself when Dad turned his head in my direction.

"What does this have to do with Ed's death?" Alfred asked.

Dad replied, "We have reason to believe that Ed was extorting money from someone. Perhaps the person who got Trudy pregnant . . . assuming Ed is not the father. Or someone else who caused Trudy harm in some way. The two of them could've had dirt on someone and that someone was willing to pay Ed and Trudy to keep it from going public. That's what we are trying to figure out. And it's why we think their vanishing act in 1978 and Ed's murder in 2008 are related."

"Is it possible they got the original five thousand dollars from the person they were blackmailing?" Alfred asked.

"Anything is possible," I said. "But we were told by a friend of Ed's that the money was given as a gift to start a new life. Of course, Ed could have made that up. Maybe they were satisfied with that meager amount back in 1978, but then had a change of heart in 1995. That's when, according to the Waltham police, the money started showing up in Ed's bank account. In October 1995. Doesn't mean he wasn't getting cash before then and simply stuffing it under his mattress. But it could also mean that their departure from the area and this mystery money are not related and, for that matter, his murder was just a random act."

"We're trying to keep an open mind," Dad said. "But the more we know about *why* they left, the greater the likelihood we find the person being blackmailed . . . and, hopefully, our motive for murder."

"All these years we didn't say a word about her being in Rochester or the fact that she was pregnant," Naomi said. "We kept our promise to Ed. Even when the police contacted us about his death, we didn't bring up their past. Didn't think it was relevant. And they didn't ask. But when you called, we figured it was time to let someone know what we knew. And if there is a connection to Ed's death, I hope we were helpful to your investigation. Unfortunately, we don't know a whole heck of a lot. We moved to Massachusetts soon after they showed up in Rochester."

"When exactly did you move here?" I asked.

"Let's see . . . that would be soon after Trudy gave birth, which was in March 1979. My husband and I moved to Hull in June 1979. Al moved to Weymouth right before Christmas that same year. My husband got a job in the area, managing apartment buildings . . . and hired Al."

"Did you have contact with Trudy and Ed when they moved to Massachusetts?"

"Not really," Naomi said. "Like I said, we were never close. They didn't even tell us they moved to the state. We found out from my mother."

"I wish there was more we could tell you," Alfred said.

"We're hoping Trudy can shed some light," Dad said. "We're going to see her tomorrow."

Naomi and Ed exchanged glances.

"Good luck trying to get anything out of Trudy," Alfred said. "We visit her once in a while. She's pretty far gone. But there are days of mild lucidity. Maybe you'll catch a break."

"Sometimes she addresses you like you're one of her friends from back in the day," Naomi said. "One day I'm Rita, another day I'm Sandra. I've even been called Maxine. I think she is conjuring up old memories and reliving them in the present." She momentarily gazed off into space, a wistful expression on her face. "I just play along so as not to upset her."

"Hmm, interesting." I lifted a second cookie off the plate, revealing the tentacles of the octopus. "One last question. Do you know the name of the adoption agency?"

"Hold on one moment." Naomi left the room. Popeye followed her.

We sat quietly for a few minutes. Dad took a sip of lemonade and a bite of his cookie.

"You should come back to Hull in the summer. Beautiful beaches," Alfred said. "Naomi loves living near the ocean. As you can see, my sister's gone a little overboard with—"

Naomi reappeared with a scrapbook and sat down between me and Dad. Popeye lay on top of her feet. She turned a few pages and pointed to a picture of Trudy, looking very pregnant and sad, and Ed, expressionless. "I couldn't even get them to smile for this picture." She leafed through a few more pages and then stopped. She pulled back the plastic coating and released a business card. "Grace Wilson Adoption Services," she proclaimed. "I knew I saved it."

"Do you mind if I take the picture of Trudy and Ed? I can mail it back."

Naomi turned back to the page with the photograph of a melancholy Trudy and a glum Ed, carefully removed it, and laid it on the coffee table next to the business card. I took a picture of the business card and placed the photo in the front pouch of my backpack.

"Are those your parents?" Dad asked, pointing to a photograph beneath the plastic sleeve.

"Yes. Amelia and Max."

"My ex-wife, Vera, is from Rochester. Her parents are Ann and Walter Sherman. Know them?"

"Dad, Rochester is a big—"

"Did your wife—sorry, ex-wife—have an older brother named Donald?" Alfred asked.

"Why yes, she did."

"I went to school with Donald, but we weren't friends. I remember the family moved away when we were in middle school. I kind of remember his parents. Our mother was like a freelance bookkeeper. If memory serves me correctly, Walter owned a hardware store—I think she balanced his books twice a year."

"That's right. He did, owned it with one of his brothers," Dad said.

"Small world, huh? I don't remember Donald's sister . . . Vera, you say. Naomi, do you remember a Vera Sherman?"

"How old is she now?" Naomi asked.

"She's seventy-five," Dad said.

"That makes her two years younger than me, so not likely we crossed paths back then."

"Where is Donald, these days?" Alfred asked.

"Unfortunately, he resides at Saint Francis Cemetery in Phoenix, Arizona."

Alfred sighed and shook his head. "When you get to be our age that's a pretty common response to that question."

CHAPTER TWENTY-TWO

Sunday, November 18, 2018

I HAD forgotten to fully close the curtains before conking out last night, and now the morning sun was leaking into the room. I lifted my head off the pillow and eyed Dad, sound asleep in the queen bed next to me. This side trip was taking a big bite out of Dad's travel budget, so we decided to share a room. It was just one night.

I quietly slipped out of bed and into the clothes I'd worn the day before, which were beside the bed, piled on the floor. I checked my weather app. The temperature was hovering slightly north of fifty degrees. Nice enough for a walk on the beach. And since we didn't get to the beach in Florida, this would have to do. A puffy coat and UGGs instead of a bathing suit and flip-flops.

When I stepped outside, the clammy, briny, sulfuric scent of the ocean invaded my nasal cavities. A contradiction in scents: refreshing and acerbic. Seagulls squawked and screeched overhead as I made my way across the beach parking lot.

The sun was low in the sky, the wispy clouds reddish orange and yellow, reminiscent of the background in Edvard Munch's *The Scream* painting. I took a selfie—a one-handed scream face and texted it to Ray. He texted back a laughing-so-hard-I'm-crying emoji.

The tide was high, crashing rhythmically against the seawall, so I walked along the concrete promenade that ran parallel to the beach. An octagonal building came into view, piquing my curiosity. I crossed back over the main boulevard and found myself standing in front of a carousel, closed for the season.

On my way back to the hotel, I passed a shuttered arcade, a couple of boarded-up ice cream walk-up windows, and a closed beachwear shop. The only other human I spied was a man walking his dog along the promenade. Beach towns were like the Catskills—bipolar. Lonely and depressing during the winter. Raucous and lively during the summer. The people who lived in these places year-round either tolerated, ignored, or welcomed the ebb and flow of tourists and seasonal homeowners.

When I got back to the room, Dad was still out cold. *Should I wake him?* I was hungry.

I whispered, "Dad? Dad?"

He groaned.

"You hungry?" I said softly. "I walked past a diner. Wanna go?"

His eyes popped open. "Yeah."

DAD NODDED off on our drive north to Trudy. Without a passenger-seat navigator, I propped my phone up against the dashboard console and tried to take it easy around curves to keep it upright. I was in a good mood. This side trip was worth the time and expense. So Trudy was pregnant. That was quite the nugget of news. If she gave birth in March 1979, she got pregnant in June 1978. Dad and I had four theories. One, it was Ben's and she did not want to raise a child with him (for which, with what her roommate Rita told us, I wouldn't blame her one bit), and Ed didn't want to raise Ben's kids. Two, it was Ed's and she didn't want Ben to find out. But if that were the case, wouldn't Ed be more inclined to keep the babies? Three, she had an affair with a man who wouldn't—or couldn't—take responsibility. Perhaps this guy was married or was a hotel guest of a higher social status. Four, she was raped. That would explain her fear, her disappearing act, and their decision to not raise these babies. It might also explain the extortion scheme. But why wait seventeen years to start shaking down the rapist?

We had the name of the adoption agency. Not sure how helpful getting in touch with them would be. Such agencies tend to be closemouthed when it came to closed adoptions. And I was not sure what legal jurisdiction we had for opening sealed files.

Between Eleanor Campbell's uncanny memory and Alfred's description of his mother's penny-pinching ways, we felt fairly confident Ed's mother was not the person who had given Trudy and Ed the money. I was more of the mind that it was the woman wearing the blue-and-white scarf who visited Trudy right before her disappearance. For that matter, it could have been her friend, Maxine. But if it was, Maxine took that secret to her grave. And honestly, did it really matter? Obviously, someone had been willing to help.

"HELLO, TRUDY." Dad pulled up a chair to face her. "How are you today?"

Trudy smiled and nodded. She looked up at the nurse standing beside her—a woman whose age was hard to peg. Could've been as young as forty or as old as sixty. There was a rumor of a mustache on her upper lip, a few stiff hairs jutting from her chin. Her gray-streaked brown hair was pulled back and swirled into a tight bun. A stray bobby pin poked out the side of it.

"Trudy. These people say they are old friends of yours. From New York." She shot me a look: *Do not upset her*.

"Hi Trudy," I said, crouching down next to Dad's chair, one knee touching the floor for balance. "Do you remember living in Brooklyn, New York?"

Trudy smiled and nodded. I wasn't sure if she was nodding yes to my question, or just nodding. I looked up at the stone-faced nurse for clarification but got none.

"New York, New York," Trudy crooned in a high-pitched, babyish voice.

I took that for a yes. Natalie thought I might be able to jog some memories if I took her on a chronological stroll down memory lane using old photographs and newspaper articles, starting in Brooklyn and winding our way to Waltham. I reached into my backpack and pulled out a stack of pictures and papers. I showed her a picture of herself and Sandra Leer posing in front of her house in Mill Basin.

"Do you recognize the people in this photograph?"

"Me." Trudy pointed to her younger self. "Sandy like the beach." She pointed to Sandra.

Sandy. Sandra. Close enough. I handed her an old postcard—the main lobby of the Cuttman Hotel.

She slowly drew the postcard close to her nose and sniffed it. She handed it back to me and smiled broadly. "Work!"

"That's right. The Cuttman. You worked there as a coffee-shop waitress. You're doing great!" Next up, an old newspaper clipping of Rachel and Stanley receiving a community award. I placed it on her lap. "Do you know these people?"

When she looked down, her smile inverted. She turned her head away. When I removed the clipping, she folded her hands in her lap. A subtle gesture, but message received loud and clear. I placed the clipping on the bed next to her and continued. I held up a photocopied picture of Scott, circa late seventies, that I downloaded from Meryl's Facebook page.

Her smile reappeared. "Handsome."

"Did he hurt you?"

She bowed her head for a few seconds. When she looked up, she said, "Helped me."

"Helped you? How?"

Trudy grinned. "Nice. So nice. Handsome. My hero."

"Can you tell me how he helped you? Were you in trouble? Was someone else trying to hurt you?"

Trudy jolted forward and back while swinging her head from side to side. The nurse cleared her throat. I looked up at her. She had that don't-push-it-or-you'll-have-to-leave expression on her face. Fine. If Trudy's mind was not playing tricks on her, she tacitly confirmed that Scott was not the bad guy. But he knew something if he helped her. I shuffled the photos and found one of Ben. I held it up.

"Ben," she said flatly.

"Did he hurt you?"

"I don't like Ben."

"Why?"

She pushed my hand away. "Leave."

"That's enough," the nurse said. "She wants you to leave."

"No," Trudy barked. "I leave. I leave Ben."

I spun back toward Trudy. "Do you remember why you left Ben?"

Trudy shook her head vigorously as though she was trying to dislodge the memory. She looked at me and shrugged. "More pictures?"

I made quick eye contact with the nurse and she nodded approval. I showed Trudy Lenny's old mug shot. "Do you know him?"

She stared at his picture for a solid minute. "Maybe."

"Maybe?"

Trudy shrugged.

That morning, Ray had texted me a picture of Renee Carter he retrieved from her missing person's file. I held up my phone. "Do you know her?"

Trudy squinted at the screen. "Pretty." She shook her head no.

"Just because she says no or maybe, doesn't mean she didn't know these people," the nurse said. "If you were here yesterday or came back tomorrow, she might have a different answer."

"I understand." I picked up a photo from the top of the stack. "This is Ben's sister, Joyce. And your nephew, Jake."

"Joyce and Jake, Joyce and Jake," she sang in a high-pitched voice. "Bowling! Joyce likes to bowl. I can't bowl."

"That's right, Trudy. She's a champion bowler. Do you know where she got her baby?"

She pointed to my stack of photos. Lenny's mug shot visible on the top of the pile.

"Him? Lenny Berman? Are you sure?"

Her face lit up. "*Shhhh.* It's a secret. I know a secret. Ben said don't tell anyone or else."

So, she knew about this. Which means Ed probably knew about this. So this could be what the extortion scheme was about. But where would Lenny come up with two thousand dollars every month? People don't blackmail poor people. Blood from a stone.

"Or else, what?" I whispered.

"They'll take the baby away! Bye-bye baby."

"Speaking of babies . . ." I handed her the photograph Naomi Resnick had given me. She glanced at it and handed it back.

"Can I ask you about this photo?"

She nodded yes.

I pointed to Trudy's distended belly. "Who is the father of your babies?"

She pursed her lips tightly, creating a thin line where her mouth used to be. Then she opened her mouth and started making a clucking noise by pressing her tongue against the roof of her mouth and releasing it.

The nurse moved closer to Trudy. "You're upsetting her."

I placed my hand on Trudy's knee and whispered, "I'm sorry."

She stopped clucking and smiled. Naomi and Alfred had told us they would ask her this question on several occasions, and she'd refuse to answer every time.

And with a few more questions to go, I did not want to risk being tossed out by this overprotective nurse. I unfolded the police sketch of Ed and handed it to her.

"Ed." She tipped her head to one side and frowned. "He's dead." She stroked his pencil mustache.

"Who was Ed getting money from every month?"

"Money?" Trudy pressed her hands against her cheeks. Trudy dropped her hands and held them palm side up. She shrugged. "No money."

"I think it's time to wrap this up," the nurse said.

I took hold of Trudy's hand and squeezed it gently. "One last question, okay?" Trudy nodded. "Who took you to the hospital after Ed died?"

Trudy turned away from me and glanced down at her bed. She released my hand, lifted her finger and pointed to the newspaper clipping of Rachel Roth. "Martha."

CHAPTER TWENTY-THREE

Monday, November 19, 2018

THE AROMA of fresh coffee was worse than the alarm clock. You couldn't just hit snooze. Unable to resist its siren call, I tossed the blanket aside and dragged my ass out of bed. I had come home late the night before and knew Ray was downstairs, patiently waiting to chat about what Dad and I learned during this trip. I reported dribs and drabs through text messages and hasty phone calls, but he was itching to add his two cents and further explore theories, motives, and whatnot.

Before heading downstairs, I scrolled through the emails that had landed in my inbox overnight. Bed Bath and Beyond coupons, Groupon coupons, CVS coupons, Banana Republic coupons, Petco coupons. Coupons I never remembered to use when I actually bought something. One real email—from Dr. Blanchard—arrived at seven o'clock this morning. It was addressed to both me and Dad, but there was no response from Dad, so he probably hadn't seen it yet (or he hit "Reply" instead of "Reply All" and his response went to Dr. Blanchard and not me). Yesterday Dad emailed Dr. Blanchard a picture of Rachel Roth hoping she could confirm that Rachel was, indeed, "Martha." The doctor came through with a definitive "yes!" Nice to have corroboration when your star witness's brain was riddled with plaque. I forwarded Dr. Blanchard's email to Dad to let him know I'd seen this and to call me later.

"Hey, sleeping beauty." Ray poured coffee into a black mug and set it down on the table. "Thought you might be in need of this."

"I got an email from Dr. Blanchard this morning. She confirmed that Martha Stuart is Rachel Roth."

"What do you make of that? Why would Rachel be checking Trudy into a hospital under a false name . . . unless she had something to hide?"

"I know. The whole thing is crazy. But it sure is reason to head down to Florida again and have a come-to-Jesus chat with Rachel and Stanley. Dad no longer has to convince me that they're up to their eyeballs in this. I mean, what in the hell was Rachel doing in Massachusetts so soon after Ed's murder? If I had to guess, making sure Trudy doesn't talk. But what was she trying to hide—Trudy's pregnancy, the extortion scheme, or Ed's murder? Are these three things even related?"

"Can we change the subject for a sec?" Ray took a sip of his coffee. "Marty got ahold of the guy who owns the company that cleared the pallets out of the warehouse. He's out of town until Sunday—spending Thanksgiving in Pennsylvania. He told Marty he's welcome to come down to his office next week and look at the work order. The guys on the job would be listed."

"Nothing against Marty, but I sure wish you were lead on this."

"Eldridge doesn't want even the slightest whiff of conflict of interest associated with this case. You know that."

The doorbell rang and Ray and I simultaneously turned our heads toward the door.

"Expecting someone?" Ray asked.

"Oh shit. Totally forgot. I told Natalie I'd watch the kids so she can do some grocery shopping." I downed the ounce of lukewarm coffee left in my mug, secured the child locks on the cabinets, and psyched myself up for a morning of *Sesame Street* and peekaboo.

CHARLIE AND Harry were napping when Natalie returned to pick them up.

"Let's not disturb them," she whispered. "Besides, I'm dying to hear about your trip." Natalie listened attentively, nodding here and there, as though I were one of her patients working through a psychological problem. *Tell me more. How does that make you feel?*

"Who do you think is the father of Trudy's twins?"

Before I could answer, Natalie put her finger up to her lips and cocked her ear toward the stairs.

"Well, I guess that's my cue to head home and get them fed. You can tell me the rest on Thursday. Come early, if you want. I could use some help with the desserts."

Natalie and I had the kind of relationship I wished I'd had with my mother. Sure, she was always an easygoing kid, which definitely helped when it came to single parenting. As a teenager, she was rarely moody or angry. And if she got upset or found herself in a funk, it didn't last particularly long. Definitely a glass-half-full person. She liked school. She was decent in sports. She had a coterie of nice friends with, as far as I could tell, minimal drama among them. Unlike most of her peers' parents, who had their children later in life, I was only thirty when she hit puberty—my own teenage years still fairly fresh in my mind. Perhaps that made it easier to be more empathetic to the growing pains of adolescence. Many a night felt like a teenage sleepover. Nail painting. Face masking. Hair straightening. Record playing. She confided things I would never have told my mother: who she was crushing on, who tried pot, who smoked cigarettes. The older she got, the less she shared, but she trusted me enough to come to me if she needed my advice or perspective. My desire to be the mom my own mom wasn't loomed over nearly every decision I made, every piece of advice I doled out. The funny thing was, she looked exactly like my mother. Everyone who saw the newspaper photo of my mother winning the Miss Monticello pageant was blown away by the resemblance.

I helped Natalie strap the boys into their car seats. They would turn one on Thursday. Which fell on Thanksgiving this year. Every year, Natalie insisted we go around the table and proclaim what we were thankful for. Let's see: I was shot. (But I survived.) I was under investigation for shooting an unarmed teenager and there was a civil suit pending. (But he might have had a gun.) And I was running around chasing the ghosts of 1978. (But I had reconnected with Lori.) It was one hell of year. But there were two little things I was very grateful for—even when one of them suddenly bopped me in the head with his teething ring.

TRUDY

"TRUDY, THIS is Belinda Mann, your new nurse," Dr. Meadows said. "She's from New York, just like you."

"Why Trudy, it's so nice to meet you," Belinda drawled.

She's not from New York, Trudy thought. Not with that accent. She sounded like that grandma on The Beverly Hillbillies. *She sounded like that woman from . . . from . . . that place.*

"Are you here for the babies?"

"The babies?" Belinda glanced over at Dr. Meadows, who nodded. "What about the babies?"

"You said I had a gift to give." Trudy turned away, toward the window. The sunlight was streaming in between the slats. Trudy

stared until it hurt her eyes, so she squeezed them tight. "You said you'd take care of everything. Isn't that why you're here?"

Dr. Meadows whispered into Belinda's ear.

"Yes Trudy, I'll take care of everything."

"Ed said this is our little secret. You won't tell anyone, okay?"

"Don't worry Trudy. I'm good at keeping secrets."

So many secrets. A person can't live with all these secrets. "Ed promised me that after we give them away, I'd get better. The pain would go away." But the pain seemed locked inside—taken root, unwilling to budge. Like when you pull an ugly weed—it was impossible to get the last little bit of the thing. It finds a way to live again.

CHAPTER TWENTY-FOUR

Wednesday, November 21, 2018

FELICIA STAPLETON placed two chocolate-frosted cupcakes on the edge of her desk. "Your last session," she said, nudging one of the cupcakes in my direction.

I leaned forward and picked it up. Felicia's farewell cupcakes were well known in the precinct. Homemade, never bought. Her bulging waistline was evidence of the hundreds of cupcakes she had served her patients—and herself. I peeled away the crinkly foil wrapper and took a bite. Although many look forward to this day, the final day of post-shooting protocol psych sessions, they would be lying if they didn't admit it was also to snag one of these glorious cupcakes.

"Y'know Susan, some people don't take these sessions as seriously as you have. I got the feeling you actually enjoyed coming here. Am I reading that right?"

I took a second bite before answering. "I went to a therapist when I moved back up here. I was trying to come to terms with my relationship with my mother. I blamed her for a lot of my shortcomings, which wasn't doing me any good. There was no real breakthrough, but airing my insecurities was somewhat cathartic. So I was pretty skeptical coming here. But, I have to say, by our third session I started to see the value in talking with you about the shooting, working through the guilt, learning how not to beat up on myself by second-guessing my actions. I think I might even miss our little get-togethers."

"We can meet again, if you like. I can arrange it with Chief Eldridge as a once-in-a-while check-in."

"Is that permissible now that I've had a farewell cupcake?"

"Only if you vomit it back up." She chuckled at her joke. "I'm curious, Susan . . . why did you move back up here? In our earlier sessions, you expressed this desire to get far, far away from here, yet here you are."

The question caught me a little off guard. It really didn't sound like the kind of question your shrink would ask to wrap up a therapy session. This was one that opened a new vein in an old mine—could keep us busy for months on end. When I first moved back, I used my father's heart attack as an excuse (when anyone asked). But there was more to it than that.

"It was a mix of things. My dad's heart attack was the main reason. But I had been thinking about it for about a year before that. I wanted to do more with my life than scout locations for movies. And, on some level, I was homesick." I took another bite of the cupcake—actually, a stall for time as I thought how best to explain the relationship with my mother without getting in the weeds. "I also wanted to repair the relationship with my mother and felt the only way to do that, and do it for real, was to be in her orbit again. At first, the two of us really tried to find a way forward, but we eventually fell back into our old patterns of bickering . . . especially when she drank. She just had a way of making me feel small. It was almost as though she took pleasure in pointing out my imperfections. In your line of work I think you call it an inferiority complex."

"Could be, if it's a defensive need to overcome her own feelings of inferiority. Her jabs at you might be a way for her to gain some control over her life. Some people belittle others in order to feel good about themselves."

"Yeah. I think that might apply to her. I tend to avoid confrontation, and so I started to minimize my interactions with her. Let's just say we tolerate each other these days. Would I like us to be closer? Sure. But until she stops drinking, I'm pretty sure that ain't gonna happen."

"What did she think about you becoming a police officer?"

"She actually encouraged it. Which surprised me, since I always got the feeling she was not keen on my dad's line of work. It's one of the few times she supported me. Follow your dream, she had said. She even went so far to tell me that I'd make an outstanding officer."

"And your dad? What did he think?"

"At first, he tried to dissuade me. But he came around. He knows it can be as rewarding as it is frustrating. He was beaming like the North Star on the day I graduated the police academy."

"Do you ever regret moving back up here?"

"Natalie really likes living in this area. So, there's that. And I get to see the twins whenever I want. I love my little house near the lake. I met Ray and fell in love. None of these things would have happened if I'd stayed in the city or moved somewhere else. So, no, no big regrets." I held up my cupcake. "And if I never came back here, I wouldn't have known the pleasure of your cupcakes."

After finishing our cupcakes, we pivoted back to the Barnes case and my on-again, off-again feelings of guilt. The seesaw in my head bouncing from *I had no choice* to *I should have held my fire*. ("This is all normal," Felicia explained at our first session.) My thoughts on the matter were still unresolved. I was hoping that if and when the Glock turned up, I'd be able to put it to rest.

CHAPTER TWENTY-FIVE

Monday, November 26, 2018

"STAY PUT," Marty said. "If Eldridge gets wind that the two of you even came here with me, well . . ." He got out of the car without finishing the sentence. He didn't need to.

I watched Marty enter the one-story brick building to meet with the owner of the company who oversaw the removal of the pallets from the warehouse. It was pretty mild for a late November morning. I rolled down the rear window next to me and tilted my face toward the sun. I didn't get to sunbathe in Florida, so this would have to do.

Marty exited the building holding a piece of yellow paper. He folded it down the center and tucked into his jacket.

"Got the names," he said when he opened the car door.

"And?" Ray asked.

"You know I can't talk to you about this. I'll drop you guys off at the station and then run this down."

With a couple of cops out on vacation this week, Eldridge needed me at the station this morning. Which was fine by me. Anything to keep my mind off the Barnes gun scavenger hunt. The Trudy and Ed investigation was at a standstill. We had no new witnesses to interview, so our best chance of a breakthrough in the case lay with Rachel.

Maybe we could even get something out of Stanley. With news that Rachel had been in Trudy's orbit as recently as 2008, we were itching to get in front of her before she got wind of what we'd found out. Dad was already looking into Florida flights and hotels. I wanted to head south right away, but he had a couple of billiards tournaments he wasn't willing to miss so he proposed we fly down on December 2.

Rachel's actions in 2008 certainly were suspicious, but it was quite possible she merely had been helping Trudy through a rough patch and didn't want anyone to know. I thought about telling Meryl about our decision to see Rachel, but I figured it was better to ask for forgiveness than permission this time around. Perhaps, as a courtesy, we would simply interrogate Rachel a bit more gently than we would otherwise.

No sooner had I settled at my desk than I eyed Eldridge headed in my direction. I braced for news about the gun.

"We got him, Susan. We got Lenny," he said, punching the air with a closed fist. "Cops picked him up in Philadelphia. He'll be back here tomorrow morning for questioning."

It took me a second to register this news.

My head was still mulling the Barnes case over what Marty was up to. "Am I stuck behind the glass?"

"Afraid so. The line of questioning is going to focus on Renee Carter, and that's Ray's and Marty's territory. If it turns out the Carter case is intertwined with the Solomon case, we'll sort it out later."

I texted Ray to let him know about Lenny. He responded: *I know*. I texted Dad. He texted me back the same exact reply: *I know*. Okay, Eldridge told Ray before me. But my father? What the hell?

MARTY HIGHTAILED it to Eldridge's office. He shot me a thumbs-up as he passed my desk. Man, I hated being left in the dark. First the Lenny news. Now this. I got it. I was not an idiot. But this was *my* livelihood at stake, for fuck's sake.

Normally, Sally would be dragging me out for a coffee right about now, but she was one of the two cops on vacation—a mini-getaway to Cancun—and wouldn't be back until Thursday. I glanced toward Eldridge's office, probably my twentieth glimpse since Marty had walked in there.

Eldridge's door opened and he stuck his head out. He summoned me in.

"We got the gun," Eldridge said, closing the door behind me.

"You made me sit out there this whole time knowing that? What the fuck, guys?"

"Easy there, Susan. We want our t's crossed and our i's dotted. I'm not even sure you should be privy to this. So, actually, I'm doing you a favor here."

"So what's the story—who had it?"

"I interviewed the two guys operating the forklifts and the guy loading the pallets onto the flatbed," Marty said. "As your boyfriend would say, one of the forklift drivers folded like a cheap suit. He claims to have found it under one of the pallets and decided to keep it for himself."

"Did he know what went down there?"

"Claimed he had no idea there had been a shooting in the warehouse. He figured finders, keepers."

"We can only make an assumption as to what happened that night," Eldridge said. "But I would venture to guess that, in the chaos, Wayne kicked Calvin's gun toward the stack of pallets hoping it would slide underneath. And it did. He must have thought he hit the jackpot when no gun was found. All he and the others had to do was stick to their story about Calvin not having a gun, and no one could prove otherwise." Eldridge paused. "Until now."

"I'm heading up to the prison now to tell Wayne the jig is up," Marty said.

"Can I—"

"Go back to your desk, Detective Ford," Eldridge said sternly. His tone softened and a rare smile escaped. "I want you as far away from this as possible. Let Marty put the final nail in this coffin."

RAY LOOKED up from his phone and yelled across the room, "Hey Susan! Just got off the phone with Marty. Seems Wayne and Melvin rolled over like an SUV doing ninety when it swipes a curb." A round of applause broke out.

Back slaps and handshakes all around as Ray made his way over to my desk.

"Let's go out and celebrate," Ray said. "Just you and me, dinner at Ciao Bella, a nice bottle of chardonnay."

I was not keen on going out to celebrate. It felt premature. There was still the hearing to get through, and there were plenty of people in town who would swear up and down this was a cover-up or insist the gun was planted. But I didn't want to spoil Ray's high. This was a big win for him. It was his idea to follow up with the company that moved the pallets out of the warehouse. He had every right to feel celebratory right now, regardless of what might happen.

CHAPTER TWENTY-SIX

Tuesday, November 27, 2018

LENNY SLOUCHED forward, his arms outstretched on the wooden table. Occasionally, his head bobbed downward. Probably didn't sleep much in the cold jail cell last night. Ray walked in with two cups of coffee and put one down in front of Lenny. Lenny pulled back the tab and took a sip.

"You tryin' to burn me, man?" He peeled off the lid and steam wafted skyward.

"If I was trying to burn you, I would have poured it over your head," Ray said. "Next time, let it sit a while."

Ray took a seat across from Lenny. He was lead on this interrogation. He had a gift for motivating people to talk, to get them to spill their guts like lava oozing out of a volcano, as he would say. He disarmed them. Charmed them. Then went for the jugular. That was pretty much how he got a first date with me.

Marty walked in, spun the metal chair around and sat on the backward-facing chair next to Ray. Dad and I were watching this unfold behind the two-way mirror. I was pretty sure Lenny knew we were behind it—he occasionally glanced in our direction and scowled.

"While we're waiting for your PD to arrive, thought we could shoot the shit a bit," Ray said. "We know for a fact that you came into possession of a baby who you pawned off on Ben Solomon. Why don't you enlighten us as to how you got to be in the adoption business?"

"I'm not sayin' nothin' 'til my lawyer gets here."

"Okay. Have it your way. But just so you know, we already got you for kidnapping—that's twenty-five years right there. And if you think your PD is going to save your sorry ass, well, go with God." Ray leaned in closer to Lenny. "So my suggestion, should you be smart enough to take it, is to tell us why you killed Renee Carter."

Lenny hooked his hands behind his head and leaned back, forcing the front legs of his chair to rise slightly. As he shifted forward, the chair clattered when the legs reengaged the floor. He took a gulp from his Styrofoam cup of coffee, now probably lukewarm. He smiled. "I didn't kill her." He ran the tip of his tongue along his yellowed teeth. "But I know who did and I know why. And I got the proof. And if you wanna know, I want some . . . assurances. A little tit for tat."

"You're in no position to bargain, Lenny," Ray said. "So why don't you tell us what you know, and then we'll decide what it's worth."

"Well, I'm not sayin' a word without my lawyer. I said enough already." He looked down at his cup and swirled the liquid. "This coffee is cold. I want another."

Ray stared coldly at Lenny while drumming his fingers on the tabletop. "Maybe when I want more coffee, I'll get you some too. Depends how I'm feeling. Right now, I'm not feeling much of anything. So, help me out here."

Lenny's court-appointed attorney, Malcolm Whittaker, stumbled into the room, breathing heavily and reeking of cigarette smoke. "Sorry. My case this morning ran late," he said with a raspy, tobacco-damaged voice. "I'd like some time with my client."

"We'll be back in fifteen," Marty said.

EXACTLY FIFTEEN minutes later Ray and Marty parked themselves across from Lenny and his attorney. Ray's take on Attorney Whittaker was pretty accurate. Not the sharpest tool in the shed. He usually picked up petty theft and DWI cases, or maybe the occasional assault and battery. But kidnapping and murder? Out of his depth. But the last thing Ray and Marty wanted was for Lenny to claim he had incompetent counsel. Which meant they would have to play it by the book. Or at least as close to the book as possible. A clean interrogation, no coercion. Disclosure of the evidence. In other words, stick to Eldridge's mantra: *t's crossed, i's dotted, don't screw this up!*

Ray directed his opening statement to the attorney. "Before you arrived, your client here was explaining that he knows who killed Renee Carter. So, why don't we start there?"

Lenny and Whittaker huddled and whispered for a few minutes.

"My client is willing to tell you everything you want to know about Renee Carter's murder for a reduced sentence on the kidnapping charge. He said he has proof he didn't do it. Once we get assurances from the DA, he'll tell you what you want to know."

RAY TURNED on the tape recorder. It had taken several hours for Whittaker and the DA to come up with a plea deal, all of it contingent on whether or not Lenny's version of events could be proven. Since there was no intent to harm the child, Lenny would plead guilty to second degree kidnapping and serve the minimum five-year sentence, with parole eligibility after two and a half.

Ray started the interview by introducing those present in the room, the date, and time, two o'clock. "So, Lenny. You got your deal. You lead us down any wrong paths or make shit up, the deal goes away and you could be looking at the maximum twenty-five on a second degree kidnapping charge. And depending on how the evidence breaks, you could also be looking at a murder charge. Got it?"

"I want a fresh cup of coffee," Lenny said. "Then you'll get your story. Black, two sugars. Real sugar. Not the fake cancer-causin' shit."

Ray tilted his head toward Marty. Marty exited the room. Ray turned off the tape recorder.

Five minutes later, Marty returned with a cardboard tray cradling four coffees. "Everyone happy now?" Marty said, placing the individual cups on the table.

Lenny flipped back the lid and blew into the opening before taking a sip. "Ahhh."

“This ain’t Dunkin’ Donuts, Lenny. Time to start talking.”

Ray turned on the tape recorder. “Leonard Berman interrogation with Ray Gorman, Marty Stiles, and Leonard Berman’s court-appointed attorney, Malcolm Whittaker. Tuesday, November twenty-seventh. Two-fifteen pm. Now, Lenny, what can you tell us about the murder of Renee Carter?”

Lenny stiffened his spine, rolled his shoulders back, and puffed out his chest. He inhaled. He exhaled. He stroked an imaginary beard. “Well, first of all, like I said, it wasn’t me. A guy named Panda killed Renee. Well, that wasn’t his real name. His last name was Pandolini or something like that. Panda was his nickname. Big, blotchy-faced, burly guy.” He slid his hands over his hair. “Black hair. In a pompadour, slicked back. Y’know, like Elvis. He was a line cook at the Cuttman Hotel.”

Panda. I remembered that guy. When I was a kid, I would sometimes see him walking his dog around the hotel. A pug with one eye and three legs. Heard it was also deaf. Sometimes it had a pink ribbon tied around its neck. It was a sight to behold. A gigantic man with port wine stains on his face and his tiny invalid dog. I once heard him call her Dolly.

Lenny took a sip of coffee, then continued: “He asked if I wanted to help him with a muscle job. Scare someone—Renee, that is—to keep her from yakkin’ about somethin’ or someone. Said there was a C note in it for me, and no one would get hurt. He said cuz I knew her—Renee, that is—I would be helpful in gettin’ her to comply. As a junkie at the time, it was hard for me to say no to quick money. But things went south pretty fast. Renee said she had no intention of shuttin’ up and she wanted the money she was owed for somethin’ or other. In the middle of them arguin’, Panda’s dog—this pathetic thing that maybe weighed fifteen pounds—starts barkin’ its head off. Renee lunged for the dog and Panda freaked out and his gun went off. I'm just standin' there thinkin', holy shit. I didn't sign up for this. Then Panda confessed to me that he was told to off her if she didn't play ball. I've never known Panda to do anythin' violent. All I could think is he must have really needed the money."

"So where can we find this Panda?"

"He's six feet under. Died a few years ago."

"How convenient," Ray said. "How do we know it wasn't you who pulled the trigger?"

"Because I ain't no cold-blooded murderer, that's why. I wanted nothin' to do with Panda after that fiasco. I dealt with the kid, and after that we went our separate ways. Once in a while, he'd come by the coffee shop to chat with Trudy."

"Trudy Solomon?"

"Yeah. That Trudy. They were friends." Lenny crossed his arms over his chest and leaned back, seemingly satisfied with part one of his story.

"Okay, Lenny," Ray said. "But I don't see how any of this helps your cause. Where's the so-called proof you said you've got?"

Lenny uncrossed his arms. "Right. Take it easy. I'm gettin' to that." He rubbed his hands up and down his thighs. "A couple years ago, Panda's sister calls me. I didn't even know he had a sister. And when I say sister, I mean *sister*—she's a freakin' nun. She lived in a convent up in Poughkeepsie. For some reason, he told her that I was his only true friend—maybe cuz I didn't rat him out—and asked her to contact me when he died. She said Panda wanted to say he was sorry for what he done to me. Then she asked if I wanted his journals. Somethin' to remember him by, I guess—like I was his best friend, or somethin'. I politely declined. She said she would hold on to them in case I changed my mind. Then she told me she had found a gun among his possessions and was plannin' to turn it over to the police. That would have been two years ago. If I'm a bettin' man, I'd bet that's the gun that killed Renee Carter."

"Is Panda's sister still alive?"

"I have no idea. But I sure as shit hope so. She said he wrote about his 'sinful deeds' in those journals. Maybe the whole story is in there, includin' the guy who hired Panda. That's your real murderer."

Ray leaned forward. "And the nun's name?"

Lenny squinted and turned his head to the left. "Um. Miriam? Yeah. Sister Miriam." He turned back toward Ray and smirked. "Pulled that one out of my ass."

"And she lived in a convent in Poughkeepsie?"

"Yeah. And Panda was livin' nearby, right up until he died." Lenny rubbed his hands together as if they had suddenly turned cold from all this talk of murder and death.

"How well did you know Renee?" Marty asked.

"What kind of question is that? You suggestin' I was one of her customers?"

"Just answer the question," Ray said.

"I seen her around. We had a few mutual friends. Why?"

"Well, we've come to learn that that baby wasn't hers. Maybe you can explain that," Ray said.

"Hmm." Lenny scratched his stubbled chin. "I'm gonna tell you somethin' that I should get extra credit for."

"Extra credit? This ain't high-school math class," Marty scoffed.

Lenny sat back in his chair and folded his arms across his chest. And waited.

Marty broke the silence. "Just tell us what you think is so worthwhile and we'll decide whether this information will help your cause."

Lenny leaned forward, squaring off with Marty. "Renee was a baby broker."

I wish I had a pin. That's how quiet the room got.

"A baby broker?" Ray asked, and Lenny turned to face him.

"Yeah. She and some lawyer friend of hers helped women who needed to find loving homes for their unwanted babies . . . for a price, of course. Usually arranged by the parents of girls who wanted to keep things on the QT. Whoever Renee was demandin' money from was probably mixed up in this baby business. We talkin' blackmail."

Ray leaned over and whispered in Marty's ear. Marty nodded.

"Well?" Lenny shouted. "Do I get a break?"

"We'll see how that bit of information pans out," Marty said.

"Fuck, man. That ain't fair."

"I've got one last question for you, Lenny." Ray stood and walked around the table to Lenny's side. "Do you know who killed Ed Resnick?"

"Man. He was a friend of mine. I didn't kill him, if that's what you're gettin' at. And if I knew who did, I would tell you. I wish I knew somethin'. But I don't. Are we done here?"

Malcolm Whittaker finally spoke. "Yeah. We're done here."

CHAPTER TWENTY-SEVEN

Thursday, November 29, 2018

AFTER MUCH back and forth, Eldridge finally gave me the green light to join Ray and Marty on their excursion to Poughkeepsie, an hour-plus drive from Monticello. Even though this field trip was related to the Renee Carter case, the Cuttman connection was deemed enough of a reason for me to tag along. I invited Dad to join us, but he declined, opting to defend his title at a Horizon Meadows billiards tournament instead.

I hunkered down in the backseat, ruminating over Tuesday's interrogation. When Ray questioned Lenny about a possible connection, Lenny claimed there wasn't one, as far as he knew. Was it just a coincidence that there were overlapping players? Both Renee and Trudy seemed to be caught up in blackmail schemes. Renee didn't get her money. But Trudy did. Did Panda threaten both women? Was Panda the person Trudy feared? But Lenny described them as friends. Perhaps Trudy was afraid of the person who hired Panda to off Renee.

Ray switched off the radio and looked at me in the rearview mirror. "What do you think of Lenny's cockamamie story?"

"It's going to be hard to prove if Panda's sister has no recollection of this, refuses to see us, or is no longer in possession of the journals. Besides, if she did give the gun to the Poughkeepsie police, there's a pretty good chance they destroyed it."

"The whole thing sounds insane," Marty said. "This repentant gun-for-hire-slash-cook character with a maimed dog. Who just happens to look like Elvis. His sister a nun, cloistered somewhere in Poughkeepsie. A prostitute moonlighting as a baby broker."

"I actually remember Panda," I said. "He bounced at some of the bars around here. And always had the dog with him. He loved that dog. Funny thing is, I always thought he was a nice guy. He might have been big, but he wasn't menacing. More teddy bear than grizzly bear."

"Catch the connection to the Cuttman and Trudy?" Ray asked both of us.

"Yup," I answered. "Did you find anything on him?"

Marty twisted around to face me. "Short rap sheet. His name is Salvatore Pandelo. A couple of drug arrests and a youthful B and E. Broke into an unoccupied summer cottage during the off-season and stole a bottle of Grand Marnier. Nothing violent. No weapons charges. Like Lenny said, his last known address was an apartment complex in Poughkeepsie, so we'll do a little nosing around there when we pay his sister a visit. Maybe he confessed his 'sinful deeds' to neighbors."

The Whitney Apartments, where Salvatore "Panda" Pandelo had resided, would be our first stop. Marty contacted the building's super and the guy said if we arrived before noon, he would introduce us to a couple of Panda's former neighbors. ("Can't promise you they'll talk," he warned.)

Getting hold of Panda's sister proved to be a bit more challenging. Ray called the Dominican Sisters of Poughkeepsie, the only convent in the area. Although there were contemplative nuns at this convent, the nun he spoke to informed him that Sister Miriam (nee Angela Pandelo) wasn't cloistered. She was an active sister who worked at the order's hospice facility. But the nun said the church officials would have to meet internally to decide whether or not to grant permission to interview one of their nuns. So this trip was a bit of a gamble. We had zero assurances that we would get to speak to anybody who actually knew Panda.

THE BUILDING's super, Chuck Worchowski, was outside when we arrived, shoveling a thin layer of snow that had accumulated in the past hour. After introductions, he leaned the shovel against the side of the building and led us inside to a small vestibule lined with metal letter boxes on one wall and a press-button intercom system on the other. Seemed no one paid attention to the "no smoking" notice taped to the glass door. Lingering cigarette smoke remained trapped between the inner and outer doors—presumably from residents who couldn't wait another second to light up before they stepped outdoors.

"I found two neighbors willing to talk to you." Chuck fumbled with the massive key ring clipped to his belt loop, isolated one key, and unlocked the inner vestibule glass door. "Mr. Dwayne Mayfield and Rose Saparelli. Both on the third floor. One across from where Sal lived, the other one two doors down."

Chuck knocked on 3A. The door opened with the chain still latched, giving us a three-inch view into the apartment, enough to see an older man with a close-cropped gray afro and small wire-framed glasses balancing on the end of a Nubian nose.

The old man, presumably Mr. Dwayne Mayfield, wheezed, then coughed. In a raspy baritone he hissed, "I changed my mind."

"We just need a few minutes of your time, Mr. Mayfield," Ray said.

Mr. Mayfield shut the door. "Go away," he barked from behind the closed door.

"Guess he changed his mind. He's a few cards shy of a full deck these days, so not sure how much he could've told you anyway." Chuck shrugged and walked down the hall.

We gathered around a door marked 3E. Chuck knocked and the door was flung open. Onion and garlic wafted out. Rose Saparelli, a petite woman no taller than five feet, waved us in. Wisps of dyed blonde hair were teased out nearly two inches from her scalp and held in place by a thick, shiny layer of hair spray. Her face reminded me of an apple that had morphed into a little old lady—an arts and crafts project where you peeled the skin, carved out the features, and placed the apple in a bath of lemon juice and salt. Once you removed it and it dried, facial features emerged on the apple, smooshed and distorted.

When Rose smiled, her wrinkles collapsed into each other. She pointed to the couch and we obliged. She sat on a well-worn upholstered chair. Chuck, his duty done, excused himself and left the apartment.

"Chuck tells me you have questions about Sal Pandelo." I was expecting a gravelly voice to match her weather-beaten appearance, but her voice was melodious and silky.

"How well did you know him?" Ray asked.

"Well enough. We were neighbors for thirty-some years. I knew he was in trouble with the law. He said as much. But he never told me why, and I never asked. Is that why you're here now?"

"Yes, ma'am," Marty replied. "We have reason to believe he was involved in a murder and we're trying to find the person who might have hired him to, uh, pull the trigger."

Rose lifted her hand to her heart. "Oh my. A murder? That doesn't sound like Sal. Always friendly . . . and helpful. Big guy, yes, but wouldn't hurt a fly."

"Did he have any visitors?"

"He pretty much kept to himself. I don't recall seeing a lot of comings and goings. Just his sister. Who is a nun. Sister Miriam. The cloistered nuns at the convent make soap, candles, hand and face creams, even honey. She'd come by and drop stuff off for him." She paused, then, with a wry smile, added, "I'm pretty sure she is not the culprit you're looking for."

"I'd like to show you some pictures, if you don't mind. Could help jog your memory."

Ray opened a manila folder and, one by one, showed Rose the photographs. Lenny. Ben. Rachel. Stanley. Scott. Ed. She shook her head when shown each photograph. Trudy. She blinked and furrowed her brow.

"Yes. Yes! She once came around here."

"You sure?" Marty asked.

"Pretty sure. But it was a long, long time ago. Early nineties, I think." She paused. "No, it was summer of ninety-five. I remember because it was right after my husband passed away. Sal introduced her as someone he used to work with. But I can't remember her name."

"Her name is Trudy. And you're sure she wasn't with this man?" Ray showed her the picture of Ed again.

"No. She was definitely alone."

"I WOULD say that was fairly unsuccessful," Ray lamented when we were back in the car. "I mean, it was a long shot that the guy who hired Panda would just show up on his doorstep, let alone that his neighbors would witness it."

"I think Trudy showing up is an interesting tidbit of info," I said. "Don't you think it's strange?"

"Maybe she was passing through, decided to say hello. Lenny claimed they got along well," Marty said. "There, on the right, that's the diner Chuck mentioned."

"She said 1995," I said.

"So?" Marty said.

"That's the year money started showing up in Ed's bank account."

"So?" Marty repeated.

"So, weird coincidence, wouldn't you say? She just happens to visit Panda in ninety-five, seventeen years after disappearing from the area, and in that same year she and Ed start receiving money, possibly in a blackmail scheme . . .which, by the way, is how Renee got herself killed."

"Only problem with that theory is Trudy wasn't afraid of him. She went to see him by herself, without Ed," Marty countered.

During lunch, Ray got a call from the nun he had spoken to the day before. The nun told Ray she'd arranged a half-hour meeting with Sister Miriam at two o'clock. She also informed Ray that the only reason we were granted permission was because Sister Miriam insisted she speak with us.

"Insisted," Ray said. "That's a good sign, right?"

WE WERE met by a young nun who introduced herself as Sister Cecelia. Early thirties was my guesstimate. Her habit, white and knee-length, was partially covered by a sleeveless black cardigan, the bottom button secured around her hips. Her hair was hidden under a simple white veil with black trim, no coif or wimple. Her face was bright and taut, with a smattering of freckles on her cheeks. She led us down a wood-paneled hallway to a library—a spacious rectangular room with five-foot-high bookshelves running along the perimeter. A couple of filing cabinets were wedged between them, interrupting the continuous flow of books. There were four long tables and four computer desks in the center of the room. On the far side of the library, sunlight spilled in through four side-by-side windows, bathing the evenly spaced potted plants atop the bookshelves.

"Sister Miriam will be down shortly," Sister Cecelia said. "I must tend to other matters."

Ray and Marty sat at the table closest to the door. Marty leaned back and closed his eyes. Ray planted his elbows on the table and cupped his chin in his hands. I wandered around the back of the room near the row of plants and peered out the window at what I assumed was the nun's dormitory across the grassy quad. Leafless maple trees lined a brick pathway between the library and the nuns' quarters. Two tall cypress bushes flanked the wooden door of the dormitory like a pair of green-uniformed sentries. I glanced back over my shoulder at Ray. He hadn't moved a muscle. Marty's eyes were still closed. Perhaps the combination of convent and library suppressed our desire to chat. The setting had a way of demanding reticence.

"Hello," Sister Miriam said. Our heads snapped around in unison. "Hope you weren't waiting too long."

"Not at all," Ray said, now standing.

Marty pulled out a chair for Sister Miriam. I took the chair next to her. Ray and Marty sat across from us. Like Sister Cecelia, Sister Miriam's skin was remarkably smooth and luminous for a woman well into her sixties. *Is this a nun thing—a life free of stress and everyday worries? Or the beauty products they produce?* I didn't see much of a family resemblance. Sister Miriam's skin was olive toned, Panda had been pasty white. Sister Miriam was thin and wiry. Panda had been heavyset and lumbering. Sister Miriam had squinty eyes, set close above a delicate nose. Panda had looked through saucer-shaped eyes looming over a bulbous nose. Perhaps different fathers.

"I've been expecting you," Sister Miriam said earnestly. "I knew sooner or later that my brother's past would catch up to him. Right before his death, he confessed to me. Told me he killed a woman decades ago. He thought about turning himself in, but with the pancreatic cancer he believed his punishment was being doled out by a higher court."

"We've been questioning someone named Lenny Berman about the murder," Ray said. "Claims you contacted him soon after your brother died. Said you offered him your brother's journals, and that you were in possession of his gun. Is that right?"

"That's all correct. Sal asked me to contact Lenny Berman. Told me he was a good friend. And to apologize for what he did."

"Do you know what he meant by that?" I asked.

"Not really. Sal did some bad things back in the day. I figured Lenny would know."

"We're also trying to determine if this case is tied to another unsolved murder," Ray said. "Do you still have the journals? There might be something in there to help us connect any dots."

"I am confident my brother confessed all his sins to me and he never mentioned another murder. But I have never read the journals, nor do I have a reason to keep them. Or the gun, of course. They're yours if you want them."

"You still have the gun?" I said. The tip of Ray's shoe gently brushed my shin.

"It's with the journals in a storage unit." She glanced around, then whispered, "A few of my old possessions are in there as well. It was hard to part with everything."

"Would it be possible to access this storage unit today?" Ray asked.

"It's not exactly my unit. One of Sal's neighbors graciously offered up some of his space. A Mr. Dwayne Mayfield. I told him that if the police ever come looking to retrieve Sal's things, he should comply."

Ray opened his folder and dealt the photographs on the table as though he was a playing a hand of Texas Hold'em. "Do you know if any of these people visited Sal since he moved here?"

Sister Miriam scanned the photos. "This is Lenny, right? Sal showed me a picture he had of the two of them. But no, I've never seen him here in person." She tapped her finger on the newspaper clipping. "Stanley and Rachel Roth. Can't imagine why they would visit Sal." She pushed the clipping aside. "I don't know him," she said, pointing to the photograph of Ed. She smiled when she eyed the next picture. "That's Trudy. I met her when I worked at the Cuttman Hotel as a maid in the early seventies. Nice girl. But meek. She once came to visit. Years and years ago." She looked at the last picture. "I believe this is Ben Solomon. He headed up housekeeping. Come to think of it, I think he dated Trudy. I've never seen him around here."

"She ended up marrying him," I said.

"Really? She didn't mention that."

"I didn't realize you worked at the Cuttman," Ray said.

"Before my calling I did a lot of things. I left the Catskills in seventy-four and entered the monastery in seventy-five."

"What was the nature of Trudy's visit?" Marty asked.

"Let me think a sec." Sister Miriam rubbed her temples, forming circles with the tips of her fingers. "She went to visit Sal, and afterward she came to see me. We spoke for a while, really just reminisced about the people we used to know. Just a friendly visit, I recall." Sister Miriam glanced at the newspaper clipping. "I think we chatted about the Roths, what it was like to work for them. But honestly, it was so long ago, I can't remember exactly what we talked about."

"How was it . . . working for the Roths?" I asked.

Sister Miriam shrugged. "Rachel was nice enough. Stanley a bit of a . . . you-know-what."

"Yeah. We know what," Marty said, winking.

"I think we can all agree with your ASS-essment of Stanley," I deadpanned.

Sister Miriam laughed. "Good one."

Ray looked up at the clock on the wall. "Well, thank you for your time, Sister."

"One last question," I said. "Is the gift shop open?"

THE SUPER buzzed us in when we returned to the apartment building. This time he was less cordial, his body language signaling we had our one chance to disturb his residents and now we were taking advantage of his generosity.

"What makes you think he's going to talk to you this time around?" Chuck asked.

"Sal's sister told us to tell him that she sent us. Said he'll be more amenable if he knows that."

Chuck knocked on Mr. Mayfield's door. The door opened with the chain engaged.

"I told you I wasn't talking to nobody." He started to close the door.

"Sister Miriam sent us," Ray said into the one-inch space. "She would like us to retrieve some of her items from your storage unit on South Road. She tells me you've got the key."

"Yeah? She said that? Chuck, is that right?"

"That's right, Dwayne. They just came from the convent. Why don't you talk to them like you said you would?"

The door closed all the way. "Mr. Mayfield," Ray implored. "We would really—"

The business end of the liberated chain scraped against the door. Dwayne Mayfield opened the door slowly and stepped back.

"You got five minutes of my time. But just one of you. You," Dwayne said, pointing to Ray. "Just you. I don't want a whole lot of strangers in my place."

BY FLASHLIGHT, Marty and I took turns reading out loud from Panda's journals while Ray drove. Two of the four journals weren't writings. They were filled with intricately detailed pencil drawings —buildings, portraits, animals, landscapes, even ordinary objects like silverware and teacups. Clearly, he had talent. The other two journals were confessional in nature: a man seeking redemption, unburdening himself of a lifetime of crimes and misdemeanors. The passage about Renee Carter's murder exonerated Lenny, assuming LB stood for Leonard Berman. As for who put him up to the murder, he referred to a DR. A doctor, perhaps? It's not out of the realm of possibility that a gynecologist was involved in this chicanery—someone who knows who's pregnant and in need of "private" services. I made a mental note to ask Clara Cole if she knew of any unethical gynos working at the hospital back in the seventies.

> *Needed money bad to pay off gambling debts. So when DR dangled this job in front of me, I took it. Wasn't my usual thing, but I was desperate. Got LB to come along for ride. He knows RC. He can sweet talk her. He didn't know I had other plans should she disobey. I didn't tell him about DR. The less he knows the better. I was supposed to put the scare in her. Thought we could play good crook bad crook. But she wanted more money or she would expose the truth about the baby. I told her I don't know nothing about that. I just went there to smooth things over. Offer her a one-time payment. Tell her to leave town with the kid. She did the calculation in her head and said not enough. She was right about that, but I would have taken it. It was something to live on for a good while. We could've talked her into it. I know we could've. LB was getting somewhere with her. But she was so agitated which made*

Dolly start barking. She told me to shut the dog up. It would wake up the baby. She grabbed Dolly and started choking her. She saw the gun in my hand but she went for Dolly anyway. She threw me off balance. It all happened so fast. The gun went off and she was dead. Shot in the side of the face. Why didn't she just take the money? She wasn't cooperating. Had to do what I was paid to do. Poor LB. Totally freaked out. He needed a fix right then and there. Then we hear the baby crying. LB said he got a plan. Said he knows someone who's looking to adopt a kid. Then we can report back to DR that we convinced her to leave town. No one the wiser. We buried RC's body along the highway. No word of it in the paper. No word about the boy. It was like no one cared. No one gave a shit about her or the baby. We said a prayer at her roadside grave. LB wanted to bury her with a cross so he tied string around two sticks and laid it next to her. We did our best to make it a decent and respectful burial.

We found one entry related to Trudy Solomon.

When TS disappeared the next summer, I wondered if what happened to RC happened to her. Maybe DR was involved in that too but got someone else to pull the trigger. No way I was going to do that again. But then she shows up at my apartment. Very much alive! Tells me she got my address from a friend of a friend. Wants to know where SR lives. I ask why, but she won't tell me about it. Besides, how would I know where SR lives? I don't even know where DR lives. I like TS. I wish her well. I hope she finds SR. Everyone has to do what they have to do. Who am I to judge?

Ray pulled into the police station parking lot at eight o'clock. I gathered up the four journals. Marty reached down between his legs and grabbed the shoebox containing the gun that allegedly killed Renee. While they reported into Eldridge, I phoned Dad and filled him in on what we discovered.

"DR and SR. Probably the fucking Roth brothers," Dad said. "Stanley and David."

"Holy shit. Forgot about him. Younger, right?"

"Yeah. Younger. He was one of them ambulance-chasing lawyers. Also did some hotel legal work for Stanley. I don't know who was the bigger asshole. Him or Stanley."

"Whatever happened to David?"

"After the hotel was sold, he went to work at Monticello Raceway," Dad said. "He had something to do with that Mohawk Indian deal to convert the raceway into a gambling casino. He was killed in a car accident several years ago. Alcohol level through the roof."

I was trying to wrap my head around how these two cases might be related. Renee was killed in 1977 for trying to extort money from someone with the initials DR, presumably David Roth. Was David involved in Renee's baby-brokering shenanigans? Lenny mentioned she was in cahoots with a lawyer friend, and David was a lawyer. Did David turn on her? It sounded like she threatened to expose their little enterprise.

Then a dozen years later Trudy shows up at Panda's apartment wanting to know where either Stanley Roth or Scott Roth lived. Why seek out Stanley? Perhaps he was also involved in this baby business, and Trudy knew that. That might explain why Stanley threatened Trudy in the nightclub. But now she had Ed to protect her, and perhaps he convinced Trudy the time was right to put the squeeze on Stanley. It's a good theory, I thought, but doesn't hold water if Trudy was actually inquiring about Scott, not Stanley.

"When exactly did Trudy go to see Panda?" Dad asked.

"One of his neighbors is fairly confident it was ninety-five. Which, if you recall, is the same year two grand started flowing into Ed's bank. Do you think that's a coincidence?"

"Hmm. Do you recall our conversation with that hotel guest, Michael Coleman?"

"The guy who said that Scott thought his dad had something to do with Trudy's disappearance?"

"Yeah, him. But something else he said. That's the year the Roths sold the hotel and the family came into a shitload of cash. Perhaps they were ripe for the picking. If Ed and Trudy had something on Stanley . . . or Scott . . . and they got wind of the fact that they were rolling in dough—"

"It would be nice to know if Stanley was in Boston around the time of Ed's murder. We know Rachel, aka Martha Stuart, was."

"But why kill Ed and not Trudy?"

"Waltham police didn't think the murder was premeditated. The knife that was used to stab Ed was from the apartment. Perhaps Ed was murdered in the heat of the moment. An argument that got out of hand."

"So, with Ed out of the picture, and Trudy in a mental hospital, no more payments. SR is off the hook."

"Have you booked our trip to the Sunshine State?"

"Sure did. We leave on Saturday. Pack your bags."

TRUDY

TRUDY WANDERED into the library. Waist-high shelves filled with books traversed across the back length of the room. Long tables, arranged in perfect rows, filled the middle of the space. A sign on a post had the image of a woman with her finger up to the lips and the word Shhhh *underneath.*

Are there secrets in this room? Trudy wondered.

The only other person in the library was a woman wearing a white scarf on her head. She tugged at her cardigan, wrapping it tightly around her torso. Trudy thought she looked familiar.

"Angela?"

"I'm sorry. You must have me confused with someone else."

"That's right!" Trudy clapped her hands. "You are now Sister Miriam."

The woman shook her head. "I'm afraid—"

Trudy took the seat next to the scarfed woman. "I'm trying to locate someone. Sal said you can help me. That you know where he is."

The woman edged away from Trudy. "I'm not Sister . . . Miriam did you say?"

"Oh. I'm . . . I'm . . . sorry. I thought you were somebody else."

"That's okay dear. Happens to all of us here."

Trudy sighed. "I was just hoping you could tell me where that one Roth lived."

CHAPTER TWENTY-EIGHT

Friday, November 30, 2018

"FIRST ROUND on me," Eldridge yelled, leaning across the bar to catch the bartender's attention. "Three pitchers of your finest beer and a bowl of pretzels."

"There's a booth," Ray said, pointing toward the back of the bar. "I'm going to snag it."

Dad, Ray, and Sally drifted to the booth. Marty and I waited by the bar. With the discovery of Calvin's gun, everyone wanted to celebrate. I wanted to roll up in a ball and go home. I wasn't completely out of the woods yet. There was still a chance the Barnes family wouldn't drop the civil suit. But at least I was at the far edge of the forest—thanks to Mordecai Little's well-placed camera and

Ray's dogged determination to figure out what happened to the Glock.

Usually we would head to McIver's Pub, but I was in no mood to get slapped on the back by every cop in this town and surrounding municipalities. Regardless of my exoneration, a kid was still dead. And I was the one who had to live with that. I preferred to simply raise a few pints with a handful of colleagues. I convinced them to meet me at the Underground, a basement bar on the edge of town. In the 1950s, this room had been a fallout shelter, the ubiquitous three yellow triangles in a black circle painted on every wall, faded but visible, so wherever you sat you saw one. No food at this bar. Just pretzels and bar nuts. This wasn't the type of place you came to eat. This was a place to drown your sorrows. No craft-brewed IPAs or trendy hard ciders. Your choices were Bud, Bud Light, Heineken, and PBR. A place where no one knew your name.

Well, at least they pretended not to. It was the consummate dive bar: murky with sticky floors and a no-nonsense bartender who was not there to listen to your sob story or dole out advice or spin a good yarn.

Above this establishment were offices for single-owner businesses. An accountant, a lawyer, a graphic designer on the ground floor. An acupuncturist and another lawyer on the second floor. The first-floor lawyer, Randy Coburn, was sitting at the bar nursing a scotch. He did some work for Dad a few years back when Dad wanted to draw up a living will and health-care proxy. He glanced my way, lifted his glass, and tipped it toward me. I nodded back. He turned away and fiddled with his phone.

The front door opened and the exposed bulb hanging just outside the bar entrance illuminated the room. When the door slammed shut, the room was plunged back into muddiness. Natalie squinted and glanced around until she spotted me near the bar. I waved her over.

"Ray's got a table in the back." I handed Natalie one pitcher.

"I'm heading over there," Marty said. "Follow me."

I waited with Eldridge to retrieve the second pitcher. Ray texted me telling me to get my ass over to the booth. I texted him back a fist with the middle finger raised. He texted a shocked face. I texted a face blowing kisses. He texted a happy face. Nothing like emoticons to bring out the teenager in you. I grabbed the pitcher and walked by a threesome of Black men, midtwenties, congregating at the edge of the bar.

One of them held his arm out blocking my route.

"You're that cop that killed Calvin," he said. "I knew I recognized you."

"I suggest you move your arm."

"You suggest, do you? You gonna shoot me if I don't?" He dropped his arm. I walked past him.

"We be watching you," he whispered to my back. He raised his voice slightly above the din of the bar chatter. "Ain't no cover-up gonna save your ass, bitch." They snickered.

When I looked sideways, I saw another young Black man heading toward me and steadied myself for the confrontation.

"Is that you, Detective Ford?" he said. "It's me. Thomas. Were those guys bothering you?"

"Oh. Hi, Thomas. Hard to see in here. It was nothing. Don't worry about it."

"I know them. They went to high school with my brother. Want me to say something? Cuz I will. They have no right to hassle you. No matter what they think you done to Calvin."

"You know about that, huh?"

"Yeah. News all over that you got yourself cleared." Thomas lowered his voice. "Didn't go over well with a lot of folks."

"And you? You think there's some cover-up?"

"I look at the facts. I learned that in my classes. If what you're saying is true, you got a solid case of self-defense. Besides, your dad is pure gold. I'm sure the apple hasn't fallen far from the tree."

"Dad's here," I said, pointing to the booth. "Wanna join us?"

Thomas shifted his eyes toward the three men at the bar. "Next time. You go enjoy yourself."

"What was that all about?" Dad asked when I set down the pitcher.

"You don't recognize Thomas . . . Mom's housemate?"

"Was that him? Man, it's dark in here. I can't even see the nails on my fingers."

Eldridge came up behind me and slapped me on the back. "Well, Ford. You dodged a bullet, you did. Drink up."

I peeked to my left. The Knicks game had captured the attention of the three men.

Eldridge continued: "Now let's get some closure on the Solomon case. I hear you're heading back down to Florida tomorrow." Eldridge turned to face me and made sure I had his full attention. He did. "Will here tells me he thinks you'll have it wrapped up by Christmas. New Year's at the latest. No pressure, guys, but tick tock. Tick tock."

"That's the plan," Dad said. "This trip to Florida is probably our last, best hope for a straight answer from the Roth clan."

With Eldridge's deadline looming, we had four weeks to figure out three things: why did Trudy flee the area (what/who was she afraid of)? Was Ed's murder tied to an extortion scheme (and if so, who was he blackmailing)? And who ordered the killing of

Renee (the most likely suspect being David Roth, now deceased)? The icing on this three-layered cake would be finding out who gave Trudy and Ed the five grand to disappear. Dad still thought it could be Rachel (she had the means), but Brian the Lifeguard had told us that Rachel thought Scott had something to do with Trudy's disappearance and, perhaps to protect him or the family, shipped him off to her sister's home for the remainder of that summer. If that was indeed the case, Rachel didn't aid Trudy's getaway. But why did she (under a false name, Martha Stuart) commit Trudy to a mental hospital? Shutting her up was the answer that came to mind.

"To hidden cameras!" Ray yelled, raising his glass, bringing me back from my reverie.

"To hidden cameras!" everyone echoed.

I glanced sideways and eyed the guys sitting at the bar's edge. Even though I was holding a cold glass of beer, my hands started to sweat.

CHAPTER TWENTY-NINE

Sunday, December 2, 2018

WE FOUND the Roths' address the old-fashioned way—the White Pages—tucked inside one of the bedside table drawers at the hotel, between a King James bible and a takeout menu from a nearby pizza place. If we had to, we could have found out where they lived through the Florida DMV database. But at this point, we didn't want to involve the local police.

Ray lifted his binoculars. He'd wanted to join us. ("What better way to use my few remaining vacation days than to sun and sleuth," he had said.) Dad sat in the passenger seat. I was behind Dad. We were all staring at a modest beige-pink ranch with a Spanish-inspired tiled roof, the last dwelling on a dead-end street. A Toyota

Camry with a dented right bumper was parked in the liberally cracked cement driveway. Weeds stood at attention in the narrow fissures. Not exactly what I was expecting. It seemed everyone in Florida who had money lived in a gated community or along the intracoastal.

But here they were, in a house on a totally accessible street. No gate. No security guard. Just an ADT sign partly obscured by overgrown bushes.

"Are you sure this is the right address?" Dad asked.

"I can see the name Roth on the mailbox," Ray said, handing Dad the binoculars.

"Do you think they fell on hard times?" I asked. "Does this make sense to you? I mean, everyone else in the family seems to be living a pretty charmed life."

"Well, there's only one way to find out," Dad said. "Let's go."

Ray watched from the car as I rang the doorbell. I waited a few seconds before ringing it again.

"Coming!" The voice was muffled, but clearly female.

Rachel Roth flung open the door. She was wearing a tennis outfit and holding one of those oversized rackets. A gym bag was draped over her shoulder. "Oh. You're not—"

"Hello Rachel," Dad said. "Do you remember me from . . . from high school?"

She stepped out of the house and closed the door behind her. She looked sternly at Dad, then at me, then back to Dad. Her face softened a bit. "I know who you are, Will. And you must be Suzie. I remember you . . . Lori's friend from elementary school." She paused, perhaps waiting for us to say something. "Meryl told me you were interrogating Cuttman Hotel workers and guests about the Trudy Solomon case. Which, if you ask me, seems like a waste of time after all these years. I hear you found her. Case closed, I guess." She twirled the racket in her palm. "Meryl told me you finished your investigation."

"Well that's not entirely true," Dad said.

"I see."

"Can we ask you a few questions?"

"Now is not a good time. I'm expecting a friend and we are heading out," Rachel said, raising her tennis racket as proof of this statement.

"We really just need a few minutes," I said. "Is Stanley home?"

"Stanley won't be able to answer your questions. He can't even remember what he ate for breakfast this morning." Rachel's phone rang and she removed it from her back pocket. "I have to take this." She walked past us onto her driveway. "Hello?"

I shifted my attention to Ray, staring at me through the binoculars. I shrugged and held my palms skyward. The universal sign indicating you didn't know what the fuck was going on. Rachel turned her back to us and continued her phone conversation. Dad was watching her intently. Probably thinking how good she looked for her age. She was trim and fit. Her still-lustrous hair was dyed dark brown, roots included. The short tennis skirt accentuated her long, toned legs. She was tan, but not in that over-the-top bronzy way. If I didn't know her age, I would have pegged her at mid-sixties, not seventy-eight years old.

"Your lucky day. My friend is running late."

"Shall we go inside?" Dad asked.

"I'd rather not. Stanley is very confused these days, and not well. He recently had a minor stroke. I don't want to agitate him, or the rest of my day will be a living hell."

"You look well, Rachel," Dad said. "Sorry to hear about Stanley."

Rachel waved her hand, shooing away an imaginary fly. "You're looking pretty good there yourself, Will." She turned to me. "And my oh my, Suzie Ford. Following in your dad's footsteps. How . . . nice."

Dad launched into a monologue, recapping our investigation from the moment the skeletal remains were found. He told her about finding Trudy after a social security number search. Our belief she willingly left the area with Ed Resnick, fearing someone or something. Rachel nodded and widened her eyes. *A pretty good poker face.* It was hard to tell if she was genuinely taken aback or feigning surprise. Dad continued the tale, telling her about Trudy's pregnancy and putting her twins up for adoption. She gasped, almost inaudibly. He told her about their move from Rochester to the Boston suburbs. He mentioned Scott visiting Trudy and Ed, and the argument in their apartment. She subtly knitted her brow on that news. Then he got to the part about the alleged blackmail scheme and Ed's murder.

She batted her eyelashes, rapidly. *A tell?* Then Dad went for the jugular.

"Does the name Martha Stuart sound familiar to you?"

"Um. Martha Stewart? The television woman who cooks and does crafts?"

"No. The Martha Stuart who committed Trudy Solomon to a mental hospital in Belmont, Massachusetts," Dad said.

"I have no idea what you're talking about," Rachel said matter-of-factly. Her voice steady and controlled. Man, she would be good at poker.

"Mrs. Roth, we have two eyewitnesses who matched your photograph to the person who signed the papers committing Trudy to McNair Hospital," I said. "You are a very beautiful woman, not easily forgotten. Are you telling us they are both mistaken?"

"You know that saying, the jig is up?" Dad said. "Well, the jig is up."

"What are you accusing me of, exactly? Helping someone in need?"

"We're not accusing you of anything. Not yet," I said. "But we are conducting a murder investigation. We know Trudy was seeking information on the whereabouts of either your son or your husband, or both, in 1995, the same year Ed started receiving money. Which also happens to be the same year you sold the hotel and walked away with a nice windfall. We have reason to believe that the person Trudy feared and had dirt on—Stanley or Scott or both—led Ed to cook up this extortion scheme. And it just so happens you were in Boston around the time of Ed's murder, committing Trudy to a mental hospital." I felt the pulse beating in my wrist and exhaled slowly. My voice was a bit harsher than I intended it to be, so I recalibrated my tone. "That is one hell of a bunch of coincidences, and we think you can help us understand what's going on here."

"Rachel, look, we don't want to hassle you, but we need to know why you used a false name to commit Trudy to care," Dad said in a soothing voice, taking the tension down a notch. "It doesn't take a genius to know you were trying to hide something."

Rachel's phone rang.

"Shit, I gotta take this. It's Stanley."

Dad and I turned to each other, confused. He whispered, "Didn't she say he was in the house?"

"I've got to go," she said after hanging up.

"Where's Stanley?" Dad asked.

"Inside."

"Inside the house?"

"Yes, I told you that already. He's in a wheelchair. He's looking for me. I have to go."

"Rachel—"

"You want to know what happened? Tell me where you are staying. I'll meet you there tomorrow at noon."

CHAPTER THIRTY

Monday, December 3, 2018

TECHNO MUSIC, set a few decibels too loud for a hotel lobby, thumped through unseen speakers. The fact that someone even chose to play electronic dance music in this hotel—mostly catering to businesspeople and families with young children—struck me as rebellious. I was curious (and annoyed). But not curious (or annoyed) enough to ask the front desk receptionist about it (let alone to lower it).

I told Dad I would meet him in the lobby at eleven thirty so we could review the questions we wanted to ask Rachel. (We decided it was best to not include Ray in this "friendly" interrogation, so he was relaxing by the pool with a paperback he'd picked up at the airport.) I glanced at my watch—eleven-forty. That gave me twenty minutes to get my head in gear for our little chitchat with Rachel. I scoped out the lobby and found a quasi-private seating area in the corner. My rear was barely in the seat when the lobby doors slid open and Rachel, clad in perfectly pressed white slacks and a lavender silk blouse, breezed through—back straight, shoulders squared. Fifteen minutes early. She spotted me and strode over. She sat down, then immediately stood up.

"I'll be right back," she said.

I texted Dad to let him know Rachel had arrived and where we were sitting. He texted back, along with a toilet bowl emoji, that he would be down in a few minutes. *Okay, thanks for sharing.* After our text exchange, I realized the music had been turned down.

"There. That's better," Rachel said, sitting down next to me on the love seat. "Now we can hear each other."

Dad stepped out of the elevator and glanced around. I waved at him and caught his eye.

"Hello Rachel," Dad said, settling into the mosaic-patterned wingback chair to the right of Rachel. He addressed her sternly but politely. Dad had more power over her than he used to, and could certainly rattle her cage, but we both agreed to treat her more like a witness than a suspect at this juncture. What he cringe-worthily referred to as his taming-of-the-shrew tactic—kill her with kindness to get what you want. "We appreciate you coming here to meet with us."

"It felt like I had little choice. I was prepared to go to my grave with this, but when Meryl contacted me about you digging around in this case, I knew it was just a matter of time before you would be knocking at my door."

"Do you mind if I record?" I asked, placing a small recorder on the cocktail table in front of us.

"Yes, I do mind. If you want to remember what I said, I suggest you take good notes."

Like a submissive child—perhaps an ingrained reflex left over from my reverence of her in my youth—I obediently picked up the recorder and deposited it in my bag. I retrieved a pad and pen. "As you were saying, Mrs. Roth. What can you tell us about Trudy and Ed—why they left the area and your subsequent dealings with them?"

"As far as why they left the area, I have no idea. In fact, I too thought she was dead or kidnapped, until Ed came knocking at our door in the fall of ninety-five."

This statement lined up with what Brian the Lifeguard had told us and further solidified my thinking that she was not the one who gave Ed and Trudy five thousand dollars.

"She wasn't with him?" I asked.

"No. He was by himself. He told us that Trudy was in Boston. And that Trudy had found out where we lived from a nun, which was odd, because I don't know any nuns."

"Why didn't you contact Monticello police when you found out she was alive?"

"Stanley told me to keep my mouth shut. Told me we risked losing everything if we reported her whereabouts." She snorted. "Yeah, well, look at us now. He managed to lose everything anyway."

"Why did Stanley tell you to keep quiet? What was he hiding?" Dad asked.

"I was not privy to whatever Ed and Stanley were up to. He wouldn't tell me and I just let it go. He convinced me that going to the police would make our situation worse. But one day, about three years after Ed's visit, I was looking through our bank records and saw a monthly withdrawal of two thousand dollars and asked Stanley about it."

"So, you didn't regularly check your bank records? You just happened to be looking at them in 1998?" I asked.

"Stanley took care of the finances. But that year he was traveling a lot. Back and forth to Monticello, working with his brother to bring gambling to the raceway. And the mail was piling up. So, I opened a few envelopes—including our bank statement—and saw the withdrawal. I snooped around Stanley's office for past statements and saw the withdrawals dating back to the fall of ninety-five."

"Stanley was working with David?" Dad asked.

"Yes. And that turned out to be a disaster." She rolled her eyes.

"Did you confront Stanley about the money?" I asked.

"Yes. That's when he admitted that Ed was pressuring him for money. When I pressed him about it, he refused to tell me more. I let it go. It was just two thousand dollars a month. At that time, it seemed like a drop in the bucket. Knowing Stanley, I figured he probably owed it to them in some way. Some business gone bad one way or another."

"I'd like to ask you a personal question," Dad said.

Rachel nodded.

Dad continued, "I get the feeling you weren't happily married to Stanley. Why did you stick around?"

"My father was old-fashioned. He didn't believe women were capable of running a hotel. When he died, he passed ownership to Stanley. And to make matters worse, Stanley and I signed a prenup before we got married. I did it thinking it would protect my assets should our marriage not stand the test of time. But it turned out that it locked me out of my rightful inheritance. If I divorced him, I would get nothing." She pulled a tissue out of her purse and dabbed her eyes.

"Don't take this the wrong way," Dad said. "But what's with the small house and beat-up old car?"

"David Roth. That's what. He convinced Stanley to invest almost all of our money in that stupid racetrack. They called it a racino. A combo racetrack and casino that was supposed to revive the area. By 2006, we had lost a boatload of money when the stock went belly-up. It was that and a whole lot of other bad investments that David talked him into."

"So I would imagine giving away two thousand dollars a month started feeling like a burden around that time," I said.

"Well, it wasn't helping matters. And on top of that, Stanley's health started to deteriorate. We had no money for quality care. Stanley refused to ask the kids for money. We don't even think they knew, or now know the extent of our loss. What was I going to do at that point . . . leave him to rot in some old-age home? We might have our problems, but . . . " She trailed off, never making her point.

"So you decided to take a trip up to Boston in the summer of 2008 and remedy the situation?" Dad said.

"Yes. We were going anyway. Josh . . . you remember Josh? . . . he was getting married at an inn in North Adams, which was a couple of hours from Boston. Our plan was to simply tell Ed that the gravy train had run out of gravy."

"And what was his reaction?"

"Well, I don't know. Stanley went by himself. They arranged to meet when Trudy was out of the apartment. I stayed back at the inn. But when Stanley came back I had a feeling something had gone terribly wrong." She dabbed again at her eyes, although I did not see any tears. "He told me to pack my bags. That we were going home early."

"I take it you didn't go home early. You hung around long enough to check Trudy into McNair Hospital."

"The murder was on the news that night. I just thought—"

Dad ended her sentence. "That Stanley murdered Ed."

"I had no proof, but I sure thought so. As you say in your world, he had motive and opportunity."

"Did you ask him if he did it?"

"I did. He insisted Ed was alive when he left the apartment."

"And did you believe him?"

"I was skeptical. But I'd like to believe that if he did kill Ed, he didn't intend to. Maybe things got out of hand . . . maybe it was self-defense. Anyway, I told him I was planning to visit a friend and needed to stay on. So he went home without me."

"He left the day of the murder?" I asked. "July twentieth?"

"Well, the next morning. The twenty-first. And then when things quieted down a bit, I went to visit Trudy."

"When was this?"

"Um, two or three days after Ed's murder."

"Go on."

"She was pretty distraught. I asked her if she knew who did it, and she said no. That she was out shopping. But I was so afraid she would talk to the police about Stanley, and they would put two and two together. So I thought, if I can get her out of the reach of the police, I can fix this mess." She paused. "That's my life . . . literally and figuratively cleaning up Stanley's messes. You can even say I was doing her a favor—she *did* need emotional support." The sliders opened and a rush of warm air filled the lobby. A rambunctious family tumbled in, startling Rachel. She abruptly turned, perhaps thinking it was the police dashing through the doors to arrest her.

"And then what happened?" Dad asked, recapturing her attention.

"Nothing. I went home. No one came knocking at our door, so I figured they caught the person who did it or they never connected the murder to Stanley. So now you know the whole story."

Dad nodded and slapped his thighs. "Okay, then." If this was someone else other than Rachel, he might have had another follow-up question, probed deeper, but perhaps he couldn't let his old feelings slide away that easily and gave her a pass. Or maybe he had some other scheme up his sleeve.

"Are you going to arrest him?" Rachel asked.

"Stanley? Even if we wanted to charge him, it sounds like he is not in any condition, mentally or physically, to undergo questioning or stand trial," Dad replied. "And really, all we have is circumstantial evidence. The body is long buried, the murder weapon never found. No witnesses. No forensics."

"If it makes you feel any better, the autopsy report points to a murderer who was shorter than Ed," I added. "More your height."

Rachel cleared her throat. "So it's quite possible Stanley did not murder him. Well, that's comforting to know." She checked her watch.

"Our original intent with this case was to find out what happened to Trudy Solomon—why she left, what became of her, and if there was any criminal malfeasance." I laid my pad and pen on the table. "We still don't know why she left, although we do know she felt threatened in some way. We have a witness who saw Stanley badgering Trudy. So I'll ask again, can you think of any reason why Ed and Trudy came after your husband for money?"

Rachel shifted slightly in her chair. "As I told you, I have no idea." She pinched the top of the pleats on her trousers and ran her fingers down the crease. "He was mixed up in a number of shady business dealings that, I will admit, I turned a blind eye to. I'm sure he stiffed Ed out of some money at some point and this was his comeuppance." She checked her watch again. "So what do you plan to do now?"

"As for Ed's murder, we'll be reporting what you told us to the Waltham police. They'll determine whether or not to close this line of inquiry, which might be the case seeing that Stanley is, well, non compos mentis."

"So that's it then. You'll leave us be now?"

"Perhaps." Dad leaned closer to Rachel. "We're sorting through some other criminal activity we stumbled upon in this investigation—the murder of a prostitute and the kidnapping of a child." Dad waited a beat. "It seems David Roth had a hand in that."

Rachel straightened her spine and rolled back her shoulders. "A prostitute? A child kidnapping? Don't be ridiculous. What would I know about that? I kept my distance from David and his henchmen, his prostitutes, and his lunatic wife." Rachel gathered her coat and purse. "Are we done here?"

Before either of us had a chance to answer, she stood abruptly and briskly made her way to the front doors.

"Shit." Dad shook his head. "I fucked that up. Man, I should have, I don't know—"

"Pushed harder? Well, I wasn't exactly putting a lot of pressure on her either—it's what we agreed to."

"She is something else."

"That's one way of putting it, Dad."

RAY FOUND a hamburger joint in a nearby strip mall, the kind of place where you "built your own burger" and were given a numbered stanchion so the server could match your order to your table when it was ready. ("This place got tons of five-star reviews," Ray informed us when we left the hotel. "It'll be worth the twenty-minute drive.") I was famished and would have been happy with Burger King or the place around the corner with a one-star review. But I didn't want to rain on Ray's parade.

Ray leaned forward from the backseat. "So how did it go with Rachel?"

Dad grunted.

I took my right hand off the wheel and gave him a reassuring pat on the shoulder. "Well, I get the feeling that Rachel is still hiding something. She's just so . . . so . . . I can't explain it." I shuddered. "I just want to wring her neck. It's like she's got a pre-scripted answer for everything."

"She should have pursued an acting career. That was some grade-A Oscar-worthy shit she was spinning. But . . . the one thing I do believe—based on my fine-tuned Spidey senses—is that she had no idea why Stanley was coughing up two grand a month."

"That's why I wanted to record the conversation," I said to Ray. "Dad and I might be a little biased in the Rachel department, and it would have been nice to get an impartial take on her story."

WE SAT in hungry silence as waiters—plates balanced on their arms—crisscrossed the dining room like wayward bees seeking a flower to pollinate. My stomach growled every time a server passed our table.

"There's gotta be another angle to pursue," Dad said. "We may be on the ropes, but I got some fight left in me."

"I don't know, Dad. I think we've reached a dead end," I said, eyeing the plates of burgers and baskets of onion rings whizzing by. "Or to stick with your metaphor, we're down for the count. We can't talk to Stanley. David's dead. Panda's dead. Trudy's unreliable. We can have another go at Lenny and Ben, but I'm pretty sure they've told us all they know."

"This is not over for me," Dad said, clearly frustrated. "We just need a little more time. We are so close. I can feel it."

"I understand where you're coming from Dad, but Eldridge only gave us two months to figure this out and we are running out of time. I can't see—"

"I suspect there is still one person who knows something about all this," Dad seethed. "And his initials are SR . . . but it's not Stanley Roth."

"He wasn't too keen on helping us last time," I said when, finally, a waiter stopped at our table and set down three hamburgers, an order of fries and a basket of onion rings. Silence once again fell over the table as we dug in.

"I have an idea as to how we might get to Scott," I said when I came up for air.

"I'm all ears," Dad said between bites.

I reached into my backpack, pulled out a small envelope, and handed it to Dad. "Go ahead. Read it out loud."

"Come celebrate. Explanation point. You and a guest are invited to attend a party celebrating four Roth milestones. Josh and Steven's tenth wedding anniversary. Meryl's retirement. Lori's fifty-third birthday. Scott's engagement." Dad paused and looked up. "Sounds fun." He continued reading, "December eighth, two thousand and eighteen. RSVP, blah, blah, blah." Dad inserted the card back into the envelope and handed it back to me. "When did you get this?"

"In early November—soon after our Facebook exchange. I thought about going, to see Lori, but talked myself out of it. Seeing we are now in desperation mode, well, maybe this is our last shot. And, this might be a way to talk to all the Roth kids, not just Scott."

"I understand your apprehension, but really, Susan, all that stuff between you and Lori is ancient history. You should have told us about this," Ray said. "Where is this party taking place?"

I was not keen on the scolding. But yeah, he was right. Because I was still chickenshit about rubbing elbows with the Roths, and coming face-to-face with Lori, I was willing to muff up this golden opportunity to get some questions answered. In all fairness, I had been planning to tell them about the party depending on what we were able to extract from Rachel.

"Vermont. At Josh's bed and breakfast."

"Did you already turn it down?" Dad asked.

"Yes, but Meryl emailed me, said if I changed my mind, she would add me back in. She said Lori would love to reconnect."

"All the Roths in one room," Dad said. "You're either walking into a gold mine or a minefield."

CHAPTER THIRTY-ONE

Tuesday, December 4, 2018

RHONDA SLID into the bench seat across from me. I was on my third (and last) cup of coffee. I wiped my suddenly moist hands with the little square paper napkin.

"Sorry I'm late," she said, slightly out of breath. "Crazy morning."

Rhonda had called me the night before. She was hoping to meet with me sooner, but I was in Poughkeepsie, then Florida, and she was caring for a sick kid.

"No worries." I stared down into my cup of coffee. "Should I be worried?"

"Hard to say. There's definitely a lot of anger in the community. Talk of a cover-up. You can't blame people for being skeptical."

"Do you think there's a cover-up?"

"You know I don't. But others are wondering why the police are not releasing the video."

"They will. In due time. There's a process. I'm not really privy to all this." I paused, modulating my voice so as not to sound defensive. "Calvin had a gun on him. You can see it clear as day."

"I'm hearing terms like *photoshopped* and *fake video*. I'm not up on the technology, but I do know video can be manipulated . . . edited."

"That video was not doctored in any way, shape, or form. Mordecai Little was present when he showed us the footage. In fact, he refused to give us his log-in information to view it beforehand. In hindsight, I'm glad he was protective of his privacy."

"I really do hope it's released sooner rather than later. Nip the rumors in the bud."

"I'll see what I can do. I'll talk to Eldridge."

"There's talk of a march."

"In support of what? Calvin Barnes?"

"Community policing reform. Calvin's mother is organizing it."

I wondered if Natalie knew about this. "When is it?"

"Mid-January. Look, I just wanted to give you a heads-up on this. Until that video is released, there's gonna be a lot of bad feelings stewing."

"Should I do something? Talk to the group?"

"I thought about that. But I don't know. Things are still too raw right now."

"I got harassed the other night. At the Underground."

"What the hell were you doing at that shithole? McIver's closed?"

"Just looking for a change of scenery that night."

"Uh-huh."

"Some guys recognized me. Gave me the 'watch your back' threat."

"Jeez. Did you recognize them?"

"No. It was hard to make out faces. That place is like a dungeon."

"Look. I'll try to calm the tensions. But do me a favor."

"And that would be?"

"Don't go to the Underground."

I HEARD a car door slam. Ray was volunteering at Better Mad Than Sad this afternoon, Natalie was at a Black Lives Matter meeting, and Dad's pickup was declared a total loss, so he was without wheels until the insurance payment came through. I peeked out the window and spied my mother making her way up the walkway. Her gait slow, limping slightly as she favored her better knee. She was carrying something, but it was hard to tell exactly what from this angle. I descended the stairs and opened the door before she had a chance to ring the doorbell.

"Hi Mom. What brings you out this way?"

"Can't a mother just visit her daughter? Does there have to be a reason?"

I softly sniffed the air around her. No alcohol on her breath. When she took off her coat, her sweater emitted an odor of cigarettes and Tide. Clearly, no amount of laundry detergent would make that sweater smell fresh again.

"I see what you're doing, Susan." She bent over and petted Moxie. She didn't seem to mind the smoky aura. "I haven't had a drink for two weeks now."

"Really?" I did not skimp on my skepticism.

"Thomas dragged me to a twelve-step program over at the Methodist church. Well, not exactly dragged. Said he brings his aunt over there every Wednesday, so he was headed there. I wasn't gonna go, but I decided last minute to check it out." She had to have seen my eyebrows arch, and added, "I know I got a problem, Susan. I'm not blind to that. The thing is, do I want to do something about it? Maybe. Maybe not. But I'm trying it out."

I knew what was driving this. Natalie and Frank put the kibosh on babysitting. Natalie told my mother, in no uncertain terms, she would not have an alcoholic watching the kids. Mom pushed back, blaming Frank. That could be true. Frank never hid his disapproval of Mom's drinking and smoking. He was quick to complain that his kids smelled like a smoky tavern after Mom watched them. That's why we called him frank Frank. You always knew where you stood with him.

I didn't want to discuss it any further. It would only give her an excuse not to go to those meetings. Her change of heart would be my fault, somehow. "What's in the box?"

"Ah, yes, the true nature of my visit. Thomas was going to bring this over to you, but I intercepted him and told him I needed to see you."

"And do you? Need to see me?"

"Not need. Want. Really, Susan. I *am* your mother. We haven't seen each other since you stopped by over a month ago. So I told Thomas I would be the messenger. Thought it would be nice, that's all."

"Uh-huh," I said, trying to keep my skepticism at bay.

"These are the pictures you asked for," she said, handing me the shoebox. "I heard Thomas moving around up in the attic this morning and asked him what he was doing. He told me you set him to this little task."

"You didn't have to come out this way. I was planning on picking them up later today."

"So what's with the photographs?"

"Meryl asked me to send her pictures of me and Lori for some trip-down-memory-lane slide show she's putting together for her party. Problem was, all my old photos were stored in your attic and she needs them no later than Wednesday, which means I need to send them out today. And since you can't climb the attic ladder with your bum knee, I asked Thomas if he could scrounge around up there. I hope that was okay."

"No skin off my nose. In fact, I asked him while he was up there if he could organize some of our old stuff. Maybe I could do some scrapbooking with old photos."

"Scrapbooking. Okay."

"Yeah. Like a hobby. A woman I met in the program traded in her addiction to bourbon for an addiction to quilting. She told me quite a few people take up a hobby of some sort to keep busy. But they're addicts, so they get *overly* involved. I've got boxes and boxes of photos and shit up there to keep me busy until I die . . . or relapse."

"Do you have a sponsor? Someone to call if you get the urge?"

"Yeah. This woman Charlene S. Not even thirty. Been through a lot though. She's sober now for three years. She started drinking when she was fourteen." She lowered her voice. "She was sexually abused by her father." She shrugged. "We all have our demons to bear."

"What was your demon?"

"Well, nothing as serious as Charlene's. Just disappointment, I guess."

I nodded, wondering if that was the extent of what she would say on the matter. But I did notice a change in her demeanor.

Perhaps it was the two full weeks of sobriety. A window opening, just a crack, to let other people in. But she said nothing more. A part of me wanted to press her to explain what kinds of disappointment required the comfort of drinking herself senseless. But this felt like neither the time nor place. *When is it ever, though?* Maybe when she hit the thirty-day mark of sobriety. Then, perhaps, it would feel real and she'd be willing to edge up that window a hair more.

I removed the shoebox lid and randomly picked up a photograph. Lori and I were wearing bikinis. Hers was blue with yellow flowers. Mine black with white polka dots. Our hands on our shapeless hips, Wonder Woman pose. Both of us flat chested. Definitely the summer between sixth and seventh grade. We were standing in her backyard, the edge of the Roths' private pool visible in the background. I peered into the shoebox. There were probably three dozen pictures of me and Lori, in various poses, in various locations, taken by whomever might have been hanging out with us that day. For my tenth birthday, my parents bought me a Kodak Pocket Instamatic camera (which I begged for every time the commercial aired). I was so excited when I saw that camera nestled inside the red velvet-like lining of the box. It came with a wrist strap, a flash Magicube, and Magicube extender. With my allowance money, I would buy rolls of 110 film and bring them back to the local drugstore for development. I kept the pictures in their original envelopes, along with the negatives. I never bothered to create photo albums—just kept them organized by writing the date on the envelopes. I would pluck one or two photos from the batch and thumbtack them to the cork bulletin board that hung over the desk in my bedroom.

Thomas must have sifted through dozens and dozens of envelopes to find all these pictures of the two of us. I wondered how much he divined about my childhood by looking through them. Did he witness the deterioration of my friendship with Lori between the ages of ten (always smiling) and fourteen (sullen-faced)?

I dumped the photos onto the kitchen table. My mother sat and started moving them around, attempting to put them in chronological order.

"I remember you and that camera. Snapping everything in sight. I thought you were going to grow up and become a spy . . . or a journalist."

Spy, journalist, cop. All the same, really. Searching for answers. For the truth.

CHAPTER THIRTY-TWO

Thursday, December 6, 2018

MOXIE STIRRED at the edge of the bed. A guttural moan escaped her throat. With my eye mask in place, I felt for Ray, then remembered he spent the night on a friend's couch in Brooklyn after an evening of bar hopping with some old friends. I peeled off my mask and eyed Moxie. She was alert now, on her haunches, growling softly. The clock read 2:06 am. She leaped off the bed and stood in front of the closed bedroom door, her tail tucked between her legs, her ears pointed forward. I reached for my pajama pants, crumpled on the floor beside me. "Shhh," I whispered. I put my ear up to the door and heard the faint noise of someone moving about the first floor.

Moxie was not exactly what I would call a guard dog. She was more likely to lick someone to death than actually inflict any harm. I pulled her by the collar into the bathroom and shut her in. She whimpered, but I sensed she was relieved to not be taking part in whatever confrontation awaited me. Returning to the bedroom, I slipped my fingers under the mattress and felt for a key. I unlocked the night table drawer and retrieved my weapon. I slowly turned the door handle and squeezed through the opening, then tiptoed down the hallway toward the stairs. About three quarters of the way down the stairs, I crouched and surveyed the two rooms I could see from this position. The living room on my right and the kitchen to my left. Nobody. Another four steps and my bare feet touched down on the first floor. I heard a drawer open. I exhaled slowly and raised my gun. I walked toward the back of the house and planted myself at the threshold between the dining room and my office.

"Police. Hands where I can see them," I said calmly to the back of the man standing over my desk.

He raised his hands, his cell-phone flashlight gleaming from his palm.

"Now turn around slowly."

I moved to the corner of the room and flipped the light switch. I recognized the man standing in front of me. I had seen his face in the local paper. Ernest Barnes. Calvin's father.

"On your knees. Hands on your head."

"I . . . I ain't carrying," he said, lowering himself to the floor. His voice continued to tremble. "I . . . I thought you were out of town."

I kept my gun trained on Ernest as I removed handcuffs from the bottom drawer of my desk. "I'm gonna cuff you. Don't make any sudden moves, okay?"

"Okay."

Once the cuffs were secured on his wrists, I helped Ernest up off his knees and patted him down. Like he said, he was not carrying. "So you want to tell me what you're doing here rifling through my things?"

Ernest shook his head and sighed. "I heard you were out of town. I just come here to find the videotape. See for myself what the police is claiming what happened."

"First of all, there is no videotape. I mean, not in the way you're thinking. It's a webcam feed, and it is password protected. And even I don't know the password."

"Why won't the police release it? It's like they got something to hide."

"It's evidence. Everything has a process. My understanding is that it will be released to your attorney early next week."

"I know my son. He just wouldn't do what you're sayin' he done."

It wasn't the first time I heard the anguish of a parent disbelieving the actions of their flesh and blood. But he didn't have to throw a stone far to hit a cop who had used excessive, even deadly, force. He had every right to disbelieve my claim of self-defense.

"I'm going to take the cuffs off, okay? Don't do anything stupid." I removed the cuffs and asked him if he wanted to sit in the dining room. He nodded.

"I really can't talk to you about this case. I'm pretty sure you know that. I am sorry that your son is dead. But I'm not sorry about trying to protect myself." I wanted to say something about how I fucked up not waiting for backup or that I simply could have walked away and opened up an investigation. But with the civil case pending, I was not supposed be anywhere near the Barnes family, let alone ask Calvin's dad for forgiveness.

Ernest bowed his head. He clasped his hands and placed them between his knees. When he looked up, he said, "I tried to be a good father to those boys. They were good boys. They got turned around by someone. They got turned around. They were no longer hanging with the nice kids they went to school with. Someone got to them. That Wayne Railman. He's no good. He turned them around."

"Like I said, I really can't talk to you about this." I stood up and crossed over to his side of the table. "I gotta ask you, Mr. Barnes . . . are you the one leaving threatening notes on my windshield?"

"That ain't me." He paused. "I swear."

"Okay. Now, tell me, what do you think I should do regarding this little situation? Should we call it a momentary lapse in judgment?"

His shoulders shuddered in defeat. "I won't bother you again."

"Go home, Mr. Barnes. Go home to your wife and your young son."

After seeing Ernest out, I trudged up the stairs and heard the faint cries of Moxie whining and whimpering behind my closed bathroom door. When I opened the door she bolted past me down the stairs. She stood at the front door, her tail wagging, probably upset that she didn't get to meet our nocturnal intruder.

THE GUN was under Ray's pillow, untouched since I tucked it in after Ernest left. It took me a while to fall back to sleep. The last time I looked at the clock it was 3:18 am. So I probably conked out soon after that.

I locked my gun in the drawer, then checked my text messages. Ray was on his way back home. Left at seven thirty this morning.

If there was no traffic, he should be walking through the door in about fifteen minutes. I told Moxie I would walk her soon. I would like to believe she understood my need to shower first—to wash away the sweaty residue brought on by last night's drama.

"Hey babe," Ray said, poking his head into the steamy bathroom.

"Welcome back," I said from behind the curtain. I had already decided that last night's incident would stay between me and Moxie.

"Running late?"

"Yeah, decided to sleep in a bit."

"I'm heading over to the precinct. Will I see you over there?"

"Yeah. Just gotta make a pit stop." I turned off the water just as Ray closed the door.

Pit stop. Actually, a conversation I should have had weeks ago.

"COFFEE?" I asked while pouring myself a cup.

"Sure."

I reached into the cabinet and pulled down a mug with Snoopy dancing on his doghouse.

"Milk? Sugar?"

"Just black," Thomas replied. "Like me," he added, then chuckled.

"The house looks nice, Thomas. I think this clean and orderly environment is having a positive effect on my mom." I placed the mug of coffee in front of him. "That, and your convincing her to go to AA meetings."

"The key to convincing someone is to make it appear as though you didn't convince them. That they came to their idea of their own accord."

"Lead a horse to water . . ."

"You can't make them drink, but if they're thirsty, they will."

I sipped the coffee. "I didn't come by to talk about my mother . . . but I do appreciate all you've done for her." I sat down at the table with Thomas. "I've been meaning to ask you something for some time now. And with that run-in at the Underground—"

"You want to know where I stand with the Barnes shooting? Like I told you, I'm swayed by the facts. Sure, when the news first broke, I was raging inside. Not gonna lie. Didn't think that would happen here. And when it did, well, I was like, this place isn't any different than all the other places this has happened. When I first met your dad, I didn't put two and two together. And we was hitting it off fine. But when he told me you was his daughter, I stormed off feeling like a damn fool. And I was like . . . what's the word? . . . yeah, conflicted. But we talked after that. He told me your side of the story. He said good detectives check their preconceptions at the door. Don't jump to conclusions. Listen to both sides. Gather the facts. Soon after that he offered me up your room."

"I got the feeling you didn't know who I was when we first met—that day in my bedroom."

"Oh, I knew. Just didn't think it was the time or place to bring it up, especially with your mom standing there. I was gonna say something when you stopped by to get your diary. But I could tell you weren't ready to talk."

"Do cops give you trouble?"

"Around here, no. Other places, yeah. But my dad could tell you stories."

"Like what?"

"He was an appliance repair guy, retired now. Drove a van all over Sullivan and Ulster counties making deliveries, installations, on-call repairs. Of the four guys who worked for Hollis Appliances, he was the only Black man. And, guess what—he was the only one that ever got pulled over by the cops—not for traffic violations, mind you, but on suspicion of being a suspect in some crime." Thomas explained this as a quiet, matter-of-fact truth. "They would hassle him as to what was in the boxes. They asked him why there was money and checks in his clipboard."

I wanted to interject here. Tell him I know this shit still happens. But, of course, he knows that. Instead, I simply nodded.

He continued, "I think the thing that really bothered him was being called 'boy,' which he said was worse than being called . . . uh, y'know . . . the n-word."

I nodded.

"When I asked him why he put up with it, my daddy would say, 'It's a white man's world, and I do my best to live in it.'" Thomas shook his head. "He was compliant. Made me mad as hell. There's no room for complacency anymore."

"Is that why you are studying criminal justice?"

"Maybe I can make a difference inside the system." I sensed a shift in his demeanor. His eyes were gleaming now. He licked his lips. "Someday . . . Maybe someday soon there will be an incident of police brutality that will get everybody's attention. It will make the Rodney King riots look like child's play." He leaned forward in his chair. "So, I gotta ask. What's up with the video?"

I gave Thomas the backstory—noticing the camera in the eaves, contacting Mordecai Little to give us access, spotting the gun resting against Calvin's hip. I told him there was more to the story, but the details—the facts—for those he would just have to wait like everyone else.

CHAPTER THIRTY-THREE

Friday, December 7, 2018

THE WAITRESS winked at Dad while pouring him a second cup of coffee.

When she walked away, I asked, "Do you know her?"

"Who?"

"The waitress. She just winked at you."

He twisted around in his seat looking for her. "No. I guess I just have that effect on women."

"Speaking of women you have an effect on . . . did Mom tell you she was going to AA meetings?"

"Didn't know that."

"Thomas takes his aunt, and somehow convinced her to come along."

"That Thomas is a good kid. I done good there, putting them together, if I do say so myself."

"Got a question for you . . . about Mom. Not sure if you even know the answer."

"Well, when it comes to your mother, I usually have more questions than answers. But go ahead, shoot."

"Why does Mom drink? I mean, what compelled her to start drinking so heavily?"

"Now that is a loaded question," Dad said, but the half smile told me I had not gone too far asking it. "I don't think it was any one thing, Susan. But shouldn't you be having this conversation with her?"

"Just humor me, Dad. What's your take?"

"Well, her father and uncles were alcoholics—that must play a part. And some of the blame certainly rests with me, and my life as a cop. The woman I married and the woman I divorced were, essentially, two different women. The woman I married was vivacious and generous. The woman I divorced was surly and isolated."

I only knew the second woman. "Generous? What do you mean by that?"

"When we first got married, she volunteered her time at the library and the high school. She actually wanted to become a librarian, but she never finished college, and then you came along. She continued to volunteer at those places, even organized their fundraisers. She also worked part-time over at Joe's hardware store, so she could have what she called 'her own spending money.' And you know what she did with that money? Made sure fundraising goals were met. If a fundraiser was shy of its goal, she topped it off."

"Why don't I remember any of this?"

"It all came to an abrupt end when you were about five. If I had to pick a point in time, I would say she started drinking in the early seventies. Usually a glass—or two—of wine at dinner. Perhaps more at a party." He swirled the last sip of coffee in his mug, then turned and signaled to the waitress who had winked at him. He leaned in closer to me, and whispered, "Depression wasn't something people talked about back then. You self-medicated. Wine morphed into vodka. The time of day no longer mattered. I think she saw her life on a slow track to nowhere. But I was so steeped in work, I was oblivious until it was too late."

"Well, I gotta tell you, I wasn't oblivious. It was pretty clear to me, even as a kid, that Mom had a drinking problem." I threw my head back and exhaled. I didn't want to end up in a fight with Dad. "Why have you never told me any of this before?"

"I don't know. You never asked, for one. And it's not something I like to talk about. I carry around some amount of guilt for how things turned out for her."

The waitress sidled up close to Dad. "Want another cup?"

"Fill 'er up."

"You just let me know if you want more, honey." The waitress flashed a flirtatious smile before leaving his side.

"You should ask her out on a date," I said.

"The waitress?" he half laughed, half snorted. "Not my type. A little too . . . skinny for my taste," he said, sliding his hands down the front of his chest.

I grimaced and glanced around to see if anyone just saw him, but everyone around us was involved in their own conversations. "Um, okay, well, I wasn't aware you had a type," I said. "So, about Mom, I know this is a tough subject for both of us. But now that she might be getting herself help, I'm willing to meet her halfway. Get to a better place with her."

"I'm glad to hear that, Susan. Why the change of heart?"

"I don't know. Maybe I'm seeing things in a whole new light these days. And a lot of that has to do with getting back in touch with the Roths . . . which, believe me, I never would have done if you didn't strong-arm me into resurrecting the Solomon case." My palms started to sweat—perhaps a Pavlovian response to mentioning the Roths, if I had to muster a guess. I grabbed a couple of napkins to absorb the moisture. "My conversations with them have been pretty mind-blowing. I really thought they were the perfect family. Sure, we had problems . . . but seems they are on a whole different level of dysfunction. And talking to Lori, hearing her perspective on our friendship, well, just proves the old adage that every story has two sides. I can't totally erase from my mind all the times Mom made me feel like shit, but y'know, I'll cop to the fact that I couldn't see past my own anger to walk a day in her shoes."

"Alcoholism is a disease, Susan. You know that."

"Knowing that doesn't make it any easier to deal with her. But, like I said, I'm willing to try."

The waitress reappeared at Dad's side. "Is there anything else I can get you?"

"How about your phone number?" Dad said.

She retrieved a scrap of paper from her apron pocket and scribbled down her number. "I thought you'd never ask," she said as she shimmied away.

"Really?"

"What? You're the one who suggested it."

I STARED at my two whiteboards. A few weeks ago, I'd moved Trudy's picture from the Victim column to the Witnesses column. In her place, two other victims stared back at me: Renee Carter and Ed Resnick. Were these cases related? The jury was still out on that.

For the moment, I just wanted to concentrate on the Trudy Solomon/Ed Resnick case. Have it straight in my head before chatting with the Roths at the party. The Witnesses column was crowded with all the people who had helped us piece together Trudy's story. I was amazed that we were able to track down a few of the original witnesses and find new ones (hat tip to Dad). I had arranged the witnesses along a time line, starting with Rita Mayer, the hotel cocktail waitress who met Trudy a few years before she disappeared and provided us with background on Trudy and Ben. The timeline ended with Ray finding Trudy at an Alzheimer's facility in Lowell, Massachusetts. In between—neighbors, friends, hotel staff, a hotel guest, a doctor, a nurse, a detective, and a nun.

The Suspects column was less crowded. Who wanted Ed dead? Who had motive and opportunity? There was Stanley Roth, who threatened Trudy in 1978 and years later was forking over two grand a month to Ed. (And, according to his wife Rachel, he left the inn the day of the murder and was gone for the entire day.) There was Rachel Roth, who wanted to end the payments to Ed and Trudy when money got tight. (But she was in the Berkshires the day of the murder.) There was Scott Roth, who also knew Ed was demanding money from his parents and made an earlier attempt to squash it. (His alibi simply meant he didn't take matters into his own hands, but he certainly made enough money to hire someone.) There was Ben Solomon, who might have exacted revenge on Ed for absconding with his wife. (As much as I didn't trust Ben, my instincts told me he truly didn't know Ed, let alone Trudy's whereabouts.) There

CHAPTER THIRTY-FOUR

Saturday, December 8, 2018

ONE YEAR before they tied the proverbial knot, the youngest Roth sibling, Josh, and his boyfriend, Steven, bought a turn-of-the-century six-suite guest house in the Berkshires town of North Adams, an historic mill town (now a tourist draw) situated in the northwest corner of Massachusetts. Steven, a Culinary Institute of America-trained chef, ran the kitchen. Josh, with a degree in hospitality from Boston University, handled everything else. They got married on Saturday, July 19, 2008, at the historic inn. It was a close-knit friends-and-family affair, officiated by a local minister. ("Low-key and joyful," Lori said.) Three months later, a fire swept through the inn. Neither wanted to rebuild, so they plowed the insurance money into a twenty-room bed and breakfast in Brattleboro, Vermont. The existing inn (called the Brattle) had a so-so reputation on travel websites, so they renamed it Blueberry Hill Inn, and now, when you googled it or searched for it on TripAdvisor, it ranked as one of the top three places to stay in Vermont. They converted a barn on the property to a year-round event hall for weddings and whatnot. They also rebuilt a dilapidated smokehouse and sold cured meats as a side business.

About an hour into our four-hour drive to Brattleboro, I rattled off this information to Ray.

"You're a fountain of knowledge," Ray said. "How do you know all this stuff?"

"Lori. She called to tell me how thrilled she was that I was coming."

"And you're sure Scott is coming?"

"Lori said he is. The brothers remained somewhat close. Lori said she doesn't need Scott's negativity in her life. My sense is that Meryl is the 'let's all try and get along' sibling, but Lori said even Meryl thinks Scott is too harsh. Says he's a grudge holder, mad at the world."

"Life's too short. I agree with Lori." Ray poked my left thigh. "I prefer to be around positive people. Spread love and good cheer."

"Is that why you became a cop?"

"Yes! Because it's our job to make peace in the valley and restore order to a troubled world."

"Really?"

"What? That's not why *you* became a cop?"

"Always the comedian." I poked his right thigh.

I spun the radio dial, trying to find a music station after the one we were listening to fell out of range. But all I could find was a country music station (Ray nixed that), a conservative talk radio station (we both nixed that), and a classical music station (Ray nixed that as well, claiming it would make him sleepy).

"Podcast?" I asked.

"That true-crime one you like?"

"Nope. This is another one, called *Serial.*"

"Let it rip."

RAY HAD booked us a room at a nearby inn, the Stone Arch Lodge. Lori recommended it based on its proximity to the Blueberry Hill Inn and its reputation for incredible pancakes. I was surprised there was a room available a few days before the party, but as luck would have it, another couple (college friends of Josh's) canceled that morning when their child came down with fifth disease (as reported to me by Lori when I told her we snagged a room). The party was scheduled to start at six o'clock, giving us a few hours to relax, shower, and strategize about how to cajole Scott. Pry out of him what he knew. We were eager to get our first glimpse of the feeble patriarch, Stanley Roth. I hoped to get some alone time with him—suss out his mental state and memory.

With time to kill, I set off to explore the grounds and to check out the majestic stone arch that gave the inn its name. At check-in, the receptionist told us it served as a photographic backdrop for many brides and grooms. ("Couples have even gotten married under it," she said.) I wandered over to the stone arch and ran my fingers along the edge of the interlocking marbled-gray rocks. It always amazed me how masons found exactly the right stones to construct these architectural marvels. At its center, the arch was about seven, maybe seven-and-a-half feet high. Plenty of clearance for even a very tall groom. I walked from one end to the other and counted out eight steps, heel to toe. Low stone walls jutted out from both sides of the arch and continued for about twenty or so feet, gently tapering off until they blended with the ground cover. I could see why couples would pick this spot for wedding photographs. Leafless, gangly branches loomed above. Vibrant evergreens, coated with a dusting of snow, in the foreground. A shiny frost carpeted the underbrush, shimmering slightly in the afternoon sun. Each season offering up its own charms. Flowers and budding bushes in the spring. Bright sun filtering through the treetops in summer. Canopies of colored leaves in the fall. With all the variations of shadow and light in this spot, you could probably take hundreds of photographs, and no two would ever be the same.

I heard rustling behind me and turned around.

"Hey, babe."

I handed Ray my phone. "Take a picture of me under the arch."

"We need to start getting ready," he said, snapping a few photos.

"Let me get a few of you." A small puffy cloud blocked the sun, suddenly diminishing the light.

"Hey, Ansel Adams, what are you waiting for?"

When the sun reappeared, I snapped a few pictures of Ray.

THE BARN twinkled. Trendy teardrop Edison bulbs hung from the rafters. String lights wound their way up the support beams. Christmas-tree lights were tucked into potted evergreens, illuminating the sharp needles. In the far corner of the barn, a string quartet was playing classical music. According to Lori, a DJ would be spinning seventies disco music after dinner. The parquet dance floor was currently occupied by mingling guests and white-jacketed servers who were passing out hors d'oeuvres and prosecco.

Seating assignment cards were displayed on a misshapen table made of reclaimed wood situated at the front entrance of the barn. *Ray Gorman & Susan Ford.* Our names expertly calligraphed on the outside of the tented card. I flipped it open—*Table 14.* Tables 13 through 16 were lined up in the back row. Each round table accommodated six people.

If everyone showed up, there would be ninety-six guests in attendance. I moved down to the other end of the card table to see if Scott had picked up his table assignment. Before I had a chance to look, I heard my name.

"Suzie!"

When I turned, I came face-to-face with her. "Lori!"

We hugged fiercely, as though the four awful years in high school never existed.

"Oh my! You haven't changed a bit," Lori said. "Well, maybe a little bit. But, damn, you look wonderful."

Lori had changed quite a bit. She'd put on about forty pounds, making her face rounder, more moon-shaped than I remembered. Her auburn hair dyed to frosted blonde. The long curls shorn, and in their place, a face-framing pixie hairdo. Pink eyeglasses, round and large, obscured the upper part of her face. She was tan, with deep wrinkles, the premature kind you get from overexposure to the sun. I had seen the changes on Facebook, but they were more pronounced in real life.

"You look wonderful, too." I said. That wasn't a lie. Yes, she had changed, and quite dramatically. But she really did look wonderful. The extra weight, the round face, the blonde hair, the funky glasses, the tan, even the wrinkles—it all worked on her. I suddenly felt Ray's presence at my side. "Lori, this is Ray. Ray, this is Lori."

They shook hands and, in unison, said hi. Ray added, "Happy birthday."

"Liam is over by the bar. I can introduce you guys later." Lori turned to Ray. "Do you mind if I steal Suzie for a bit?"

"Go ahead. Enjoy, *Suzie*, I—"

Before he could finish his sentence, she hooked my arm and led me to the front tables near the string quartet.

"Look who I found," Lori said.

Josh stood up from his seat at Table 1 and stared at me for a few minutes. "Suzie Ford?"

"This is the surprise guest I was telling you about."

"So, you're the reason Lori and Meryl insisted on being in charge of table seating."

Unlike Lori, Josh hadn't changed all that much since I last saw him, which would probably be when I left for college in the early eighties. He was still slim. He held onto his hair, with slight receding at the temples. Just a few wisps of gray visible. The wire-frame glasses were similar to the ones he wore as a teenager. He was a cute kid; he had grown into quite a handsome man.

"I'm going to rescue Liam from my mother. If you'll excuse me for a minute."

I watched as Lori made her way to the bar and spotted Rachel talking to an older gentleman, easily twenty years older than us. Liam, I presumed.

"So, Suzie. What are you up to these days?" Josh asked.

I decided to let the whole Suzie thing slide. I knew it was bound to happen. On some level, it was actually endearing. "Living in Bethel. I'm a police detective."

"Holy shit. Wow. Your dad was a cop, right?"

"Detective. Will Ford."

"Yeah. Yeah. I remember him. Nice guy. Still alive?"

"Alive and kicking. Enjoying his retirement."

"And your mom?"

"Very much alive. And very much kicking. And you? How's life?"

"Crazy, but I love it. I'm living what I dreamed. Can't wish for anything more than that."

"And your family? I heard it's been a while since you've all been together."

"Ten and a half years, to be exact—when Steven and I got married. Those days we were more like the Ewings than the Brady Bunch. I'm not sure things have improved much."

"Lori filled me in on some of the family drama. You were living in Massachusetts at the time, right?"

"Yeah. We were running a small inn in the Berkshires. It's where we got married. The wedding was a bit of a fiasco. Scott wasn't speaking to my father. Still isn't for that matter. Lori wasn't speaking to Scott. And Meryl was pissed because Scott bolted from the reception before the toast to catch a plane to some dealership conference." He paused to catch his breath.

I nodded. This bit of information lined up with what Detective Flannery had told us. Scott couldn't have stabbed Ed because he was headed to Las Vegas at the time.

Josh continued, "I was in a bit of a rift with my mother. And my father had not exactly warmed to the idea of a gay wedding. And then Dad got ill. Blamed the food—although no one else got sick. But it might have been a blessing in disguise. Steven insisted on taking care of him that day, and they bonded a bit. Over baseball, no less. Red Sox versus Mariners. Still fresh in my mind, I guess."

"This happened the day after the wedding?"

"Yeah. July twentieth."

"So your dad was stuck at the inn that entire day?"

"With his head in the toilet."

"And your mom. Did she help out?"

Josh snorted. "Claimed she had to meet a friend in Boston. Left early that morning and we didn't see her again until later that night."

I scanned the bar area looking for Rachel. Instead, I saw Lori talking to Ray. Rachel *had* lied about her husband having gone to see Ed that day.

And with such conviction. I was still kicking myself for not pushing her harder when we had the chance. I had to keep reminding myself I wasn't thirteen years old and she no longer had enormous power over me—but it somehow still felt that way. I had a few more questions for Josh, but thought better of conducting an inquisition while guests milled around us. There would be time for that.

"Well, everyone's here now. That's all that matters. And I have to say, the setting is gorgeous." When I turned around, Rachel was standing next to me. *Stay cool.*

"Why, hello Suzie. I didn't realize you were invited. You two catching up on old times?"

"I was just complimenting Josh on how beautiful this place is. Such a perfect setting for a party." I turned back to Josh. "It was so lovely seeing you again. I'm sure you have lots of guests you want to chat with." Luckily, Josh acted on my cue and beelined it to a guest on the other side of the table. The last thing I needed was Rachel alone with Josh, asking him what we were just talking about.

"Funny. You didn't mention you were attending this shindig when we met last week," Rachel said.

I smiled warmly. "Last-minute decision to come. It's nice to see everyone again. Now, if you'll excuse me, Mrs. Roth, I just spotted Meryl and I haven't said hello to her yet."

I eyed Ray coming toward me and, when we met on the parquet floor, I steered him toward the far side of the barn, where Meryl was standing with four guests. Meryl had aged well. Out of the four siblings, she most resembled her mother in her Rachel-like glamour. When she lifted her martini glass to her lips, she spotted me and excused herself from the group.

"Well, as I live and breathe. Suz . . . oops . . . Susan Ford. Lori was telling me how great you look. And you do! And you must be Ray." Before Ray could answer, she asked, "Have you seen everyone yet?"

"Just quick conversations with Lori and Josh. But the night is young."

Meryl lowered her voice and leaned in. "Scott just arrived." She pointed toward the entrance. "The gang's all here."

Ray and I snapped our necks around. Scott reached for his table card, glanced at it quickly, and tucked it into his sport-jacket pocket. Behind him, his daughter Mandy. At his side, the high-heeled, pencil-skirted woman we met at his car dealership. Christie Lamont. Well, well . . . this family was full of surprises. For this occasion, Christie was dolled up in a tight black dress, her breasts swelling over the V-neck plunge.

"To tell you the truth, I'm surprised Scott is here. He can't stand to be in the same room with my father," Meryl said. "It took a lot of convincing. But I think it was his fiancée who pushed him to come. I think she was curious. This family is like a car wreck. It's hard not to rubberneck. I think she wanted to see what all the fuss was about. I'm sure Scott has given her an earful as to how insane we all are."

If Meryl knew I'd gone to see Scott last month, she kept that fact to herself. But Scott might have had his own reasons for not disclosing our meeting to her. Besides, her beef was with me talking to her parents—and she hadn't mentioned that either. This family feud definitely worked in our favor. They were not all on the same page.

Meryl turned to her right. "See that gorgeous hunk over there?" She waved at him. "The tall one. That's my husband, Mike."

"Easy to spot in a crowd," Ray said. "Six five?"

"Six seven. He was a tight end in college. Probably could have played pro, but medicine was his calling. The cheerleader and the football jock. So cliché, huh?"

I glanced at Ray and raised my eyebrows. He grinned. If we were by ourselves I'm sure he would have pretended to barf.

Mike wove his way toward us, first dodging a server, then gingerly stepping around a young girl darting through the crowd, leaving defenders in the dust. For a big guy, he was pretty deft.

"Hi, hon. Old friends?" Mike held out his beefy hand.

After introductions, we chatted for a while. Family, careers, weather. Typical party banter. She pointed out her three daughters, who were standing together near Table 4. I asked her if Lori's daughter was at the party, and she told me she was on her way but running late. ("Breastfeeding!" Meryl said, offering this as an explanation.) When we ran out of small talk, Meryl held up her empty martini glass and excused herself for a refill. Mike fell in line behind her as she moved toward the bar.

"Ray, we gotta talk. Somewhere private."

"Follow me."

I followed Ray to the back of the barn, where intimate seating areas had been arranged.

I filled Ray in on the conversation with Josh. "What do you think?"

"Sounds like we got ourselves a new prime suspect."

"She certainly had a motive."

"Yeah . . . to stop the payments. Then she committed Trudy to a mental hospital, tying up loose ends."

"Before we confront Rachel, I would like to know what that blackmail money was all about. And, as Dad would have said, my Spidey sense tells me Scott knows something."

"What makes you think he'd be willing to talk to you this time?"

"Something Trudy said to us that I think will get him to open up."

"And that is?"

"That he was her hero. Came to her rescue. Maybe he's willing to do it again."

"Good luck trying to get him alone."

A server, carrying a tray of pigs in blankets, appeared and asked if we would like to indulge. We each took a napkin and a toothpick, stabbed a pig and dipped it into the little bowl of mustard.

"I have an idea," I said, holding up my mustard-slathered mini hotdog encased in a pastry puff.

RAY POKED four blanketed pigs with toothpicks and dipped them—generously—in the mustard. I watched him hurry over to Scott and, pretty convincingly (in a Chevy-Chase-as-Gerald-Ford kind of way), accidentally trip and smear the mustard across Scott's sleeve. Ray apologized profusely and pointed in the direction of the bathroom. Now the two of them were heading my way. That was my cue to duck inside.

The door to the men's room swung open. Scott's initial expression led me to believe he probably thought he'd walked into the ladies' room. He glanced at the urinals. He looked at me again.

"What the hell?" he roared.

"You don't want that mustard to stain." I jutted my chin out toward the sink.

Scott grabbed a handful of paper towels, ran them under the water, and started mopping up the mustard. "What the fuck are you doing in here? Is this another one of your ambushes?"

"Look Scott, I only need a few minutes of your time. We went to see Trudy and she said you can help us. Like you helped her all those years ago."

"I have no idea what you're talking about."

He turned to leave, but when he opened the door, Ray was standing there, blocking his escape route.

"Scott, I'm not sure who you think you are protecting," I said. "But, the truth will come out. We have reason to believe that your mother killed Ed and committed Trudy to a mental hospital to put an end to some blackmail scheme."

"That can't be. My mother had nothing—"

I waited for him to finish the sentence, but he did not. "Go on, Scott. You were saying."

"Not in here. I'm parked right outside the barn."

Ray and I followed Scott through the barn. Guests were beginning to take their seats. He passed Christie and whispered into her ear. When we got outside, he unlocked his rented SUV. I climbed into the passenger seat, Ray sat behind me.

"I'm not sure why you think my mother is involved in all this. The bad guy in this story is my father."

"Why are you protecting him?"

"I'm not protecting him. I'm protecting my mother. He can rot in hell for all I care. I kept quiet to spare her from his atrocities. She wanted to pretend everything was hunky dory, and I gave her that."

"Atrocities?"

"You want the truth? Here's the truth . . . my father raped Trudy."

I heard Dad's words in my head: *Poker face. Poker face.* "And you know this . . . how?"

"I witnessed it."

"You witnessed your father raping Trudy?"

"Well, not the actual rape. The aftermath." Scott tapped on the steering wheel, thrumming a Morse code-like pattern. "Trudy was on night patrol that night."

"Night patrol?" Ray asked.

"It was a service for parents who wanted to go to the nightclub, but were too cheap to hire a babysitter. Trudy would walk around the hotel grounds and listen in at their doors. She wasn't allowed to enter, but if she heard crying or something, she would alert the bellhop station. A dollar a door, so you could make good money on a busy night."

"Okay. Go on."

"It was mid-June, before the start of the summer season. I saw my father come out of a guest room—one of the Skybridge Terrace rooms—and skulk away. I figured he was fucking a guest, as usual. But then I heard sobbing. When I opened the door, I saw Trudy on the bed, disheveled and crying. She said he threatened her to keep quiet and begged me not to say anything."

"So that's why you thought your father killed Trudy?" Ray said.

"When she disappeared, I confronted my father. He swore up and down that he did not kill her. He knew she had run off with someone . . . heard it from this guy who used to work in the coffee shop. I thought, good for her. If she wanted to disappear and make a new life for herself, who was I to convince her to file a sexual-assault charge—"

"Where people would be more likely to take Stanley's side over Trudy's," I interjected. "Your father could have claimed it was consensual."

"Exactly. This is 1978 we're talking about," Ray added. "And Stanley had resources and friends in high places."

"Look, I need to get back to the party," Scott said.

"We're not done here," I said. "What do you say we meet after dessert?"

Scott nodded, pulling on the door latch. "Sure." He paused. "And you're wrong about my mother."

WE MISSED the salad. As we settled into our seats at Table 14, the waiter placed a shrimp cocktail appetizer in front of us. Four enormous shrimps lounging on the lip of a glass dish with a couple tablespoons of cocktail sauce at the bottom of the bowl. I introduced myself to our table mates. To Ray's right, Marisa and Cameron. And to my left, Carol and Mason. We learned Marisa and Carol were Meryl's friends from the literary agency where she used to work.

"We were hoping that whoever sat with us also had the first initials *M* and *C*," said Carol. "That would have been funny."

Mason rolled his eyes.

Once the shrimp was cleared, the waiter asked our preference for dinner: a spinach-stuffed chicken breast, filet mignon with garlic herb butter, or a vegetarian option of grilled vegetables. The men opted for the steak. The women chose the chicken. Marisa and

Carol tried to include me in their conversation, asking questions about family ("Wow, twin grandsons!"), career ("Oooh, you're a cop. How badass!"), and how I knew the Roths ("Sounds like a fun childhood"). When I told them I was friends with Lori, Marisa lamented that none of Lori's friends came because of the distance. ("California to Vermont in the dead of winter, and right before Christmas, is probably tough to manage.")

I was eager for dessert. The conversation was pleasant enough, even interesting at times, but I was afraid Scott would bolt if he got the chance. Carol was mid-sentence when Meryl tapped on a microphone, yelling "Testing, testing, is this thing on?" Table by table, the buzz of conversations subsided.

Meryl started her speech by thanking everyone for coming. She joked about the mishmash of celebrations—a birthday, a retirement, an engagement, a wedding anniversary. She mentioned a few other Roth milestones that had occurred earlier in the year—the birth of Lori's granddaughter, her own daughter's recent engagement, her parents' fifty-eighth wedding anniversary. She directed guests to the back of the barn where they could view old photos of the Roth clan. She let everyone know that after dessert the DJ would be spinning tunes, and dancing was mandatory. She said there were no planned speeches—besides the one she was giving.

A slice of cake was nimbly placed at each of our settings by stealthy servers.

Meryl finished up by adding, "I had hoped to regale you all with the history of the Cuttman and Roth ancestors, but alas, Ancestry dot com must be extra busy these days, cuz I'm still waiting for the results. In the meantime, I built a little family tree going back to my great-grandparents, and if you're interested in our history and the history of the hotel, you can find that among the photographs."

I remembered Meryl had mentioned this family-tree project, back when we first exchanged messages. Dad thought about finding long-lost relatives through one of these DNA databases, but that inclination lasted a hot second. ("I'm not thrilled with the relatives I got, so not keen on finding more Fords," he semi-joked.)

Ray gently kicked my shin and tilted his head to the side, signaling Scott's movement to the door. He whispered, "That's our cue."

Ray and I excused ourselves from the table just as the DJ put on a David Bowie song and yelled into his microphone, "Let's dance!"

THE TEMPERATURE in the car had dropped since the last time we sat in it, about an hour ago. Scott pressed the ignition button and blasted the heat.

"Just so we are clear—I'm not going to sit on some witness stand and repeat any of this. I thought about this a whole lot since your little ambush down in Florida. I'm done with the charade. But if you want to hear my story, this is the one and only time I will tell it."

I had no authority to agree to his conditions, but I figured I could sort that out later.

As though reading my mind, Ray said, "Can't make any promises on that, but we will do what we can."

"You've already told us that Stanley raped Trudy," I said. "Is that what the blackmail scheme was all about?"

Scott sat silent for a few minutes, obviously weighing his options. We let him mull.

"Yes."

"Was your mother in on it?"

"Doubt it."

"Do you know that for sure?"

"Pretty sure."

I felt like I was shaking a Magic 8 Ball, with Scott coughing up short, nebulous answers.

"Can you just tell us what you do know?" Ray said.

I was expecting Scott to say, "*Reply hazy, try again.*"

Instead, he said, "With all the police hanging around that summer, Dad was afraid I would say something. Even though I told him I would not. Which, by the way, was mainly because I was worried about my mother getting dragged into all this. I was also concerned how it would affect hotel business. In hindsight, I might have done something different, but I was just a dumb eighteen-year-old kid then. And he swore he would stay away from Trudy." Scott fiddled with the temperature controls on the console. "My mother actually thought *I* had something to do with Trudy's disappearance. She shipped me off to my aunt's house, afraid I would confess I did something to Trudy. Ha!"

"So that's why you think she didn't know what Stanley had done, and therefore couldn't be in on the extortion scheme."

"Yeah. That and the fact they lived pretty separate lives back then."

"Okay. So, jumping ahead to 2007. Why did you go see Ed and Trudy? How did you even know where to find them?" Ray asked.

"My mother called me in early 2006 asking to borrow money. And I'm thinking, what the fuck? They had millions. That's when I learned the truth about their dwindling finances, heard she'd stumbled upon the extortion, and figured out Trudy and Ed's whereabouts. Anyway, my mother opened a secret bank account, and every month I gave her money. At the very least, it allowed her to keep up appearances, with nice clothes, some jewelry, and a tennis membership."

"And Stanley didn't notice this?"

Scott snorted. "He wouldn't notice her if she stripped naked and pole danced."

One of Ray's eyebrows arched. "Okay. So, then what? A year later you decide to take matters into your own hands and threaten Ed to stop with the extortion scheme?"

"My mother thought I could appeal to Trudy. Explain my parents' current financial situation. I am pretty damn sure my mother had no idea why my father was giving them money, and I think she didn't want to know. But I had a different agenda. I wanted Trudy to expose my father. I was even willing to act as a witness. I figured my mother was better off with him behind bars."

"I guess you didn't factor in Ed's sway over Trudy," I said.

"He went ballistic. Said I didn't know the whole story. And that Stanley caused a lifetime of pain and suffering for Trudy."

"Do you know what he meant by that?" Ray asked.

"That she never fully recovered from the assault, I presume."

I looked at Ray and he nodded. "Trudy was pregnant when she fled. And if what you said is true—that your father raped her in June—she was probably carrying *his* babies—"

"Babies?"

"Twins. According to Ed's siblings, the strain was too much for her. She was institutionalized for some time after their birth."

"Where are they?"

"That's the sixty-four-million-dollar question. They were put up for adoption. Records sealed."

"Holy shit. Holy fucking shit."

"And you're sure Rachel knew nothing about this?" I asked. "Can you be sure that your mother didn't take matters into her own hands, killed Ed and admitted Trudy to a mental hospital?"

Scott pressed the ignition button. The engine quit. Without the heat humming, I could hear Scott breathing rapidly. He opened his door, stepped out into the darkness, and slammed the door behind him. He turned to look at us. For a second there, I thought he was going to lock us in the car. No click. Ray and I scrambled out of the car.

We hurried back to the barn just in time to see Scott storming over to Stanley, who was going nowhere, trapped in a wheelchair near the bathrooms.

"You piece of shit. You goddamned piece of shit." Scott was leaning over the wheelchair. His face two inches from his father's face. Nose to nose.

Ray grabbed Scott by the elbow and pulled him back.

Scott whirled around and snarled, "You stay out of this. This is family business."

"What the hell is going on here?" Meryl muscled herself between Ray and Scott.

"Fuck this!" Scott yelled. He sprinted over to his table, said something to Christie and Mandy—they stood up, retrieved their coats, and walked out of the barn with him.

"What was that all about?" Meryl demanded. "Does this have something to do with that case you were working on?"

The music was blaring and I wasn't sure if Meryl was raising her voice to get above the thumping bass notes or if she was incensed. Her expression was more aghast than angry. I led Meryl away from Stanley and from the corner of my eye, I saw Lori rushing toward us. I moved toward the entrance, away from the loudspeakers. Lori caught up with us near the seating-cards table.

"What just happened there?" Meryl asked. Her voice quieter, but definitely oozing indignation.

"What's going on?" Lori asked.

"I think this has something to do with the Trudy Solomon case," Meryl said. "Am I right?"

I thought to myself, *just tell them, Susan. Lay it all on the line.* "I'm sorry. I can't get into it with you right now. But new evidence has come to light that, um, implicates, um . . . your parents."

"I thought you found Trudy. I thought you said nothing happened to her," Meryl said.

"I never said that," I said. "She's alive, but in the course of our investigation, we uncovered . . . well . . . other things."

"Other things? Is that police jargon?" Meryl's voice ratcheted up a hair more. "I want to know what you think my parents did."

"Is this why you got in touch with us, Susan?" Lori asked. "Is this why you accepted the invitation? To dig up dirt?"

"I . . . I . . . " That phrase—*at a loss for words*—popped into my head. Or maybe it was more like *a deer in headlights*. Either way, I felt cornered. "No . . . and yes. I first turned down the invitation, because we were knee-deep in this investigation. But new information came to light last week, and I was actually excited about the prospect to see you all again, and so—"

"This was my idea." Ray suddenly appeared at my side. "I'm the lead detective on another case that intersects with the Trudy Solomon case."

I glanced up and saw Rachel making her way toward us. *Great.*

Rachel directed her ire at me. "What's going on here? Stanley nearly had a heart attack. I thought you said you were done harassing my family? You said you were closing all lines of inquiry."

"Mrs. Roth—" Ray began.

"Who are you?"

"I'm Ray—"

Rachel held up her hand, palm flat, as though she was being sworn into office. "Actually, I don't care who you are. I think it's time you both leave."

THE COATROOM was on the far side of the barn, to the right of the entrance. While Ray headed off in that direction, I hurried over to Table 6.

"Where was Rachel sitting?" I asked the lone man at the table.

He pointed to the empty chair next to him. I picked up a discarded napkin.

"Thank you," I said, gingerly picking up the lipstick-stained, empty wineglass positioned in front of the half-eaten dessert. I wrapped the glass in the napkin and made for the exit.

TRUDY

TRUDY REMOVED the panties she was wearing and tossed them into a laundry basket filled with other dirty clothing. She opened her top dresser drawer and took out a clean pair of underwear, then hurried back to her bed and slid underneath the covers. She reached toward her toes and inserted a foot in each opening. She slowly inched the panties up from her ankles to her thighs, then stopped abruptly when she heard footsteps in the hallway. Is that him? Is he back? A deep moan escaped as she tried to catch her breath. Trudy slowly sat up and leaned her head against the headboard. She smoothed her hand over her nightgown, tugging at it until it covered her knees. Then she quietly sobbed into her curled fists.

A rap at the slightly opened door startled her.

"Is everything okay in there?" Dr. Meadows asked.

That wasn't his voice, she thought. She quieted her cries, hoping whoever it was would go away. But the tears continued to flow and her breathing picked up pace, betraying her resolve to remain silent.

"Trudy? Are you all right?"

"Yes," she croaked. "Please leave me alone." She glanced up at the door. She couldn't see the room number, but she remembered: 226.

"Trudy?" The man said as he slipped into the room.

Trudy blinked furiously in an attempt to clear the tears. Before her stood Scott Roth. She pulled her knees up to her chest and wrapped her nightgown tighter around her thighs.

"Are you sure you're all right?" Dr. Meadows asked.

Trudy shook her head. "He told me to shut up. He told me I can't tell anyone. Or else."

"Or else what, Trudy?"

Trudy remained silent. Rocked back and forth, her nightgown tight around her thighs.

"Whoever he was, he's gone now. And he's not coming back," Dr. Meadows said, attempting to cajole Trudy back to the present. "Shall I call a nurse to stay with you?"

"You just saw him, didn't you? Crossing the skybridge."

"He's no longer here. He can't hurt you."

"I can't tell anyone—" She pressed her lips tight.

"Trudy, Nurse Mann is here now. You're safe."

The tears started up again.

CHAPTER THIRTY-FIVE

Monday, December 10, 2018

"SUSAN. IT'S Meryl. Please call me when you get a chance. We need to talk." I replayed the voice-mail message for Ray.

"I'll call her later this afternoon."

"Why the wait?"

"Maybe by then I'll have the fingerprint results. Detective Flannery said I'd get them later this afternoon. If the prints we lifted off Rachel's wineglass match the latent prints lifted from Trudy's apartment, at least we'll have some concrete evidence to prove we aren't barking up the wrong tree. I just want to know if there's a match before I call her . . . in case she accuses me of harassing her family for no good reason."

"Gotcha."

"And I'd like Dad in on the call."

"What about Stanley's fingerprints?"

"I couldn't figure out which glass was his. But his prints showed up on AFIS because he was involved in the racino. State law requires all people working at gambling operations to ink and press. I sent those to Flannery as well."

Ray stared at my whiteboards.

"Where are you on the Renee Carter case?" I asked.

"We're just wrapping up. The case seems pretty straightforward—David sent Panda to do his dirty work. Panda enlisted Lenny's help. He confessed to his sister about killing Renee. We know Lenny gave the kid to Ben, who in turn gave him to his sister, Joyce." Ray downed the rest of his coffee. "And we got the gun."

"Will there be a search for Jake's birth parents? I mean, it's quite possible they put David up to this, no?"

"We closed the case, Susan. Eldridge told me to put it on the back burner. You know we ran his DNA through our database and nothing came up. It would be a huge undertaking to try and find whoever David brokered babies for back then. Besides, didn't you say that Jake is doing his own DNA sleuthing? If he finds something, I can revisit the idea."

I got the message loud and clear, and backed off. Ray had enough on his plate with current cases. Resources were tight. We had to pick and choose our battles. Last week's murder of a twelve-year-old girl was foremost on Ray's mind. This baby business was yesterday's news.

Hashtag WhoIsBabyDoe no longer trending.

AT FOUR o'clock, on my way to Horizon Meadows, I got the call I'd been waiting for. Detective John Flannery confirmed that the fingerprints on the purloined wineglass were a match to fingerprints the Waltham police lifted from the inside doorknob. Even more damning, the fingerprints on the counter were inches from the knife block. Of course, it was possible Rachel was in that apartment just prior to the murder, said her piece, and left.

But why would she lie and say Stanley went to see Ed on the day he was murdered? And in the process, give herself an alibi? I'd seen my fair share of cases where guilty people find someone they can pin the blame on. Especially when that someone else was unable to speak or defend themselves, let alone remember what they ate for breakfast. There was no evidence of Stanley being in that apartment. Sure, he could have been wearing gloves, but it was July. And with the evidence suggesting the murder was spur-of-the-moment, the chance of him having gloves handy fell into the slim-to-none column. Then there was the stabbing trajectory—Rachel was about three inches shorter than Ed. Everything pointed to her.

I had texted Meryl a few hours earlier to let her know I would call her when I got home at five o'clock. Ray wanted to listen in on the phone call, so I needed enough time to pick up Dad, drive home, and settle my nerves with a glass of wine before hearing what it was Meryl wanted to tell me. I was fairly sure I was going to get an ear load about ruining the party. But all I thought about was what I planned to unload on her.

Ray's Jeep was not in the driveway. In its place: a silver Audi. When I killed the ignition, both the driver-side and passenger-side doors to the silver Audi swung open. *The guys from the bar?* I glanced at the glove compartment, my gun nestled inside.

"You have company," Dad said, reaching for the door handle.

"Dad, don't get out—"

Two women emerged from the Audi. Meryl and Lori. *What the fuck?*

When I cut my headlights, Ray's Jeep turned in, re-illuminating the driveway. Meryl stepped into the Jeep's headlights. Dad and I opened our car doors as Meryl approached.

"Sorry to barge in, but we really needed to speak with you... and thought it would be better to do so in person."

Dad crossed in front of my car, his hand outstretched. "Well, look at you two. All grown up."

We were all plunged back into darkness when the Jeep's headlights automatically switched off.

Ray walked toward us and flicked on his flashlight. "Let's all get inside before we freeze to death."

"CAN I get you anything?"

Meryl and Lori glanced at each other. "A glass of wine, if you've got it," Lori said. "It's been a long day." Meryl nodded in agreement.

"Where are you staying?" I asked.

"In Bethel, an Airbnb near the festival site," Meryl replied.

"I'll open a bottle," Ray said. "Susan?"

"I'll pass. Gotta drive Dad home later."

"I'll take a beer, Ray. One of those fancy IPAs you got. I'm not the designated driver," Dad said.

"Two glasses of wine and one IPA coming up."

"Before you tell me what you want to tell me, I want to apologize for using Josh's barn as an interrogation room," I said. "We crossed the line. We could have handled it a different way."

"Look. We know our family is the epitome of dysfunction. I threw that party hoping to bury old feuds. Call me a cock-eyed optimist. As Lori predicted, it was an utter disaster. After you left, well, let's just say it went downhill from there."

Ray entered the living room and placed two glasses of wine on the cocktail table. "Be right back."

Meryl continued: "If our parents or Scott are mixed up in something, we want to know about it. I am not trying to help anyone shirk responsibilities. But that's not why I called you."

Ray reappeared, this time with two pilsner glasses, and handed one to Dad. "I think you'll like this, Will. It's called Arrogant Bastard." He smiled at Meryl, signaling her to continue.

"I think I mentioned to you that I was doing a family genealogy project." Meryl plucked a piece of paper out of her pocketbook and placed it on the cocktail table. "This is the profile of a man whose DNA suggests he is our half brother. Which, knowing my dad, didn't surprise me as much as you would think. But look at his name."

I spun the piece of paper around. *Jake Solomon*. Holy shit.

Now we knew why David sent Panda to silence Renee. Gave new meaning to being your brother's keeper. Renee wasn't going to expose David's role in her baby-brokerage business. She was going to expose his brother, who had obviously fathered more children out of wedlock than Trudy's twins.

MERYL AND Lori stood motionless in front of my whiteboards as I explained the two cases and what we discovered about Scott's and their parents' involvement. I chronologically retraced the steps of our investigation so they understood how each rock was turned over, leading us to where we currently stood. The final rock—the party. Scott revealing to us the incident—the rape—that set Trudy's disappearance in motion. The reaction from Meryl and Lori was not what I expected. Both stone-faced, no tears, no hysteria. No pushback. They knew their father well. They knew he was capable of this.

When I hesitated, Meryl prodded, "Go on."

I launched into the story of Renee Carter.

Ray scrolled through his phone, looking through the uploaded pages from Panda's journal, then read the entry related to Renee and David Roth.

"Maybe David was helping Stanley sell his child. And if Renee knew the kid was Stanley's she might've wanted more money," I said.

Meryl turned to Lori. "Do you think Mom knew about Dad's affairs?"

Lori shrugged. "How would I know? Besides, do you really think she gave a rat's ass? She wasn't exactly the doting housewife."

Meryl snorted derisively. "Well that's the understatement of the century."

Lori spun around to face me. "My mother had her fair share of dalliances." She shook her head. "And yet, we all pretended to be the perfect family!"

"So I take it Josh told you about Mom's affair with David." Meryl looked at her sister.

"What? No!" Lori shouted. "Uncle David? Are you fucking serious? Jeez. Why am I always in the fucking dark in this family?"

"You're in the dark because you choose to be in the dark," Meryl snapped back. "You made yourself an outsider. You moved out to California. You changed your appearance. You married outside the religion."

Lori sat down in the chair next to Dad. She folded her arms across her chest and sighed. "While your life has been all sunshine and lollipops, my life has been a struggle. But you don't bother to know about that either. You don't even try to understand why I wanted . . . no, why I *needed* to make drastic changes in my life." Lori unfolded her arms and leaned forward. "Do Scott and Josh know about this?"

Meryl nodded. "Josh and I came home early from school one day and we saw them. I'm pretty sure Josh still hasn't forgiven her. We thought it was best to keep that affair to ourselves. If it makes you feel any better, I never told Scott. And whatever it was between Mom and David, it was short-lived."

"Like all her affairs," Lori mumbled. "I knew coming here was a mistake." She turned toward me. "I don't mean here in this house, Susan. I mean here, back home, where my fucking family is involved with murder, kidnapping, blackmail, adultery, and who knows what else."

Dad banged his fist on the dining-room table. "Time out!" He stood up suddenly, then sat back down. "So your family's fucked up. Whose isn't? Though I have to say, yours is a doozy."

"Lori, I'm sorry," Meryl stammered. "I didn't mean to say all that. I did see what you were going through. I'm just . . . I'm just a little tired. Which is no excuse."

I was not sure what I was witnessing, but I felt like I was sitting in the audience of a Dr. Phil show. The knives were out, and Dad's attempt to steer this back to the Trudy and Renee cases landed with a resounding thud and a detour into Rachel's extramarital liaisons. My turn.

"Lori. Meryl. I'm not gonna pretend to understand what's going on between you two, but some pretty shocking shit just came to light—and obviously unearthed some deep resentments here. But we're all here now, in the same room. Can we try to figure out how all these pieces fit together, and where we go from there?"

For roughly thirty seconds, the only sound I heard was the wind whistling through a hairline crack in the dining-room window, which I should have fixed months ago.

Lori sighed. "Just so you know, Meryl, I had my own issues with Mom. Remember the time she claimed she needed alone time and dumped us with David and Diane for six months so she and her sister could frolic down in Florida for the winter? I had gotten into a fight with her right before she left and I heaped a ton of guilt upon myself thinking her desire to get away from us was my fault."

"Yeah, I remember. She took off right after the high holidays and came back just in time for the Passover opening," Meryl said. "I'm pretty sure it was not your fault. You were too young to see it, but the strain between Mom and Dad at that time was quite palpable. Y'know the cliché, 'the tension was so thick you could cut it with a knife'? Well, a hatchet couldn't even slice through what hung in the air between them."

Meryl gazed at Jake's picture taped to the whiteboard. "I think it's important we focus on why Lori and I came to see you . . . which, in light of your investigation into Trudy Solomon, was why we wanted to tell you about Jake Solomon."

Okay. We were back on track. Somewhat at least. I told Lori and Meryl about my conversation I had with Jake—his desire to find his relatives and my suggestion he get a DNA test. Which, obviously, he did.

"Can we rewind for a second?" Ray said. "This affair between Rachel and David got me thinking. Maybe David felt guilty about betraying his brother and was willing to be the heavy . . . or the fall guy. DR gave Panda the order, but maybe SR was really behind this."

"There's another possibility," Dad chimed in. "Perhaps it was Rachel pulling the strings. Especially if she knew Stanley had a child with another woman."

I was leaning toward Dad's theory. "Rachel could have convinced David to help her get rid of this problem. A kid who would one day want a share of the inheritance. A kid that wasn't hers."

"Also, we shouldn't rule out that it might have been both of them, together, pressuring David," Ray added.

"Too bad Renee's landlord isn't still alive," I said. "We could have asked her if she'd seen any of the Roths in Renee's orbit."

"There might be another avenue we haven't explored," Dad said. "Renee lived on the first floor of a duplex and the landlord lived upstairs. She had a son, who I believe was living with her at the time. He might have seen the Roths lurking about. He was late teens, early twenties back in seventy-seven, so he would be in his late sixties, early seventies now." Dad tapped his right cheekbone. A habit when he was trying to remember something. "Karl. Karl Houser."

"I'll run that down," Ray said.

"That's the problem with really old cold cases," I said. "Everyone is dead. Or too old to remember anything. Like, I wish we could talk to your dad."

"Go ahead. Talk to him," Meryl said. "I'm not interfering in your investigation anymore."

"This has nothing to do with you granting permission. I'm not sure how much he can tell us based on his limited mental capacity."

"His limited mental capacity?"

"Your mom said he had a stroke and his memory is shot to hell."

Meryl and Lori squinted at each other, eyebrows knit.

"Jesus Christ." Lori snorted. "What a bunch of malarkey."

"He had a small stroke a few years ago. He slurs a bit. Hard of hearing too. But his memory is just fine," Meryl said.

"Why is he in a wheelchair?" Dad asked.

"He fractured his ankle a few weeks ago," Meryl said. "He's milking it to get my mother to do his bidding."

Dad twisted around to face me and raised an eyebrow. He was definitely thinking the same thing I was: *it was time to have another chat with the Roths.*

But this time . . . the kid gloves were coming off.

CHAPTER THIRTY-SIX

Tuesday, December 11, 2018

RAY SWAGGERED over to my desk. “Got a line on Karl Houser. Get this . . . he was a narcotics officer on Long Island.”

“Was? Is he dead?”

“Retired. Agreed to a phone call with us in fifteen minutes. We’re just emailing him some photographs of Rachel, Stanley, David, Ben, Lenny, and Panda. We’ll see if he recognizes any of them. You’re welcome to join us.”

Just try and stop me.

After introductions, Ray briefed Karl on the Renee Carter case.

“Did you get my email?” Ray asked. “The pictures?”

“Got ’em. I’m lookin’ at ’em now.”

"Do you remember seeing any of these people visiting Renee?"

"The guy with the long hair, definitely," Karl said, referring to Lenny. "I think he was a customer of hers. Although, you rarely saw johns around. I think she used one of the motels up on Route seventeen. So maybe they were just friends. Those four other guys don't look familiar."

"How about the woman?"

"I've never seen her," Karl said, referring to Rachel. "And I'm pretty sure I would remember someone who looked like her. But there was another woman who came by quite a few times."

"Hold on," Ray said. "Emailing you another photo now." He sent Karl a picture of Trudy.

"No. Not her. The woman I remember was kinda heavy. Probably midthirties. Not too attractive. Had a mole on her chin. The kind where hair grows out of it. Like I said, not too attractive."

"Do you remember when you saw them together?"

"Renee went missing in seventy-seven, right?"

"Yeah."

"I was taking classes at Orange County Community that year. I would have to say around spring break, when I was home."

"You said you saw the woman with the mole a *few* times. Can you be more specific?"

"I would say three or four times over a two-week period."

"Were you interviewed by the cops back then? After Renee disappeared?"

"No, but the cops spoke to my mom. Everyone was under the impression she just up and moved away. Not exactly stellar police work, huh?"

Good thing Dad wasn't on this call to hear that remark. Ray ignored the barb and asked, "Did it strike *you* odd that she just left without telling a soul?"

"Not really. She told me she was coming into some money—an inheritance she said—and couldn't get out of this town fast enough."

Ray asked Karl to contact him if he thought of anything else. And like that, we were back to square one.

"A woman with a mole. Well, that narrows it down," I said sarcastically. "Think she has something to do with Renee's murder?"

"Could be a woman who was buying or selling a baby. Perhaps a friend or fellow prostitute," Ray said. "I'll have that rookie page through prostitute mug shots from back then. See if he can find a woman with a hairy mole on her chin."

"THE SILVER lining in all this is that it's given us a chance to get reacquainted," Lori said as she rearranged the pillow on my sofa to better support her back. She had texted me around 3:00, shortly after the phone call with Karl Houser, and asked if I would be interested in getting together. Just the two of us, to "talk things through."

I handed Lori a glass of chardonnay and sat next to her.

"Cheers!" Lori exclaimed, clinking her glass to mine. "To renewed friendships."

"I'll drink to that."

We sat quietly for a few minutes, each nearly daring the other to speak first about the revelations of the last few days. As a trained interrogator I had a tendency to remain silent, create an air of discomfort that occurs in the silence, forcing the other person to blurt something out when the quiet becomes unbearable. But in this instance, I was just trying to think of the right thing to say . . . to sound more like a friend with a shoulder to lean on than a cop with an itch to solve a case.

"What will happen to my parents if they are involved in either Ed's or Renee's murders?"

"Well, we are not even sure they had a hand in Renee's murder. David, your uncle, certainly could have acted on his own for reasons unknown. As for Ed's murder: well, there is certainly a lot of circumstantial evidence implicating your mother. But without hard evidence and witnesses, it will be awfully hard to mount a case against her."

"What about Trudy's rape?"

"Even if your brother is willing to provide testimony against your father, without Trudy's statement and evidence of assault, your dad could assert consent. He can even claim that someone else raped her and he was merely comforting Trudy when Scott saw him leave the room. Now, if we found the twins, we could, at the very least, prove he did indeed have . . . have sex with her. But those records are sealed. Which was a pretty common practice back then."

"So now what? You're going to confront my parents with what you know? See if you can get some answers? Goad them into a confession?"

I downed the rest of my wine. I thought about refilling it, but instead put my empty glass on the coaster in front of me. "It's a long shot, but yeah. And I'm probably the last person who should be interrogating your mom. Every time I talk to her I feel like my thirteen-year-old self. Rachel—the glamorous and wealthy matriarch of the Roth clan—honoring me with a word or two. At least that's how I perceived things when we were growing up."

"And that's exactly what she wanted you to see. What she wanted the world to see. But there were two Rachel Roths. The public-facing Rachel—poised, gregarious, generous. And the private-facing Rachel—manipulative, duplicitous, selfish." Lori's lower lip quivered. She gnawed at it gently. "The one thing both Rachels had in common was that they were intimidating."

"Yeah, to say I felt like a tiny gnat in her presence is not an exaggeration. You just respected someone like her. Like, she could do no wrong."

"Oh, she did plenty wrong. But I was blind to it myself until my freshman year in college, when I was no longer in her orbit. Not being around her opened my eyes. And Meryl was kind of right . . . I chose not to see. It made life easier."

"I just had it in my head that Rachel was this doting, attentive mom—obviously, I had no idea what was going on behind the scenes."

"No one did." Lori scooted forward and set her now empty wineglass on the coffee table next to mine. We sat silently for a few minutes.

Lori slapped her palms on her thighs. "Hey! Before I forget . . . I have the photos you gave Meryl for her trip-down-memory-lane display—they're in the car. Besides, I could use some air. I'm not much of a drinker these days, and that tall glass of wine went right to my head."

As we walked over to the car, Lori linked her arm in mine. I was barely inebriated, but felt light and giddy. We broke into a skip and giggled like preteens. She flung open the rear door and the dome light illuminated the posters leaning against the backseat.

"Are those Meryl's ancestry posters from the party?"

"Yeah. She was going to bring them to the inn and give them to my parents."

"I never did get to look at them. Mind if I take a peek?"

"Be my guest."

I leaned into the car and pulled one out. Lori activated the flashlight on her phone and illuminated the poster.

"I remember these boys. Your cousins, right?"

"Yup. My mother's sister's kids, Matt and Andrew. My aunt died a few years ago, but they came to the party."

"Oh my, who is this character with the handlebar mustache and monocle?"

"Ha! He was a character all right. That's my grandfather's brother, Isaac Cuttman.

"When was this one taken, the four of you by the pool?"

"Hmmm, probably seventy-eight . . . before my boobs exploded."

I scanned the pictures. "Meryl did such a great job with—" I leaned in closer and pointed at a woman on the poster. "Who is this?"

Lori shone the flashlight directly where my finger was pointing. She squinted, then said, "My Aunt Diane, David's wife. Why?"

CHAPTER THIRTY-SEVEN

Wednesday, December 12, 2018

DIANE ROTH was still alive, living in Goshen, New York. Just thirty miles south of Monticello. As this was Ray and Marty's case, my presence was simply to observe, listen, and ascertain whether Renee's murder was connected to Trudy's disappearance.

Diane led us into her living room. The room was sparse with cheap Scandinavian furniture positioned willy-nilly, as though we had interrupted her while she was rearranging the pieces. The blinds were nearly drawn, forcing the intruding sunlight downward onto the cream-colored carpet and creating a lined pattern—a stark contrast between shadow and light, reminiscent of the art direction in an Alfred Hitchcock film.

"Man, I was wondering when you'd be knocking at my door. Took you this long, heh?" Diane slid out from her forearm crutches and slowly lowered herself onto a glider recliner. "MS. A bitch of a disease." She stretched out her legs and moaned. "Sit. Sit. Over there," she said pointing toward the couch.

"So you know why we're here?" Ray asked as he lowered himself onto one corner of the couch. Marty and I squeezed in next to him. The futon couch felt as though it would collapse under our combined weight.

"I read you found Renee's body. I figured it was only a matter of time until you came to question me."

"Renee's landlord's son mentioned you hanging around the duplex," Ray said. "We came here hoping you had some information that could help us with our investigation. Were you friends with her?"

Both of her unplucked eyebrows rose in unison and her thin lips parted, forming a little o. I couldn't quite discern if her facial expression was a sign of confusion or surprise. "Friends . . . with her? Is that what the landlord's son said?"

"He simply mentioned you came around a few times," Ray said. "Well, he didn't actually know who you were. He described you and we found a picture of you among the Roths' family pictures."

"Ha! I bet the mole gave me away. Shoulda had it removed years ago. So three of ya here to question me. Seems overkill. I ain't running nowhere, that's for sure." Diane patted her crutches. "Well, you caught me at a grand time. I'm in a confessing mood. I'm not long for this earth, and it's time for a cleanse, so they say. Right? I was even thinking of coming to see you when I heard about Renee's body surfacing. You just saved me a trip up to Monticello. So where to start?"

"The beginning is always a good place," Marty said with a wink and a quick smile. "Just lay it out for us."

"My husband was a bastard. B-A-S-T-A-R-D. His brother, Stanley, even worse. Peas in a fucking pod, those two. But you know who I really couldn't stand? Rachel. The high and mighty, Rachel Cuttman. Ha! Y'know what I called her? Rachel Cuntman." She snickered. "I'm sorry, am I offending you?"

Ray shifted and knocked my shoulder. "It'll take a lot more than swear words to offend us," Ray said with a forced laugh.

"A little color commentary never hurts, am I right?"

"Right, you just tell it like you want to," I chimed in. "All we want to know is how Renee ended up with Stanley's baby."

"Stanley's baby?"

Ray and I exchanged glances.

"That screaming bundle of joy wasn't Stanley's baby." She stared at us as if we were crazy. "I thought that's why you were here. Cuz you figured out that it was my deadbeat hubby who spawned that kid."

"David's child? How can that—" I clapped my hands, turned to Ray, and saw an expression I can only imagine was similar to mine.

CHAPTER THIRTY-EIGHT

Thursday, December 13, 2018

DAD, RAY, and I formed a semicircle around the fireplace in the parlor of the Blueberry Hill Inn. I was not sure if my hands were sweating from the roaring fire or the looming inquisition.

Josh emerged from the dining room. "They're seated. Meryl said you should go in." Josh hastily retreated to the kitchen. Last night he told Meryl he didn't have the stomach to be part of this confrontation.

Stanley was at the head of the table, slumped in his wheelchair. His outdated necktie was askew and mismatched with his shirt, a poor choice perhaps made by Rachel to humiliate him. He lifted his head slightly and scowled as we entered the room. Lori twisted around in her chair and gave a subtle nod. Meryl wore a Zen-like calm, perhaps resigned to the fact that her parents were due for a reckoning. Rachel chewed at her lower lip and fingered the silverware. Her expression changed from surprised to pissed in a matter of seconds.

"What's going on?" she said, removing the napkin from her lap and tossing it on the plate. She moved forward in her seat, about to stand.

Meryl put her hand on her mother's forearm and, in a tone that would freeze water, said, "No one is going anywhere until we get some issues cleared up. Please sit, Mother." Rachel settled back into her chair.

Stanley tried to roll back, but he failed to release the brake, and remained motionless. "What in cra-sha is gowin on here?"

"It's cre-a-tion, Stanley. Cre. A. Tion," Rachel admonished. "Jesus Christ, Meryl. Can't you see you are upsetting your father?" Rachel picked up the linen napkin, smoothed it out, and placed it back on her lap. She leaned forward and whispered to Dad, "Stanley had a stroke recently. He slurs his words when he is upset."

Dad leaned forward in his chair. "Rachel, why did you tell us that Stanley was incapacitated?"

"Are we actually going to be served lunch or is the idea to starve us until we answer your inane questions?"

"Mom, Josh prepared sandwiches. We all have a few questions we want answered, that's all."

"What is this? Gang-up-on-your-parents day?" Rachel looked around. "Where is Josh? I'm feeling lightheaded. I need to eat."

"Mom, answer Will's question. Why did you tell them Dad was mentally impaired?"

"Well, he is. Look at him, for goodness sake."

All heads swiveled toward Stanley.

"For the wuv of gawd, Rachel. What the hell is gowin on here?"

A waiter entered the dining room with a platter of sandwiches and set it down in the center of the table. A waitress, carrying bowls of potato salad and coleslaw, squeezed between Dad and Ray and placed the side dishes in front of them.

"Can I have an iced tea, dear?" Rachel said to the waitress.

"I'll bring out a pitcher, ma'am."

"Well, isn't this lovely," Rachel said, examining the sandwiches. She picked up a roast beef sandwich. "Dig in everyone. This might be our last meal together for a while," she mused without a hint of irony.

"Does this have to do with what happened at the parhy?" Stanley shouted. "Scott's outburst?" He shooed away the server hovering over his shoulder, nearly knocking the pitcher of iced tea out of her hand. She retreated to the corner of the room.

"Now, now, Stanley. Settle down. You know what the doctor said about your blood pressure. Do you want the roast beef or the turkey?" Without waiting for a reply, Rachel placed a turkey sandwich on his plate. She picked up the spoon buried in the potato salad and plopped a dollop on Stanley's plate. "No coleslaw for you. You know it won't agree with you later."

"Mr. Roth, we are investigating several—"

"Who the hell are you?" Spittle formed in the corner crease between Stanley's upper and lower lips.

"Ray Gorman. I'm a detective with the Monticello police department. We are investigating three cold cases involving Trudy Solomon, Ed Resnick, and Renee Carter."

Dad added, "We've come to learn that these folks have various connections to the Roth family and—"

"Who?" Stanley glanced over at Rachel. "We don't know any of those people."

Dad kept his eyes trained on Stanley. "That's odd, because when we spoke to Rachel in Florida, she had plenty to say about Trudy and Ed."

Stanley leaned closer to Rachel. "What did you say to them?" But Rachel didn't answer. She sat stone-cold still, her eyes glassy but tearless, staring straight ahead. Stanley twisted around to face Dad. "Well, I have no recollection of them."

"Well, let me refresh your memory." Dad licked his lips and rubbed his hands together like he was about to feast on an oversized turkey leg. I'm not a mind reader, but I would bet he was thinking: *I'm going to nail these sons o' bitches.* "In 1978, Trudy Solomon—one of your coffee-shop waitresses—disappeared from the Monticello Hospital parking lot. Our investigation turned up bupkis, and it was shelved. But here's where it gets interesting, Stanley. New evidence came to light this past September. And guess what? We found Trudy Solomon. Alive. Living in Massachusetts. And being the stickler I am for wanting to know what happened, we sought to find out if she was kidnapped or left the area of her own volition."

"I don't have to lishen to this bullshit. Rashel, get me outta here."

Rachel stood up.

"Mother. Sit. Down." Meryl reached out to grab her mother's arm, but Rachel yanked it away.

"It's here or the Monticello police department," Dad said. "Take your pick."

Rachel sat back down.

Dad continued: "Turns out Trudy ran off with Ed Resnick. Ed did some work for you, Stanley. Heating systems, I believe. Someone sympathetic to Trudy's situation gave them five grand to start a new life, and they settled in Rochester. Trudy gave birth to twins in March 1979, then they moved to the Boston area and in 1990 they moved again to Waltham, Massachusetts. Fast-forward thirty years and Ed is murdered in his apartment and Trudy is committed to a mental hospital."

"What does this have to do with me?" Stanley tugged at his hideous necktie making the knot smaller and smaller with each pull. His rising anger made his face redder and puffier.

"I thought we cleared up this matter back in Florida." A bead of sweat appeared above Rachel's upper lip; perhaps it was just the heat from the fireplace making its way from the parlor into the dining room, but no one else was sweating.

"We don't think you were completely forthcoming," I said to Rachel.

"Are you suggesting I was somehow involved in this murder? That's ludicrous."

Lori slammed down her glass, the water splashed out onto the platter of sandwiches. "Well if you weren't involved, why were your fingerprints found in Ed and Trudy's apartment?"

"My lord, Lori. Calm down. I already explained this to Susan. I was at Trudy's apartment *after* the murder." Rachel rolled back her shoulders and sat up a little bit taller. "I touched things. I helped Trudy pack."

"The Waltham police lifted the prints the day *of* the murder," I said. "Before you went to—"

"I was at the inn the day of the murder," Rachel stated firmly.

"Were you, Mom?" Lori hissed. "You might want to rethink your alibi."

"You are mistaken. I don't know what *they* are telling you." Rachel pointed her chin toward Ray and Dad. "I was at the inn."

"Not according to Josh," Lori countered. "He said *you* were out and about, gone for the entire day."

"I . . . I . . . Josh is confused." Rachel tightened her grip on her napkin. "I was at the inn all day. I'm sure I was. Ask Josh. He'll tell you."

"Jesus Christ!" Meryl jumped out of her chair. "Has it not yet dawned on you that Josh isn't even in the room? Of course not, because you are so wrapped up in your own little world, trying to figure out how to weasel out of this. Josh despises you," Meryl spat. "Despises!" she repeated slowly. "He arranged all this, y'know. But in the end he just couldn't stand to be in the same room with you . . . to hear all this, and have to listen to more of your lies. Josh told us that Dad had his head in the toilet, sick to his stomach, on July twentieth, and you took off to Boston to meet a friend."

"This is crazy. You're all making this up to get back at me for . . . for . . . I don't know what. For not being the perfect mother?"

"I would have settled for a mediocre mother," Meryl muttered under her breath.

"Excuse me?" Rachel snarled. "Show some resp—"

"We believe that the day after Josh's wedding, *you* went to see Ed and Trudy," Dad interrupted. "To explain to them that the—how did you put it, Rachel?—that the gravy train had run out of gravy?"

"That's ridiculous." She bowed her head slightly, then suddenly jerked it back up. "Oh yes, now I remember. I went to visit an old friend. But not in Boston. She lived in Worcester."

"Oh please." Lori shook her head. "Like we're to believe that."

"I visited my friend Gloria," Rachel asserted. "I've had enough of these unfounded accusations. Are you done yet?"

"Oh, we're just getting started," Dad said with bravado in his voice. He spent his whole life being pushed around by the likes of Stanley and Rachel, and he was warming up to give them their just desserts. "And here's the real interesting part . . ." Dad leveled his gaze at Stanley. "Rachel told us that *you* went to see them."

Like a listing ship, the attention tilted away from Rachel toward Stanley.

"What? I never went to see Ed and Trudy." The spittle lodged between his lips went airborne. "Why would I have anything to do with those two?"

"So you do know them?" Dad asked.

Stanley grunted. "I have a vague memory of them."

Lori pounded her fists on the table and rose suddenly, bending over the table toward Stanley. "A vague memory? You *raped* her!"

"Rape?" Rachel shrieked, sounding genuinely shocked, and the room listed back toward her. "That's why they wanted money from you?" Her hands trembled as she brought them up to her cheeks. "You *raped* that girl? Ed wanted retribution?"

"It wasn't rape," Stanley huffed. "Who said it was rape? She was a willing participant."

"What bullshit! You wouldn't be giving them money if you simply had a consensual quickie. What an idiot I've been. I turned a blind eye as you chased every skirt that set foot on hotel grounds. I was willing to put up with your gallivanting, but rape?"

"Gallivanting? Well, that's the pot calling the kettle black." Stanley wagged his finger at Rachel. "Was there a male guest under thirty you didn't screw?"

"Or a lifeguard? Or a waiter? Or a bellhop?" Lori seethed. "Did you ever think how embarrassing you made our lives?" Lori glanced in my direction. Perhaps she was remembering the time she and I saw her mother canoodling with a dining-room waiter in the kitchen. We went in to steal some pastries. When Lori spotted them she grabbed my arm and steered me back out, muttering "fuck her" under her breath, then storming off, later to laugh it off and tell me that I misunderstood the situation.

"What I did is nobody's business. At least I didn't rape anyone." She turned to face Stanley. "*My* lovers were *willing* partners."

"Maybe you didn't rape anyone, Mother," Meryl said, brandishing a fork in her mother's direction. "But what you did was equally reprehensible, discarding a child like a piece of trash."

"Child?" Stanley barked. "What child?"

Rachel glared directly at Meryl, her fury clearly overflowing. "I did no such thing. I mean, I did the right thing. I took care of the situation and no one got hurt. I did what was best for every—" The sentence came to a screeching halt. Her eyes blinked furiously with the sudden realization she had slipped up, that she had vomited out a confession brought on by anger and exasperation.

"What child?" Stanley repeated, but Meryl and Rachel ignored him.

"What do you mean you took care of the situation?" Meryl shouted.

"I'm not feeling well." She stood suddenly and her chair crashed behind her. "I'd like to leave now."

"No one is going anywhere," Ray said. He walked to the back of the room and lifted the poster board that was leaning against the wall.

"Are you planning to arresht us? I've had nuf of this. I want my lawyer."

"We don't have a lawyer, Stanley," Rachel snarled, reaching down and righting her chair. "We barely have two nickels to rub together."

"Please sit down, Rachel," Dad said, striking a balance between civility and disdain.

Rachel looked squarely at my Dad, clearly attempting to reestablish control. But he stared back, rattling her. Her gaze darted to the poster in Ray's hand. "More so-called evidence?" she scoffed.

"As a matter of fact, yes."

Rachel sat back down with an audible moan, crossed her arms in defiance, and leaned back. Ray propped up the family-tree poster on the chair he'd occupied, then positioned himself against the wall facing Rachel. "Susan."

I CLEARED my throat, then stood up and walked over to the poster. I trained my eyes on Rachel for a few seconds. She didn't blink. I wasn't going to let her unnerve me. I glanced over to Dad, who winked and nodded.

"A man named Salvatore Pandelo, known to his friends as Panda—who, by the way, kept a very helpful journal—was hired by someone with the initials DR to offer a lump sum cash payment to a woman named Renee Carter and threaten her with bodily harm if she didn't leave town. Only the situation got out of control and Panda killed her."

"Killed her? That can't—" Rachel bit her lower lip.

"You were about to say something?" I asked, giving her a few seconds to finish her sentence. "No? Okay, well, we know this because, in his journal Panda confesses to murdering Renee Carter."

"So what dush this have to do with ush?" Stanley said brusquely.

"Good question. We asked ourselves that. We surmised that DR was David Roth from other references in Panda's journals."

"Yeah, well, I didn't know everything my brother was up to back then."

"Okay. But what about you, Rachel? Think you might be able to shed light on this?" I asked.

"What would I *possibly* know about it?" Rachel bristled.

"Oh, you know plenty, Mother," Meryl said. "We know what you did and we have proof."

Rachel pursed her lips. "Again with the proof. What proof? I didn't do anything to that woman. Why would I. I've never even met her."

"Mom, stop the charade." Meryl's gaze rested on her mother for a moment, spewing disdain and impatience at the same time. "I discovered your dirty little secret when I took up genealogy to look for long-lost relatives." She shook her head. "I sure did find some. In fact, I came across a man who presented as a half brother." Meryl let that sink in for a few seconds. "So given Dad's well-known philandering ways, naturally we first thought that man was Dad's biological son."

Stanley thumped his open palms against the arms of his wheelchair. "What? That can't be. I was never with that woman."

"Yes, we know that now," Meryl said and nodded in my direction.

"We got a tip that a heavyset woman with a mole on her chin was seen hanging around with Renee Carter right before she supposedly ran off." I watched the blood drain from Rachel's face. Her brows knitted, her lips forming a frown. "And look who I found right here in your family tree," I said, pointing at the picture of Diane Roth. "A heavyset woman with a mole on her chin. So we decided to pay her a visit."

Rachel squinted. "She's a lunatic. You can't believe a word she says."

"Go on. I want to hear thish," Stanley said.

"How much longer are you going to go on with this nonsense?" Rachel said, fanning herself with her napkin. "I'm not feeling well."

"Like when you weren't feeling well the winter of 1976?" Lori jeered. "When you needed a break from your family? You returned right before Passover in 1977. No one the wiser about your condition." Lori air-quoted *condition.* "David told you about Renee's services and he arranged everything."

"What in the goddamn world are you talking about!" Stanley barked.

Rachel suddenly wheezed and reached for her glass of iced tea.

Lori waited until she had Rachel's full attention again, then continued, "Mother knows what I'm talking about. Right, Mom? Don't bother answering because I'm pretty sure whatever comes out of your mouth will be a big, fat, fucking lie."

"You have no right to talk to me that way. I did what I did to protect this family."

"Oh that's rich, coming from you," Lori spat.

Stanley leaned forward and slammed his hands on the table with such force the plates and silverware rattled. "What the fuck is going on?" he roared, drawing everyone's attention back on him, stunned expressions all around.

Then, as if on cue, everyone in the room turned to me, six pairs of eyes begging me to continue, to pull the Band-Aid off and get this over with. But this was no minor cut—this was more like sawing off a cast and revealing the milky, sore, atrophied skin underneath.

"As I was saying, we paid a visit to Diane Roth—who, by the way, is not exactly a fan of yours, Mrs. Roth." A part of me wanted to repeat Diane's nickname for Rachel, but even I felt that was crossing the line. "Seems she and Renee cooked up a scheme to extort money from you, threatening to expose a secret about you and David to Stanley and your kids." I glanced over at Stanley, who appeared impatient, agitated, and confused. Meryl must have noticed this as well.

"For God's sake," Meryl shouted. She leaned over Rachel to face Stanley. "Just in case you didn't get it yet, Dad . . . Mom and Uncle David had an affair, Mom got pregnant and arranged, through

David, to sell the baby." Meryl turned to Rachel, her pointer finger aimed at Rachel's jugular. "Isn't that right, Mother?"

"You had an affair with my *brother*?" Stanley was bouncing around in his chair, clearly frustrated at his inability to stand and, perhaps, squeeze his hands around Rachel's throat. "You could have fucked anyone you wanted. Hey, you did fuck anyone you wanted. But my brother?"

To think this family was the object of my envy. The grass was not greener on their side. It was scorched and swampy and trampled on. Was it possible that when Lori could no longer hide her family's grotesque dysfunction, she cut ties with me to save face? Maybe not consciously. But if I was embarrassed about bringing friends over to my house because my mother was out cold on the living-room couch, I can only imagine the lengths she would go to keep what was going on in her family out of public view.

"Rachel," I began. "We spoke to Diane. We know what went down."

Rachel turned toward me, completely ignoring Stanley's outburst. "What do you think you know? David and I had a short-lived . . . relationship. So what?"

"Stop it, Mom. We know you parted your legs for everyone who'd give you the slightest bit of attention," Meryl said, her voice now steady, cold and steely.

Rachel glanced at Lori, then Meryl. Perhaps realizing she'd been defeated, she took a deep breath before she spoke. "Fine, I'll tell you what went down, as you so eloquently put it." She looked at me with all the disdain she could muster, but unlike the past, she no longer made me feel unworthy of being in her queenly presence.

"By the time I figured out I was pregnant, I had no choice but to go full term. David told me he knew of this woman . . . some kind of baby broker. We paid Renee very handsomely to quietly make arrangements." A single tear rolled down Rachel's cheek. "I had no choice! If Stanley found out about the affair and the child, he would have divorced me and I would have lost everything." She flicked the tear from her face.

Rachel paused, perhaps waiting for Stanley to refute that last statement. But he said nothing.

"Whatever arrangement she made fell through and she was in the process of finding another couple. Then David, half in the bag, blabbed all this to Diane. David told me that Diane was so pissed off she initially wanted to expose the affair. She went to see Renee to convince her to go public, but Renee had a different idea. Demand more money and she'd split it with Diane. Diane liked the sound of that and told David to squeeze more money from me. I upped the offer and that's the last I heard of it from anyone. David told me Renee accepted the payment and left town, Diane would keep quiet, and everything was hunky dory."

"Hunky dory? Hunky fucking dory?" Lori seethed. "David sends his goons to threaten Renee, one of them kills her and gives away your baby, and you think this is all hunky dory?"

Meryl piled on. "Do you even care what happened to the child, or are you so twisted with vanity and selfishness you never gave it a moment's thought?"

Rachel, breathing heavily now, turned her head to the side, pursed her lips, then let out a sigh. "Yes, I want to know. What happened to my . . . the boy?"

Rachel fussed with her wedding band as I told her about Jake Solomon. When I finished talking, the only sound I could hear was the whir of the wind against the windows. The few moments of silence were shattered by Stanley tapping on the armrest of his wheelchair.

"I knew I married a whore," Stanley spat at Rachel. "But to shack up with David and sell—"

"You raped someone," Rachel hurled. "You have zero moral high ground to say anything to me. I'm sick of this. You want to know what happened? What you forced me to do because you mismanaged my father's money and squandered it away? I thought I could reason with Ed. That's why I went to see him. I thought this was about a business arrangement in which you owed him money. He threatened me. He said nothing was going to stand in his way of getting the money he deserved. He charged at *me,*" she hissed through clenched teeth. "I . . . I had no choice—"

"So you killed Ed and tried to pin this on me?" Stanley rocked in his wheelchair.

"I've paid for your malfeasance and crimes long enough." She dabbed at her eyes and gently blew her nose with a hankie that magically materialized from inside her cuff. "When Will and Susan started snooping around I needed to get them off my trail. And just so we're clear here, I acted in self-defense. If we are assigning guilt, the bigger heap should fall at your feet."

"Wow! It's finally happening," Meryl said. "I never thought I'd see the day."

"What day?" Rachel asked.

"The day the two of you finally realize how much you hate each other and ruined each other's lives . . ."

"And ours," Lori added.

"Can I be excused now?" Rachel said, pushing back her chair.

No one answered.

"Well then." Rachel tossed her napkin on her plate, stood up and click-clacked across the hardwood floors. She swiveled her head when she got to the dining-room doorway. "I'll be up in my room, resting."

"I think we can all use a rest," Meryl said, standing abruptly.

Josh suddenly reappeared. Probably heard his mother leave the room and decided it was safe to come back in.

"Any chance you have a spare room, Josh?" Meryl asked.

"Come with me."

Meryl and Lori exited the room with Josh. A bewildered Stanley remained, picking at his lunch.

THE ROTHS were all upstairs in their respective guest rooms. Stanley had fallen asleep in the dining room and no one bothered to wheel him out. Dad, Ray, and I stood silently in front of the fireplace. I could only imagine what was going through the minds of the Roth kids, perhaps each one trying to come to terms with what happened in that room. In some magical way, I hoped the heat from the fire might cauterize their wounds. An unlikely possibility, for sure, but it was nice to think that there might be a way for them to feel whole again. Perhaps forgiving each other over time. I glanced over at Dad and Ray, both looking solemn, befitting the day's dark mood, but I had a feeling if we were anywhere but here, they would be high-fiving each other.

I elbowed Dad gently. "Well, Dad. You did it. You found out what happened to Trudy Solomon."

Dad turned and hugged me, tight. "*We* did it, Suzie-Q," he said with a satisfied smile. "*We* did it."

CHAPTER THIRTY-NINE

Saturday, December 15, 2018

THE STATION was quiet. It always was the week or so before Christmas. We had arrived home late the night before and decided to come in early in the morning, file our reports on the Trudy Solomon case. We ended up sticking around the inn for an extra day, extracting statements from Stanley (who—surprise, surprise—insisted the sex was consensual) and Rachel (who gave us an Oscar-winning performance). As Dad predicted, Rachel played her self-defense argument to the hilt. Claimed Ed lunged at her, began choking her, and she had no choice but to reach around him for the knife. Said she didn't intend to kill him, just nick him, but inadvertently hit an artery. It was a masterclass in femme fatale acting, on par with Lana Turner in *The Postman Always Rings Twice.* She also claimed she knew nothing of David's intentions to off Renee, believing it was handled in a—as she put it—civilized manner. I called up a lawyer friend of mine who explained that baby brokering—euphemistically called private adoptions—was not criminal in the state of New York in 1976. ("Distasteful, yes," he lamented. "But illegal, no.")

Eldridge slid a chair up to my desk and sat down. "What about Diane? If what she is telling you is true, then she was part of the extortion scheme that got Renee killed."

"She's got terminal cancer," I replied. "Six months, tops, according to her doctor."

"And she told you Rachel knew nothing of David's plan?"

"She couldn't say for sure whether Rachel knew that David was willing to resort to violence to clear up this matter," I said. "David told both Diane and Rachel that Renee took the money and left. But when Diane read the news about Renee's murder, she was pretty sure David had lied all those years ago."

"Oh well." Eldridge stood and shrugged. "Sometimes people get away with murder. This is one of those times."

"Yeah, well I was hoping someone would be held accountable for what happened to Jake—being sold like a piece of meat."

"Lenny got a couple of years, there's that." Eldridge patted me on the shoulder before retreating to his office.

I actually felt sorry for Lenny. I believe he didn't know what he was in for when Panda dragged him to Renee's that night. But nonetheless, he was an accomplice. Ray put in a good word with the district attorney about his cooperation with us. I think that helped his cause.

Jake had called me the night before. He had seen the match on the Ancestry website and wanted to contact me before he got in touch with Meryl. Get my advice. (I should have warned him I was the last person on this planet to give advice on family matters.) I filled him in on what had transpired these last few days and told him that Meryl was eager to speak with him. Lori and Josh said they needed more time to process the events of the last few days and weren't ready to meet him. But they were open to a future reunion . . . when the time was right. According to Meryl, Scott was in no mood to deal with his parents, let alone a newly discovered sibling. ("He threw up walls like he always did," is what she related to me.) As for Rachel, her desire to meet her son remained a big question mark. Meryl had yet to address it with her, the wounds still too raw. But if Jake and the Roth kids managed to eke out a relationship, and Rachel wanted to repair her relationship with them, she might have no choice but to welcome Jake into the family fold. Or at the very least fake it—and she was good at that.

Eldridge released the Barnes video Thursday afternoon knowing I'd be in Vermont, where no one could find me. I picked up a voice mail from Rhonda on Thursday night, telling me that between the video, the warehouse guy's statement, and Marvin's confession, the civil suit against the county was likely to be dropped. There hadn't been any menacing windshield notes since the one placed under my wiper in early December. Perhaps Ernest Barnes did know something about that. I took his word he wasn't the culprit, but had a feeling he knew who was and had a hand in stopping it. Rumor had it, it had been Calvin's cousin. Ernest's brother's kid.

Ray came over and sat on the edge of my desk. "What you say we get something to eat?"

"Can't. Told Thomas I would stop by the house."

Mom had jogged my memory the other day when she mentioned my penchant for sneaking around and snapping pictures. I had this fuzzy recollection of taking pictures the day I came home early and found the man and my mother chatting in the kitchen. If I had a photo or two of him, maybe Mom could tell me who he was. After seeing what secrets can do to a family, I could not let this stand between us. So I called Thomas to ask if he happened to come across any photos from the summer of 1978 when he was looking for pictures of Lori and me, and he said that indeed there were a couple of envelopes from July and August.

I sensed Ray was mildly disappointed. He thought I was done with the past. Moved on. Said I'm picking a scab that would heal faster if I left it alone. "We can meet later, if you want," I offered.

Ray shrugged. "Call me when you're done chasing ghosts."

"HELLO! ANYONE home?"

"Up here, Detective Ford," Thomas shouted. "In the attic."

The attic was accessible through a push door in the ceiling, located on the second floor about five feet from the landing. I climbed the pulldown ladder. Thomas stood on the far side of the attic, near the cobweb-filled, moon-shaped window, sifting through some boxes. The air was chilly but not cold enough to see your breath. Enough heat rose from the lower portion of the house to keep this room bearable. I removed my knee-length puffy coat and dropped it through the hole in the floor. It caught on the second rung.

The floorboards creaked as I walked toward Thomas. "What did you find?"

"Over there," he said, pointing to a little table pushed up against the back wall. "I also found some old letters from that summer, so they're over there as well. They were wrapped inside a scarf."

There were two mustard-yellow envelopes on the table. In my preteen handwriting, one was marked August 3, 1978, the other July 15, 1978. They both contained about fifteen pictures. If memory served me correctly, I usually got anywhere from twelve to sixteen pictures from a roll of 110 film. The negatives were tucked into their own narrow sleeves within the envelopes. I pulled out the July photos. This envelope contained photos taken at Old Falls and a few photos of my Uncle Donald, Mom's brother. He would visit occasionally. I was pretty sure he was not the mysterious guy I'd seen on the porch or in the kitchen—Uncle Donald was burlier and shorter. I put the pictures back into the envelope and opened the one from August.

On top, a photograph of my mother standing in the kitchen. Judging from the angle, I was pretty sure I shot this picture from the top of the stairs. The next four photographs were also of Mom, in various poses. All from that same downward angle. In pictures six through ten, the perspective changed. It appeared as though I had positioned myself in the dining room. In these photographs, Mom was seated at the kitchen table and a man's legs were visible under the table—the rest of him out of the frame. It would have been impossible to capture the face of the man without being seen, which might explain why I couldn't get a clear shot. In the next two photos, the angle suggested I was back on the stairs, probably about halfway up. The man was standing now, his back to the camera. A hat askew on his head.

The last picture of the bunch was blurry. Fearful of being caught, I probably started to move up the staircase. But the man had turned around, enough for me to capture his profile. His bushy mustache was very distinctive. There was no doubt—I was staring at a blurry Ed Resnick.

What the fuck?

I unfolded the blue-and-white kerchief and leafed through the three letters that Thomas had found. The handwriting was compact and graceful. All brief, written on a single side of lined notepaper.

"Did you read these?" I asked.

"Nope. None of my business. But I saw the dates on top and figured you might want to see them. They're from that same summer and fall."

I turned away from Thomas and started to read.

"HOLY SHIT." Clutching the letters, I reached into my back pocket for my phone. It wasn't there. "Shit." I frantically looked around, then realized it was in my coat pocket at the bottom of the pulldown stairs.

"Detective Ford? Are you okay?"

I scrambled down the ladder, and from the fourth rung reached down and grabbed my coat. I retrieved my phone and dropped the coat onto the floor below. I cradled the phone in my hand, wondering who I should call first. Ray or Dad?

"I take it you stumbled onto something," Thomas said, poking his head through the opening.

"You can say that. Do you know where my mother is?"

"She left here about fifteen minutes before you showed up. Said she had errands to run. But I think she'll be back within the hour."

Fuck it. I knew what I had to do and it didn't involve calling either of them. It was Mom who had some explaining to do.

I SAT with my back to the kitchen entryway, so when Mom walked in, all she saw was my ponytail hoisted high on my head, not the indignant expression on my face. The three letters laid on the table in front of me, the top third and bottom third of the stationery bending up from their creases, forming three little paper boats. I fingered mom's blue-and-white silk kerchief, trying to make sense of all this.

"Susan?"

I twisted around in my chair. She shifted her gaze to the table, then back to me. Was that panic in her eyes or relief? Perhaps a mixture of both.

She lunged forward and snatched the letters off the table. "You have no business—" She folded the letters and stuffed them into the back pocket of her jeans.

"What? Are we going to pretend like I haven't seen this?"

She flung open a drawer and pulled out a pack of Marlboros and a red Bic lighter. "So you've seen it. Now you *know*." She fumbled with the lighter. As she brought the cigarette up to her lips I noticed a minor tremor in her hands. It took three flicks of the wheel before the flame escaped and she could light up.

"I don't *know* anything. I don't know what warped thinking it took for you to hide this from Dad. To make him feel like a failure. And worst of all, allow Stanley to get away with what he did to Trudy."

"How dare you judge me?" She sat down across from me and leaned over the table. "You wanna know?" she taunted. "You *really* wanna know?"

Did I? I didn't answer immediately. I let her defensive fury wash over me. I knew there would be no future relationship with her if I walked out the door right now. But that was the old Susan.

The Susan who avoided confrontation. The Susan who kept her mother's problem at arm's length. I knew deep down that I needed to hear her side of the story.

A loose cough rattled in her chest. "Well?"

"Yeah, I want to know."

She took a long drag off her cigarette and blew a line of smoke sideways. "After Ed's father died, his mother told him about her affair with my Dad . . . and—as you read in the letters—that I was his half sister."

"Naomi Resnick told me about their mom being your dad's bookkeeper. Guess they were doing more than number crunching."

"You make it sound like a fling. It was not. According to Ed, she was deeply in love with my father. But when my dad moved away from Rochester, she knew the affair was over and she carried on . . . like lots of women did—and still do. Anyway, Ed rang me up soon after his mom confessed all this and we just hit it off."

"When was that?"

"Oh, I would say midseventies—1974, I think. Anyway, I convinced him to move to the area and he did, in 1976."

"Why so secretive about it?"

"When I confronted my father with this bit of news, he begged me to not tell anyone. Especially my mother. At first, I was none too thrilled to keep this from her. But what was I going to do? Upend their whole marriage? Even Ed's siblings didn't know that Ed wasn't their full brother and he wanted to keep it that way—he promised his mom he wouldn't tell them. I guess she was ashamed." Mom tapped the long accumulated ash onto a saucer. She took a short drag, then snubbed out the nubbin. "Ed said the less people who knew, the better. On some level, I liked having this little secret. Just something shared by two people."

"So where does Trudy factor into all this?"

"Trudy and Ed met at the hotel in early 1977. Ed really liked her—he was always trying to cheer her up." She opened the lid of the cigarette pack, then closed it and pushed it away. I flashed a closed-mouth smile to let her know I was happy with her decision not to start a new one. She continued, "And then her world came crashing down on her when Stanley Roth . . . well, you know. When Ed came to me with his plan to leave the area to get away from all this, I saw myself in her situation. What I wouldn't have given to start a new life where no one knew me and I could reinvent myself."

"What was so bad here? So Dad was a workaholic? You had friends. Dad said you worked part-time. And there was me."

"Who doesn't think that sometimes?" Mom eyed the pack of cigarettes. "You wouldn't understand, Susan."

"Try me."

"I got married young. You were smart enough to get out of your marriage early when you knew it wasn't working. Maybe that's a generational thing. I was beautiful. I had some smarts. I had the whole world in front of me. I met your Dad and fell in love at twenty. Got married at twenty-one. Had you at twenty-two. But I let my dreams fall by the wayside. And I don't even know what those dreams were. To be an actress? Maybe a teacher? I started drinking. A sip here and there, until it felt good to feel numb. To not think about what could have been." Her eyes got glassier as she spoke, her voice raspier. She coughed up some phlegm, then choked it back down.

I rose and walked to the kitchen counter, where I tore a piece of paper towel off the roll. I pulled my chair around closer to Mom and handed it to her. She blew her nose then tucked the paper towel into the pocket of her cardigan.

She pulled the letters out of her back pocket, laid them on the table and smoothed them out. "I didn't know Trudy very well. I went to her house a couple of times. We chatted. She was married to a bully of a husband who made it clear divorce wasn't in the cards. And what if Stanley wanted another go at her? I felt compelled to help."

"Why not just report the rape?"

"Oh Susan. You're not that naive." She lowered her chin and peered over her glasses. "That's not how it worked back then. I'm not even sure that's how it works now." She fiddled with the pack of cigarettes. "Who would put themselves through that shit, especially when you're up against some powerful folks. The victim gets victimized all over again." She snorted derisively. "Me Too wasn't a thing yet."

"Well, after reading these letters from Ed, I'm not so sure her life got a whole lot better."

"You're wrong about that. Sure, having the twins was a low point and she had bouts of depression throughout the years. But she led a fairly content life. She wrote me once in a while, kept me up to date on their whereabouts." She ran her fingers through her hair, dislodging a few knots. I noticed her nails were newly painted and her roots matched the rest of her hair. I guess that was the errand Thomas alluded to earlier. "She was a good person who deserved a good life. She couldn't take a real paying job because she would've had to file taxes and risk being found. So she volunteered at soup kitchens and such. And I bet you didn't know she was artistic. She loved to paint and Ed would buy brushes, canvases, acrylics and she would go to town. You know that covered bridge painting in the living room? The one you like?"

I nodded.

"That's hers. Her initials are on the bottom right."

"Did you know Ed was extorting money from Stanley and was murdered because of it? That Trudy ended up in a mental hospital with early-onset Alzheimer's?"

"I never knew about the money thing." She picked up on my skepticism and quickly added, "Cross my heart. I mean, I knew Ed was murdered, but had no idea about the extortion scheme. When I didn't hear from them for a while, I called a neighbor Trudy had mentioned in one of her letters—luckily back then everyone had a landline and a telephone listing. Anyway, this neighbor told me of the murder. But she didn't know what happened to Trudy. So I called Ed's sister, Naomi. Told her I was an old friend of Ed's and Trudy's and she filled me in."

"Why did you keep this from Dad?" I threw up my hands and they landed with a crash on the table.

She jolted back slightly, and brought her hand to her heart. "For a whole host of reasons. One of them being that I didn't think he would have been all that keen on me giving five grand to a couple on the run forty years ago. Especially because I kept complaining I needed more child support."

"I think you're wrong about that."

"Do you, now? What makes you an authority on that subject?"

"Something he said to me recently. One of the things he admired about you was your generosity."

She chortled. "Yeah? He said that? Well, it would have been nice if he said these things to *me* once in a while."

"Maybe he did. You have to admit you were out of it quite a bit those days."

"Well, it wasn't just the money. I know your Dad. He would have pressured Trudy to pursue a rape charge. He would have loved to have nailed Stanley, but at whose expense? She would have suffered more."

"So why keep up the charade? Why didn't you say anything after Ed's death? Why didn't you say anything when we reopened the case?" With each question, my voice boomed louder and my palms got wetter. "Do you really think he would still be miffed over the five thousand dollars you gave them? And Trudy probably . . . hopefully, has no recollection of the rape."

She reached for the pack of cigarettes, opened the lid, and pulled one out. "I was afraid your father would never speak to me again."

I could certainly understand her thinking that. Some part of me entertained the idea of keeping this from him. He was helping Mom again. She was going to AA meetings. And they were getting up there in age. They would need each other. It was not far-fetched to believe he wouldn't speak to her again. He might never forgive her. This case consumed him back then. And it had made him feel like a failure.

"So, how exactly did this plan work?"

"It was all pretty simple." Mom gazed down at the kerchief. "A week or so before they left, I paid a visit to Trudy to give her the cash."

"A neighbor saw you. She described the blue-and-white headscarf," I said, pointing at it.

"The woman with the parrots?"

"Budgies."

"Budgies?"

"They're called budgies."

"If you say so. Anyway, a guy Ed worked for, this George Campbell fellow, waited for Trudy to get out of Ben's car. Once Ben was gone, he made sure no one else was around, and picked up

Trudy. He later reported to me that Max Whittier, y'know, the old postmaster, was in the parking lot at the time, but he was pretty sure Max didn't spot him."

"He didn't. He was interviewed in 1978—claimed to have seen Ben drop Trudy off and drive away. But he didn't see anyone else lurking about."

"George worked at the hospital, in maintenance, so even if someone saw him there it wouldn't be odd. Anyway, she got in his car, and the rest—as they say—is history." She brought the cigarette to her lips, lit it, and inhaled deeply. "Are you going to tell him?"

"Dad?" I paused, then put my hand on hers. "No. You are."

EPILOGUE

June 10, 2019

EVELYN WORE her dark curly hair short. Vivian wore her dark curly hair long. This was the only way to tell them apart. Trudy sat at the head of the picnic table, flanked by the twins. Scott and Meryl were seated beside Evelyn. Lori and Josh facing them. Dad, Jake, and I sat in white Adirondack chairs surrounding them.

Meryl arranged this gathering after I had found the twins, which turned out to be surprisingly easy. I ran both Trudy's and Stanley's DNA through our system and got a match. The girls were part of a New York State police DNA project to help forensic experts discern differences in DNA should a twin get nabbed for a crime and try to pin it on their sibling (or fog the courtroom with an argument of reasonable doubt). They claimed they did it for the money, but also thought it would be fun.

They grew up on Long Island. Their mother was an elementary school teacher. Their father a sales executive at a printing press. ("A pretty ordinary life," Evelyn said.) They knew they were adopted from an early age. ("We had each other," Vivian said. "I think that had a role in curtailing our desire to find our birth parents.") When I contacted them, they were immediately curious but a bit reticent. Clearly, they weren't going to do this unless they both agreed. ("I'm game if Vivian is game," Evelyn said.)

It was Scott who suggested this reunion to Meryl. Which definitely surprised me. Meryl told me that after Scott finally confessed at the party, he yearned for the family to find a way to heal. At first, it was simply going to be a gathering of the siblings—whole and half—at a restaurant in the city. But when the twins mentioned to Meryl they were curious about Trudy, she contacted the memory care facility to see if there was a way to have a get-together on their grounds. ("We have picnic tables on the back lawn," the director informed her.) Lori was the only holdout, until her daughter persuaded her to come. Lori said she would only come if I made an appearance.

So here I sat with the Roth and Solomon clan, listening to them catch each other up on their lives. Trudy didn't speak. But she was nodding and smiling and laughing.

My phone, facedown on the arm of the Adirondack chair, vibrated. I flipped it to face me. The word "Mom" splashed across the screen as it continued to vibrate. I let it go to voice mail, although I was pretty sure she wouldn't leave a message. Who did these days? Besides, if it was urgent she would text me. I glanced over at Dad and smiled. He still had no idea. Once in a while, Ray brought it up. ("I don't know, Susan, this secret can explode in your face," he warned.) Mom said she needed more time. She promised she would tell Dad everything once she hit her six-month sobriety mark—her self-imposed deadline shortly approaching. She had stuck to her promise to attend AA meetings, and although I couldn't be with her twenty-four seven, I was well versed enough in the signs to know she was on a path to sobriety. Whether that path was smoothly paved or littered with rocks was hard to tell, but at least she was on it.

TRUDY

THE AIR smells sweet, *Trudy thought. Blades of cut grass carpeted the lawn around the picnic table. She breathed in deeply. And smiled. She looked around the table at the guests assembled before her.*

"Hello," she muttered, mostly to herself.

The women on either side of her looked alike. But different. As they spoke, Trudy moved her head as if she was watching a tennis match. They finished each other's sentences.

She stared at Scott. I know him, *she thought. She squeezed her eyes tight trying to surface a memory, but all she got was a good feeling.*

She decided that was good enough.

The other two women and the younger man sitting at the table were complete strangers, but they all seemed to resemble each other in some way. She couldn't even conjure up a feeling about them. But she loved listening to them chatter. Chatter. Chatter. What a lovely day!

The very tall gentleman perched on the edge of the Adirondack chair looked vaguely familiar. He said his name was Jake. Or was it Jack? She knew she should keep a secret about him. Something about bowling. Maybe.

When the older man in the white chair spoke, everyone turned toward him. Then laughed. The dark-haired woman sitting next to him slapped him playfully on the arm.

Oh what a day! She clapped her hands together. The guests turned their attention back to her. She tried to speak, but the words sat still on her tongue. This is best day of my life, *she thought.*

ACKNOWLEDGMENTS

THERE ARE so many wonderful people who helped me bring *The Disappearance of Trudy Solomon* to life.

This book might have never seen the light of day if it wasn't for PitMad, a quarterly Twitter contest for authors to pitch their novels to agents and editors. Helga Schier, editor at CamCat Publishing, "liked" my 280-character query and requested the manuscript. I knew from our first correspondence that Helga totally got my story and would push me to make it as good as it could possibly be. She suggested ways to vastly improve the plot lines, encouraging me to ratchet up the fraught dynamics of a dysfunctional family. I couldn't have asked for a more insightful and imaginative editor.

The folks at CamCat Publishing are a dedicated bunch, who are deeply invested in their authors' success. Thank you to Sue Arroyo and Laura Wooffitt for your tireless effort in getting my novel into libraries, on bookstore shelves and e-commerce platforms. Thank you Maryann Appel for wrapping my words in your artful design of a time-worn hotel hallway at the fictional Cuttman Hotel.

Thank you to my early readers and beta readers: Patti Daboosh, Shelly Strickler, Sari Breuer, Peter Dill, Vickie Baumwald, Mia Rosenberg, Jade Rosenberg, Louise Smith, Arlene Weinstock, Stacie Spencer, Lauri Kahleifeh, Alissa Locke, Marie Joyce, and Karyn Anastasio. Your critiques were invaluable, many of which you will find incorporated into the novel.

2020 was a tough year to write and edit a book. There were plenty of distractions: a global pandemic, the presidential election, social unrest and protests. It's hard to stay focused when you are doom scrolling on Twitter between chapters. But that's where my family comes in. When the world around you feels like it's coming apart at the seams, these are the people I can count on to make me feel secure and loved: my parents, Larry and Shelly Strickler, my sisters, Karyn Anastasio and Sari Breuer, my daughters and stepdaughters, Hayley Dill, Taylor Dill, Molly McCreary, and Hannah McCreary. (So thank you Zoom and FaceTime).

I dedicated this book to my dad, Larry Strickler. He was the consummate tummler at both the Hotel Brickman (1965–1986) and Kutsher's Country Club (1987–2013). The Hotel Brickman was my summer home away from home from 1965 until 1982. It truly was "the time of my life." I knew I wanted to write a story in this setting, but the question became . . . what story/what era . . . A coming of age? A romance? A memoir? Then, in 2017, I came across an article about a woman (a coffee-shop waitress at one of the hotels) who disappeared from the area in the midseventies and was found forty years later in an Alzheimer's facility (in Massachusetts) through the fluke of a social security number search by a detective. She was unable to tell the detective what had happened to her in the intervening years. That was my eureka moment. I was intrigued by the idea of fictionalizing this woman's story—filling in the forty-year gap between disappearing and being found. Throw in a father-daughter detective team and I knew I had my story.

My husband, Lew McCreary, a brilliant writer and editor in his own right, was my mentor and writing coach. Whenever I read a passage out loud to him, his response would inevitably be, "There's a way to make that sharper." And of course, he was right. Lew, there is not enough space in the acknowledgments section to describe how much I love you. So I will not gush all over these pages but simply let you know that you are *the best husband in the world* ("Is that too cliché?" I would ask. He would say, "Yes, you can do better." My response, this time: "Well, too bad, I'm keeping it in.")

FOR FURTHER DISCUSSION

1. This novel plays on the changes that afflicted a rather distinct geographical area. Do you think the demise of the Catskill resort area affected the characters and story? How?
2. Did the socioeconomic divide between hotel owners and workers (and townspeople) play a role in Trudy's disappearance?
3. Was Susan justified in using deadly force during the drug deal? Does unconscious bias play a role in behavior toward minorities/POC?
4. How did Susan and Lori perceive each other's lives and how did that make them feel about their own lives? How did it affect their relationship?

5. For someone who has lived a traumatic life, is Alzheimer's a blessing or a curse?
6. How do you feel about Vera's betrayal of Will? Should Will forgive her? Or are some things unforgivable?
7. Is it possible to recover from a no-holds-barred outing of secrets in which the dereliction of family duties is exposed for all its ugliness?
8. Susan flirted with disappearing and it was a secret desire of her mother's as well. Were they jealous of what Trudy actually did? Do you ever think of just disappearing, starting a new life where no one knows you and you get a clean slate? Do you think that there are quite a few people who harbor fantasies about running away and becoming someone else?
9. Even though Susan perceived Ray's family as "perfect," it was filled with eccentricities. Is there really a "perfect" or "ideal" family?
10. Susan is a procrastinator, putting off the inevitable in both small ways (repairs needed around the house) and big ways (talking with Thomas, meeting with Rachel/Stanley). How does this character trait get in the way of the investigation?

ABOUT THE AUTHOR

MARCY McCREARY grew up in Brooklyn, New York, and moved to the Boston area after graduating from George Washington University with a B.A. in American Literature and Political Science. With little interest in pursuing a career in politics, Marcy stumbled into the marketing communications field. For twenty-five years, she occupied marketing and sales roles at various magazine publishing companies (Cook's Illustrated, Sky & Telescope, CIO, Technology Review) and content marketing agencies.

When laid off from a job in 2016 and looking for something to do to keep busy and challenged, Marcy decided to write a novel, something she had been itching to do for years. Marcy's novel *The*

Deeper You Dig was self-published in April 2020 after relentless badgering from friends and family to make it available in book form. Soon after typing *The End* on that book, she started writing *The Disappearance of Trudy Solomon*.

With two daughters and two stepdaughters living in four different cities (Brooklyn, Nashville, Madison, Seattle), Marcy spends a lot of time on airplanes crisscrossing the country. The ocean is her happy place, so she lives at the seaside in Hull and Nantucket, Massachusetts, with her husband, Lew, and black lab, Chloe.

If you enjoyed
Marcy McCreary's
The Disappearance of Trudy Solomon,
you'll enjoy
The Ghosts of Thorwald Place
by Helen Power.

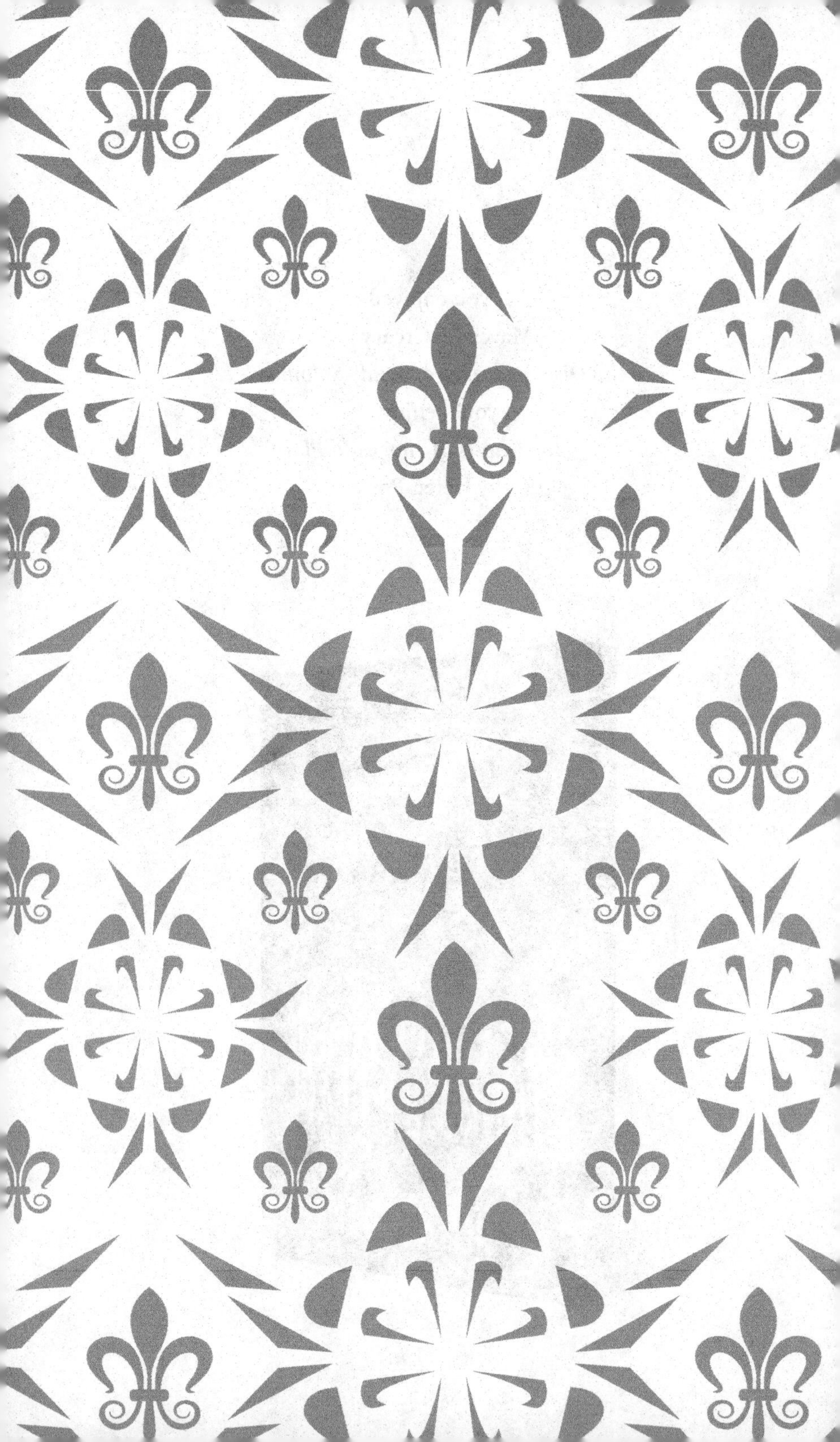

CHAPTER ONE

"I THINK he's going to kill me." The voice is barely above a whisper.

I grip the telephone and take a deep breath. My eyes skim across the page in front of me. I know I should use open-ended questions, but I already find myself going off-script.

"If you believe your life is in danger, you need to call the police."

"No! I mean, no. I don't think my life is in danger."

I frown. It's not uncommon for callers to make grand, sweeping statements about murder or conspiracies and then recant moments later. But there's something different about this caller. There's something in her voice that makes me think she might have been telling the truth the first time.

"You can be honest with me," I say. "Tell me about your husband."

She pauses. "Well, he's really sweet. He's handsome. Generous. He buys me everything I could ever want . . ."

"But?"

"He gets horrible mood swings. He gets so . . . *mad* for no reason. I never know when he's going to snap. I think he's been having trouble at work, but he won't talk to me about it."

I bite my lip. "Has he ever hit you?"

The silence stretches like a yawning chasm as I wait for her next words to either topple me over the precipice or guide me safely away from the edge.

"No."

My heart skips a beat. I don't believe her.

"I wouldn't even consider leaving him if it weren't for . . ."

"If it weren't for . . .?"

"If it weren't for Shane."

"Who's Shane?"

She doesn't respond.

"Is Shane your son?"

I worry that she might hang up, but she finally answers.

"Yes."

"Has he ever hurt your son?"

"No."

My frown deepens. Is she lying? "Listen . . ." I falter. Normally I would use a caller's name here, to cement the trust I'm trying to build, but she refused to give it. "I think you should call the police."

"I—can't. I won't."

I want to push her—this might be my only chance to convince her to get help—but instead, I give her a list of places she can go, emphasizing the discretion of the different women's shelters that are strategically located around downtown Toronto, where she has alluded to living.

"You can call any time you need to talk. Ask for Rachel, and they'll connect us if I'm working," I say. "I usually work a little later than this—from twelve to four."

I hear a muffled thump on the other end of the line.

"I have to go. He's awake."

My heart leaps into my throat. I open my mouth, but I'm cut off by the dial tone.

I reluctantly return the phone to its receiver, the springy cord of my vintage, black telephone snapping tightly into place. I take a deep breath and arch my back, stretching my arms to the ceiling. Some—but not all, never all—of the tension releases from my body.

I flip through the pages of the binder back to the first page, ready to start the process over again. I've been volunteering at the distress line for almost fourteen months now, but it never gets easier. The service helps all those in crisis, from teens who just want information about mental health programs to the elderly who are grieving the loss of loved ones. We also get many calls about domestic abuse. Too many. Unless the caller explicitly gives us permission, or if we have reason to believe that someone's safety is in immediate danger, we aren't allowed to contact the police.

Sometimes, I hate this rule. But one of the reasons people feel comfortable enough to reach out to us is because of our discretion. Still, it's hard to hang up and let go of someone who needs my help. I may never hear from this girl again. I may never know the rest of her story.

I make a note on the call log, both online and in my own personal records. I put down my pen and stare at the phone for several minutes, hoping that I can compel the girl into calling back. But it's nearing the end of my four-hour shift, so I likely won't hear from her again tonight.

Housebound, I volunteer for four shifts a week. Usually, I take the most unpopular shift of midnight to four, but tonight I'm working from eight to twelve. Because of my flexible schedule, the hotline has made an exception, and I'm allowed to work from home instead of at the busy call center. Of course, I didn't tell them the real reason why I can't leave my apartment. They think I have mobility issues, which I faked during the company's mandatory therapy sessions. I was given a clean bill of mental health. Ironic.

I head into the kitchen and turn on the kettle. I grab a box of Earl Grey and drop a bag into my favorite mug. The mug is plain and brown and has a tiny chip on its lip, but it reminds me of home, and I always use this one, even though I have a dozen other mugs crammed onto the shelf. I hug my arms across my chest as I wait for the water to boil. My wool sweater does little to warm the chill that has permeated my bones.